For ourselves

and Alison

Darling Bay Park

C.P. Bishop

First published in Great Britain in 2018

Copyright © 2018
C.P. Bishop

Cover illustrations 2018 by
C.P. Bishop

mavenwriters@hotmail.com

A catalogue record of this book
is available from the British Library.

ISBN: 978-1-9164030-0-0

Printed in Great Britain by KDP

This novel is entirely a work of fiction. The names, characters and incidents portrayed in it, while at times based on historical events and figures, are the work of the authors' imaginations.

First Edition

*They all say the same things, in different ways,
with different words, occasionally pausing for
nodding heads and rapturous applause.*

*Though who am I to question legacy and
promise of centuries past, I am but a person
amongst people, with liberty of voice and breath.*

*Many minds far exceed mine but I can still
think, many a chorus is louder than I but I can
still verse, many tears have fallen harder than mine
but I can still cry, many lead lives richer than I
but I can still smile.*

*Questions are not invitations for the titled to
dwell upon, nor for those who have read the most
books, they are for the pauper who is free of preach
and dictatorship.*

*Answers are not storied by curly white wigs
upon thrones fit for kings and queens, they are
voiced by those upon green grass, who worry not of
power and consequence, but of a place called home.*

Chapter One

Benedict Maven walked a treacherous path through city streets lined with fiery rivers that were running away from the furnace that had swallowed Central Park. The streets were his and his alone. Fire filled his eyes. It was beyond beautiful. A devil's utopia. The blaze began to spread further through the Big Apple, clinging and stretching to the oxygen that swirled around it.

Its self-perpetuating flames grew outwardly like a blossoming flower. The familiar noises of New York City had been replaced by a fizzing, crackling roar. Benedict continued to walk between the walls of the inferno, revelling in the warmth and tranquillity, alone with only his thoughts and his soul.

He had almost forgotten the rain that fell like suicide onto the scorching surrounding scenery. The drizzle was supremely inferior and would require drastic thickening to tackle its nemesis. It continued to fall, pointlessly; its only purpose was to tighten Benedict's clothes and allow him to occasionally and subconsciously lick his lips.

The rain had caused his hair to flop onto his forehead in such a way that allowed heaven's water to trickle along a fixed course down his angelic chiselled face before tickling his top lip. Benedict savoured its annoyance and its flavour before he swept it away with his tongue.

And so, with dripping hair and soaking wet clothes that clung to his body, he walked on.

A storm was gathering in the distant sky—high above the Atlantic coastline, poised for an impending battle. A war of water and flame. An ordinary man would undoubtedly appear disheartened, dishevelled and dreary—a walking metaphor of pathetic fallacy. Yet the weather hadn't dampened this man's spirits. Benedict was far from an ordinary man. He was significantly the contrary. The type of man who deserved to be the subject of story.

Chapter Two

SOLITARY

She was drawn to the adorable child

Natalie wasn't one for physical contact. She didn't despise it, she just needed time to prepare for it and then cleanse accordingly—the type of person who ogled bleach bottles and enjoyed the ambience of clean places. Her desk at the New York Social Services department was immaculate—everything had its place and there were always sticky notes evenly placed and full of joined-up writing.

The air conditioning unit at the workplace was undoubtedly the cleanest of all such establishments across America. Natalie was solely responsible for this undesired accomplishment—in her two years at the office she had filed seven complaints about its dust. Natalie followed her mother. She was slightly taller than average, had flowing, rich-auburn hair and oozed personality. She would often break the silence with strangers in elevators and—put simply—she was as pleasant as chocolate.

Benedict had been institutionalised for nearly two years before Natalie first visited him. The Windham Orphanage of New York City had provided shelter and supper to suckle, but the elder children there were disillusioned, dysfunctional and damned. They were categorised unknowingly according to God: the unwanted, the uncared for and the unfortunate. It was the age-old debate—was it better to have dead parents who had loved you or living ones who didn't? It would ultimately be the undoing of most of the state's children. The unloved carried an unwavering bitterness towards life and those who had lost their family cared little for consequences thereafter. The toddlers still had a chance. Benedict still had a chance.

He had been a part of Natalie's daily routine for nearly a month and, despite prior warnings, she was drawn to the adorable child. It was inevitable; clever children are charming. Benedict found solace in the sweet lady's soothing voice and vixen hair; however, Natalie's bond with the boy was tarnished with despondency, owing to the advice given to her by her mentor, Jayne Dartmore. When Natalie had first wandered into the dusty office, Jayne had urged her to '*care for them but do not get emotionally involved—they are not your children.*'

Jayne's words were not quite her own, but the moral of her statement was summed up by the impersonal pronoun: them—a fundamental justification of detachment. It was ruthless and yet tinged with tenderness.

Natalie's three-year study of social and emotional development had not prepared her for the first time she had entered the Windham residence; there was an aura of attachment disorders and a palpable objection to authority. But, despite the disobedience of frantic children, there was a sadness in an orphan's eyes that could not be documented. It would infinitely spoil their beauty. Like ink in milk.

Natalie unbuckled Benedict's seatbelt and looked to the moment that she had rued for the last few weeks—introducing Benedict to his new home. She fixed her skirt as she stepped from her Bobcat car. Her cream blouse fluttered in a softening breeze. She was more than presentable. She lifted Benedict from the car and pushed the door shut with her foot. The car was battered—one more footprint wouldn't hurt it.

Natalie walked a few steps before she reached the porch of Mr and Mrs Jackson's home. She refrained from knocking the door for only a second or two, allowing the child in her arms to be embraced for a moment longer. Jayne's words echoed in her head and she hurriedly knocked the door, forcing her to put down her delivery. Both were immediately met by an eager Mrs Jackson. Mr Jackson was standing just behind his wife, his elbow perched on the stairs' balustrade. Mrs Jackson allowed Natalie and Benedict into her home with an elaborate, 'Hello,' but there was a nervousness to her welcome.

Natalie despised the formalities but felt obliged to shake Mrs Jackson's outstretched hand one last time. Her weathered gardening hands were grainy and dry to touch, and scratched against Natalie's tropical-scented skin. It was the initial greeting months before that had made the handshakes customary, and thereafter, it was Natalie's professionalism that made her continue despite her displeasure.

Mrs Jackson knelt beside Benedict. She rubbed at his cheek; her fingertips roughed his silky skin. 'Hello my darling.' She hugged him snugly and lifted him skyward.

Mr Jackson stepped forward and ruffled Benedict's hair. 'Alright boy,' he offered, before walking to the kitchen—he seldom allowed himself to display public affection.

A searing stuffiness shrouded Natalie and she wondered how Benedict would cope with the stifling humidity and clinging warmth. She longed for her air-conditioned office and watched Mr Jackson filling the kettle. She instantly thought of bleach and had palpitations just *thinking* about cleaning Mrs Jackson's kitchen. Benedict smiled in all the excitement.

The penultimate handshake had landed on the day of Mr and Mrs Jackson's final scribble. Mr Jackson's signature was untidy and barely legible, owing to his lack of education. His scrawl appeared beneath an off-straight print of his name: Mr Gerald Jackson, and that was it—as soon as Sally Jackson's swooping signature landed on the paper, Benedict's future was signed and sealed.

The Jacksons were a typical inner-city family. Their car was too long for Sally to park. The Chevron estate was old, worn and paint-stripped after too many winters. The Jacksons lived in a home that was too small for them, with a television too big for an Elvis-themed living room. Mrs Jackson was a mother to two children, Brad and Jay; they were grown up and lived with their father in Texas. Sally had stayed and remarried the uneducated but loyal Gerald. They fostered four children, three of which were still in their care; the other had landed in Orange County state prison due to a gang-related offence. This was by no means a reflection of Mrs Jackson's mothering capabilities, and the social services knew this.

Mrs Jackson and Natalie were awkwardly smiling at each other. The kitchen smelt of fried food and the surfaces were lightly coated in grease. The Jacksons liked their tea strong and sweet. There was a nervousness in the room that only a warm drink could cure.

'Would you like a cup of tea, dear?' Mrs Jackson offered.

Natalie responded blankly, 'No thank you, I'd better be going,' not wanting to prolong the goodbye.

Benedict was still perched upon Mrs Jackson's left arm, nestled nicely into her knitted cardigan. Natalie was languishing between happiness and sadness. Benedict liked the warmth of the place—the orphanage was always cold. Natalie reached to Benedict who had turned to the sound of her shrinking voice. The temperature was still annoying her and the rattling of tea cups compounded her agony.

'Goodbye, Benedict,' she whispered as she stroked the left side of his face with a tenderness that you couldn't find in textbooks.

Benedict followed the touch of Natalie's coconut fingertips and her voice. Her gentleness was something he had become accustomed to. Benedict twisted in Mrs Jackson's arms and looked at Natalie as she backed away. She raised her right hand, waved it playfully and whispered, 'Bye-bye,' to the boy.

There followed a collision of goodbyes—almost in sync, Mr Jackson, Mrs Jackson and Natalie respectively.

Natalie stepped onto the Jacksons' porch and closed the door behind her. She was weakened by her sadness. A breath of air had been zapped from her. She fidgeted as she walked back to her car—she couldn't wait to get back to the office to wash her hands.

Chapter Three

DESIRE

Spoiling the pattern of ticking time

The school was ageing but its foundations were solid—laid by labourers of yesteryear, its characterful features were scarred and jagged. The gargoyles perched upon pillars had been nibbled at for over two hundred years; their devilish smiles had been softened by centuries of being exposed to the elements. Students scuttled beneath the high ceilings and heard their voices swallowed up by the cavernous space above them. Mrs Flynn was unfortunate enough to sample the chaos of the sound before it disappeared to the rooftop. She often longed for the queasy heights of her own seventh-floor sanctuary.

Today's class of excitable whippersnappers deafened her. She wanted to shout at them all but couldn't summon the energy to chastise them, knowing that her lack of gusto would be stifled by the continuous yak of chaotic children. The weather was undecided, caught somewhere between sunshine and rain. An incandescent light permeated through the sash windows and seemed to radiate from the annoying children's bellowing cheeks. The strobing daylight collided with Mrs Flynn's headache and upset her more than the chatter. She cowered away from it and, with difficulty, reached to the window— the blinds were a fiddle to draw, her dexterity eluded her. Finally, the teacher settled in the shade and her school day had begun.

She watched the miserable humdrum outside and strangely she longed to be amongst it. Beyond the window, a statue of Abraham Lincoln looked back towards her, the rain gnawing at its tarnished exterior. Mrs Flynn was oblivious to the boisterous banter being shared between overexcited and unseated students. Some of the children told tales of the weekend—drastically embellishing each story to gain the approval of William Benter, the boy who balanced on the rear two legs of his chair.

Billy was quintessentially a *Jack the Lad* character, empowered by the acceptance of his momentary mini-gang. His unkempt appearance reflected his carefree attitude and a hollow confidence— a pretentious projection of his insecurity. His fellow miscreants fell for his deception, looping around the trailblazer, mimicking his cult status.

Mrs Flynn longed for her bed. Her own space in the high-rise building, sandwiched on the seventh floor of the Belle Vue block and decorated subtly with reasonably priced Swedish furniture. It was her haven. It was quaint, quirky and quiet.

She scratched at the back of her hands, an itch caused by the humidity. Soon her skin was soothed by a breeze that filtered into the classroom from the ajar window beside her. She closed her eyes and allowed the draught to pass over her face.

The racket in class plagued her relaxation and she clicked back into the day by forcefully declaring the date to the children, 'Monday, May 16, 1983.'

Mrs Flynn quickly skipped through a head count and ignored the formalities of the register; she counted twenty-five heads at the desks and quickly lined the twenty-five names on her dated sheet. She was already exhausted and it was barely five minutes after nine. Her declaration had signified the beginning of the school day and those who were standing and chatting scattered to their specified seats. The resulting silence did not appease her—today the teacher had no desire to teach, only a desire to observe. Mrs Flynn's epiphany excited her and she proclaimed, 'Exam time.'

One of the twenty-five children sat with perfect posture, poised and attentive, in spite of the uncomfortable wooden chair that was bolted to the desk. Undeterred at the prospect of examination, Benedict Maven was nearly eight years old. From behind his awkward desk he gazed at the copper statue of Abraham Lincoln—copper turned ocean-green courtesy of coastal rain. Benedict was well presented; his sweater and trousers were immaculate. He was a particular student. Punctual. Polite. His legs dangled from his chair and his body sat tall with his head bent slightly, like an italic question mark.

The silence was blissful. Last night's socialising at Bar Forty-One had already spoiled the teacher's morning and would ultimately define the rest of her day. She vowed never to drink red wine again. Her mouth was dry; she sipped at her water, captivated by the confusion of the weather and the children she had inadvertently punished for her own drunken escapades.

Three of her students huffed in protest at their inability to answer the questions of an exam that had originally been pencilled in for the following week. Benedict was in his element, sailing in the consummate ease of elementary work. A triangle of disgruntled students peered over his shoulder. His position towards the front-right of the class didn't overtly allow them to copy his work, or even land a long stare upon it. In fact, they never saw anything that they could not work out for themselves with a little application.

Mrs Flynn scanned the classroom and wallowed in the hush, choosing to ignore the clusters of scheming students. Billy had no one looking towards him for inspiration and resolutely puffed out his chest in defiance. His pen was largely a lollipop throughout his lessons. He had chewed its edge so much one particular day that ink had blotted his lip. He had smeared more onto his mouth in an act of insolence, attempting to make the class believe it had been a deliberate act.

Mrs Flynn had refused to join the class in the chorus of laughter—she knew the future he was destined to have and had shouted at him in an attempt to steady his life. Her reprimand was as loud as a gunshot on that day, causing the birds resting upon Abraham Lincoln's shoulders to scatter into the sky.

The exam room was tense, and yet Benedict exuded a mature calmness. His rollerball pen glided smoothly over the off-white paper. He turned the question paper with his left hand and jotted the answer with his right. Effortlessly. The square Newgate clock that hung above the board sounded with each passing second—the other children were sure they could feel it tick in tandem with their racing hearts.

Mrs Flynn looked up at the same clock, believing that the seconds were ticking too slowly, contrary to the children. Her body was beginning to ache in protest at its dysfunction and disuse. It ordered her to stand with the tightening of her muscles; she stood tentatively to prevent her dehydrated legs cramping and walked down the aisle between her students. She peered over the melee of scribbling hands and stepped slowly in her heels. They clicked every time they landed on the chessboard-tiled floor, spoiling the pattern of ticking time. Mrs Flynn settled at the back of the classroom, focused on the clock and drifted to a daydream. The break-time bell sounded, stirring the teacher to remember her role.

'Pens down, time for recess,' she croaked.

The synchronicity of pencils dropping and papers shuffling was as wonderful as an orchestra's four-beat. The students and the teacher welcomed the rustle. Mrs Flynn allowed the children to filter from the room before she clumsily collected all the exam papers and placed them in a messy pile upon her desk. Billy was first out of the room, circumventing the jostling stragglers blocking the doorway.

11

Benedict avoided the stampede and was the last to leave. Mrs Flynn was just in time for a mid-morning breeze to welcome her back into her chair. The students careered from the class to the playground and, on the way, enjoyed the promise of lunchtime delights, courtesy of the odour which floated like a vortex down the hallway—spicy meatballs.

The day's warmth clung to Mrs Flynn, who still nursed a dull headache. The thought of marking the exam papers strewn on her desk did not excite her. She looked to Abraham Lincoln for a boost in resolve and took a deep breath.

Chapter Four

HELPLESS

Her floral rose and jasmine scented perfume fanned over her son's delicate nose

Benedict's baby blue eyes were only nine months old. They watched the raindrops outside slowly streaking along the car window, captivated by the patterns of inclement weather and the beauty of such moments. Soon his impressionable eyes were clogged with tears. They began to tumble in tandem with the rain, but there was no tantrum. He dismissed the watery moment and stole a glance of his mother and father from the confines of his baby seat. He could barely hear the car's engine; it was drowned out by the frantic windscreen wipers.

His mother was playful in her posture and she gazed adoringly at her husband who was snuggled neatly in the driver's seat beside her, with one hand gripping the steering wheel and the other entwined between her dainty fingers, resting upon her lap. Benedict's dad was a confident driver and a competent husband. Benedict began to sob for no particular reason. His mother unclasped her seatbelt and turned towards her boy, causing his dad's doting hand to slip from her knee; he took hold of the steering wheel with both hands and concentrated his attention on the road and stormy weather. Benedict's short meaningful cry was answered by loving arms—a warm cuddle from his outreaching mother who had clambered awkwardly between the front seats. It was a stretch, but the momentary closeness comforted him, his tears soothed by her voice and touch.

'What's the matter, Ben?' She wiped his soft cheeks dry with her sleeve. She paused as if she expected an answer, while she steadied her balance by resting her elbow upon her husband's headrest. She was perched, protective. She lightly caressed Benedict's cheek with her thumb, and a waft of her floral rose and jasmine scented perfume fanned over her son's delicate nose. It was his favourite fragrance. It widened his eyes with pleasure. His mother smirked and straightened the white shawl that nuzzled him, before lightly tickling his ribs. It was a sure tactic and caused her son to smile. Her smile was infectious.

His father was focused on the highway ahead; the rain was falling heavily on the car. Visibility was mediocre. She jostled back into her own seat after tending to her only child and fidgeted with her seatbelt. His father maintained his two-handed grip of the wheel. 'Is he settled now, darling?' he questioned without even looking towards her, conscious that the weather was worsening.

'Yes, dear,' she replied succinctly before looking intently at her husband. She had the luxury of looking away from the windscreen, but her drawn gaze caused her to further fumble with her seatbelt's clasp.

A wretched screech muted the mutter of minimal conversation between parents. The reality of an oncoming vehicle silenced them both. Its snaking was audible. Benedict was silent. His dad's hands reacted by trying desperately to pull the steering wheel to the right, but the propulsion of forward motion didn't allow it—the car strained and attempted to veer right but the speed was too much, causing it to suffer from severe understeer and stiffen into a straight line.

Benedict's dad reached out one hand to his wife to protect her, but the impact was inevitable. His blocked hand across her body was fruitless. The sheer collision instantly drained the family car of its air, exhausting it with a solemn breathlessness like the spent chamber of a gun. The snaking vehicle hurled the family car into a flip as it wittingly avoided being crumpled by the opposite force. His dad's once-steady hands flapped in hope and prayer.

The driver's-side suspension had buckled grossly under the impact, arching the wheels that had fought desperately to remain grounded into the air—ripping with it Benedict's mother as her unbelted body tried desperately to defy gravity and remain in contact with her seat. She collided heavily with the vehicle's ceiling which knocked her unconscious instantaneously. Her cataleptic body was sent flailing, colliding harshly with her husband who was pinned to his seat, before meeting the top of the driver's side window. It buckled under the collision and spun shards of glass like confetti through the interior of the family car. The mosaic sharps ripped indiscriminately through anything in its path—the fabric of seats, the felt of the ceiling and the flesh of the front-seat occupants. A series of deep-red droplets rebounded within the spinning space, staining Benedict's rosy cheeks and speckling his white shawl with crimson.

In the whirlwind of weightlessness, Benedict's mother spun helplessly like a falling die towards the windscreen. Unstoppable. Nature's cruel power.

The roof buckled like a piece of cardboard as the tarmac broke its fall. The spin continued, jolting violently and intermittently as the tyres screamed in an attempt to cling to the road. The four wheels bounded harshly again and again, struggling to gain equilibrium, but they were at the mercy of revolution. The vehicle leapt three times from the sanctity of solid ground. The front and back suspension jostled softly in tandem with each other as the vehicle eventually slowed and settled to a smoky standstill.

The horn reverberated inside the vehicle as his father's limp body slumped against the steering wheel for merely a moment. The vehicle's instruments, dials and windows screeched and clanged to a climax.

The baby seat had been fastened tightly prior to the road trip. Benedict's dad had secured it solidly to the rear seat behind his own. He had pulled it, pushed it and prodded it prior to presentation—his wife's standard was always the sternest of tests. She inspected it thoroughly every time that the family travelled. On this day, she had nodded in approval to her husband before landing a deserved kiss upon his lips. She then plucked herself away from him and, as soon as she was wholly satisfied, she placed her son into the sturdy, well-studied seat. Benedict cried throughout the preparation, wriggling profusely, but his mother set him within each clasp with consummate ease. She then took a white shawl and wrapped it around her son, who still sobbed in protest.

The seat met all national approvals, which was entirely the reason Mr and Mrs Maven had bought it, protruding in all the right places. Benedict was truly enveloped within it like a precious pearl in its shell. When the car had begun its tumble, the seat stood up true to form and promise, barely moving and casually absorbing the forces that threatened it. It did shuffle slightly to the left, taking with it Benedict's timid body, but comfortably defied the grotesque power that had dismantled the car and his family. The baby merely rocked back and forth like a barrel jumper beneath a waterfall, untouched but for a tickle of foreign softness on his skin—his parents' blood. When the vehicle finally settled like a coin on the surface, the event had pickpocketed the oxygen from his tiny lungs for more than a few seconds. The baby looked to the sound of the horn, dazed and in a flurry of shock, as if he had been dunked into ice-cold water.

Benedict's dad was lifeless, and his contorted body finally fell away from the steering wheel, slipping to his left as his heart struggled to beat. The orchestra's finale wailed to a hum before silence surrounded the sorry scene. There was no fantasy in the last moments. The wreckage of the two vehicles involved offered little hope. Entangled momentarily, they had separated violently as the family car took flight. Both were now separate entities scattered across the highway. Exhausted.

The windscreen before Benedict was a blur of cracked glass— shattered but in situ. The weather began to seep through. Blood trickled onto and into the windscreen. It thinned in the rain, translucent like watered-down cordial. Beyond the pale, cherry-stained mosaic was the offending vehicle; the teenage driver was slouched against the driver's side window, unconscious and within a bubble of smoke. The only occupant.

They had collided with such force that the brunt of kinetic energy had spun it laterally several times. It had spun like a roulette ball off the road, through a sludge of mud and grass before nudging a set of trees that befriended the highway. The vehicle hissed in pain, resting in plain view of the devastation it had created, and looked on with a ghoulish glare.

Benedict's mother lay motionless on the dashboard with blood seeping from her hairline. Her thick hazel hair was scarlet and matted. His dad's cadent eyes flickered as the last of his life left his body. A father powerless to comfort a baby dyed red. Benedict turned to his right, clinging to the outdoors and earlier moments. The rain had wilted to a softening drizzle like desiccated coconut. The baby had already seen the devastation before him. A spectrum of oil and blood and rain caked the road. The pattern of inclement weather and fatality was quite something. Benedict closed his eyes.

Chapter Five

SUFFERING

There was no inherent reason for his violence—it was hereditary

A veneered desk and chair unit sat symmetrically in the square room. There were exactly twenty-five—all varying in their neglect. The lack of ergonomic design spurred an upright, attentive attitude, but the prickly posture caused each student to slump, opposing the desire that the chair craved to instil. The history of Lincoln Elementary was far more important than comfort; it had been this way since the school's opening at the height of the American Revolution— stubbornness would prevail.

Its esteem and values prepared children for adulthood and it was every history teacher's wish that the desks be kept and maintained; they were martinets who valued historic artefacts and wallowed in the room's ambience. Each of the surfaces had been carved and tagged over the years and still they sat in a muddle of muskiness—the scent of damp had seeped in and amalgamated with the cleaner's morning bleach. The patina of the pine floor was dark, swirled with eighteenth-century grain and grime. The classroom was dated, riddled with aesthetic history, historic posters, and the historic Mrs Newman.

Mrs Newman was in her forty-ninth year at the school. Her floral cream blouse rested softly against her pleated ankle-length grey skirt, accompanied by her silver bobbed hair and caramel glasses. Her appearance hadn't changed since the fifties, apart from the colour of her hair, of course. Her appearance was generational—she wore what her mother had always worn. She was the sternest of creatures and had an unfaltering passion for history.

Mrs Newman sat upright; her wrinkly fingers held her current novel a whisker away from her face. She squinted habitually to see the words—she needed new glasses, but she liked their colour and didn't care for the inconvenience of conversion.

Mrs Newman enjoyed the quietness of being early. Her struggling eyes swallowed each sentence of *The Invasion of Amada*—she had read it so often that she could recall whole paragraphs with ease. She was enthralled by its words and barely noticed the bell that sounded for the start of the day. She creased the top corner of page ninety-three and gently placed the book into her drawer. It would return to her hands for morning break with the regular accompaniments of strong tea and fruit cake.

Soon Mrs Newman's ears tried desperately to drown out the noise as a gang of children spilled into her classroom. She stood in front of the class, armed with an unyielding presence. She peered over her glasses at the horde and focused her tirade upon the leader, Billy Benter. 'Children, will you please be quiet and listen, I will not ask you again,' she warned in her croaking old voice.

Each student adhered to Mrs Newman's demands—no one wanted to stay in school longer than was necessary, knowing that Mrs Newman felt at home in her classroom. She would often remain at her desk with her book between her fingers, irregularly but loudly sipping at her lukewarm tea and no child wanted *that* for company. She had once kept a young boy in the classroom until eight o'clock in the evening for failing to adhere to her commands. This was one tale that the classes of Lincoln Elementary would always recall. It had filtered its way through generations and, like campfire folklore, it had the desired effect.

The subsequent ghostly silence was interrupted only by Mrs Newman's chalk; a wretched screech caused the class to wince at its sound and significance. The children felt their skin tremble until finally the thick white capitals of 'THE AMERICAN CIVIL WAR' spanned the board.

Billy was seemingly uninterested by Mrs Newman's aura and the sound. He looked menacingly towards Benedict at the front of the class—jealousy had engulfed him, and soon his hand grasped an eraser from a table adjacent to him, squishing it tightly in his right hand. He rolled it beneath his index finger and thumb for a few seconds. He dragged his right arm back over his shoulder and hurled it at Benedict.

It tumbled through the air, end over end, narrowly missing Benedict, and struck Mrs Newman on her back. It jolted her in shock more than severity and caused her to joggle forward momentarily, enough for the chalk she was holding to break in two against the board. One half of the chalk fell to the floor.

She immediately turned to the chorus of laughter, red-faced with white fingers. She dropped the broken half of chalk that still powdered her fingertips and picked up a board eraser, the nearest thing to her whitened hands. She slammed it onto her desk. Wood on wood. The clap was thunderous. It reverberated around the classroom, causing every student to jump into silence. White chalk powder puffed into the air.

Mrs Newman shouted an open question, demanding its answer. 'Who just threw that?'

Hush filled the room. White powder began to settle onto Mrs Newman's desk. The children all knew the culprit but were silenced by the repercussions of truth.

Mrs Newman continued to taunt the class. 'I will only ask you once more—who threw the eraser?'

'Billy, Mrs Newman,' answered Benedict.

Billy followed the words Benedict delivered and saw them land upon the teacher's ears.

'Mr Benter. Get out of my class,' she snarled. Billy shuffled in his chair. She barked at his insolence, 'Get out of my class!'

Billy puffed his cheeks. His desk grated against the floor as he bundled into it with a degree of petulance. He walked methodically to the front of the class, dragging his feet. He peered at Benedict as he passed, his eyes narrowed, his fists and teeth clenched. Benedict sulked over his desk; Billy's anger absorbed Benedict and sucked the energy out of him.

Billy opened the classroom door, causing a slight draught to whisper inside and sting the silence. The aftermath of Billy's departure was uninspiring. The clock dared to tick. Even when Mrs Newman had left the room to escort Billy to the office, the class remained silent for fear of her imminent return.

Mrs Newman did return. Billy did not. She ordered the class to read their text books like a military drill ma'am before she leaned to Benedict and whispered to him, 'Benedict, I know what Billy does to you. I'll arrange for Mr Hart to speak with you later, OK?'

'OK, Mrs Newman,' muttered Benedict.

The shiny gold letters that adorned the heavy grained oak door smelt of paraffin and lemon. It read boldly, with stature and authority, *Mr Hart, Principal.*

The bench in the hallway was old and uncomfortable and groaned with Benedict's subtle movements. The walnut was a deep ocean of colour. Its circular grain curdled like custard beneath the polished surface. It was craftsmanship at its finest; it commanded respect, as did the principal.

Billy was sitting on the other side of the door, in a chair far too big for him. He looked away from the principal, choosing instead to look at the speckled black wallpaper that lined the office walls. He was consumed and immersed in the fizzle of black and white dots, slowly drowning out the crackly voice of the principal.

Speckles of black, white and grey fizzed from an old television like a fresh glass of pop. Millions of circles jumbled and jostled like magnified atoms on the screen. Billy's eyes were captivated by them. The TV aerial poked outward from its top like a wire coat hanger. He pressed at the heavy buttons that protruded in a column from the TV's panel. The picture fragmented, distorting Billy's desperate eyes as he wiggled the aerial in anguish, searching for a solid picture. The television's background noise crackled from the mono speaker to its side. Frustratedly, he began to twist and turn the aerial recklessly until gunfire could be heard from the speaker. The picture followed soon after and an old western movie shook into view. Billy's smile widened in his delight, his eyes comforted by the flashes of gunfire.

Quickly he returned to his seated position on the tacky auburn patterned carpet in his living room. He was all alone. He watched cowboys on horseback chase a wagon of moustached men out of town, and felt himself drifting into the action, away from his home.

The surrounding walls that encased Billy were a dirty shade of magnolia; the sofa matched the carpet—worn and tattered. He sat with his back against the sofa for fear of ripping the material that was already frayed and thinning. He had propped a single cushion behind him that pushed softly against his back. It was his only comfort. To his right stood a grimy coffee table, its surface stained with last night's beer. Sticky. The murky room stank. Billy had become immune to it, but on occasions, when he had returned home on sunnier days, the smell seeped through his nose and floundered in his throat.

The room was dark; today's smell was particularly bad due to the suffocating afternoon sunshine. The pong had soaked into every porous surface. Billy's eyes battled his nose. They were captivated by the melee of gunfire and destruction. Each explosion enthralled his craving and took him further away from the smell that surrounded him. He would be the cowboy in his daydream, cocking his finger like a pistol shooting at the Indians. He would always be the cowboy. Always the goodie. Alone in his children's fantasy, Billy sat like this for hours, flipping his hands like guns from his waist and making the sound effects of firing colts. He enjoyed these hours the most.

He cowered as the front door was unlatched abruptly. His spine tingled as the door swung open, clumsily crashing against the living room wall that was only really fit for death. His father fell into the door which rebounded off the wall and bounced himself back into balance. He was drunk. He was always drunk. He had long since forgotten the smell of this house, whatever the weather. Plaster crumbled to the floor. It rested amongst plaster from identical days and weeks before. The hole in the wall eroded a little bit more daily.

Billy shimmied down in front of the sofa, shuffling in an attempt to be just out of sight. He hoped that his dad would stumble to the staircase, stumble up the stairs and stumble into his stained bed. Billy sat silently. The cowboys were still firing in the background. Billy sat rigidly, wishing that the cowboys would put away their guns. Slowly he looked to his staggering father, peering carefully above the ripped sofa arm.

George had surprisingly maintained the balance of the bottle in his spare hand. He staggered from the doorway to the first step of the stairs and slightly tipped the bottle of beer. Alcohol spilled from its spout and splashed on the uncarpeted stair. George paused for a moment and watched the beer splash and drip over the stair's ledge. George heard the gunfire. He planned a route to the sofa; his soiled boots scraped across the floor. Billy winced as the footsteps approached him and the TV. George turned and reached to the front door that was still recovering from being bashed against the wall. His large hands put down the bottle, which wobbled on the floor before falling. The contents seeped out and puddled against the staircase.

George grasped the door in one hand and threw it shut. A heavy draught swept into the room. It caused Billy to shiver.

George stepped towards Billy—appearing larger with each step. He was tall, wide and had hands like sledgehammers. He was known unimaginatively in his local bar as Goliath. It was understandable why a child would be frightened of this man. George saw a blurred image of his boy sitting against the sofa and belched as he approached him, managing to step to the side of his son before falling into a seated position on the sofa. Billy didn't move an inch, even when his father's knee collided with his shoulder. It was still digging into Billy's shoulder when his father asked him, 'What's up, boy?'

'Just watching the TV, Dad,' Billy quipped in his cutest voice.

George pushed his hands down onto the unpadded cushions at his side and sat upright. His mood changed upon hearing his son's voice. Drunkenly he delivered hiccupped words. 'What have I told you, boy—no watching TV when I come home.'

Billy was petrified; he recognised his dad's mood change. It was instant. He tried to pull his father away from the dark mood that he was wandering into. 'I'm sorry, Dad, it won't happen again.'

His father didn't come back to the light and delved further into his internal drunken anger. 'I know it won't—you just don't listen, DO YOU?'

George slapped Billy across the back of the head with his large shovelled right hand. Billy jolted forward sharply, falling in a heap before his father's knees. He held the back of his head with his one hand, ridding the stinging sensation from his skin.

'Get to your feet, boy,' thundered his father.

Billy trembled. His master's voice pierced his little eardrums and caused his head to shake further. He stood sharply to attention before his dad and tried to steady himself in case there was another cheap shot. He was resigned to the future event; it had happened before, it would happen again. He had once run from his dad when he returned home drunk, but it had only delayed the beating until the following day. Billy had suffered three cracked ribs as a result of the previous escape.

It'll be over soon, Billy told himself. Helpless, he stood before his father and listened as the sound of a leather belt slid through his dad's denim belt loops. George staggered to his feet by leaning forward from the sofa. He wrapped his belt around his right hand. He steadied himself by pressing his left hand on Billy's head, before pulling the other end of the belt tightly. George cracked the belt against his alcohol-soiled jeans. Once. Twice. Billy shuddered at the first crack. He shuddered at the second crack. He had turned around forcefully as his dad's left hand again landed on his head. His dad spat, 'Turn around, boy. I'm going to show you what my father, your grandfather showed me—some discipline.'

Billy was consumed by the thought of imminent pain and tensed his body. He gritted his teeth as if he were in a family photograph. He had never met his grandfather but cursed him for making his dad so angry. Billy stood rigidly, his balled fists clasped tight against his belly. His body began to tire with the anticipation. His dad swung the belt and it cracked and wrapped around Billy's back and chest. It was as relentless as hailstones.

Billy quivered in between the slaps; he winced with every strike. The pain was overwhelming. He thought of the cowboys. Grimacing, he fell to the floor, pawing at the shredded carpet for some solace. It was too worn, the pile far too thin to grasp. Billy's face was wet, shiny with tears. The belt arced over him. He cried out as the pain engulfed his body. 'Stop, Dad!'

A wheezing George stopped after delivering three more blows to his boy. This was to remind him that he stopped when he wanted to and not upon request. George threw his belt to the corner of the room and fell backwards into the sofa, gasping for breath. The belt slapped off the wall and slid down it into a collection of green beer bottles stacked at the edge of the room. The bottles jingled as they collided together. It was strangely comforting. 'Get out of my sight, boy,' George snapped, his voice spoiling the chiming of glass.

Billy edged to his feet. Battered and bruised, he walked gingerly to the staircase. He was oblivious to where his footsteps landed as the pain rippled through his small shell like a trapped fly. His right foot landed in the spilt beer that George had left at the stairs' edge. Billy didn't acknowledge it as it soaked into his sock. He began to creep up the stairs to his bedroom. His back was awkwardly arched over as it tried to absorb the force of the blows that had been dealt upon it. Billy didn't make a sound. His right foot led him to his bedroom. It squelched silently as it landed on each tread.

He crawled timidly into his bed. He pulled his grubby bed sheet over him, wrapping it around him like a cocoon. He tucked his knees into his chest and stiffened his body beneath the sheets into the shape of a question mark. His body revelled in its solitude, but still battled to release the pain trapped within it. Achingly, Billy fell into a deep sleep that lasted all night.

He woke from his slumber to the sound of cheering coming from downstairs. He struggled to unwind his body that had set like baked clay. He delicately unwrapped himself and cautiously made his way down the stairs that he had found so difficult to climb yesterday. His dad was collapsed on the sofa, a fresh bottle in his hand. The small television speakers threw loud chanting into the room as an American football game played out. George looked away from the stadium colour towards Billy, who was creeping down the stairs. George was sweating as yesterday's booze oozed out through his pores.

Billy timidly sat at his father's feet, carefully resting his shoulder against his dad's knee, his shoulder blades and back sore from yesterday's beating. His dad saw Billy shuffling for comfort. He too had known that pain and the awkwardness of the following day.

George knew that Billy's bruises and welts would fade in time, but that the scars within him would permanently etch themselves onto the memory of his childhood. George shared the same internal scarring. They never faded. They were only forgotten when the alcohol blinded him.

George looked lovingly at his son. Tears forged in his eyes, glazing them. Billy looked directly at the TV and enjoyed the colour of the weekend game. George ruffled his son's hair in his shovelled hand, running his fingers through it. There was no inherent reason for his violence—it was hereditary, and it was fuelled by his alcoholism. George sighed before resting his hand on the top of his son's shoulder as they watched the sport together, deep into the afternoon.

'Benedict!' bellowed Mr Hart.

His voice tugged Billy from his daydream and back into his office. The door groaned open in answer to the summons. Mr Hart ushered Billy from his office with a simple hand gesture and nod of his head. Benedict walked into Mr Hart's office, passing Billy in the grand doorway. Mr Hart paced around his office, stopping proudly at his plaque—*Principal of Lincoln Elementary*. 'Sit down, Benedict,' he commanded.

Benedict immediately sat down in the black leather chair in front of him, his back cushioned by the back rest, his hands grasping at the arms. Photographs, sheets of paper and a Newton's cradle decorated Mr Hart's desk. Its veneered surface reflected the room's surroundings like French-polished shellac.

Mr Hart turned towards Benedict. 'I'm finding it hard to figure you out, Mr Maven. Mrs Newman tells me that you're doing very well in class, but you seem quite distant from the other children. It seems like there's a lot on your mind?'

Benedict leant forward and pulled the end steel marble dangling from the Newton's cradle. The marble swung in a pendulum motion, crashing into the remaining four that dangled freely; it caused the opposite end marble to crash into momentum courtesy of physics. It continued like a ticking clock, which fascinated Benedict.

'Benedict!' shouted Mr Hart, peeved by his insolence.

Benedict's blank expression irritated Mr Hart.

'I just asked Billy the same question I'm about to ask you. Where do you see yourself in ten years?'

Benedict ignored the meaningless words from the worthless man and instead fixed again on the Newton's cradle's gravitational momentum, thinking of the words that rattled around in his head— *every action has an equal and opposite reaction.* Mr Hart could never fathom the thoughts that Benedict pondered, and instead, the principal wallowed in the sound of his own voice. Benedict ignored the chastisement and drifted on the principal's monotone drone, imagining Billy's life and not his own.

'Benedict—Benedict!'

Mr Hart nudged Benedict's shoulder. Benedict looked at the fringe of hair dangling over him. It smelt of tobacco. He was confronted by Mr Hart's large beady eyes, overhung by greying bushy eyebrows. He felt suffocated.

'Now, back to why I brought you here in the first place, and why Mrs Newman is concerned about you—is Billy bullying you?'

Benedict thought of his normal routine as it had played out that morning. He had taken two of the five one-dollar notes out of his duffel coat pocket and stuffed them into his sock. The playground was awash with children still waking up to the day. The majority of them were running around with sleep still in their eyes.

Billy trudged into the playground and instantly sought out Benedict, as he did every day. Benedict watched Billy enter the playground and could see the other children fanning away from him, like a bad smell trickling through a room. Benedict stepped out into Billy's view.

Billy hurried to Benedict, grabbing at his duffel coat. Billy frisked the coat's pockets, oblivious to the boy inside the coat. He didn't even ask for his dinner money anymore and Benedict didn't even ask for Billy to leave him alone. This was their routine. They fell into the movements like veteran actors. Billy took the remaining three notes from Benedict's left pocket and pulled them away aggressively. The notes crumpled in his hand. He stuffed them into his well-worn trouser pocket. It caused the pocket lining to loosen more than it already had.

It was almost identical to the first time it had happened. The only difference being that Benedict had pleaded with Billy when Billy first demanded that Benedict give his dinner money to him. After a short conversation that was dominated by Billy's voice, Billy shoved Benedict to the floor and towered over him while he pulled three one-dollar notes from his coat pocket. Billy's pocket lining was taut on this occasion. It had housed the dollar notes comfortably. Nearly three months later, Billy's pocket was buckling under the strain of his hand ramming the notes into it every morning.

Billy pulled his hand back out of his pocket and walked away from Benedict and the playground towards the main entrance of the school. The bell sounded. The school day had officially begun.

Benedict looked at the principal and answered profoundly, 'No, sir.'

Chapter Six

RESOLUTION

I work on something that you will always take for granted

Benedict's upbringing was largely uneventful. He was an introverted boy and consciously drew very little attention to himself. Mrs Jackson was neither a bad person nor a bad mother, but she often lacked attentiveness, unable to focus her attention on one single child when there were so many chores and children to chase. But, in her defence, there was always warm food, warm rooms and a warm television. The Jackson children realised from an early age that Benedict's presence in their home was merely that—a presence. He had a knack for isolating himself and enjoyed spending most of his evenings cooped up in his bed, engrossed in books of fantasy, oblivious to the screaming and clanging of his siblings' arguments.

The Jacksons did not pay Benedict too much attention, nor did he crave any; he didn't quite fit the Jackson regime of microwave meals and afternoon game shows. The Jacksons would sit with fold-up trays full of processed food, riveted by the flashing lights of *Jeopardy!* and *Spin-a-Win*. They seldom knew the answers, but on occasion Mr Jackson would mumble a guess between sips of strong tea and broken biscuits. There was a simplicity to the family, but they held a kindness that could not be argued with. They didn't know much, but knew enough to marvel at Benedict's abilities from afar—the first of which was when he swooped, hooped and looped his shoelaces at the tender age of two. The feat was met with nothing more than a ruffle of his hair and a momentary look of acknowledgement shared between Mr and Mrs Jackson.

One morning, after a particularly blustery night, Benedict stirred, still snuggled in his toasty cream quilt. The dew of the misty morning was beginning to replace the frost that had clung to each and every surface overnight. Benedict folded his arms, scrunching the pile of feathered cotton between his fingers, pulling the softness tighter to his frame. It enveloped him. Benedict appreciated the serenity; he listened to the leaves rustling in the morning's squall while tweeting birds shielded themselves amongst groves of cherry blossoms. Everything was grey with dashes of vivacious pink. It was a bleak but beautiful morning.

'Benedict—time for school!' yelled Mrs Jackson from the confines of her kitchen.

Her voice stung Benedict's ears. The clamour of pots and pans and a whistling kettle was unpoetic. Mrs Jackson slaved as she prepared the morning's breakfast of sweet treats and cups of tea.

Benedict peered reluctantly at his digital alarm clock and cursed how early it was. He adored his comfortable bed. He nestled his head deep into his soft pillow and scrunched his quilt, wrapping himself in a cocoon full of warmth and softness. The clang of Mrs Jackson's wretched voice cut into Benedict's bones. 'BENEDICT!'

Even Mr Jackson, the soundest of sleepers, stirred. Mrs Jackson screamed again. 'BENEDICT!'

Benedict rolled out from beneath his warm bedding, yelling back, 'I'm coming!' It was the way the Jacksons spoke—loudly.

Mrs Jackson listened to Benedict's careful footsteps that creaked against the rickety floorboards on the landing's edge. Her kitchen was a muddle. Utensils of all shapes and sizes hung over a greasy range cooker. Her eagerness to purchase items she had seen on television soon cluttered up any last bit of available space. Amongst the clutter stood a stack of pancakes on a plate, with maple syrup trickling down over them like hot glue. 'You're late again,' lamented Mrs Jackson.

Benedict ignored his mother's words and leant over the sweet treats. He took a slice of toast from the counter buttering board and swallowed a large bite of the crusted edge. The butter was silky and strong. Before Mrs Jackson had a chance to lecture Benedict, he threw his schoolbag over his right shoulder, opened the front door and mumbled, in between his munching, 'Love you, Mom.'

The door closed harshly, leaving Mrs Jackson bemused by Benedict's charm—it only lasted a moment until her screams reverberated in the ears of her other sleeping children who held different regimes. They were, unsurprisingly, already awake.

Benedict's steps were precise—they needed to be. The cobbled stones that paved his route to the bus stop were treacherous, especially so as they were coated in last night's frost. The heavy mist of clouds opened occasionally, gracing both Benedict and the street with the morning glow. It warmed Benedict's skin momentarily like a theatre lamp. Benedict waltzed atop the camber of cobbles and took the last bite of his toast. He listened to the stampede that intensified behind him. Scores of children skidded on the slippery surface while Benedict's schoolbag bounced in time with his steps; the other children's schoolbags bounced in time with theirs. It was a mad dash, a percussive two-beat.

'We're gonna miss the bus,' they shouted. It was a moment of excitement before the mundane and almost prison-like school register.

Benedict smiled and strolled on, unaffected by the vigour of youth. In the distance, on the opposite side of the street, a yellow bus hissed to a stop. Thick, bold, black letters beneath the square windows read *School Bus*. The suspension groaned in defiance. The bus was old, but the exterior was well cared for. Immaculate. The scurrying children failed to appreciate it; they barely looked at it as they scampered onto the bus in between their foggy, panting breaths. Benedict watched on from afar as the column slithered like a snake onto the bus. His strides were unaffected and, without breaking rhythm or tempo, he stepped aboard.

'Morning, Mr Tom,' Benedict said to the driver.

'Morning, Benedict,' replied Mr Tom.

Tom had been the only black student in Albuquerque School and had been bullied continuously for being 'different'. His mother and father had little money, but what they did have to give Tom was stolen from him on a daily basis. He too kept a dime or two in his holey socks and never told a soul of his losses. He was the minority. Tom was a sweet and caring child but never made any friends—the colour of his skin and the parents' prejudices had brainwashed those around him. The teachers, too, cared little for colour. Black was the plague and the young boy dwindled in his own company for years.

'End of the line, children,' joked the driver in his Texan rasp.

They rushed like a mischief of rats towards the glass-fronted Lincoln Elementary School. Benedict was the only passenger remaining. The driver's bright white eyes peered through his black stubbly eyebrows to the large rear-view mirror in front of him. He looked at Benedict and the bag that swung from the burgundy leathered seat up onto the boy's shoulder. It reminded Mr Tom of the cruelness of children. Benedict landed beside the driver's cabin, 'Have a nice day, Mr Tom.'

'You too—lucky I was late today, son,' quipped the driver. Benedict smiled and offered a gentle ruffle to the man's shoulder. 'Luck—you need to alter your alarm clock, Mr Tom.'

Benedict stepped away from the chuckling driver who was humbled by the simplicity of kindness amongst people.

Jimmy scribbled on a doodle-covered, red-lined piece of paper. He peered out through the condensated glass towards his rebels' corner;

his spiky, dyed red hair reflected softly in the glass. The faint sound of the less-than-authoritative teacher murmured in the background, murky and undecipherable. With an impassive attitude, he scribbled until the lead crumbled to charcoal on the page. His shirt was unbuttoned; his denim jacket hung over the back of his seat, torn and scuffed.

The teacher stared at Jimmy—both pairs of eyes wallowed in the other's insignificance.

'It's nice of you to join us today, Jimmy. Your attendance leaves a lot to be desired recently.'

He looked up momentarily before peering back towards his desk's surface, unmoved by the teacher's words. Throughout the morning, he daydreamed, muting the teacher's words, blurring the room to a fine haze.

The corner was full of discarded cigarette butts and colourful graffiti. Fellow smokers met up at break time and shared exaggerated stories of their mischievous mornings. Wasted youth.

Jimmy snatched at his Marlboros and flicked the top open like a treasured pocket watch. He dealt the cigarettes out like cards in a poker game. When all were dealt, he flicked his own cigarette up, catching it in his mouth. No one watched but everyone saw his smirk. It was his party trick, but it had been overused and nowadays failed to enthuse his friends. Jimmy rasped his match against the matchbox strip, and cupped it in his hands as the flame flickered over the cigarette, making its tip glow ruby red. The smoke from the group swirled like a hurricane and hid Benedict's uninvited entrance. As the smoke cleared, Jimmy looked at Benedict, who had infiltrated his group and was boldly standing in front of him. Behind Jimmy were his friends—his gang—forming a semi-circle.

Without warning, Jimmy flicked his cigarette at Benedict. The red ash scattered and sparked. It was a gang thing. Benedict landed an explosive, single clean slap to the side of Jimmy's neck. The blow instantly caused Jimmy's body to wobble; the wobble became a sway and the sway became a tumble. He fell to his left; his arms were too slow to react and failed to break his fall. His knees hit the ground first and scuffed as they skidded slightly with his momentum. His body followed and his forehead landed with a nasty thud on the concrete.

Benedict didn't watch Jimmy as he fell; instead, he walked towards the music hall. The semi-circle was stunned. Jimmy stirred on the ground, his arms paddled on the concrete as they tried to lift his disorientated body up off the floor. A pool of red began to clog next to his head, as if his hair was shedding its colour. His knees and flailing arms eventually allowed him to lean back into a kneeling position; the blood from his hairline left a trail that ran down his face and into the pool of blood on the ground, like a string tied to a red balloon.

Benedict was dwarfed by a grand piano. He played the score exactly as the composer had written it. A harmony surrounded Benedict as the orchestra joined in. Mrs Newman walked in abruptly, stomping towards the music teacher who was busy conducting his musicians. His arms waved theatrically to the score. Mrs Newman tugged at the conductor's right arm, spoiling his motion and the music. He called a halt to the proceedings and the tangle of untimed instruments clanged to a silence. Mrs Newman looked towards her shy, star student, fresh with the knowledge of his break-time misdemeanour. Her scolding was succinct.

'Fighting will not be tolerated. Your hands are for playing music, not punching Jimmy Thatcher. Dr James, four o'clock, physics, room one.'

Dr James sported a greying beard. It rounded his face, making him look older than he actually was. Often, he would stroke his soft bristles philosophically. It was a habit he had become accustomed to. He wore the same clothes; he wore the same face. His tweed trousers and woollen russet cardigan were old and tattered. He always wore them together. Mrs James always put them together. Dr James was comfortable and unexciting.

Folded neatly in his pocket was always a scrap of paper; whether it was the start or end of the day there were always equations written on its surface. This was another one of Dr James's habits. It had always been this way for him since his introduction to algebra at the tender age of five. His childhood had been spent solving mathematical equations, not partaking in childhood adventures. He didn't have friends. He had never needed them. His best friend was the mystery of algorithms.

Dr James's passion allowed him to study at Harvard and pursue his dreams, but it was a dream named Roselyn that had captured his untouched heart; it was love at first sight. She often related her psychology studies to their relationship and her philosophy studies to fate. Dr James was the same; he tried to correlate their relationship mathematically—it was an equation he would never solve. They were meant for each other like F equals ma.

Both their studies suffered as a result. Dr James's more so. He never achieved his potential, but they were happy. It was only when Dr James joined Lincoln Elementary that his passion for non-relativistic physics reignited. It was detention and evenings at his home laboratory that pained him the most. It was here that he concentrated on his dwindling future.

Dr James was never late. He looked at his battered wristwatch and struggled to see the time beneath fifteen years of scratches. Mrs James had bought him the watch for their anniversary. The hands crept to just a shade past four o'clock, and Benedict was yet to make an appearance. The other detainees had turned up on time and sat quietly amongst numerous equations plastered and chalked on every available surface. Einstein watched over the classroom from behind framed glass, and over Benedict as he strolled in late. Dr James stood up and instructed, 'Take a seat. You are late.'

Benedict's eyes fixed on the only empty desk in the middle of the classroom. The other twenty-nine seats were occupied by whispering children. Benedict sat behind his desk to the chorus of students' huffs and puffs, which aired their dissatisfaction without truly making it public.

Dr James stood over his desk and lectured the children. 'Ladies and gentlemen, evidently your time is as precious as mine and that's why you are here. All I ask is, while you are here, you are quiet and that you don't interrupt me while I work on something that you will always take for granted.'

They understood Dr James's words precisely—the majority had heard them before and would undoubtedly hear them again. Dr James sat before the thirty children that scribbled quietly onto their text books to pass the time. Dr James didn't mind the occasional mutter, but when it troubled his soul he could command a person with a solitary glance. He looked slightly dishevelled but that was his strength. Someone who cares little for appearance often cares little for consequence. The teacher wrote slickly but he was very vocal in his frustrations. The children pretended they didn't hear; they were frightened without really knowing why. Dr James was like a madman at times, crumpling the written notes and tossing them violently towards the wastepaper basket beside his desk.

He shook his head in annoyance as yet another ball of paper landed in the bin. The children looked at the second hand of the round black clock above the blackboard. Dr James kicked his chair from underneath him and stood up, facing a blackboard chalked with numerous equations. He quickly scribbled on the board, cancelling the terms of an equation to solve the unknown conundrum. Again, he had failed; the children didn't know the reason for his failure, but his body language suggested wild disappointment. Dr James sat behind his desk, perturbed, discouraged—but undefeated.

Benedict looked at Dr James scribbling frantically onto a fresh piece of paper, smirking at his frustration. Further notes were tossed into the bin, eventually making it look like a caged icicle. The five o'clock bell was enough to spark the children into life—it was home time, and they were free. Tables scraped, and schoolbags were hurled onto young shoulders. Benedict scribbled quickly onto his exercise pad and tore at it indiscriminately. He walked amongst the fleeing children and placed the note onto the teacher's desk.

Dr James was immersed in his work and ignored the children leaving the classroom. The last of the them were filtering out as Dr James thumped his desk in anguish, knocking pens and books to the floor. He tended to his precious books remorsefully and placed them back onto his desk, lovingly brushing their spines.

His grief was soon absorbed by the torn note on the edge of his desk. He held it up, formulating its message; his eye movements questioned it. He kicked his chair from beneath himself and rushed to the classroom door. He desperately looked up and down the hallway, but the children were gone.

Chapter Seven

LIBERTINE

A hot knife through strawberries

Las Vegas at night was spectacular. Benedict surveyed the city of lights from the panoramic window in his plush penthouse suite. Everything was a glossy black and white. He strolled to the suits that hung perfectly in his wardrobe. The apartment's lighting enhanced his already beautiful frame, which was reflected exquisitely in the expanse of glass that delivered a deep, delicious night sky. He selected the black. It fitted perfectly, hugging his thin waistline and wide shoulders. His frame accentuated the cut of the suit. Lastly, he closed the clasp of his diamond watch and stepped from the comfort of his apartment to his personal elevator.

The soft carpet of the ground floor greeted his tan soles. The heavy-patterned, primary-coloured carpet complemented the surroundings and clashed with a crowd of multi-coloured fashion delinquents. Benedict strutted confidently across the casino floor. His patent shoes reflected fruit-machine lights like colours from a rainbow. Tourists and gamblers alike shovelled coins and notes into hungry machines.

Benedict stood and surveyed the feeding frenzy. Croupiers chorused in segmented cadence, 'Place your bets now.'

There was heartache and ecstasy in the cauldron of loss and relief. Whether they were high-flying businessmen or high-on-luck tourists, everyone lost, and lost relative to their worth. Benedict meandered through the tourist-filled fun to the solemnity of the private poker tables. The mahogany double doors were guarded by casino security. White shirts, a black dicky bow and a black three-piece. The minimum buy-in stake was fifty thousand dollars, which had to be arranged in advance.

Benedict sat at the polished ebony table and pressed his hands onto the bright-purple cloth. He was surrounded hexagonally by oil tycoons, property investors and stockbrokers. There were too many egos in too small a space.

The trading pit was a complete paradox. It was a muddle of the lonely and the powerful. It was a cattle market, and people jostled and bustled into position to buy and sell. Stockbrokers did not care too much for personal space; they cared more for possessions.

Benedict stood out from the cut-throat circle. His blazer was jet blue, with a heavy yellow trim that lined the blazer's lapels. He looked important. He was important. He flicked his fingers like a seasoned bookmaker at the races. He bought. He sold.

The pit rarely relented; it chewed people up and spat them out again in plain view of everyone. Benedict witnessed swarms of traders physically living out their investments. As stocks rose and fell, traders scampered around the pit, falling over one another to regain parity or make even more money. They were like heroin addicts, constantly looking for the next high. You couldn't tell who was winning and who was losing. It was a free-for-all. You could only tell them apart at the end of the day when faces and shoulders hung heavy, heaped with disappointment, while those who had made a profit stood tall, towering over the unfortunate ones.

The pit was decorated with a rainbow of coloured blazers, and the floor was spattered with white tickets like snowflakes on a winter's day. Computers hummed to a close, screens fit for cinemas that had been full of numbers were now blank, printers ticked to submission and the lights buzzed as the last of the stockbrokers left the room. The revolving doors came to a standstill. Benedict had made plenty of money. He had invested in coffee.

Benedict walked from Wall Street to a quaint area of the financial district. The streets were littered with men with briefcases and women in suits. He escaped the busyness and slipped down a darkened alleyway.

A large man stood in a rustic doorway. The hinges of the oak door towered above both Benedict and the doorman. He looked immoveable. His shoulders seemed never-ending underneath a black jacket; his white shirt was unbuttoned at the top for comfort, revealing a neck twice the width of most men's. His face was weathered, stern. Benedict looked to the doorman, acknowledged his size momentarily and then revealed a glossy white card to him. The doorman elegantly stepped to one side, pulled open the door, and ushered Benedict through it before shutting it behind him. Benedict found himself standing in a long corridor. At the end of the corridor, next to an elevator, stood another man, almost identical to the doorman in stature. Benedict approached him; no words were exchanged, they merely nodded to one another with mutual respect.

The doors opened. The attendant delicately pushed button two and stepped back out of the elevator. The mirrored walls reflected onto and into themselves, creating eight different views of Benedict. He glanced at each one with a single look. He looked immaculate and he knew it. The blazer was striking. Its fit was a tailor's dream.

Benedict stepped out onto a marble-tiled floor; the spotlights above sparkled like diamonds upon its polished surface. Benedict's traditional brogues tapped the tiles as he approached the bar. Soft rock music reverberated around the plush nightclub. Burgundy chesterfield sofas lined the walls. It was a cosy retreat. Beautiful people sipped at champagne, quietly bragging about their successful days on Wall Street. The dress code was smart. Men wore suits and the ladies wore Chanel. Overpowering jewellery glistened like the dance floor that was largely empty. It wasn't an establishment that concerned itself with dancing duets of drunken damsels. It was exclusive, revered by the entitled few.

Benedict glanced left and right, scanning the place for beautiful women. He found them all looking back at him. His left hand fell softly onto the bar. He nodded to a suited bartender and uttered, 'Bourbon on the rocks.'

The barman slid the bourbon across the bar as a twenty-dollar note slid towards him. Benedict lifted the tumbler and held it to his mouth. He felt the ice soothe his lips, as the smokiness soothed his palate. His body was arched over slightly, his head down. Within moments he caught a brunette staring at him from the end of the bar. He stared back. Attraction was all in the eyes. His blues were piercing; her silky browns were softened by his stare. They were full of reverence.

Benedict turned back to the barman, who was now standing across the bar from the brunette. He gestured to the barman with a single lift of his left index finger and thumb, and he mouthed, 'White wine,' flicking his finger in the direction of the brunette.

She nodded. She understood. The barman delivered a glass of white wine and she sipped it provocatively. Benedict walked towards her and slid another twenty dollars to the grateful barman, who had seen this move many times before—the mysterious man in a bold blazer buys a pretty girl a drink, tells stories of his money-making day on Wall Street and then whisks her away in a sports car for drinks at his bachelor apartment. Tonight was no different.

Benedict introduced himself. 'I'm Benedict.'

She delicately whispered, 'Raffaella,' in his ear as the soft rock music became louder.

Benedict felt her lips touch his ear and her breath tickled the back of his neck. He looked at her intently. She was electric, an olive-skinned Italian girl of twenty-three, her hair was bobbed and shimmered in the shiniest of blacks, her little black dress hugged her everywhere it should.

She playfully whispered again into his ever-grateful right ear, 'Do you come here often?' and giggled at its delivery.

Her Italian accent enunciated every vowel impeccably. Benedict laughed with her.

'Not often enough,' he quipped, and rested his right hand onto the small of her back.

The barman looked on, counting the minutes until Benedict offered her the inevitable ride home in his sports car. Benedict altered his cuff. It revealed his Breitling watch. The detail in its craftsmanship was plain to see, to even the most untrained eye. She saw it—she had seen many watches before. Benedict leant towards her, she tilted her head. His spiced aftershave hypnotised her. He whispered sensually, 'Should we get out of here? I've got my other Italian sweetheart outside.'

Raffaella giggled in delight. The barman smirked to himself, relishing the game of cat and mouse. Benedict looked towards the man who hung on his words and actions and smiled back. Raffaella took one last sip of her wine before placing the glass on the nearest table. She reached for a small black bag with a golden clasp and slipped it onto her tanned shoulder. Benedict put a strong right hand onto her other shoulder and led her towards the elevator.

His brogues and her heels ticked in melodic fashion. Benedict walked slowly and looked back at the barman who was clearing away Raffaella's half-empty glass. Benedict had left another twenty dollars on the bar. He clicked his fingers once, grabbing the attention of the barman, and pointed to the note.

The mirrored elevator reflected never-ending images of these two beautiful people. They were like a glossy magazine advert. Benedict's perfect jawline, Raffaella's flawless skin. The elevator slowed to a stop. The attendant smiled at them both and, in a husky voice, wished them goodnight.

Benedict tipped his head and handed him twenty dollars. Benedict yearned to touch Raffaella's back again, but instead he allowed her to walk a half-step in front of him while he drank in her beauty. The doorman opened the oak door and was paid twenty dollars for the gesture. Benedict rested his left hand upon Raffaella's back and began to stride in time with her.

A red Ferrari F40 graced the cobbled street. Benedict had requested it be parked outside ready for his exit. It had the desired effect. The engine was still warm. Benedict helped Raffaella into the passenger seat and ogled her legs as her dress rose momentarily. He glided into the driver's seat and ripped the ignition into life. The engine roared. Benedict looked in the rear-view mirror and could see the large man beside the oak door. An italic sign above the door read *The Pink Cadillac.*

Benedict woke; the quilt of his bright-white bed was dishevelled on one side. The other side hugged his muscular body. It was a typical bachelor apartment; everything in it shone with narcissistic power— everything was glossed; there was a subtle nuance of industrial shades and the occasional hiccup of flamboyant colour.

On the black side table were two champagne flutes, one of which had a smudge of scarlet lipstick on the rim. Raffaella was perched on the balcony, looking out onto the metropolis that was New York City. Central Park pleased her eyes.

Benedict looked over to her; she was wearing his blazer. Its shoulders draped over her petite frame and her incredible sun-kissed legs disappeared tantalisingly beneath the bottom of it. She casually smoked a cigarette. Her vantage point allowed the sunrise to grace her. Her beauty was becoming of a fairy tale.

Benedict closed his eyes again for a few minutes; he opened them as he felt Raffaella kiss his forehead. He smelt the cigarette smoke on her breath. She turned away from him and walked away, her stilettos dangling between her painted finger nails. She slipped the blazer off her back with a simple shrug of her shoulders and announced, 'Check the inside pocket, mister.'

She strolled out of his view with a confident swagger and closed the door to his apartment behind her. Benedict stretched out to reach his blazer that now lay in a heap on the tiled bedroom floor. He reached into the inside pocket. A white serviette was inside, embossed with the Pink Cadillac logo. The serviette was stained with scarlet-red lipstick; the Italian lady had left her number and a note— *Raffaella the Rodeo x.*

He smirked and remembered the previous night's misdemeanours.

His Ferrari F40 was one in a long list of classic sports cars that he had acquired. The others were stored under lock and key code by the Hudson Harbour at City Island Park.

His Ferrari smelt of Raffaella—infused with the sweet and seductive. It cornered like the sports car it was and what it professed to be. Its curved shell danced on the ocean roads. It purred as he stopped at the harbour. Even after the engine was turned off, the car grumbled and groaned in its disappointment.

A uniformed man greeted Benedict, who dropped the Ferrari's keys into the welcoming man's hands. The valet's hands then caressed and squeezed the Ferrari's steering wheel. The car came to life and was driven steadily to a large hangar-type structure ten metres away. Benedict walked behind.

The valet, Mikko, prised his hands off the steering wheel and typed seven numbers onto a keypad beside the car. A garage door opened slowly and Mikko carefully parked the Ferrari. Benedict walked to a separate door within the hangar and inputted his own seven-digit code into another keypad attached to a reinforced modern door.

'Mikko—keys!' shouted Benedict.

Mikko was busy ogling the pale-blue-and-orange Ford GT40 parked beside him. He reluctantly threw the Ferrari keys a few feet to Benedict, who caught them effortlessly. Mikko lacked coordination, but he had never seen Benedict drop a set yet. He hung them beside six other sets of car keys. The horse on the key fob rocked back and forth for a second or two.

Benedict high-fived Mikko as they left the classic-car compound. Mikko giggled like a child. 'Which car you taking home next, sir?'

'Don't know yet, I'll decide later—look after them for me in the meantime,' Benedict instructed. Mikko enjoyed this playful delivery.

The harbour was picturesque. The sun was strong. Benedict reached into his denim jacket and pulled a pair of aviator sunglasses from a stitched pocket. He slipped them on smoothly and strutted onto the pier.

The harbour was decorated with sparkling yachts. Ocean spray tickled Benedict's face. Droplets appeared on his sunglasses. A soft mist of sea water was the backdrop to a handshake between Benedict and an elderly man wearing a captain's cap. To their left, a tall white yacht harboured ten scantily clad women. The women all looked towards Benedict and the elderly male, trying to overhear their conversation, but it was already over by the time one of the girls turned down the soul music that resounded from the bottom deck of the yacht. Benedict stepped aboard and saluted a goodbye to the elderly man in the cap, who saluted back.

Benedict's yacht sliced through the ocean like a hot knife through strawberries. The shore had long since disappeared. Benedict was stranded with only ten bikini-clad girls for company. The girls were sipping champagne and nibbling diced strawberries. Soul music played in the background.

Benedict looked over his sunglasses towards the beautiful women. Two of them playfully fed each other strawberries and looked to Benedict for approval. Both were tall and slender. Both were blonde. Both wore bikinis. Both approached Benedict. They laughed, seductively aware of their provoking tease.

'Heads you get me, tails you get both of us,' and with that one of the blondes threw a dime towards Benedict. He caught it.

He held it in his right fist as they continued to prance towards him. He opened his hand as they knelt beside him. Franklin's head looked back at them.

'Heads,' Benedict sighed.

The other blonde interjected, 'No, turn it over,' and winked.

Benedict stood and began to follow the two blondes to the lower deck of his yacht; his body was illuminated by the sunlight reflecting off the sea. Benedict felt the dime in his hand and rolled the coin over each of his knuckles in turn. He looked at the yacht and the girls that pranced around him and thought only of his early gambling years and his first six-dollar combine.

Benedict was dressed in his school clothes. He gently stroked the coin's ridges, dents and imperfections as he selected the dime from his right pocket. He shuffled the coin back and forth between his index finger and thumb in anticipation of his throw. Pitch-and-toss had long since been a tradition at Lincoln Elementary. It had cost students their dinner on many occasions but, on the flip side, it had allowed students to dine like kings with their winnings.

The game was a simple one, a game of skill with a pinch of luck— to throw a coin at a specified wall, in an attempt to land *said coin* as close to *said wall* as possible. Each player would take their turn in trying to move another player's coin, or simply trying to beat another player's coin. The player to pitch or toss their coin closest to the wall took the other players' coins as a reward and retained their own. Benedict had never lost.

His eighteenth birthday began early. He threw on a pair of jeans and yesterday's T-shirt, and carefully retrieved his cotton sack full of dimes and dollars. Benedict crept across the landing, beneath the multi-coloured birthday decorations that were pinned to every available space, and carefully tiptoed to the Jacksons' front door.

The old, beat-up betting shop was a thorn in the sidewalk of Sixty-Third Street. The neon sign shone brightly, and its hum echoed up the empty street. Metal horizontal bars protected the expansive windows that had further neon signs to attract gamblers' eyes.

Benedict pulled at the weighted door that screeched as he stepped inside. Smoke clouded the room and its occupants. It clung to every surface and drenched the room in an amalgamation of tobacco and alcohol. It was desperately bitter. Shreds of torn newspapers lay at the entrance and stuck to Benedict's soles as he entered.

His eyes were stung by the smoke. He rubbed at them before looking towards the gamblers sitting opposite him. Not a single word left their lips. Benedict fought the haze and quickly scribbled on a betting slip at the counter.

The cashier towered over Benedict in height and breadth. His suit struggled to fit his heavy frame; his shirt button was on the brink of popping from the cotton. His tie matched his suit—it was black. Buck always wore black. Buck talked the way he looked; he was loud and overpowering. His mother and father were the same. They enjoyed eating burgers and fries. Everything was a greasy comfort. No greens in sight. They ate from the comfort of their sofas in front of the television.

Benedict placed his betting slip on the counter and rotated it to face Buck, who peeled himself away from the small black-and-white television beside the counter and took the slip. 'Six-dollar combo?'

'Thought I'd try my luck,' quipped Benedict.

Benedict dug into his heavy pocket, that hung lower than it should, and pulled at the cotton bag like a fisherman at his catch. The coins jangled as he emptied them onto the counter.

'There's one hundred dollars there,' said Benedict.

Buck laughed to himself and found the inventiveness to crack a joke. 'Raided your savings, have you?'

'I have.'

Behind Buck's brash exterior was a caring soul. He remonstrated with Benedict, 'You sure you want to spend all your savings, son? The odds are not really in your favour.'

'I'm sure.'

Buck shook his head and reluctantly collected the coins. He counted and stacked them quickly considering the fatness of his fingers. With one sharp stamp, the bet was placed, and the haze was sucked from the murky room as Benedict's feet graced the street once more.

Buck was watching his black-and-white television. The room hadn't changed. The same old gamblers sat on leather stools surrounded by the smoke from their cigarettes. The smoke irritated Benedict's eyes again. The whir of an oscillating fan clouded Buck with unconditioned air. It cooled him and swirled the smoke-filled room into a backdraft.

'Hi there,' said Benedict.

Buck jumped from his chair, startled by Benedict's stealthy appearance. 'You—you won, boy,' stuttered Buck.

Benedict stood in an unfazed arrogance. Buck was too excited to notice.

'I can't believe you won. One in a million that, boy—well actually, it's one in fifty-eight—wait here, I've got your winnings out back.'

Buck waddled to the back room and returned with a bag full of fifty-dollar bundles. 'There's five thousand eight hundred there, boy. I had the machine count them.'

Buck placed the bag onto the cashier's desk and Benedict shovelled the bundles into his rucksack.

'Oh, I almost forgot. Here's your stake—couldn't give you your coins back, could I? I'd have to count them again.' The chubby man laughed before handing Benedict a fresh hundred-dollar note.

Benedict trod barefoot across the oak-floored deck, arm in arm with Miss Heads and Miss Tails. There wasn't a cloud in the sky to diminish the evening's bright moon. Ripples on the dark ocean twinkled as far as the eye allowed—3.1 miles to be exact. The girls failed to appreciate the mystery of the ocean surrounding them; they treasured one thing and one thing only, the enigmatic man that spoiled them. Benedict graced the deck and sank into his cream leather sofa as gorgeous girls danced around him. Some wore bikinis, some did not.

The yacht swayed on the ocean's current as the music rippled across the water, dissipating in the lightest of breezes until the party darkened into moonlight.

'To the bedroom!' shouted Miss Heads as the moon set over the yacht.

The morning after the night before saw Benedict snuggled amongst a cotton quilt and naked girls. He awoke to the sounds of seagulls squawking outside and the waves that rose and fell against the stern. An ebony girl was lying provocatively next to him, asleep. Her slender thigh and shimmering back were visible against the white cotton quilt. Benedict tickled both sensually before making his way to the deck. The rising sun beamed off his tanned physique as he walked slowly to the bow's edge. The previous night's flutes, champagne bottles and bikinis were strewn over the oak deck in dramatic fashion, dumped wholly in that order. Olive-skinned beauties bathed in the sun, soaking up the morning's indulgence, readying themselves for what the day had in store—or, more so, what Benedict had in store for them.

They marvelled at their captain as he graced the deck with his charming presence. They couldn't take their eyes off the man that spoiled them, and pampered their deepest, darkest desires.

He stood at the bow of his yacht and looked over the crystal turquoise ocean that swelled to the edge of the earth. He paused for a moment as the topless girls admired his physique. He brushed the hair from his eyes, relishing the attention of the beautiful women. His outstretched arms bulged in the definition of his pose and the sunlit morning. He stretched his arms into a crucifix, squatted slightly, and sprang into the ocean air. His elegant entry into the cool water hardly caused a splash. Bubbles encapsulated his body as he sank deep into the crystal-clear abyss. He kicked sharply towards the surface. He studied the sun that shone into the ocean, fragmenting on the ripples overhead. Benedict broke the surface and a yellow warmth embraced him. He swam towards his adoring spectators—all aboard ogled at his beauty from a yacht named Acquiesce.

Chapter Eight

HEARTLESS

Like the speed of sound chasing the speed of light

Benedict stood like a solemn soldier, allowing the shower's water to douse and caress his chiselled face. The droplets ran frantically along his hardened cheekbones and jawline before finally falling to the marbled shower floor. His body was hugged by a white vest, spoiled with bright red blood. The blood was several shades of red, caused by the water that seeped into the fabric like a discoloured jellyfish. His hands hung by his side and allowed the water to cascade down them simultaneously. The water knotted the open flesh wounds of his bruised knuckles.

As the water gained momentum it gained blood, before twisting and swirling into the plughole. Benedict watched the whirlpool. He reached to his face with his right hand; he tipped his head ever so slightly and brushed his hair backwards. His fingertips ran smoothly through his hair as he closed his eyes.

The punch bag was heavy; it looked heavy. It thudded and winced with every blow that Benedict landed upon it. He stung a combination of left and right punches into the bag's midriff, in a hundred and one different places. Benedict weaved into position and pounced on the defenceless leather that swung desperately in an attempt to evade more punches. He caught the bag in both hands as it swung towards him, deftly laying it to rest. The sweat glistened on his skin before dripping onto the boxing gym mats. He removed the gloves that had peppered the punch bag and gripped a skipping rope between his wrapped knuckles.

Soon enough, the snap of the skipping rope was tamed like a serpent; it arced through the air and disappeared beneath Benedict's dancing feet and crossing hands—the rope only reappeared when he slowed to a dancing skip. He stopped and exuded calmness; his heart rate was smooth, settled and undaunted. He clenched his hands and opened them, feeling his fingertips stretch. He allowed his left hand to caress the top of his right hand. They were as smooth as his heartbeat.

An array of glamorous cars had been parked inward-facing, creating a large circular barrier. Behind the vehicles stood a large hangar that dwarfed the beautiful women and suited men who looked towards the centre of the makeshift ring their cars had created. The nose and cockpit of a private jet poked out of the hangar, the wheel chocked to the tarmac as it watched over the large, lit-up, runway fighting ring.

In the middle of this opening stood a monstrous figure who twisted his neck left and right before snarling at his slender opponent. His jawline was sharp. His name was Frank. The crowd sizzled in anticipation of this David and Goliath duel. The suited men made bets with touts and with one another. To the objective eye, the odds were heavily stacked in Frank's favour. He was huge. He was hungry. He had never tasted defeat.

Frank shouted at Benedict; saliva spat from his mouth and travelled with his words. 'I'm going to make you ugly, pretty boy!'

Frank was mindful of Benedict's looks and had an insatiable desire to destroy them. Frank clenched his fists and scowled. The duo walked with purpose towards the referee, their eyes fixed on each other. Benedict smiled casually, Frank roared back.

The referee was a shadow of the two men that sandwiched him. They towered over his outstretched arms that were holding them apart. Despite his lesser presence, the referee spoke with aplomb and authority. 'When I say fight, I mean fight. When I say break, you break, and when I say it's over—it's over.'

Frank exerted his authority and declared unequivocally, 'It ain't over till I say it's over.'

Benedict stepped forward. Frank was steadfast. The referee pushed at Benedict's chest and gestured him backward. Their eyes pierced each other's. The atmosphere electrified everyone involved. The referee stood amongst it; his skin trembled, but he was warmed by the streams of light that flooded onto him from all directions. He pointed to Frank, he pointed to Benedict. He drew both his hands down, gesturing for these men to meet in the middle—for them to fight. They obeyed and walked forward.

'You ready, you ready—fight!'

Frank sprang towards Benedict. He was sharp and deceptive. His deception had fooled many opponents, over many years. He was built like a rhino but had a light-footed pounce. Frank sucked at the open air, taking in the oxygen needed to deliver the first and pivotal punch. It was his sole tactic, mastered with violence. His opponents, stifled by his speed, would invariably scrunch up into a ball to protect everything that mattered, but the sheer and unparalleled power of this titanic man would rip deep into the soul of his opponent and devour their spirit.

Benedict, the significantly smaller man, failed to underestimate the colossal figure that overshadowed him, and the jackhammer of his right hand. He slid to his right like a Motown dancer, and whipped a counter right hand from his right hip to his left ear. The sheer momentum and accuracy of the uppercut sliced through the shimmer of lights and landed square onto the encroaching jaw of his opponent.

Frank's teeth were the first part of his body to absorb the blow. His ears were next, with the sound of his teeth that wretchedly shattered like a mosaic vase. The watching piranhas indulged in the gore, craving more blood. It took Frank a second or two to sense the destruction, but it wasn't this that affected him—his body was thrown into a frenzy. His toes tried desperately to cling to the ground as the aftershock of Benedict's blow echoed around his mind in cataclysmic fashion. Frank stumbled towards the blinding frog-eyed headlights of a parked 1971 Ferrari 308 Daytona. It was inevitable—Frank was on a collision course of destruction. The weight of his impact buckled the bonnet into a muddle of cubist red.

The voluptuous blonde that stood next to the Italian supercar was horrified, stumbling backwards on her sparkly heels. The owner of the car watched through heavy-rimmed glasses—geek chic. He grinned from ear to ear, relishing the theatre of the occasion. He cared little for possessions.

Frank shook his head to rid himself of instability, and covered the red Ferrari in his blood, spoiling the freshly waxed surface like cherries amongst strawberries. He staggered to his feet as the suspension groaned in relief. He pawed at the blood that continued to gush from his mouth; it started to slow as it congealed in a gloopy mess and hung down from his chin like thick snot. He looked at the blood on his clenched hand and gritted his mouthful of mutilated teeth in rage, spitting out four that scattered between a gladiator's footsteps and diamond heels.

Despite Frank's lack of wisdom, he swiftly realised that Benedict was much the quicker man and refrained from running; instead he walked slowly towards Benedict. He had never been on the back foot. He had never lost any teeth. He took calculated steps. He was frightened.

Benedict smirked at the man that feared him, whose steps between his fallen teeth were littered with apprehension, and

Benedict chose to exploit his fear. He goaded the stumbling mess with a simple gesture from his finger. The crowd fizzed around him. Frank remained steadfast. Benedict gesticulated again, forgetting his subtleness and instead screaming in rage, 'AARGH—COME ON!'

Frank had never been belittled in his life. He was too big for that, but he could see the sympathetic stares of flash men in flash suits and extraordinary women in astonishing outfits. He would have chosen to lose more teeth rather than be pitied by them.

Benedict began to bob and weave, circling like a professional boxer. His graceful shuffle was interrupted by two stinging jabs that sprang from his hip. They landed with precision and power, both rocketing Frank into a wild spin. Frank's delayed reactions left him swinging a right hook before he had even registered that Benedict had landed two punches on the bridge of his nose. His body eventually caught up with his injuries, like the speed of sound chasing the speed of light.

Benedict rolled under Frank's baseball hook to the opposite side of Frank's body and delivered two devastating hooks to his ribcage. Frank winced while falling and skidding to a heap at Benedict's feet. Frank was confused as to which injury he should protect first; he opted for his body. He struggled to breathe amongst the brooding blood. He was drowning. He sucked desperately at the night air for oxygen and wished the man standing over him would leave him to lie there in peace. The pain in his ribs was unbearable. Two were broken. He wheezed in pain between his arduous breaths. He begged between his coughs, while curling himself into a foetal position, 'Please—please…'

The baying crowd laughed at Frank's weakness, but by this time Frank didn't care. Benedict ignored his words entirely. His plea was more in hope than belief. Benedict didn't allow the man to surrender and instead stamped on his face while the downed monster clutched his ribcage. His head crash-landed onto the bloodstained runway, causing his blood to spatter over Benedict's shoes and white vest.

The businessmen roared at the heartless stamp while the ladies adorned with jewels turned away in disgust. It pleased Benedict.

Benedict knelt down and callously spat at the bludgeoned face before him. The watching crowd loathed the vile act, but Frank's torment wasn't over, and strangely the referee failed to step in; instead he watched the white-vested man continue to attack his stricken opponent. Benedict continually crashed his fists into Frank's already broken ribs. They began to crumble like concrete and blood congealed within them. Benedict sneered as the man coughed to avoid suffocation. He gripped at Frank's mouth and squeezed it shut—stealing away his pathetic breaths. He looked into his eyes and viciously declared, 'Now it's over.'

Benedict rose to his feet and was immediately confronted by the referee, who threw Benedict's arm up into the air. His knuckles bore open wounds, his vest was stained red. Frank's body was battered, ruptured and covered with blood.

Chapter Nine

CONSEQUENCE

A place called home

Benedict's bloodstained white vest was crumpled in a heap, unwittingly spoiling the cream granite tiles of the bathroom floor. Benedict stood beside the dampened bloody mess and acknowledged it before looking at his bare body in a misted mirror. He held up his right hand and reached out to the steamy haze, arcing his palm over the blurry view of his face. He looked down and scanned the heavy bruising and raw skin on his right knuckles and elbow. He took his battered and bruised hands to his pristine wardrobe where his shirts and blazers hung immaculately—in order of colour, preference and importance. He delicately pondered over which shoes, shirt and suit would soon grace his body before a mist of Caron Poivre dampened his neck. It was spicy, enriched with woody and floral base notes. The mercurial perfume suited the man that oozed confidence. Benedict wore it audaciously.

The cold air of Fifty-Fifth breezed past the rose-and-clove-scented man, rushing down the street in time and in tune with Tuesday's traffic. A taxi swung across to the beautiful black-suited man. Benedict acknowledged the driver as he entered a cab ordinarily full of nonsensical chatter.

Bob had been doing this for twenty-three years. He had studied the warrens of the city and told tales to tourists eloquently. He had a predilection and talent for cryptic crosswords. Bob had always been the most intelligent occupant of his taxi. He had carted successful businessmen and politicians through the city for over two decades and marvelled at how they would often lose themselves in their self-importance during phone calls in the back seat of his cab. Quite often Bob thought to himself, when they were busy ignoring him, that the loudest man in the room was not always the most powerful. Knowledge was power. Bob knew better. *Proverbs 24:5*, recalled Bob. Benedict allowed Bob to think the same on this occasion, but couldn't help peeking over the driver's shoulder at his folded crossword. They both enjoyed the silent journey.

Bob rolled the cab to a gentle stop and Benedict leant forward to hand over the fare to his deliverer. The neon reflection of a news studio glimmered off the internal taxi window as Benedict opened the sturdy door. Before he closed it, he leant his head into the taxi and waited until Bob turned to see him, then offered the driver some words. 'Couldn't help but see six across—somnambulist—a night and daze walker. Somnambulist.'

Benedict closed the door as Bob watched the charismatic man disappear behind revolving doors. Humbled, he unfolded the crossword that rested on the front passenger seat.

Benedict walked into a studio that was bold in colour and scale. He climbed carpeted stairs and then onto the second tier of the auditorium. He sat in a kitschy, uncomfortable chair that overlooked hundreds of people below him. The audience sat quietly, nervously, on the soft but unshaped burgundy seats. A table at the front of the elevated stage was illuminated by a theatre lamp. Two seats and two glasses of water were set either side of the light that drew the audience's gaze to it like a moth.

A studio producer stood at the front, blocking the light for those in the low-level seats. A red and yellow sign blinked when he threw his hands in its direction—*Applause*—he swivelled to his left and right in time with the organised applause, gesturing for the star in the wings to enter to raptures. The applause grew as the familiar figure of Christopher Casey stepped into the studio lights. George Wainright followed Casey's footsteps and enjoyed the studio cheer which was as false as canned laughter.

George was a ruthless, self-opinionated politician; he shifted in his seat as he wriggled his overweight frame into it. He was both liked and disliked by many of the voters he served. His brutal honesty was admired and loathed, and his straight-to-the-point brash way divided opinion. Controversial. Cocky. Conniving.

Casey allowed George to wriggle one last time before he took his seat like a gentleman. Benedict and a three-hundred-strong crowd watched the formalities and accolades play out. An industrial-size camera aired the show live to a million New Yorkers, who watched from the comfort of their sofas.

Casey pointed to Mrs Keegan, who was holding her left arm aloft in the fifth row. Geraldine had been a carer for almost thirty-five years; she was a grandmother, mother and a widow. Her job title perfectly complemented her worth. She was a delightful person. Her aqua blouse had landed her the question. Her wrinkled eyes widened as Casey spoke directly to her. 'Yes you, just there, what's your question for Mr Wainright?'

'Hello. Please forgive my frustrations, but how is it possible that we live in such an advanced society yet we have such a poorly performing, inefficient medical system?'

Her left hand clutched at her neck as she felt it redden under the spotlight of the studio and the gaze of the people around her. Her articulate question surprised a few, but not her daughter April, who was there in support beside her. George began to speak with aplomb as if he were singing in his shower. 'We have an excellent health service, which you must pay into; if you have no insurance then unfortunately that failing can only be attributed to oneself.'

Mrs Keegan, who had stood to deliver her question, had by now eased back into her seat. Her hips hurt from old age and a lifetime of bending to another person's need. She looked to her left, to the younger version of herself; they both shook their heads and held each other's hands—words failed them. Most of the audience were angered by Wainright's cut-throat answer. It was echoed by a jostling of bodies and murmurs that amplified their disapproval.

Benedict watched Geraldine and April hold hands throughout the following quick-fire questions that George batted away like an all-star baseball player. The questions were cut and curved and screwballed at him, but he dispatched each like a Babe Ruth moonshot. A trickle of George's fans and acquaintances that were tactically placed in the crowd applauded, but the majority disapproved. Casey had chopped at least three outbursts by raising his voice as the studio microphone that hung over the crowd was temporarily turned down.

Mr Gillard stood and raised his hand; Casey offered him a voice. The audience mic was turned up as the shocked man slowly lowered his raised hand. He was not dressed for the occasion—especially for this prime-time slot, but his worn jeans and dishevelled T-shirt portrayed the stereotypical worker he was.

The big man had worked for a multitude of building contractors since he had left school at fifteen. His hands were like shovels, big, tough and weathered. He was an honest man with a laugh unfitting for his frame. Mouse-like. He had travelled to his twenty-second-row seat via two subway trains. The television cameras played out nearly ten seconds after real time, allowing the camera to zoom to Mr Gillard as Casey still held the screen; his words were delivered with authority. 'Next question—you at the back…yes, you. What's your question?'

The large man chuckled nervously, summoning up the courage to speak. 'Hey both, I'm Gareth.' He shuffled slightly as soon as he realised the camera and light were upon him.

'Hello, Gareth,' they replied in chorus. Casey took back the screen, which then panned to show the audience and the politician.

'What's your question to Mr Wainright?'

Gareth eased into his surroundings, took a deep breath and spoke. 'Well, I'm concerned about the politicians like yourself there, constantly telling us that it's our problem. The working folk of this country, like myself, who work all the hours I can—to make ends meet, to provide for my family—we are then told that due to government expenditure we will have to pay more tax to subsidise the excessive spending of government officials like yourself there. Who fine-dine, live lavish lifestyles and claim expenses unnecessarily. So, my question to you, Mr Wainright, is—why are we being punished for your misdemeanours?'

The audience applauded as the big man landed himself back into his seat. His words still echoed throughout the hall. His body fizzed with adrenaline. His taking of his seat was less than graceful. An unknown hand settled Gareth as he tried to quash the shaky feeling that cascaded over his skin. The hand patted his large shoulder endearingly. Gareth turned and followed the arm, seeing a like-minded and like-dressed man at the end of it. They both grinned in mutual agreement. Mutual respect.

The politician spoiled their moment with perfect and pronounced English. 'The simple answer to your question, Gareth—can I call you Gareth?' His question was merely a polite gesture and he continued without waiting for an answer. 'I chose to further my education to make choices, sometimes difficult choices, for the American people. For those difficult decisions that I make I get paid a lot of money and decide to live the way I do. If you wanted to further your education and make something of yourself, you too could make pivotal decisions like I do, and live—like you say—lavishly.'

Gareth felt his hoi-polloi blood boil. The builder shuddered out of his man-to-man moment and bit back from his seat. 'At least I can say my living is an honest living. Can you say the same there?'

The adrenaline fizzed again, demanding that his body stand up. Instead he shuffled to the edge of his seat to contain his emotion and remembered his children were watching their daddy from home.

The frustrated members of the debate jostled in the free seats offered to them by local unions and friends of friends. Their dissatisfaction was palpable, sandwiched between an unhappiness about Wainright's jab and yet enthralled with Gareth's counter-hook. Ringside whispers began to resonate throughout the lower tier; before the whispers rose to chants, Benedict interrupted the melee. He stood up as the murmurs, moans and mumbles stirred in the cauldron beneath him. The microphone operator had witnessed Benedict's black suit shimmer as he stood up. There were only a handful of people in the upper tier—the overflow was dotted sporadically throughout the top section.

The boom man had been working at the studio for less than two years; Jarrod had a steady hand and a degree in sound engineering. He was an ambitious person. He lived with his boyfriend of three years who was an aspiring actor in a city full of actors. Jarrod had seen many beautiful people in his life, owing to his boyfriend's profession, and when Benedict stood, Jarrod knew that this man was fit for the screen.

Jarrod also knew that there had yet to be an upper-level question and drifted the boom microphone up towards the gorgeous man. He felt his skin tremble in the moment. He steadied it close to the edge of the upper tier, close enough to catch Benedict's words and to amplify them to the hundreds in view and the millions unseen.

Benedict spoke eloquently. 'They all say the same things. In different ways, with different words—'

His words caused the people seated in the lower level to turn and look up to this elevated man. The chatter ceased completely. Jarrod wobbled slightly as he watched the floor cameras spin and point to the man in the upper tier. The television personality, the audience and the politician listened intently as Benedict started again.

'They all say the same things, in different ways, with different words, occasionally pausing for nodding heads and rapturous applause. Though who am I to question legacy and promise of centuries past, I am but a person amongst people, with liberty of voice and breath. Many minds far exceed mine but I can still think, many a chorus is louder than I but I can still verse, many tears have fallen harder than mine but I can still cry, many lead lives richer than I but I can still smile. Questions are not invitations for the titled to dwell upon, nor for those who have read the most books, they are for the pauper who is free of preach and dictatorship. Answers are not storied by curly white wigs upon thrones fit for kings and queens, they are voiced by those upon green grass, who worry not of power and consequence, but of a place called home.'

As the last of his poetic words left his lips, Benedict stepped past both empty chairs and occupied ones. His black shoes slid onto the red carpeted stairs that led to the balcony door. The nineteen-month boom man was proud of his initiative. Casey looked across the stage to him and offered him a wink in appreciation of the television moment. It aired just as Benedict left the studio in real time. The audience were gleeful at the prospect of a response to Benedict's rhetorical riddle. George Wainright felt the studio lights for the first time and reached for the glass of water beside him. George failed to realise that he had drained it long ago. The image of him holding an empty glass and stuttering was one that would endure. It was symbolic. It was prime time. Casey smiled.

The amalgamation of the warm studio air and the cold of the street confused Benedict's body. His words still lingered in the ears of the speechless audience as he began to walk briskly away from them to combat the cold. His shoes no longer felt the comfort of the red carpet and instead strode through city crowds over uneven concrete. His celebrity had passed. He was a stranger amongst strangers.

The evening had yet to stray into darkness and was still caught between blue and black. The metropolis beneath the troubled sky was a New York City cliché, normally represented in modern and reasonably priced artwork. Yellow taxis tussled for position with aggressive driving and frequent bad language; other drivers beeped in defeat as the cabbies dominated the road. Pedestrians adhered to the walk/don't walk signals. From beneath a green and white street sign, behind a beaten-up stand, a flat-capped New Yorker named Gerard sold hot dogs and newspapers. His cheeriness and salesmanship deserved better, but it lent itself perfectly to the expression *as keen as mustard.*

Benedict strolled past the flaming hot dogs that crackled and spat as Gerard flipped them while fiddling with his flat cap. The aroma clouded the street, teasing customers until they parted with two American dollars.

Benedict fought the urge to delve into the mid-street snack; instead he wandered away from the hustle of the vehicles and street vendors to a less-travelled road. A yellow cab spotted his mooch onto the sparsely populated street and followed him with a drastic spin of the steering wheel. The taxi slammed to a halt beside Benedict and, without breaking stride, Benedict reached out his hand and popped the door handle of the dirty yellow Ford Crown Victoria. The driver's words flew out of the open door, as if they had just been granted freedom, in order to expedite the process of travel and tip.

'Where to, sir?'

Benedict paused as the words cantered towards him, momentarily focusing on the conscious change of wind direction. The faint smell of burning wood overpowered the fried onions and sausages of Gerard's stall. The infusion of fire rose up into Benedict's delicate nostrils and clawed at the back of his throat. He could taste the bitterness. He slammed the taxi door shut in a defiant refusal of custom and began to chase the smell that scratched his palate.

Benedict bounded over the uneven concrete slabs and disregarded the advice of street signs. He crossed the road to a deluge of disconcerted drivers who voiced their opinions with some dazzling language. The profanities were lost amongst the screeching of brakes and slammed horns. Benedict ran into the wind, searching for the tang that taunted him, a journey seemingly embroiled with fate.

Flames engulfed a suburban home. A crowd had gathered to witness the inferno. Black smoke and fire billowed from the windows and the withering porch door. A local resident, paralysed with fear and consumed by her own words of terror, declared to everyone and anyone, 'There's someone in there!'

Benedict slipped past the shouting, statuesque resident and cut through the posse of people as if a religious figure had parted them for him. He pulled the bottom half of his jacket up over his face and leapt onto the porch that had been transformed into a tunnel of fire. Benedict felt the heat prick his body like needles as he ducked into the hallway. The living room sofa was blistering spitefully as it was torn of its colour. It spouted toxic fumes into the air, which clouded the ceilings and charred the walls, buckling them slowly like torture. Benedict shielded his eyes further, bowing to regain his wilting composure. A submissive act to this violent creation.

The landing window shattered, spinning shards of glass onto the staircase. A blast of oxygen was sucked into the house like a suffocating dragon. It exhaled and bowled a ball of flames out into the street. The crowd shrieked in unison.

Benedict sprinted up the nineteenth-century oak staircase that swayed under his weight and the unbearable temperatures. The fiery beast threw its wings out to its sides, smashing the balustrades as the animal tried desperately to escape the house that caged it. Its tail whipped in a frenzy at the staircase Benedict had treacherously scaled. It obliterated it with one fell swoop, causing it to crumble and pile like jenga pieces. Benedict gasped for breath beneath his suit jacket and chewed at the material trying to salivate his mouth and rid it of its charcoal dryness. He barged into the bedroom door that was scarred courtesy of the flames that softened and warped its texture. The frame buckled, causing Benedict to fall into the bedroom.

Pockets of air spun like shrapnel, causing the door to slam violently behind him and a confusion of colour to rapidly attack the landing rooftop. The flashover was beautiful. Flames hung on the ceiling like inverted lava. Fire dripped to the floor, fusing upstairs and downstairs. In a haze of smoke, Benedict reached the woman lying on the bed. Benedict's eyes had blurred uncontrollably with tears and reddening; he felt the quilt beneath her and grabbed it with both hands, cocooning her tightly. He spluttered. 'You're safe—you're safe.'

The female's only breaths were powerless coughs. The smoke was busy clogging her lungs as well as her home. The quilt ironically offered a suffocating release. The tail of the dragon whipped in rage. It thrashed at the door and the body of the house. The upper level began to crumble, imploding under a series of mini explosions like fireworks that devastated the structure and sentiment of the woman's home. The tail wrapped back to its body and again lashed at the fractured frame and, with the power of a waterfall, the structure toppled. The second tier crashed onto the weakened first and sank into it. Benedict hurled his body and the quilt he was holding through the bedroom window that was a block of soot.

Benedict landed feet first on the lawn, still cradling the woman in the quilt. He allowed his momentum to crash and dissipate by instantaneously rolling onto his side. The lawn had been fried to a brown colour, thanks to the transfer of heat and malice. His first breath of clean air was silky. Benedict let go of the quilt, which unfolded, comforting the woman in a heap on the floor. He looked up at the dragon that broke free, exploding into the darkening sky.

Benedict was rushed upon by a flurry of people. Several arms reached in to pull him to his feet. He felt them pull him, in and out of time sequence, causing him to stand in an unbalanced fashion. He stirred as his feet settled onto the beige grass. Two paramedics ushered unwanted hands away from the hero and leant their trained hands to the woman in the quilt, quickly rushing her into their arms and then into their waiting ambulance.

Blue flashing lights and whistling sirens intermittently echoed from every surrounding nook and cranny. The avenue was submerged with emergency vehicles. The fire truck stood the tallest and was coloured a vicious red. The fire that it battled was reflected magically in its paintwork. The sound of the water wailed and frothed as it doused the dwindling dragon. Onlookers hustled onto tiptoes, trying to see into the back of the ambulances that had converged on the scene. Each had been tactically parked and prevented the concerned crowd from causing chaos.

Elisha, the damsel in the duvet, was lying in the back of Tom and Jerry's ambulance. They had gained those nicknames when they had first paired up as paramedics nearly five years ago. It was Thomas's fault; he had joked that Ryan was the Jerry to his Tom when the customary workplace banter had played out—and it had stuck. Ryan had been renamed; even his wife called him Jerry now.

Elisha's frame was lying on an uncomfortable bed that she could not properly feel. Her body was riddled with smoke. She had a couple of small cuts from the death-defying window leap that she had known nothing about. Benedict took the brunt of the impact; the quilt softened the rest, at least enough that her only real treatment now was an oxygen tank that diluted the smoke in her lungs. Her wheezing, whistling breaths were pacified by a transparent mask that she had originally tried to pull off her face in panic when she had regained consciousness.

Benedict was perched at the rear of the ambulance. He was exhausted, overcome with adrenaline, fear and heat. His body levelled itself with a slowing heartbeat and thanked the night for providing a cool breeze. Tom wandered away from Jerry and could see that Benedict was recovering from his ordeal. He rubbed at his shoulder before asking him, 'Are you coming with us?'

'I'm good, thanks. I don't even know her,' Benedict whispered, his eyes still glazed with a film of water.

'Well, that truly is one hell of a thing you did, risking your life for someone you don't even know,' Tom joked in a serious tone.

Benedict got to his feet, dropping the white blanket that had caped him. 'You don't even know the half of it.'

Tom looked back and scampered back towards Jerry who was reassuring Elisha as the oxygen cleaned her lungs. He turned and nodded to Benedict. 'She's in safe hands now.'

The night had yet to descend to darkness and was the deepest purple it could be before black. Smoke filled the street downwind of the emergency services as silhouettes of people bounced in excitement and nosiness. The powder-grey smog had a ripple of emergency-blue drizzled within it.

Benedict saw that the paramedics were busy treating and ushering rubberneckers who had wandered too close to the blaze. Benedict seized his opportunity to leave the scene, much like he had entered it—with purpose. The indigo sky and dry-ice mist of dispelling smoke was reminiscent of a fantasy novel. Benedict wandered into the darkness.

Chapter Ten

FORTUNE

It was the colour of dark chocolate

The quiet hum that reverberated inside the mirrored elevator resounded in Benedict's head. The sound was strangely soothing. The after-effects of last night's heroics had caught up with him. He was exhausted. He pushed himself against the aluminium handrail, allowing the tubular chunk of metal to tickle his lower back. He was unable to rid himself of the smell of last night's fire that still seeped from his skin.

The elevator's citrusy cleanliness was overpowered by the pong of smoked wood—a distinctive smell that had been tasted and spat out by sommeliers the world over. It was the story that accompanied the scent that was the most pleasing to the taster—the tale of the woman and the dragon.

A robotic female voice sounded. 'Ward C. Please mind the doors.' The smell of the ward seeped into the elevator and mingled with the other odours.

A light tap at the door disturbed Elisha from her afternoon nap. A man came into her distorted view and she tried to focus her eyes on him. She shuffled up beneath the tight bedding and fixed her bedridden hair. It was the colour of dark chocolate.

'Hello,' Benedict said sheepishly.

'It's you,' she responded in a dozy moment of disbelief.

Her eyes couldn't hide the recognition and blinked in order to zoom in on the man. Her hair had fallen into place.

'Sorry if I woke you,' he offered humbly.

'It's fine, I was just resting my eyes,' she joked, and blinked again.

'How are you?' he asked sincerely.

'I'm OK—smoke inhalation and a few burns and bruises. I think they want to keep me in for a few days, but it's all pretty much precautionary. I feel filthy, I can still smell the smoke on my skin and in my hair.' Elisha realised the impertinence of her misguided perspective and instantly corrected herself. 'Listen to me—I wouldn't even be here if it wasn't for you. I'm sorry—I don't even know your name and here I am wallowing in self-pity.'

Benedict refrained from addressing her melancholy and simply introduced himself. 'I'm Benedict, but you can call me Ben.'

She interrupted him impishly, 'No, no—Benedict is fine by me...it's charming. Hello, Benedict, and—excuse my ignorance—how are *you*?' she questioned, accentuating every syllable of his name.

'I'm fine, they gave me the once-over last night—all buzzes and beeps, numbers and figures...' he answered half-heartedly.

Elisha nodded and spoke again. 'I guess it is all pretty overwhelming...' A wave of breathlessness sailed over her, a sudden realisation of where she was and how she got there. She waved it away instantly to dispel her inner anguish. 'I don't know how I could ever thank you,' she said, then playfully quipped, 'My hero.'

He smiled.

'Benedict...' She spoke slowly and eloquently. 'From the Latin, *benedictus*—the blessed one. That Sunday-school Latin served me well,' she announced confidently.

Benedict raised his eyebrows, impressed by the bundled but beautiful girl before him. '*Certe*—indeed it did, Elisha.'

Elisha mirrored him, raising her eyebrows. 'How do you know my name?'

He toyed with her and paused wittingly. 'Umm, it's written on your notes,' he said as he pointed to them.

Her quizzical squint leaned into a coy smile; they had been properly introduced.

An experienced nurse entered and dissected the conversation between the two beautiful people. Polly had served the hospital for eighteen years; it had ultimately cost her a marriage, but she cared little for that now. She had acquired a wisdom that was often in demand and always had a pocketful of lollipops for the children. Polly announced her entrance into the room with typical spark. 'Hello dear, how are we today?'

Elisha beamed. 'Polly…I'm feeling great, thank you.'

Polly looked across at the man beside the bed but didn't address him; instead she mumbled to herself, 'I bet you are.'

She looked intently at Elisha and fixed her pillow with accomplished grace. 'And who is this handsome young devil?' she teased, like an embarrassing relative.

Elisha answered frivolously, 'This is Benedict—the reason that I'm still here.'

Polly studied the man. 'Quite the lead character,' she proclaimed.

Elisha agreed, 'Indeed.'

Both looked adoringly towards him. Benedict didn't flinch; he enjoyed their attention.

Polly tampered with a beeping machine momentarily and picked up a chart that balanced on the beam of Elisha's bed. 'Well…the numbers and figures say that you are on the mend, so I shall leave you to it—I will pop back later to check on you…and perhaps I'll check you as well, mister.'

She flashed a cheeky smile in Benedict's direction. 'See you later, children.'

Benedict's reply staggered her exit from the room. 'Thank you, Mary.'

Polly was a woman who always spoke first, and last, in any conversation. She peered from the edge of the doorway and responded playfully, 'Only my mother calls me Mary, dear.'

Polly had been born Mary Leila Earls, the only child of a devout Irish Catholic family. Her grandparents had sailed the choppy waters of the Atlantic many moons ago, docking in New York with nothing but a suitcase and a smile. Polly had inherited their charm.

She closed the door behind her and watched Benedict and Elisha fall into conversation like reunited sweethearts. The man was captivated by Polly's recovering patient, who, despite her ordeal, still looked fit for Broadway. They both twittered like lovebirds. Polly was absorbed by their interaction but could not hear a word of it. It was in that solitary moment that she longed to be young again. She missed her husband.

The quiet hum that reverberated inside the mirrored elevator annoyed Andy and caused the cups of coffee in his hands to shake. He was not the most intelligent of people. He was fortunate in that respect. If he had been a thinker, he would have drifted into an overthought depression long ago. He'd had a far more difficult childhood than his peers. His father had worked away a lot, was seldom home and had died far too young. He too had been in construction, laying railroads for affluent people.

His death had gone largely unnoticed. Not that the immediate neighbourhood didn't know; they had been kind, often bringing a plate of food to Andy and his mother for months thereafter. Beyond the neighbourhood, it wasn't big news. It wasn't the kind of place where a sense of community thrived. Too many strangers who barely had time to acknowledge each other's presence, let alone share stories of their days. It wasn't like the movies—people didn't stop each other in the street and say 'Have a nice day.' The pace of life didn't allow it.

Andy missed his father. An absent father, absolved the moment he returned home and left his work boots by the stairs. Andy's mother remarried just under five years later. Her extended family and her heart welcomed it, but it never quite sat right with Andy. He was a young man with a young, narrow mind. On the day of the wedding he had been courteous and restrained but crippled inside. He may not have been academic, but he did have an uncanny ability to be a different person at different times.

A robotic female voice sounded, 'Ward B. Please mind the doors.' In stepped a nurse casually sucking on a lollipop. Their eyes met momentarily.

Andy quipped at the stranger, 'Want a cracker?'

The middle-aged nurse heard him but pretended not to, taking the orange lollipop from her mouth. 'I'm sorry?' she said bluntly.

Andy repeated himself wearily, knowing full well that she had heard him the first time. 'Want a cracker?'

The elevator was a confined space. The doors had closed and it had begun its ascent. The robotic announcement of this fact had been promptly ignored, owing to the increasingly awkward human exchange. It continued. Andy felt obliged to explain his attempt at a joke. 'Polly want a cracker?' There was nothing in return.

He continued like a scorned child. 'You know…like the saying.' Andy looked sheepishly at the nurse's name badge and tilted the right-hand cup of coffee towards it. She scrunched her face in disapproval. He understood that at least.

The robotic female voice sounded, 'Ward C. Please mind the doors.'

Polly stepped out without the usual acknowledgement that concludes elevator rides with strangers. She turned right as she exited. Andy shook his head and watched the nurse put the lollipop back into her mouth. She didn't look back. He stepped out of the elevator and walked without care in the opposite direction.

The door jolted open, causing flowing conversation to halt. In stepped a man whose gifts invigorated the room with the aroma of strong coffee. 'Hello darling,' uttered Elisha.

'Hi sweetheart.'

Andy looked uncertainly towards the man that stood to his right. It was territorial. He turned to Elisha. 'How are you feeling?' he asked, and kissed her on the forehead before placing the coffee cups on the bedside table.

Elisha answered immediately and introduced the man with a sharp jawline and imposing physique who was standing at the bottom of her bed. 'I'm much better, thank you darling. Andy, I'd like you to meet Benedict. He's the man who saved my life.'

Some of the tension in the atmosphere evaporated. Benedict looked at Elisha and smiled at her quaint introduction. She spoke again as the two men closed in on each other. 'Benedict, this is Andrew.'

Andy corrected her, and introduced himself, 'Andy.'

Benedict leant forward and shook his outstretched hand, 'Nice to meet you, Andy. I've heard a lot about you.'

Andy found a joke amongst the firm handshake, 'All good, I hope?'

Benedict returned to the bottom of the bed with two steps backwards, 'Of course, of course—hospitals are holy ground, nothing sacrilegious is ever said.'

Andy didn't quite understand what Benedict meant but tittered anyway. He wasn't one for formal introductions or long words, but he had sanctioned his innermost etiquette and continued with his gratitude. 'I can't thank you enough...wouldn't know what to do with myself if I lost this girl.' His gaze washed over Elisha.

Polly returned to the room. All eyes turned to look at her. Again, she mumbled to herself with her mouth almost fully closed, 'Ah, the plot thickens.'

She casually walked beyond the two men to the far side of Elisha's bed—the only space left. Andy acknowledged the nurse with a single nod of his head. Benedict followed his movement. Elisha sensed the tension and spoke in order to correct it. 'Polly, this is Andy,' before nodding in the direction of the man beside her.

Polly was effortlessly loud. 'Ah, the joker and the prince,' she announced in a jovial manner.

Elisha was confused but didn't address it. Benedict could see that Polly's attendance was not just a social visit and that he was obviously encroaching on Elisha's impending care. Polly was playful but professional. There was a degree of animosity between the nurse and Andy.

Benedict addressed the awkwardness and announced his departure with kind words. 'Polly, 'twas lovely to meet you.'

The subtle Irish word softened her heart. She smiled at him. He rested a strong hand on Andy's shoulder and said, 'Andy—you take care of her, OK?'

'I will,' he assured the well-wisher and then confirmed Benedict's departure. 'Thank you, Ben—see you again.'

Benedict acknowledged Elisha as he approached the door. She spoke sincerely and strongly. 'Thank you, Benedict.'

Benedict turned away from the door and theatrically swung his right arm across his body, looked at Elisha and bowed. 'My pleasure...*convalescas ex aegroto mox.*'

Polly and Elisha swooned as the door closed behind the gorgeous man. Andy looked bizarrely at Elisha. She steadied his confusion. 'It means get well soon—it's Latin.'

Andy watched Benedict walk in the direction of the rumbling elevator. He looked back to Elisha as soon as the visitor had completely disappeared from his view. 'I didn't know you spoke Latin.'

Chapter Eleven

ENLIGHTENMENT

Mr Hatten's writing hand was firm and heartfelt

The hardened soles of Andy's heavy rigger boots clobbered down the American oak staircase to the newly polished parquet flooring and Elisha's presence in the kitchen. He peered over her curvaceous frame, his gaze caressing her lazy morning attire. She had been living with him for the past week. Andy's house had finally become a home.

He had moved into Elisha's house shortly after their relationship blossomed. Since then, his house had solely been used as a weekend retreat for his drunken friends to watch sport. But since Elisha's family home had gone up in flames, this was the best of a bad situation.

Andy bumbled quietly towards Elisha; his tiptoed steps were clouded by the clanging of the kitchen and Elisha's dreamlike thoughts. Even in her comfortable clothes she exuded an understated sexiness. Andy wore a red-chequered fleece shirt, which was unbuttoned at the top, displaying a white vest, and scuffed denim jeans. He owned six of each of these items of clothing. He reached out gently to Elisha, who was preparing breakfast; his fingertips tickled her hip as she jumped in both pleasure and fright. 'Andy!'

'Good morning, darling,' he chuckled.

'You frightened me,' quipped Elisha, playfully slapping his shoulder.

'I meant to.' Andy reached beyond Elisha and grabbed a slice of warm buttery toast. 'I love you, darling,' he said.

These words were seldom spoken by him and he knew that. Recent events had really put things into perspective for him. Elisha was flummoxed and stood silently. Andy was completely unaware of what such simple words could evoke, and took a large bite of his toast and wiped his buttery fingers onto his jeans. The richness jolted his taste buds and tangled with the peppermint toothpaste that still clung to his lips. Elisha gathered herself as Andy grabbed his ready-made sandwich box and cradled it under his arm. He pulled out the slice of toast that dangled from his mouth and kissed Elisha on the lips. She too tasted the peppermint. Before she had a chance to respond to his earlier surprise words and wish him a good day, the front door swung open and Andy shouted, 'You meeting Benedict later?'

'Yes, I am—take care, darling!' she hurriedly replied, as the front door slammed shut on her words.

Benedict's tailored woollen trench coat comforted him as it hugged his frame. The satin shine from the dark grey material was peppered with a red haze from the crackling neon sign of Maggie's Diner, as he absorbed the hustle and bustle of the busy street from the sidewalk. He peered through the swarm of yellow taxis that buzzed before him. His eyes were appeased by the intermittent glimpses of Elisha who was standing opposite. She wore a double-breasted winter coat, its fabric a delectable shade of lilac. On its front were six black buttons stacked like dominoes. It had the desired effect; those who looked at her toppled at her beauty.

The street appeared duller against her presence; she was New York's lady in lilac. Elisha caught a glimpse of Benedict; his stare caused her eyes to widen. He gasped, captivated by Elisha's wavy bronze and hazel highlighted hair. He was already addicted. Elisha's footsteps were crisp and slow. The street's busy bees stopped and admired her. She focused her attention on crossing the street in her tanned leather Eskimo boots. It was only when she stepped onto the sidewalk that she looked at Benedict again. Her eyes were a deep chocolate. Marbleised. Benedict's blues melted into hers; it was then that he fully appreciated the sparkle that he had already imagined. She cutely bit at her lip before Benedict greeted her. 'Hello stranger.'

Elisha spoke softly in return. 'Hello. Sorry I'm late, have you been waiting long?'

Benedict looked slowly to his watch, with his fist tightly closed, and whispered, 'Long enough to learn this magic trick.'

He blew sharply into his cupped hands—his breath fogged in the afternoon's chill. A pink flower emerged from beneath his fingers. He had learnt the trick many moons ago and had performed it for many women on many occasions. 'For you, madam.'

'Not a red rose?'

'It lacks originality—the sacred lotus cares little for its own indulgence.'

'Well, thank you, kind sir,' replied Elisha.

'The pleasure is all mine.'

Elisha smiled and clung to the feelings the act had produced. Benedict opened the door to Maggie's Diner and the jangling brass bell welcomed them.

The diner was largely empty. Vintage burgundy-leather bench seats sat back-to-back. Fixed between the seats were blotchy laminated tables, hosting regular assortments of condiments, with an extra helping of ketchup to the centre. The diner was symmetrical. The floor resembled a chessboard.

Mr Hatten was stooped upon the second stool to the right of the cash register. He was a particular gentleman who habitually wore a tweed three-piece suit. Between his short sips of tepid coffee he read articles of prominence. He enjoyed a structured life, never squandering his precious time. He had no time for inconsequential chatter or falseness; he was a straight-talking retired journalist whose words had been chewed up and spat out a million times.

Much of his best work had been his depiction of American troops who had died during the Vietnam War. He had captured the loss and the grief felt by the soldiers' families. His articles were personal, often written with consent over coffee with widows. He felt that kind but impersonal words written on US Army headed paper were meaningless, and he hated the generic nature of them. Mr Hatten had lost count of the articles he had written—it was never about him.

It was the new millennium that this humble man felt had brought the most disgrace to his profession. The accumulation of front-page articles that celebrated celebrity lives and meaningless gossip had buckled his spirit. One major newspaper had once dedicated its front page to a celebrity pet, causing this retired journalist to be lost for words. America had lost its direction and he was saddened for the future of his beloved country. He sipped at his coffee as New Yorkers passed by outside, unaware of his past, his words and his intelligence. They were a generation lost.

The dining room and kitchen were open-plan, a trend that would soon grace regular homes across America. Customers cherished Maggie the owner, Maggie the cook, Maggie the general dogsbody. She was a delightful person. Mr Hatten could have written a book about her spirit and warm heart. The retired journalist enjoyed Maggie's company and Maggie would often blush at his courteous head-tip and over pronounced *ma'am*.

They seldom shared words, not for Maggie's want of trying, but owing to the fact that Mr Hatten chose his words carefully after spending the best part of fifty years tussling with them.

Maggie was old-fashioned and cherished chivalry. Since the untimely death of her husband she had single-handedly raised her only child. Maggie's grief had been internal, geared solely to affording her daughter the opportunity of furthering her education through her work. Margaret missed her husband, but those who knew her as Maggie would never know it. She always made time between orders to discuss her *customer's* problems. Maggie was as tender as the steak she served.

A middle-aged man named Michael, who was not a regular customer, was slouched on a stool at the counter. His dark silvery suit was pressed, his black leather shoes buffed at the tips. He heard the bell jangle and peered over his shoulder at Benedict and Elisha as they entered. He watched them secretly as they strolled to the window seats. He thought of his wife at home. His gloomy disposition oozed from him like the cheese that smothered the diner's quarter-pounders, and Mr Hatten had noticed it.

Mr Hatten got up slowly from his stool and walked towards Michael, and rested his hand against Michael's shoulder, the same way he had done to comfort the families of unforgettable soldiers. He recognised his solemn demeanour. Mr Hatten's writing hand was firm and heartfelt as it landed upon Michael's shoulder. Michael drew breath but did not speak. Nor did Mr Hatten.

Mr Hatten tipped his head towards Maggie as she stood in the kitchen. 'Ma'am.'

Maggie sparked into life amongst a steamy haze.

'Have a lovely day, Mr Hatten, I look forward to seeing you tomorrow.' She smiled and turned back into the steam.

Benedict and Elisha landed in the window seat as Mr Hatten left to the tinkle of the bell. Benedict's courtliness wooed Elisha as he gently placed her coat on a nearby peg.

'Well, thank you,' she acknowledged.

But Benedict didn't reply; he was staring at Michael, who was leaning on the counter, his hands comforting his head. Benedict absorbed his sadness, only to be jolted by Elisha's words.

'What's wrong, Benedict?'

Benedict turned to Elisha, who had nestled snugly into the leather seats, and then threw his eyeline back towards Michael. 'Seems upset over there—the weight of the world, I guess.'

Elisha followed Benedict's eyes and agreed. 'I know, poor thing. I wonder what's wrong?'

'People's problems. Wait here and I'll get this show on the road,' he said, not wanting to dwell on the sadness of the stranger and his newspaper.

Elisha's question had been rhetorical, and she soon forgot about the man with shiny shoes at the counter. 'Don't be long—I'm hungry.'

Elisha chuckled as Benedict turned mid-stride and shook his head at her cheekiness. He strolled towards the waitress standing behind the counter, lost in the importance of her newly painted nails. A 1950s cash register sat between them. Natasha was oblivious to both the beautiful stranger and the sadness of the man to her left. Benedict cleared his throat. Natasha looked up. Her eyes lit up in astonishment. Her smile invigorated her mood.

'Don't concern yourself with your nails, they're perfect,' said Benedict.

Behind him, Elisha inspected her own freshly painted nails as she toyed with the blushing lotus flower. She questioned her presence, even if the man before her had saved her life. Benedict looked over his shoulder to Elisha. Natasha's mood dulled. Elisha looked up at the man smiling at her—it caused her heart to flutter the same way it had when she had heard his voice the night before.

'Hello?'

'Hi.'

'Who's this?' quizzed Elisha.

'It's your charming, intelligent hero from the other night.'

Elisha sniggered shyly into the telephone handset, realising who it was. She had longed to hear his voice again since the day they had met for the second time. 'Oh, hello Benedict, how are you?'

'I'm good, thank you. More importantly, how are you feeling?'

'I'm much better thanks—plus my hair no longer smells of smoke.'

'Well, I'm glad you still have your faculties and priorities in order.'

Elisha propped herself up on the edge of her bed. Attentively, she replied, 'A girl has to feel good you know—anyway, more to the point, how did you get my number?'

'I will explain all if you accompany me to this fabulous diner on Catherine Street—Maggie's Diner. You'll love it.'

'Is that so?' Elisha paused for a moment, allowing her playful words to settle. 'And how do you know that?'

'Because I know everything.'

Elisha giggled and shook her head. 'So, if you know everything, Mr Confident, what's my response?'

'Yes, of course.'

'What if I say no?' she replied flirtatiously.

'You won't. See you tomorrow at four, Elisha—don't be late.'

'But—but I...' stuttered Elisha, before realising Benedict had already hung up.

She placed the handset back on its base and fell back onto her soft bed, smiling. She lay there for a moment, only to feel a sharp twinge of guilt that caused her to sit up again. Andy was at work. She wondered if she had done anything wrong—after all, this man on the telephone had pulled her from a burning building. She reminded herself that Andy wouldn't have a girlfriend if it wasn't for Benedict, and so she slumped back onto her cushioned quilt, wondered what to wear, and wondered how to tell Andy.

Elisha fixed her collared cream dress and dismissed her scruples. Benedict leant forward slightly and whispered into Natasha's ear. Natasha acknowledged his words and replied seductively, 'That's no problem. Take a seat, sweet tooth, and I'll be with you shortly.'

'Could I have two menus, please?' asked Benedict.

Natasha looked baffled but didn't question his request and handed him two menus. He slid them under his arm and marched towards Elisha. Elisha watched him, Natasha ogled him. He sat beside Elisha and handed her one of the menus.

'I'm so hungry,' Elisha childishly proclaimed as she took hold of the red leather-bound menu full of italic scribble.

'I know…you've told me once already,' replied Benedict with an undertone of sarcasm.

Elisha scrolled up and down at what the menu promised, before informing Benedict proudly, 'I'm done.'

She peered over the top of the menu and caught Benedict's bright-blues fixed upon her. She smiled and playfully popped a question at him. 'Are you done already?'

'Of course.'

'A latte and pancakes with maple syrup for me, please,' said Elisha.

Benedict deliberated, 'A sweet tooth?'

'I *love* pancakes,' enthused Elisha.

'Perfect choice,' said Benedict, insinuating the same choice.

Elisha enjoyed his gaze and sarcastically quipped, 'Very original.' She smiled before Benedict stood and walked to the counter.

Benedict nodded at the waitress who purposely brushed his hand while taking the money and the menus.

She cursed her current predicament. Her skin was tainted with grease. Her pink-chequered pinafore lacked sexiness. She had failed to make an impression as she watched the man walk back to his seat. The remainder of her day would be consumed by thoughts of the stranger and of different places, different circumstances. Maggie slid the order across the counter. Natasha plonked it onto a tray and followed Benedict back to his seat. Natasha placed the tray on the table between Elisha and Benedict. She looked at Benedict and begrudgingly addressed the girl in his presence. 'Enjoy your meal.'

Elisha acknowledged her politeness and smiled, but threw a puzzled look towards Benedict, confused at the speediness of the delivery. Elisha stumbled over her words. 'That was so quick!'

'Told you this is the best diner in New York.'

'Oh, I forgot to ask you. How did you know I would turn up?'

'Because I, my sweet tooth, know everything.'

'Do you now, mister? So I guess you knew my number as well?'

'Of course—I may have had some help from the lovely receptionist, if I'm being truthful.'

'I'm sure that's illegal—patient confidentiality, you know,' claimed Elisha.

'It is, but he just couldn't resist my charm.'

Elisha's laugh ricocheted around the diner. It caused Natasha's finger to snag while curling her hair. Even Maggie looked over from the heat of her kitchen, drawn to the sound of laughter and smiled in its direction. Elisha blushed at her outburst. Michael stood sharply, dragging his stool across the tiled floor, and made his way to the restroom.

The biting cold of the street cut a homeless man to his core. His loafers had been battered by the streets, causing his sockless toes to poke through. He was cold from his feet to his face. His body shook uncontrollably in his thin, rigid, dishevelled green coat. The hooded peak tipped over his brow, covering his face and darkening his features. The fabric was hardly fit for New York's winter but unfortunately it was the only coat he owned. Beneath the worn fabric his knitted maroon sweater failed to warm his cold, dry skin. He hugged himself, desperately wishing the warmth would sink to his bones like hot treacle.

He meandered sluggishly through the hordes of commuters that rushed to a schedule—a regimented nine-to-five. Slowly, the pale, grotty fingertips of the man lowered his hood, allowing his hardened features to greet his enemy—the cold.

Billy's eyes hadn't changed. They were still inherently unloved. At twenty-five years of age, Billy was a troubled soul who found solace in substance. His cheeks were as rough as a coastline crag, protruding horribly. Gaunt. Malnourished.

Empty plates of devoured pancakes sat upon the blotchy table. Creamy remnants of latte lightly stained the inside of two coffee cups. Benedict stood, holding Elisha's coat as she wriggled from her seat to her feet. He tenderly placed it around her shoulders and, as she buttoned it and adjusted the collar, she murmured, 'Thank you.'

'I'll meet you outside,' said Benedict.

'It's OK. I owe you five minutes—remember?' said Elisha, walking with her words to the front door, while Benedict strolled to the row of stools at the counter.

The bell above the door jangled, announcing Elisha's exit to the sidewalk. She didn't mind the cold; it gave her time to think.

Benedict stood at Michael's empty stool, quickly scanning through the discarded newspaper. He nodded at Natasha but looked towards Maggie. 'Thank you, Margaret.'

Maggie's heart fluttered—she hadn't heard anyone call her by her full name since her husband's passing and quickly responded, 'Have a lovely day, sir.' Her voice crackled with emotion.

'You too, Margaret.'

Natasha was jealous. She failed to find any words and instead watched Benedict walk out of her daydream and out of the diner. Michael returned to his stool and reached to his newspaper. He was relieved to see that the giggling couple had left.

Benedict watched Elisha inhaling the scent of her lotus. The petals pushed gently onto her lips. The rush hour had died to a simmer, but the frost was unrelenting. A flurry of New Yorkers trudged along the sidewalks beside the East River. The place was a painter's dream, but for every quaint perspective there were the shady alleys that harboured the undesirables.

Billy plodded the street until the same red haze shone over his faded coat. He too entered Maggie's Diner. His ears tingled as his face was hit by the warm air that was sucked outside by the sidewalk chill. Billy closed his eyes and felt the warmth that comforted him briefly.

Michael snapped his head towards the stranger at the door. Dejectedly, he turned back to his newspaper, engrossed in the words. Billy walked gingerly to the counter and Natasha, who watched him approach. She asked coldly, 'Can I help you?'

'Cup of coffee, please,' asked Billy, shivering uncontrollably as the warmth of the diner stung his cold skin.

He scrambled deep into his pocket to the sound of jangling coins. He scooped in hope at the change he had begged for that morning. He emptied the entire contents of his pocket onto the counter in front of the jaded Natasha. She was glad she didn't have to touch him. It eased her tension. Maggie looked over as Billy rushed to catch the coins that rolled precariously towards the edge of the counter. He bumbled at them frantically and instantly knew he was short of change. Maggie sensed his agony from the kitchen. Natasha was unmoved. Maggie looked on amongst the steam and shouted, 'This one is on the house, sir.'

Billy's eyes welled in response to her compassion. 'Thank you, miss,' he shyly replied, before carefully collecting his morning's work.

While Billy's cold fingers struggled to secure his coins, Natasha placed a paper cup of coffee before him. His reactions and mannerisms were those of a man fifty years his senior. The streets had aged him horribly. Billy offered a look to the waitress but she dismissed it with an insincere, 'Have a nice day.'

Billy shovelled five scoops of sugar into his coffee before grasping the cup and leaving the diner. Natasha was thankful he had left.

Billy traversed the streets full of people wearing thick jackets and hats, and sipped his sweet coffee. He rummaged through sidewalk garbage cans, uncaring of the eyes that scrutinised him. He tucked wasted food into his jacket and soon slithered into a darkened alley. He was home. Away from the world. He took another sip of his coffee before he wedged himself through a boarded-up door.

The haze that clogged Billy's thoughts was similar to the mist that clogged the East River. It was overbearing, atmospheric and powerful. It was late in the day and still the frost clung to the darkening December air. The paved promenade glistened like scattered glitter. For brief moments, the murkiness decided to reveal the splendour of the icy river.

The bridges of Manhattan and Brooklyn disappeared into the distant sky. Above the suspending structures, the evening was blessed with a full moon. It scattered light onto the lady in lilac and the man in charcoal. They indulged each other like high-school sweethearts and sat snuggly beneath the impending cloak of night.

The bench that held the pair was perched upon the promenade and overlooked Wallabout Bay. It was a romantic cliché. Benedict smiled at Elisha, who was lost in the moonlight, and interrupted her thoughts gently. 'Beautiful, isn't it?'

'It sure is.'

Elisha caught Benedict looking at her and returned his smile. She enjoyed her clandestine thought as the moon reflected within her eyes. 'I've always wondered if we really did land on the moon.'

Benedict looked at the reflection in her eyes as she peered into his. 'Well, wonder no more,' he proclaimed.

'And why is that?' questioned Elisha.

'Because I know everything.'

Elisha snuggled further into Benedict and responded, 'So, Mr

Know-it-all, did we or didn't we?'

Benedict leant towards Elisha, lifting her woolly hat slightly. Elisha felt his cheek brush against hers and his warm breath that tickled her ear. 'Can you keep a secret?' he whispered.

'Yes,' she replied softly.

Benedict looked dramatically left and right. Elisha giggled. Benedict cupped his gloved hands over her ear, soothing her from the cold and whispered softly. Elisha sprang back in disbelief. 'Really?'

Benedict nodded. 'Really.'

Chapter Twelve

SENTIMENT

A puzzle that will last forever

The charred blistered remnants of the front door lay where the jute welcome mat once did. Elisha's family home was ruined. Andy delicately leant his arm over her shoulder and cuddled her gently. 'Don't get upset.'

They both stepped carefully inside; their feet crackled upon the broken glass and charcoaled wood. Elisha looked over to the fireplace in what had been the integral room of her home. The chimney breast was the sturdiest structure of the house—it was buckled badly but it still stretched to the upper floor and stood like a beacon amidst fallen walls. The fireplace had been burnt by a sibling of its own creation; a much more powerful sibling that had risen and demolished all that Elisha had treasured and loved. She had warmed herself during cosy nights by the fire, dealing cards and sipping hot chocolate. The fire's warmth had been evocative of their family's love.

The fire was rippling and crackling with intense but controlled yellow flames. Elisha's six-year-old eyes were captivated by them. Transfixed. Her father nudged her from her fiery trance; she shuffled on his lap until she was facing him. He was a handsome man with jet-black hair, slicked back, revealing his teddy bear face. Paul, her eight-year-old brother, was oblivious to his father's cheeks and the flickering fire; instead he was captivated by the toy soldiers on the floor around him. Machine-gun sounds bubbled from Paul's mouth and, with a sweep of his right hand, he knocked some of the standing soldiers to the floor, simulating their death. The open fire cast a soft glow over the battleground where these plastic soldiers had fallen.

Christmas stockings dangled from the fireplace, high enough that they wouldn't be caught by the flames. The Christmas tree crowded the corner of the room and screamed for attention with a body full of baubles and an angel sparkling at the top. Traditional decorations overloaded the room—the scene was fit for a Christmas card.

Elisha's mother entered the scene with a trayful of mugs brimming with hot chocolate, and carefully placed it on the coffee table. She gestured to Paul with her hands and, in the most delicate of voices, said, 'Come on, Mommy's little soldier.'

She sat beside her husband who was still delighting in Elisha's innocence and beauty. Paul edged between his mother and father on the sofa. The whole family were cuddled together. Elisha's dad balanced his daughter with one hand and reached out with the other to retrieve something from under the tree. He was clutching a box no bigger than the size of his palm. It was wrapped in golden paper that perfectly complemented the glow of the fire. He handed it to Elisha. She began tearing at the paper without being prompted. Her father steadied her as she rocked back and forth in the effort to reveal her present. Her eyes were wide with anticipation. In her small hands sat a Rubik's cube—six sides, each one a different colour and each face split up into nine squares. Elisha was baffled. 'What is it, Dad?'

'This, my dear, is a puzzle that will last forever,' he answered, and gently took it from her delicate hands. He quickly twisted and turned the cube in several directions, causing its colours to jumble completely, and then offered it back to her.

Elisha was oblivious to her outstretched hands that had followed the movements of her daydream. She was interrupted by Andy's soft words. 'Are you OK, darling?'

The stench of burnt wood had soaked into their clothes, enough that Elisha was aware of it. An echo of dripping sounded from upstairs, causing Elisha to look up towards a destroyed ceiling. She walked cautiously, but with purpose, towards the oak staircase that had tumbled like a house of cards. The rubble had piled beneath the landing; it enabled them to climb carefully up to the landing that was shattered but still delicately in situ. The building creaked in pain.

'Be careful, darling,' whispered Andy, recognising that they were not strictly allowed inside the taped-off house.

The bedroom was largely empty. Black glass was spattered around like confetti unfit for celebration. The walls displayed beautiful patterns, caught between an overload of fire and water. Sooty shapes and shadows were muddled like the surface of the moon. The disjointed pile of bedroom furniture lay beneath the least damaged wall, which was the furthest from the door. It was an ugly scene.

The room housed an unearthly contradiction of a dampened and yet burnt smell. It was foul. Elisha's frustration caused her to push at a cabinet on the outer edge of the pile. It rocked back and forth before falling beside her. Soot flew up from it.

'Careful!' Andy scolded her.

Elisha ignored him and took a deep breath in; she stretched her wet, blackened hand into a small crevice beneath an overturned chair. Her fingertips rolled a cubed object towards her until she was able to grab it entirely. She exhaled as she pulled it out. The cube was blackened but her grasp had rid it of some of its black exterior to reveal a mix of squared primary colours.

She marvelled at it for a second before taking another deep breath and stretching her arm back into the gap between the chair and the cluster of furniture. She arched her back to gain a few more inches of reach as she attempted to retrieve a photo frame from the darkened cove. She could feel the frittered glass, as she slid it towards herself, before she was able to grip the edge of the frame between her thumb and forefinger. She pulled it towards her and stood up as soon as she had satisfied herself that her grip was solid.

Andy saw Elisha shuffle to her feet and stepped behind her, recognising that she had momentarily lost her balance. She was oblivious to Andy's body connecting with hers and rubbed her forearm over the cracked glass frame. Andy could see Elisha sitting with her mother, father and brother. He thought that she must have been about seven years old.

Elisha was light-headed, caused mainly by stretching and holding her breath simultaneously, but ever so slightly by the emotional impact of gathering her belongings from her fire-ravaged family home. She picked up the Rubik's cube that she had set at her feet and began to shuffle slowly towards what was left of the entrance to her bedroom. The dripping could still be heard, but the source could not be seen.

Back on the ground floor, Andy allowed Elisha to pick up the cardboard box which she had left by the fireplace. He sensed it was all beginning to overwhelm her, so, with a 'Come on, honey,' he ushered her out onto the street.

Andy steadied the box in Elisha's hands and then cocooned her as he helped her to his car, parked in front of the house. Neighbours watched Andy lift a flimsy tape that ordered persons not to enter the house and it fluttered behind them in the lightest of breezes as they arrived at the car.

Andy placed the box on the back seat before he settled Elisha into the front passenger seat. Elisha felt pitiful, but with a sharp breath of fresh air she tried to snap herself out of her dark slumber; she gently pushed Andy's hands off her shoulders and reassured him, 'I'm OK.'

Before Andy could start the engine, Elisha blurted out, 'Paul!'

She hadn't spoken to him for months; his last letter had displayed a foreign postmark. The letter had said little, but it was never the words that pleased her; it was the sight of the sealed envelope with her name and address scribbled on it. Elisha turned to Andy. 'What if Paul writes a letter to be delivered here?' she asked in a worried voice.

Andy reassured her, lending his hands to her shoulders and his words to her ears. 'It's OK, I'll speak to the postal service tomorrow and get them to redirect any forthcoming mail to my address.'

'But I don't want to tell him, Andrew, not while he's away.'

'Come on, honey, I'm sure he'll be OK—he's a marine.' Andy chuckled.

Elisha followed his lead and chuckled her way out of her sombre mood. Andy rested his hand on her knee and accelerated in the direction of his home. The radio was playing a song about a cowboy and whiskey. Andy continued to jest between the lyrics. 'I think we could both do with a bourbon,' he said as his voice began to croak and spoil the country heartbreak song.

Elisha's mind had already wandered; the memory was fused into her mind—the auburn cardigan day. The day she had been told of her parents' tragic death.

Since that day, Elisha had drifted through school in a cocoon of self-pity and pity projected upon her. It was understandable. It was awkward. Friendly conversations didn't flow like they always had before. She had dabbled with rebellion for a time, but her inherent angelic personality would always correct mistakes and undo the done. She had been an above-average student, but ambivalent about learning, with a wisdom withdrawn; in fact, the only lessons that had offered themselves to her interest were literature and art. She liked to read. She liked to draw. She had felt safe in fiction and free in creativity. Elisha had all the qualities required to be a charity's marketing officer. She had used buzzwords during her interview, but there was substance to her exposition. The cause was just and it drew on her innovative, creative and vivacious talent. The egregious stories of famine and affliction fuelled Elisha's drive, but it was a builder who had steadied her sorrow.

Elisha had stumbled upon Andy for a second time at the White Heart conceptual event involving a collaboration of charities, united in rescuing Third World countries. It sure had eclipsed their first meeting beside the apples at the local supermarket. Colourful banners and trimmings had been draped around a sturdy stage. Elisha had been frantically twisting white ribbons. Andy had been setting the last of the poles into its truss. Their hands met before their hearts. Andy had opened the conversation. 'Our hands need to stop meeting like this.'

It was a good line. She had found solace with the man with a 'heavy handshake'. That was how Paul had described it after he had first been introduced to the construction worker. 'You can't go wrong with a man with a heavy handshake,' Paul had advised during his weekend leave.

The military maketh the man and he had been rattling off one-liners like a seasoned drill sergeant. Andy became a regular fixture at their house. Fixing pipes and sockets. Their grandmother, Evelyn, doted on him.

Elisha was wrapped in a multi-coloured throw that barely reached her feet but adequately hugged her body. The day had been long. Darkness had descended outside. She looked out at the evening from the comfort of her chair and then across to Andy who looked the epitome of comfort, monotonously humming the tune to the cowboy song that had played during their mid-morning journey. It frustrated her. His humming seemed insensitive. Elisha took the Rubik's cube from the cardboard box that was next to her chair. She began to twist and turn the cube of colour that she had earlier cleaned. Its darkened cove had protected its shell perfectly from the fateful flames that had destroyed her home. It was as if it was *meant to be*.

Elisha pondered this as she shuffled into a more upright position that allowed her to concentrate more intently. She placed her feet on the wooden floor. It was cold and sticky. Andy glanced across from his two-seater sofa at Elisha's sudden movement. His feet were crossed and perched on the coffee table. A baseball game on the television lit up the room. Elisha felt a surge of ambivalence overwhelm her. Her house had indeed been that, a house, but it held the last memories of her mother, father and brother. She battled internally to convince herself that it was just a house, but with each turn of the cube she felt herself being drawn back to the notion of home. This was not the time for the completion of this puzzle, but nevertheless she attempted to solve the algorithms.

Andy was in a fruitless position. He was aware that Elisha was fragile; his earlier sentiment had not been wholeheartedly received. He sensed that, with every arm of comfort he had offered or sentence he had softly uttered in her direction, she had received his gestures and words tentatively to avoid conflict instead of willingly in consolation. He was damned if he did and damned if he didn't. He plucked up the courage to make one last-gasp attempt to bring Elisha back to normality, jokingly spurting out, 'You're never going to complete that silly thing.'

He had failed to realise its importance to Elisha. She had never told him the Christmas story that she had earlier wandered into. His joke would ultimately mean that she never would, and yet, with a determined and facetious giggle, she replied, 'I will one day.'

Chapter Thirteen

HUMILITY

Benedict twisted the cube until it held six sides of block colour

Benedict sat on the soft colourful floor of a preschool classroom. His fellow classmates were sitting beside him, forming a circle. They were captivated by their teacher. Her enthusiasm was infectious, and it allowed the children to forget the rain outside, mesmerised instead by her manner and movement. Mrs Harding's hands flew back and forth like an interpretive dancer. She transferred the book that she was reading from hand to hand, allowing the other hand to swing free; it drew the gaze of the children as her animated words nibbled at their imaginations.

Benedict looked intently towards the woman before him who was busy conducting the class. He acknowledged her ability to teach. He was conscious of it. He too was drawn to her movement and pronunciation of the storybook's words, until a bell interposed and cut short Mrs Harding's lesson.

'Playtime,' she pronounced elegantly, and clapped the book shut with both hands.

Like magpies, the children scurried to their feet in search of their next wide-eyed attraction. They swarmed towards a large oak box in a corner of the room. Dolls, balls and toy cars were pulled out indiscriminately. Other children picked their playtime toy according to preference and clutched it to their chest before sneaking off to a quiet space in the classroom. The biggest and brightest toys gradually disappeared from the box and soon there remained only small toys of subtle colour. A chunky boy was the penultimate prizewinner and bumbled to the box in an awkward manner. He reached lackadaisically into the box and pulled out an ugly plastic hexagonal object. The panels had been scribbled on, but its shape transfixed the big droopy eyes of Charlie Smith.

Charlie rolled the misshapen object and watched it stagger in fifteen different directions before waddling after it. Benedict dodged Charlie and meticulously reached into the box. He rummaged through unwanted clutter. The object he found was slightly too big for his palm and he lent his other hand to it before it slipped from his grasp. He cradled it and made his way to an unused corner of the classroom.

Charlie had caught up with his hexi-ball and fell onto his behind to rest from his ordeal. There was a loud ungraceful thud. Benedict sat in silence and chose to ignore the thud that caught the attention of the other children. Benedict sat with his legs crossed in perfect posture beside paint-pot corner—he wouldn't be bothered there. In his small soft hands, he held a Rubik's cube. Full of randomised colour. He studied it. His nimble fingers began to twist the stiffened cube that had fused with disuse. The sound of bickering children around him was louder than the storm outside, but Benedict was oblivious. He was engrossed by the puzzle.

It wasn't ordinarily meant to be in the box. The since-departed caretaker had been tidying the corridors after last year's end-of-term bonanza. The teachers had brazenly sipped cherry brandy and had cared little for the consequences of crazed children. The caretaker was too old to study the range of toys strewn about his hallways. The cube had been swept up and piled into a large oak chest with a selection of other colourful toys. Its colours clouded its complexity, but Benedict twisted the cube until it held six sides of block colour.

His accomplishment was met with a sly grin that only he saw—reflected several times by the shiny squared stickers of the toy before him. Benedict did not marvel at himself for long and, without care, began to jumble the coloured squares, distorting the conjoined pattern.

Mrs Harding was impervious to her surroundings, and the boy genius beneath the paintbrushes. She was lost in the fantasy of an after-school activity. The teacher was finally jolted from her reverie by another colossal thud, courtesy of Charlie Smith's bottom. Her attention zoomed beyond him to the far corner of the room. She marvelled at Benedict who was sitting in a bubble of silence far away from his squabbling and sobbing peers. Mrs Harding stood up and wandered over to him. Benedict was denying the cube of its completion and stopped only to look up to his teacher. 'Hello, Mrs Harding,' he said sweetly as she knelt down beside him.

'Hello, Ben. Pretty tough puzzle you've got there, perhaps we'll have to try this one again tomorrow.' She reached out and allowed him to roll the cube into her slender hands before getting to her feet. 'Thank you,' she continued, and then offered a free hand to Benedict. He took hold of his teacher's palm and she eased him up off the paint-stained floor. She turned back to her tumultuous class and planned a route through the girls and boys and toys. A beaming smile lit up her face, in admiration of Benedict's puzzle attempt. It allowed her to skip through the class as if she were crossing a river's stepping stones. She decided to gather up the toys before setting about soothing a class half-full of crocodile tears. 'Playtime is over, children,' she said with purpose.

The bell sounded in recognition of her proclamation. The class shuffled into small chairs. Each one scraped as the children tucked themselves behind their respective group tables. Benedict heard the large oak box close as Mrs Harding's hands delivered the final toy into the sacred chest. Charlie Smith was the last one to sit down.

Chapter Fourteen

SERENITY

The old man was as much of an attraction to them as the towers and trees

An aroma of cedar and freshly mowed grass complemented the morning breeze. Elisha and Benedict walked towards the park. The smell opened their lungs and hung on their hair. The sky was idyllic, dressed in an unapologetic blue. Elisha's eyes were wide as they absorbed the colour, the calm and contrast. Pedestrians were heading in different directions, each beginning their respective days. Benedict sidestepped to allow an elderly man to pass by.

The retired restaurateur held a newspaper in his left hand; he tipped it in acknowledgement of Benedict's swayed step. Mr Truman's footsteps crackled over fallen twigs and leaves. An etched trail marked the history of his strolling off the beaten path. It led him to a small bench that was overhung by a kind umbrella tree. This tranquil haven looked out onto a picturesque backdrop of New York's avenues and high views. Mr Truman would routinely read his newspaper, studying each story and watching shadows spin around the park. The early morning tiptoed towards mid-morning and the hustle and bustle of the Big Apple was faint in the background. It reminded Mr Truman of his once-busy business.

A Danish couple passed him as he neared the seat that had been his, unofficially, for nearly eight years. The students were blonde and spritely; they both had satchels and thick-rimmed glasses. The taller of the two offered a heavily accented welcome to the elderly man. 'Good Morning.'

The shorter student just smiled meaningfully. It was the first time that they had been in the park; the old man was as much of an attraction to them as the towers and trees. They both studied his New Yorker appearance.

The bright-smiled, bright-eyed Stewart Truman revelled in his role of being the local-of-the-day and delivered a perfect 'Good Morning. Have a nice day,' before he sat down on his bench.

The couple continued to walk along the trodden line that swirled to the official path. They looked back. The old man opened his paper. It flapped into a large broadsheet and, as he creased it open, he chuckled to himself.

Benedict had watched and enjoyed the international hello. Elisha was busy herself—watching a robin darting from tree to tree, chirping at every checkpoint. The sun filtered through the trees, casting shadows on the leaf-stricken green grass. Elisha moved her gaze from the tree-tops towards the mini-league baseball game that was in full swing. The ball was already in flight; it was the ping that had caught Elisha's attention. She now watched the batter skip over first base, and then second, his own checkpoints. His hard hat bounced upon his head; his delicate hands tried to hold it down as he ran. He wore a red pinstriped strip, clay-stained.

Elisha was captivated by this magical place. Benedict felt that she was about to speak—he could see it in her eyes.

'Isn't this lovely? It's so peaceful,' she said.

He had already prepared his answer, sensing that this beautiful place was due a compliment. 'Indeed it is—exactly how this life should be.'

Elisha was drawn to his sentiment and his effortless charm. 'Quite,' she pondered, before she sought another moment. 'So what have you got planned for next Sunday? Andy's with the boys—again.'

'You are high maintenance,' Benedict quipped, recognising that she was purposely damning her partner.

Elisha interrupted his playful gesture. 'I am, and fortunately for you that's my only flaw—or should that be unfortunately? Anyway, have you got anything planned for us?'

'I have, as a matter of fact, but that is a surprise and I couldn't possibly tell you. You will have to wait until Sunday,' Benedict cheeked.

Elisha sighed theatrically, already wishing the coming week away. 'So I'll have to wait until Sunday, then?' she pleaded.

Benedict nodded before he confirmed, 'Indeed you will,' then suddenly grabbed Elisha by the arms before she had a chance to reply. He shoved her to one side as a football flew past, narrowly missing her.

Elisha looked towards the group of children that had sent the wayward football in their direction. The child responsible had winced as he watched the football fly past Elisha. He sheepishly ran after the ball and muttered a 'sorry' to Elisha as he passed her.

Elisha barely noticed him; instead she looked deep into Benedict's eyes. She felt safe in his arms. 'You're making a habit of this, aren't you?'

'I guess I am.' Benedict loosened his grip of her arms but held her stare.

'Thank you,' Elisha offered.

Benedict stepped back and bowed theatrically. 'My pleasure.'

Elisha laughed and held her arms back out towards him— yearning to be held again. She embraced him lovingly and whispered over his shoulder, 'You are just too good to be true.'

Chapter Fifteen

SECRECY

There was deadly silence—it was strangely peaceful

The underground car park was as gloomy as it was grey. Overhead lights flickered like a fly-catcher, strobing shadows in dark places. Tuesday night, it was closed to the public. The yellow barrier that shut off the entrance was controlled by the security guard, Kirk Sanders. Kirk, the inside man, was given charitable donations by the businessmen that arrived in flash cars accompanied by beautiful women.

A bracelet of luxury motors formed a circle on level three, the largest section of the underground car park. Headlights threw welcomed light over the space. It illuminated a makeshift ring the size of a theatrical stage. It was close. It was tense. The arrangement was professional, a clandestine *cash only* affair. The risk-takers flicked through bundles of notes, waiting impatiently—overcome with bloodthirst and trepidation. A suited man holding a briefcase passed a packet of cash to a banker.

The noise from the gambling circle dwindled to a hum as Benedict walked through the crowd towards the centre of the pit. Dwayne Trigg approached from the opposite side of the ring, his frame cutting through the beams of light. His shadow stretched out across the open space. Dwayne stood six-feet-five tall. He dwarfed Benedict and the spectators. Dwayne was edgy. Athletic. His jawline pulsed, his gold teeth glistened as he ground his precious mouthful of metal together. His black skin camouflaged his facial tattoo—there was nothing artistic about it; it was plain and simple and had one meaning. It was his gang's signature. A circle and a triangle.

The referee was dressed in black. He pointed to Benedict and shouted, 'The CHALLENGER!' Then, sharply, he pointed to Dwayne and proclaimed, 'And…the…CHAMPION!'

With outstretched arms he directed them to move to opposing sides of the ring. Dwayne exuded confidence, owing to previous victories and perilous violence. Benedict was calm and composed.

The referee threw his arms to the floor. The signal was understood. Dwayne shuffled to his left slightly, before edging towards Benedict. The smaller man mirrored his movement.

Benedict's bright blue eyes reflected Dwayne's formidable frame. The vehicles and crowd beyond had faded to peripheral vision. Benedict replicated Dwayne's initial spring towards him. Critically, it fractionally preceded Dwayne's lunge, and a disguised short-armed elbow shattered against Dwayne's rugged jaw. Bone on bone. The impact shook the champion to his core. His body buckled and leaned dangerously towards Benedict. It allowed the challenger to land a series of frantic elbows, both left and right, to the stumbling champion's face. Unremitting. Unforgiving. Benedict's cutting swipes split Dwayne's face like cracked crème brûlée. Each elbow was delivered forcefully, causing the champion to slump further. Dwayne's blood oozed from his open wounds and swelled inside his mouth.

The crowd, hidden behind headlights, jeered at the violence, fully expecting the larger man to be revived by his anger and the taste of his own blood. Benedict chose to edge away from the man who could barely stand. There was no revival. The barrage of blows had sunk the unsinkable man. Dwayne dropped to his knees before the callous challenger, and saw his blood congeal like caramel on the floor.

Benedict approached the kneeling man and pushed at his chest, upsetting the last of his equilibrium. The champion fell, crumbling to the cold ground of the concrete car park. He was no longer able to defend himself. His arms flailed at his sides, his body entangled in a twisted mess.

Benedict knelt slowly over Dwayne. He evaluated him briefly before brutally crushing another elbow against the engorged features of his face. It was barbaric. Onlookers were sickened by Benedict's savagery but relished the gladiatorial gore. Benedict basked in the moment that surrounded the blood. He rose to his feet and stood over the battered and helpless thug. The monster cowered like a child on the floor, his hands covering the wound to his face. Benedict kicked his victim's hand away to reveal the disfigurement. There was deadly silence—it was strangely peaceful. Spoiled only by a sickening stamp and the sound of shattering teeth.

Chapter Sixteen

COTOPAXI

Anyone who dared to speak, spoke in a whisper

The Sunday morning sun bathed Benedict in a glorious shower of golden colour. His presence in the suburban street went largely unnoticed by Timothy and Bradley, who were pedalling frantically in the excitement of their tricycle chase. Their grandparents, on the other hand, looked on from behind their garden fence through judgemental shaded eyes.

Benedict's introduction to the street had alarmed them. He was a stranger with an extravagant car and a tailored suit, but it was the sports car door that opened to the sky and the click of his brogues on *their* sidewalk that irritated them the most. It irritated them that they knew nothing about the man who had arrived in *their* neighbourhood.

His presence had cut short their critique of their neighbour's plum jam from yesterday's jam club and, instead, they chose to scrutinise the stranger. They couldn't help but stare at his flamboyance and the sun that seemingly shone only upon him.

Benedict knocked and waited. The sash window scraped open and Elisha peered out from the confines of her bedroom. Benedict looked up as she cutely reprimanded him. 'You're early.'

'I couldn't sleep—we have an exciting day ahead.'

'You and your Sunday surprise!' She smiled and shook her head.

Benedict was transfixed by her flowing hair as she spoke again. 'The door's unlatched, come inside and make yourself at home—I'll be right down.'

Benedict opened the door as the window slammed shut. He was confronted by a contemporary living room. The walls were London grey, the sofa a darker grey. There were sporadic dashes and splashes of pink flowers and cushions.

It was Elisha's decision to brighten the place up a little after moving in. Andy disposed of empty beer cans and bottles while Elisha gave it a spring clean. The log fire was picture perfect and, even before she had unpacked her clothes, she had placed photographs and keepsakes on the railway sleeper above the fireplace. Beneath the sash window that overlooked the garden sat an upright piano. It took centre stage—a recent gift from Andy. It was homely and quaint.

Benedict walked towards the oak mantel that displayed photographs of Elisha's family and a slightly charred Rubik's cube. It sat incomplete and still smelt of the night they met.

Benedict held the cube between his fingers and methodically twisted and turned the jumbled colours, before laying it back to rest, still jumbled, beside a holiday photograph of sun, sea, sand and Hawaiian shirts. It was a happy picture of a family holiday. Benedict inspected it, only to be interrupted by Elisha politely shouting from upstairs. 'Is everything OK?'

'Yes, everything's fine. Who's this handsome fella in the photograph?' quipped Benedict.

Elisha giggled.

'Stop it, that's my brother, Paul…' She paused for a second, before walking to the edge of the staircase; she peered over the wooden balustrade at Benedict and playfully threatened, 'He's a marine, so no upsetting me, OK?'

Benedict turned sharply to her mischievousness as she hung her head over the bannister. He snapped his feet to attention and saluted the beautiful girl. 'Yes, ma'am.'

Paul had swallowed the tears that had welled up within him from the moment his grandma had cuddled him and his sister into her auburn cardigan. After that day, he had spiralled into a cantankerous spirit. He was compelled by his grief and his unwillingness to display it. It created an anger within him that neither his sister nor grandmother could control.

The first time Paul was properly collared by a cop was on a Thursday evening, owing to a misdemeanour—a petty theft and disorderly conduct. He had been forcibly dragged away from his wayward peers and ended up between his grandmother and the fireplace. The victim had refused to prosecute the disillusioned young man, courtesy of the cop's influencing words and the shopkeeper's own troubled childhood.

The fire was lit but Paul felt a coldness overcome him as he saw the disappointment cloud within his grandmother's eyes. It had been six months since his parents had passed, but it felt like yesterday— every day. A family photograph was on the mantlepiece.

The gnarly, weathered police officer knew of Paul's predicament and was the only one in the living room who chose to look at the picture. It was with a humble and heavy heart that he had collared the boy at the precinct and delivered him to his next of kin.

Paul had been banished to an upstairs bedroom while the officer and the elderly lady spoke beside the flicker of flamed light. Paul adhered to orders. He was shattered by the emotion of the evening and knew that the officer was strong beyond his measure.

The officer spoke softly, in complete contradiction to his frame. 'The boy needs direction—he needs a draconian routine to tame his grief, it's compelling him, Mrs Bryson. He requires a purpose.'

The police officer had known Evelyn's late husband, George. His father had shared bitter beer with Georgie on more than one occasion and had taken a back-pew seat on the day of his funeral. Mrs Bryson leaned towards the officer and offered her gracious hand to his shoulder. 'You're a good boy, Tommy,' instantly humanising the badged man. 'Thank you for bringing him home.' They were kind words by a truly kind lady.

Benedict continued to mosey around the living room until the mahogany piano grabbed his attention. He lifted the leather stool and placed it in position beneath him. He sat, poised. His fingertips caressed the keys. They were silky soft and cold to touch. Elisha heard the first note; she was struck motionless by her favourite melody. She listened to the sound as it drifted up the stairs towards her. She hurried to the top of the staircase. A pleated grey skirt hugged her hips and thighs. She clutched a cream blouse and slid it on over a black brassiere.

She stepped down the staircase and quietly approached Benedict, then placed her quivering hand onto his shoulder. She closed her eyes and listened intently to the melody, drifting on its beauty until the last note resonated softly.

'*He Sleeps*—James Newton Howard.'

Benedict swivelled on his stool to face Elisha. 'You know it?'

'Doesn't every girl?' she asked. 'You're full of surprises.'

'I am.'

'Indeed you are,' she replied provocatively. 'Where did you learn to play?'

'Lincoln Elementary.'

'Not a music school?' Elisha quizzed.

'No, just a plain old elementary school.' Benedict smirked. 'I guess I'm just a natural.'

Elisha was aware that his piano-playing prowess was more than just school-taught and questioned him. 'I don't believe you.'

'Ask Alessandro.'

Elisha laughed. 'Alessandro? Who's he?'

'My music teacher—the Italian heartthrob,' joked Benedict.

Elisha chuckled and tried to picture the man as Benedict began to reminisce.

'I can recall how the weighted keys felt against my fingers, how the sound rose to the high ceilings and how the Italian man danced around me—from that moment on I was hooked.'

Polished oak and the scent of bleach wafted around the rectangular hall. Benedict settled himself on a stool and shuffled closer to the shabby old piano. The hall's ceiling was high above the little boy. The wooden sash windows threw welcomed light across the room, allowing the mist of dust to float like a daydream. Sunlight bathed the ebony and ivory keys as Benedict caressed them; the sound swallowed both him and the hall in an acoustic wave. Each imperfection on the piano's surface showed signs of the abuse at the hands of ignorant children over the years, highlighted further by the unforgiving light and the shadows of the hall.

Alessandro, the Italian music teacher, had the glossiest black hair. He conditioned it daily. It rested softly against his white pointed-collared shirt and his velvety black blazer. His olive skin and silver cross peeped through his unbuttoned collar. Each of his four fingers of his right hand wore silver patterned rings, and his fingernails were perfect.

He would often stand with a feminine posture, clutching his hip with one hand while grooming his beard with the other. He hadn't quite grasped the English language, but his pronunciation of simple words left his female colleagues wanting more. He oozed a sexiness that they found difficult to resist. Even his cologne was feminine. He was a beautiful man with gentle ways. His students marvelled at his ability and the encouragement he gave them.

Alessandro skipped across the wooden floor in a tarantella two-step, hypnotised by Benedict's majestic rendition. He was enthralled by the notes that sprang from the piano strings and echoed throughout the expansive hall. Benedict's fingers titillated each key and Alessandro's heart.

Alessandro revelled in the sound that took him back to his small home town, Vogogna. It was there that he had found his true love, beneath the wondrous green mountains and the Visconti Castle. Lincoln Elementary was a far cry from Vogogna, but it was simply the music for Alessandro—it always had been.

Alessandro danced as if he were in a musical theatre production as he landed beside the piano and rested his hand on the dull mahogany top. His fingernails tapped in rhythmic frequency, in time and in tune with his Italian heart—thumping in harmony with every vibration. He closed his sparkling eyes.

His eyebrows were as defined as his fingertips. They twitched uncontrollably as the octaves coursed and melodies meandered throughout his body. He was rendered motionless, in awe of the child prodigy.

Alessandro slowly opened his eyes, succumbing to the irrepressible flutters and exhaled a breath of complete satisfaction. The subtle shake of his head preceded his rapturous applause. His Italian heart was overcome.

'*Sorprendente*, Benedict, *proprio bella*—just beautiful,' he declared in a tangle of Italian English.

'And there you have it, a beautiful man with beautiful eyebrows and fingernails taught me all that I know.'

'I'm glad—thank you, Alessandro,' Elisha replied, glancing at her own fingernails as she gestured for Benedict to inspect them by holding her hand out before him.

Benedict stood, taking her outstretched hand between his

fingertips and said, 'Beautiful—are you ready ma'am? Your chariot awaits.'

'I am.'

Benedict released her hand to open the door and stood back for Elisha to step outside. He closed the door behind him and the sun shone exquisitely over them both. He took her hand and guided her down the concrete steps to the sidewalk. An alpine-white Ferrari graced the road. Each curve majestically created. It was a thing of beauty. It sparkled like a sunlit glacier.

'Wow—is that your car?' said Elisha.

'Only for today.'

Elisha giggled and preferred to take pleasure in it rather than ponder it.

'Please,' said Benedict as he opened the passenger door.

The door sprung upwards; Elisha's eyes followed the white door that reached to the sky. The two nosey neighbours had barely taken a breath, frantically discussing the activities inside Elisha's home. It was only when the spaceship-like door folded to the sky that they were left speechless. Elisha edged carefully into the tanned, stitched and embroidered leather seat. She looked around at the interior as Benedict walked to the driver's side. She wallowed in the beauty. The car. The man.

Benedict's door opened and he slid into the seat beside her. Elisha was conscious that she was swooning and tried to guide the conversation away from complimenting the man beside her on his gadgets. She shot a question at him instead. 'So where you are taking me?'

Benedict started the engine.

'Well, that's a surprise. I couldn't possibly tell you that, could I?'

'Of course you could, if I asked nicely,' she said, leaning her head to one side as she fluttered her eyelashes.

'That may work on other boys, but my lips are sealed, miss.'

The twenty-four-cylinder V10 engine roared. Its purring prevented Elisha from responding. It was intentional. The car scooted into life as he pressed progressively onto the accelerator. Elisha was finally able to hear her own voice as the engine balanced its power. 'It seems like an eternity since last Sunday.'

'I agree,' Benedict replied.

Her eyes were fixed on him as he drove the white beauty. He slowly turned towards her, sensing that she was about to speak.

'So—are you going to tell me where we're going?'

His eyes pierced her spirit; they were as beautiful as an Edgar Allan Poe poem. They softened her before he spoke. 'Patience is a virtue.'

Each time Elisha looked in a different direction, she drew in a deeper breath. It seemed that each original painting and sculpture in the place battled intensely with all the other artwork for favour. New York Museum was bustling with visitors, all adoring the brilliance of artists.

The museum was largely silent. The halls and arches were tall and stretched high into the sky. The ceiling was a muddle of contemporary and old. It was lit with modern spotlights but held together with old sturdy bricks and topped with tiles. Anyone who dared to speak, spoke in a whisper for fear of their words resounding along the halls and echoing loudly above and around them. Elisha softly broke the silence. After pirouetting like an excitable child, she caught sight of Benedict and voiced her feeling. 'Wow, this is amazing.'

Benedict grinned. 'Thought you might like it.'

Elisha barely allowed him to reply before she declared, 'Like it? I love it.' Elisha wandered away from Benedict while they conversed lightly. She was caught up in the majesty of the museum.

Cotopaxi by Frederic Church hung on a grey shiny wall. It looked small in its surroundings, but its image sucked in all those who dared to peer at it. The remnants of the painted sunset were slowly being overshadowed by an erupting ash cloud that cloaked it. Elisha stood in awe, transfixed on the setting sun beneath cloud. Benedict was behind her. Close enough to feel her happiness. He too was drawn to the oil painting and stepped in front of her, purposely and playfully blocking her view. Elisha put her hands over Benedict's eyes and started to giggle. For a moment, all that Benedict saw was blackness, broken by a shimmer of light that had slipped between her fingers. He reached for the hands that were softly resting on the bridge of his nose and gently pulled them downwards, away from his face. He turned his head to face her. They smiled. The oil on canvas painting had become momentarily invisible.

Elisha spoke profoundly, in a more settled tone. 'Thank you for bringing me here, it's beautiful.'

Benedict's eyes had glazed over. His forehead crinkled and his eyes widened. The subtle movements gnawed at Elisha's attention. The seriousness on his face was apparent.

'There's something I need to tell you.'

Benedict took a breath. A Chinese art student passed them. A Mickey Mouse rucksack adorned her slight shoulders. Benedict saw her, Elisha saw her rucksack. Benedict leaned his head close to Elisha's. The student wondered what whispers they were sharing. Lovers or art lovers? The painting had earlier stolen a little over four minutes from her day.

A moment later, Benedict turned and ran from Elisha. The confused student looked at Elisha and then walked towards the trail of echoes. Elisha shouted, her words ricocheting through the vastness, 'Benedict, be careful!'

Benedict didn't look back. He navigated the halls and corners towards the grand museum doors. He slipped through the arched hallway and leapt out onto the museum's concrete steps. He landed with poise and purpose, leaping again and again until he was at street level. Benedict dashed beyond a telephone box and towards a street packed with pedestrians and vehicles.

Elisha left via the same exit as Benedict and spotted the phone box beyond the splendid entrance. She made her way down the museum steps quickly but safely. She reached the phone box and picked up the receiver, frantically pressing the digits.

'911, what's your emergency?'

Elisha composed herself. 'Police—there's a man with a bomb on the bus.'

The operator rapidly digested her statement and raised her voice in her reply. 'Which bus, ma'am?'

'Accordion Bus. D60. Red roof. Outside New York Museum.'

Elisha looked back at the museum, dropped the phone, and ran towards the street. The operator continued to shout but her words were not heard. The art student was sitting at the top of the steps next to her Disney rucksack. She was doodling intently and was now wearing a pair of oversized headphones. She was engrossed in her music and imagination, oblivious to the swinging phone and dashing girl a short distance before her.

Benedict raced across the busy road, which was full of cars and people edging their way through the traffic. A taxi driver beeped continuously at Benedict as he applied his vehicle's brakes sharply to avoid the crazy man. His two foreign passengers jolted forwards from the back seat. Benedict cared little for their inconvenience and slipped between the taxi and a slowly moving green Chevrolet. His hand grabbed hold of the curved handle of a bus door. He ripped the door open and jumped aboard. It was full. Women, children and men.

Benedict disregarded the flummoxed driver who began to shout unprofessional expletives at him. He was driven by his focus and rampaged to the back of the bus. The commuters were shell-shocked by the impassive passenger, caught between fear and confusion.

A male in the rear quarter of the bus was drenched in perspiration. He stroked his bushy, tangled beard and fidgeted with a bag upon his lap. Benedict was unchallenged. The passengers remained frozen.

Without introduction, Benedict landed a sharp elbow to the temple of the bearded male, knocking him out instantly. He slumped in his seat; the black sports bag on his lap bobbed back and forth but remained in place. The crowd were ready to castigate the stranger for his untamed violence, but Benedict bellowed at them, 'EVERYONE OFF THE BUS!' He allowed his command to resonate before delivering the uncomfortable message. 'THERE'S A BOMB ON THE BUS!'

A wave of panic rippled through the bus like firecrackers. The seated passengers jumped to their feet and bundled their way into the shuffling standers. Benedict watched them ebbing like a mudslide to open water. An elderly man was the last to clamber out. A succession of faraway sirens descended upon the drama. The racket had caused the bearded man to stir slightly. He was viciously elbowed again.

Chapter Seventeen

TRUTH

I know everything

Benedict's back was as stiff as morning arthritis. The old wooden chair had been nibbling the arch of his back since the officers had left exactly forty-seven minutes ago. Since then, he had sat in silence. The cold, clammy room was full of earthy grey colours. Benedict ignored its tastelessness.

The ploy was to allow guilty thoughts to simmer, but their tactic was counterintuitive. The detectives batted insults at the beautiful man from behind the protection and secrecy of the two-way mirror. Benedict stared at the jovial detectives hidden behind his reflection and leant forward slightly, which allowed his back to breathe. He began to tap his fingertips on the table beside an empty mug that held heavy coffee stains—the remnants of previous questioning. It was bribery at its best. A comforting gift that allowed detectives to inveigle the truth from those who normally lied. Benedict pondered the imminent interrogation and purposely cajoled his body into a state of cosiness. The smell of bitter coffee wafted into the room.

The coffee carriers had dovetailed for the last fourteen years; they were seasoned veterans of the law game. Burnett spoke with aplomb, often plucking at fantastical words and phrases to confuse the confused. He read books; he usually had two on the go at any one time.

Dobbs' vocabulary was plain and boyish; in figurative terms he was several coffee beans short of an espresso, but what he lacked in grammar he made up for in gusto. He truly believed in justice. The detectives enjoyed their coffee bitter and cheap. They were perfect partners.

Benedict was focused on Burnett, who had taken an aggressive lean, a trick perfected with practice. It ordinarily made a suspect uncomfortable, but Benedict chose not to be fooled by silly games. Burnett placed the mug of coffee onto the table like an invitation; the steamy mist drifted up towards the low ceiling, accentuated by the cold air. The detective looked through the mist and zoomed deep into the suspect's eyes. Benedict was quiet.

The detectives' carefully crafted plan was to always remain silent for the first minute; normally, the accused would demand an attorney, or the power of silence would lead to a tirade of truth. Benedict basked in the peaceful harmony and joined the detectives in observing a practised virtue. Burnett noted Benedict's insouciance. Dobbs toyed with his pen. Their plan had already started to unravel. Burnett jerked his chair slightly to stifle the downward spiral. The feet of his chair screeched harshly within the claustrophobic room, causing Dobbs to fumble his pen onto his lap and then to the floor. It fell at Benedict's feet. Dobbs followed the pen with his eyes. The other two chose to overlook the calamity. Burnett stood sharply. Oppressively. Dobbs wondered whether he should reach for his fallen pen. Burnett swung out his right hand, crashing it into his idle coffee cup. The cup and its contents catapulted across the room and burst upon the wall. A stain of brown liquid offered some colour to the bland room. Its bitterness trickled like treacle to the floor, but Benedict was unflustered.

Burnett was embarrassed by his own lack of discipline and wandered away from his partner and the accused. He gathered his composure and spoke eloquently while pacing. 'We have received confirmation from our bomb squad that an explosive device was located on the bus. Do you have anything to say about that?'

Benedict addressed Dobbs instead. 'Here's your pen, detective,' he said as he rolled the ballpoint across the desk.

Burnett ignored the nicety and spoke slightly louder than before, directing his question at the subject. 'Can you please enlighten us, Mr Maven? You sit there unperturbed—something that I find quite difficult to comprehend considering your involvement in a terrorist attack, and this is all you offer us, this insolence, this silence.'

Dobbs failed to fully understand the words his partner had spoken. He simplified the narrative in his own mind like a conversation in broken English.

Benedict allowed the words to settle before he replied, 'I smile at your lack of professionalism and knowledge. I smile at your arrogance and your overuse of extravagant phrases. You naively believe your intelligence supersedes mine and yet it's as artificial as the coffee you drink,' nodding to the coffee-stained wall.

The cops had been reprimanded, and they sat in solemn silence.

Benedict spoke again. 'What happened to one of the most sacred principles in the American criminal justice system—innocent until proven guilty?' Benedict paused and allowed the words to resound around the room.

'You preach such values that you fail to instil—it upsets me. I saved hundreds of men, women and children today—and still you treat me with contempt.'

A room at the opposite end of the station, with a window overlooking the street, housed their captain, who was occupied in the buttery sweetness of his afternoon pastry. Captain Emery munched on a croissant in an office too small for his podgy belly, where pictures of him shaking hands with distinguished officers lined the walls.

Edward Emery was the son of a baker. His lack of a stable diet combined with a sweet tooth caused his pale-blue shirt to cling to his skin. The lower buttons failed to clasp shut over his belly, like a busted sofa, hanging horribly over his trousers. Pastry was a regular indulgence. He always licked his fingers clean.

His career had begun in the seventies, when he enrolled at the School of Public Affairs in Washington DC and studied at the Department of Justice, Law and Criminology, graduating with flying colours beneath the stars and stripes that fluttered softly against the Washington sky. His parents had watched from the seated crowd, proud of their son who sported a flat cap and slender waistline.

The tension had settled. Benedict was no ordinary suspect. He addressed them both but Burnett was the focus of his delivery. 'Gentlemen—like I said, I know everything. Now, Marion—would you be so kind to inform Captain Emery that I have information relating to the murder of Zoe Lynch?'

Dobbs rallied to speak, but was restrained by Burnett, who reached an arm across the path of his looming words. Burnett tipped his head towards the door, a simple gesture that Dobbs understood, and said, 'Let's get the captain,' as he stood sharply.

Dobbs shot a maddened glance at Benedict before he followed his partner. The door closed soundly behind the pair and Dobbs immediately began an internal interrogation. 'Who's Marion?'

Burnett reluctantly replied, 'Me.'

'You?'

'Yes, me. My father named me after the Duke.'

'The Duke?'

'John Wayne.'

Dobbs repeated the name, puzzled, 'John Wayne?'

'His Christian name…Marion.'

Still the pendulum swung inside Dobbs' head.

Burnett fired, 'My birth name is Marion, John Wayne's birth name is Marion.' He reloaded. 'Make sure he doesn't leave. Can you do that? I'll get the captain.'

'So, you believe him?' questioned Dobbs.

'Strangely, yes—only my parents and I know my birth name.'

Dobbs looked at his partner and addressed him formally. 'Marion James Burnett,' he said, pointing in the direction of the captain's office, 'Well, giddy up, cowboy.'

Emery detested small talk. He dealt in facts not fiction. Burnett and Dobbs were mere onlookers; they were frightened to sit with the dogmatic man. The captain thrived on confrontation and pulled his seat towards Benedict. He placed a hefty file on the table and spoke without any introduction. 'Tell me what you know about Zoe Lynch.'

Benedict repelled Emery's instruction and chose to take ascendancy of the conversation. 'First, captain, I will tell you about Mohammed Al Yaidi.'

Mohammed was known as a recluse amongst his fellow civil engineer undergraduates, often referred to as an illegal alien. His freshman year consisted of scribbled nothings on his notepad and thoughts of his parents in Pakistan who had afforded him the opportunity to study in America. They were proud parents, but Mohammed hated the country, its culture, its existence.

His Muslim faith required him to pray. It was in his religion and solitude where he found his saviour, an individual that preyed on lonely souls. Abdul Aziz preached fictitious verses and empty promises that nibbled on Mohammed's naivety.

The impressionable young man soon felt a radical sense of purpose—to destroy the Western way of life, all in the name of Allah. Al Yaidi's relationship with Abdul flourished, and soon he was able to recite hate at his mentor's request. He read sections of the Quran at prayer and soon the imam afforded him the opportunity, just like his parents had done, to make him proud.

Mohammed had chosen his month of sacrifice. He was handed a blueprint and began to gather regular amounts of ammonium nitrate. It was this one simple ingredient, known as fertiliser, that was the core element in his volatile concoction. Walmart supplied the rest with an uneasy helping of four-inch nails. Carefully, and in the confines of his student accommodation, he built an explosive device large enough to devastate his chosen target.

The street was lively on the day that he marched towards his target. Disillusioned and programmed. He suckled on the words of his mind's corruptor and was impassive to the politeness of people. The sunshine had failed to unravel the radicalised soldier and he slithered onto the D60 bus—its destination: *New York Museum.*

Benedict studied the painting *Cotopaxi.* The colours began to arc, twist and distort as an explosion shook the painting from its mounts. The power deafened Benedict as whistles reverberated inside his head. The aftershock of the explosion hit the museum; Benedict's knees buckled. The shockwave crashed into the structure. The large monasterial pillars shook while roof tiles fell like confetti onto the congregation below. The wave rushed through the gallery, throwing every person onto the floor simultaneously.

Benedict and Elisha tried to scramble to their feet while priceless paintings fell from the walls. The modern lights flickered as panels were ripped from the ceiling and thrown onto the uneven floor. The remainder of the ceiling was hanging perilously.

The climax continued. Benedict leant over to Elisha and lifted her up. The museum was a cacophony of screams and groans. The constant whistling inside Benedict's head numbed his wits.

Outside, bodies were strewn all over the street. Some were bereft of life, some clung desperately to it. Dust tried to settle around the living and the dead, but the chaos caused it to swirl uncontrollably. A Chinese art student entangled in a Mickey Mouse rucksack lay bloodied at the base of the museum steps. Benedict stepped beside her, pulling Elisha with him. The sound within his eardrums softened to a dull murmur. Elisha could barely stand; the sounds around her were amplified and magnified her imbalance. She clung to Benedict. They ran down the museum steps but her feet stumbled. Benedict pulled at her, enabling her to remain standing. He propped her up beside a telephone box; she slumped into a seated position with her knees high, tucked into her weary, spluttering chest.

Benedict looked at the street beside the cultured district. There was not much left to distinguish what used to be a bus. It was distorted horribly. Pedestrians were busy dragging blackened bodies from the bus and the blast site. Shop fronts and office windows were torn and shattered. Occasional swathes of unbroken glass reflected an image of terror. A large city bus had been ripped apart by a detonated device. There was a mass of pierced passengers contorted amongst the wreckage. Blood and fire immersed them. The murmur inside Benedict's mind grumbled on. It augmented as he ran towards the broken bus.

Vehicles adjacent to the blast were ablaze and upside down in the street. A crater could be seen on the tarmac which separated two halves of the bus. The severity of the blast had left dozens dead and hundreds wounded. There was mass confusion. Panic. Benedict slowed to a walk as the catastrophe overwhelmed him. He looked back towards Elisha. She was in state of shock, unmoving beside the phone box. Benedict absorbed the devastation that surrounded him and took a deep breath.

The listeners absorbed Benedict's description of his premonition. Al Yaidi was already in police custody and under twenty-four-hour guard. Although nobody had been injured, Benedict's words had documented the terrorist's intent. His story had maddened the three men and a torrent of retribution raced through their veins. Emery understood that the justice system cared little for the prosecution of intent. Benedict answered the unasked questions. 'Mohammed Al Yaidi will be deported in just under a year, according to the impending Patriot Act of 2001, and will pay with his life two months later—dying slowly under the hex of an American airstrike.'

The cops were astounded by Benedict's apathy. He addressed the captain. 'On April 16, 1994, at 19:42, twenty-one-year-old student Zoe Lynch was fatally stabbed in an alleyway off West Tenth Street.'

Benedict was the ultimate raconteur; the captain and the detectives were pinioned by his words and didn't dare interrupt his revelations. He spoke slowly and methodically.

Zoe Lynch was an effervescent, cultured student who always travelled on the subway. She defied the stereotype, always wearing red lipstick, and her chosen tipple was red wine. She alighted the train at Franklin Street Station. The station clock read 19:25. The evening was typically cold.

Zoe graced the bustling street and taxis were plentiful. Many of the drivers gawped at the beautiful blonde, but it was taxi number fourteen that swung to the kerbside and hailed the young lady's custom. Her voice was soft. 'West Tenth Street, please, sir.'

The driver was pleasant, offering warmth and custom with assertion. 'Of course, my darling, cold one tonight.'

'It is indeed. I'm exhausted. And the closure of Houston Station isn't helping.'

'I guess not.' The taxi driver took heed of the adjective; he recognised those who cared for dialogue and those who cared only for delivery. He had a proclivity for reading people and politely drew the pleasantries to a close. 'Well, let's get you home then, darling.'

Six minutes into the journey the traffic had congested to a stop. Zoe was lazing nicely, pondering the day's interview. The taxi driver voiced his frustration at no one in particular. 'Jesus Christ, only in New York.'

Zoe looked at the standstill traffic and thought better of waiting in it and watching the meter. She longed for a hot bath and her bed. It had been one of those days. 'I'm good here, thanks.'

'You sure, darling?'

She looked at the laminated identification card pinned to the driver's sun visor. 'Yes, thank you, Mr Maplin, how much do I owe you?'

'Call it a sawbuck, darling, and please—it's Kurt.'

She reached into her bag and passed the pleasant man a ten-dollar note, knowing that the ride thus far was worth more than that. 'Thank you, Kurt.'

'Good evening, ma'am.'

Zoe edged from the taxi and wandered beyond a coppery coloured car. The driver of the VW Beetle looked back at the blonde. She was a sight to behold, curved wonderfully like the car he was in. John probably looked for longer than he should have, but luckily for him, Mrs Paul was tucked up at home caring for their toddler twins.

The captain was entirely convinced at the precision of Benedict's account. Edward Emery had been the lead detective in the murder investigation. He opened the file for his detectives and scattered the evidence across the table like a tarot reader. Photographs of the girl, statements and CCTV stills. He shuffled the papers and indicated two of the names atop the evidence with a simple finger movement. The detectives zoomed in on the words that had been referenced so confidently by the storyteller—Kurt Maplin and John Paul. The captain reached for the photographs and delved through them—the stab wounds, the hair matted with blood, and a black stiletto, pictures that defied logic and seamlessly exhibited the evilness of humans.

The pictures reminded Emery of his daughter, a daughter in university who regularly travelled on the subway. During the four-year investigation, he had worked tirelessly, often reeling into the early hours, sifting through evidence and religiously observing streams of the young lady's last steps. It was fair to say that the case haunted him.

'Hey there, sexy,' rasped a deep voice. The sleaziness of its delivery rumbled against the walls of the narrow alley.

Zoe looked back and was immediately consumed by fear; she was too far from the entrance of the alley and too far from the exit. She decided to run. Her heels clipped across the cobblestoned alley but the predatory male shouted again and began to jog towards her. 'Hey, I'm talking to you!'

Zoe's right stiletto twisted and then tumbled from her foot. It caused her to fall heavily onto her right side. She skidded to a stop on the unforgiving surface and threw out a wretched, piercing scream. 'HELP…SOMEONE HELP ME!'

The girl stoically scrambled to her feet but panic had poisoned her. It had sucked the energy from her lungs and the hollow alley had swallowed up her voice. There was no intervention. The man sunk a knife into her body. The blade lodged between her ribs and the last spark of hope was stolen from her. She fell to her delicate knees. The blade was snatched harshly from her flesh and driven back into her by the crazed man. A flurry of blood clogged in her throat. She coughed it out.

The stones beneath her were blood-red. The man slowly lowered himself before the bloodied blonde and brushed her hair to the side. He suckled on the spicy, scented perfume at her neck and ripped the blade from her weakening body. He delivered it again into her stomach and waited patiently for her groans to fall silent. The girl sunk to the stone floor, drained of life. The man leaned over and reached for her bag, untangling it delicately from her shoulder. The gentle gesture epitomised his madness.

Benedict looked at the captain. 'Mark Bill Withers.'

Chapter Eighteen

REVELATION

Chad Aprilsun...the fastest man in the world

The glare was unsettling. The frenzy of intermittent flashes rebounded off every shiny surface and struck Benedict directly between his beautiful blues. There was a smell of anticipation and polish. A young reporter marvelled at the grandeur of the entrance of The Plaza. She had never been in a place like this before. Her stories had only ever encompassed small-town fame, the type which Warhol would suggest lasts only fifteen minutes. On this day, she had been entrusted to capture the words that this conference promised. The words that Benedict Maven promised.

Jennifer jostled for position within a crowd of reporters that moved sluggishly through the polished foyer and into the main conference room. She drew her startled eyes away from the glamour and glitz of the hotel, and instead concentrated her attention upon her size four plimsolls. She moved her feet slowly, hindered by the slugs around her; it was more of a shuffle than a step. The bundle of reporters and photographers squeezed through the oversized doors and then dispersed into the array of seats and spaces that the room offered.

Benedict was in an elevated position, above the crowd, sitting at a table that stretched across the width of the stage. He nursed a glass of ice-cold water and savoured the chill on his lips. Benedict was not alone at the table, but he was the focus of the floor and the lights were entirely upon him. The other suits at the table fanned out from Benedict, who shimmered like a perfect sun on the horizon. He was poised and photogenic. The frantic cameras snapped like firecrackers. Jennifer was lost behind the parapet of paparazzi, who were all hoping that their picture would be front-page news.

She managed to sit, rather ungracefully, on quite literally the furthest seat away from the stage, but at least it allowed her dainty feet to rest. Jennifer placed her scruffy rucksack between her ballerina-like feet and unclipped the buckle. She dipped her shaky hand into the bag, and brought out her pencil case, which was a fluffy lark-blue and gypsy-pink colour.

Its appearance was met with a patronising look from a seasoned reporter who was standing beside her. The pencil case screamed *amateur*. The leering professional consulted his inner monologue— *and to think that SHE got a seat*. He replied to himself with a simple shake of his head, noticed by Jennifer, and which, in essence, said it all. Jennifer refused to let the man intimidate her. This may have been her first paid article, but it was the words that mattered, not the weird old man beside her, shaking his head like a disappointed parent. Benedict felt the anticipation of the room rumbling like an unfed stomach. A man to his right stood and cast a powerful voice over the room. He was a broad-shouldered man, a significant figure in the FBI. 'Quieten down, find a seat or a space and do what you do best, write and not talk.'

Jennifer didn't know the man castigating the crowd. She turned to the old man beside her and saw him scribbling intently. He had captured the turn of her dyed blonde hair in his peripheral vision and he spoke without invitation.

'Louis Fitzgerald, the director of the FBI, a very puissant man— P U I S S A N T, puissant—to have great power or influence.' He had enunciated each letter. He couldn't resist.

Jennifer was thankful and annoyed all in one moment. She clicked her pen and wrote the name down quickly. Louis Fitzgerald spoke in a monotone voice, the kind that could make you sleepy. He pronounced every syllable like an elocution lesson.

'Ladies and gentlemen, it is not often that this divine country is graced with such a radical prophecy. Yes, there have been preachers who have preached and presidents who have presided, but today belongs to one man, an American man, who will assist the FBI and serve his country greatly. You have gathered here today to witness a phenomenon that will make this great country greater—this great man is Mr Benedict Maven.'

Louis was blinded by his own patriotism and, when nervous, tended to repeat superlatives. He bumbled on but was aware that he had used the word great far too many times; he steadied himself by gesturing to Benedict. 'Shall we take it to the floor, Mr Maven?'

Benedict was bored of the brilliant man's voice. And Fitzgerald *was* a brilliant man—a Harvard graduate whose hobby was building model ships and who had once memorised pi to one hundred and forty-three digits. Benedict threw his hand out like a fishing rod to the sea-full of press and raised fins beneath him.

A juggle of journalists looked at each other, all of whom were in the general direction of Benedict's pointing hand. One stepped forward and plucked up the courage to speak to the fanciful fisherman. 'So, how are you going to prove to America—' he corrected himself mid-flow, 'No—the world, that you know *everything*?'

The journalist had perfected the art of undertone; the last word of his question was a jibe at the quote on the enlarged television screen at the side of the stage. He even finished the question with a delightful dip of his head in the direction of the lavish screen. BENEDICT MAVEN—THE MAN WHO KNOWS EVERYTHING.

Another cunning reporter climbed aboard the satirical train that threatened to derail the conference, announcing his boarding to Benedict with a condescending quip. 'Perhaps you could enlighten us as to next week's lottery numbers?'

The journalists tittered. Laughter began to cloud in the crowded hall. Benedict joined the chorus of chuckles, but the microphone in front of his mouth caused them to focus on Benedict's laughter and forget their own. Benedict spoke purposefully into the device before him. '23, 21, 9, 41, 33 and 49.'

Jennifer jotted the numbers into her notepad. Her mother had bought it for her. The older reporter found himself looking at the 'new job' notepad and tried to decipher the first two numbers she had penned. She noticed the movement of his floppy, but receding, brown hair and tilted the notepad to his vantage. He copied the first two numbers down onto his own notebook whimsically. He had managed to catch the last few. Jennifer whispered to him playfully, 'Did you manage to get all the numbers?'

His eyes and voice softened, 'Yes, thank you. I'm Ralph.'

'Jennifer.'

The conference continued. Ralph and Jennifer quickly forgot their introduction and looked to the stage. Despite Benedict's confident prediction, the satirical train still moved onwards, picking up another passenger from the back of the room. The man shouted at Benedict, 'So, Superman—can you dodge a bullet?'

Louis Fitzgerald was outraged at the lack of order, the sarcasm and the threatening undertone that poisoned the room. He stretched out his big hand to cover Benedict's microphone as if urging him not to answer, and for order to prevail. He scowled in the direction of the voice but could not pinpoint its deliverer. Benedict touched the model-maker's hand softly, reassuringly. 'It's OK, sir.'

Mr Fitzgerald slid his hand away from Benedict and took a sip of the ice-cold water. His hand dwarfed the glass. He scouted to see where the voice had flown from but felt his anger soothed momentarily by the refreshing drink. The lotto man, who had spoken moments earlier, had enjoyed the ripple of laughter his first comment had won him, and decided to satisfy his predilection for sarcasm with another quip before Benedict could speak again. 'You'd have to be the fastest man in the world to do that.'

The two journalists were revelling in the theatre of the conference, but Benedict cut short the satirical train ride and interrupted their contemptuous conversation with a name. 'Chad Aprilsun.'

'What?' replied the reporter who had originally been undetected in the crowd.

Mr Fitzgerald spotted him and felt his anger bubbling. Jennifer and Ralph were enjoying the drama. The voice was that of a sad middle-aged man who always saw the doom and gloom before the dream and gleam. Benedict saw Mr Fitzgerald attentively staring down at the man; a few of the heads in the audience had also turned to see who was behind the pessimistic voice. Benedict spoke again. 'Chad Aprilsun…the fastest man in the world.'

The man in Fitzgerald's firing line diced with death again.

'What—who is Chad Aprilsun? How is he the fastest man in the world?'

Benedict answered clearly. 'He has the highest percentage of fast-twitch fibres of any human on this planet.'

The reporter continued to speak in a patronising manner. 'So where is he now? And why haven't we heard of him?'

Benedict's response was unfathomable. 'England. Because he just doesn't know it yet.'

Chad Aprilsun was a slob. A happy slob. He slept too much and didn't eat vegetables. Chad had been unemployed for eight months, although he was far from unemployable. It wasn't all down to his gluttony; it was that he had been mothered too much and fathered too little. He was as bright as a button, quite a lovely person who had a flair for computers.

The screen sparkled into life. Sunlight tried to peer though his bedroom blinds and Chad tugged them closed, protecting his haven of hi-tech gadgets. His den of delights.

Chad was part of the Amiga generation and refused to fall into the venomous flytrap of corporate gaming. He was true to the original pixel form, and with each computer he had ever possessed there was an obligatory keyboard. Chad was a touch typist with round eyes, despite his mother having warned him continuously that '*those eyes of yours will turn square if you keep on playing those video games*'.

Chad had never known his father and never really asked about him. He knew enough to know that his mother was better off without the adulterer and that he had left prior to Chad being welcomed into this world. His mother loved him twice as much as most mothers loved their children. Food was always prepared. Always eaten.

Chad's mother had left their home at an ungodly hour to complete a day in retail. She was polite, punctual and podgy. She was a great mother but had figuratively used up enough cotton wool to fill a warehouse in wrapping up her boy. Chad hadn't really experienced much of life and was often lost in worlds within a computer screen.

His black T-shirt clung to his frame; his belly protruded more than it should for a boy of twenty, but less than it should for the copious number of cheesy snacks he devoured day after day. A crumpled, empty packet lay beside the black leather computer chair. The short journey from his bed to the blinds and to the chair had taken its toll on him. He squeezed into the discoloured chair and landed his lardy limbs onto its worn arms. He fidgeted until he was eventually jammed in, like sweets in a jar.

He pulled down his T-shirt that held the crumbs and stains from last night's treats. The backs of his legs were sticky; his boxer shorts hadn't quite prevented the cold leather from touching his skin. Soon enough, Chad had forgotten the stickiness and was engrossed in a screen that displayed more colours than an artist's easel.

Chad was, however, distracted by a noise outside; it was enough to make him pause the game and turn his head inquisitively to the window blinds. He was reluctant to investigate the sound of rushing vehicles, and he allowed the noise to progressively intensify before he unstuck his legs from the seat and landed his heavy frame onto two large feet. He stomped to the window and parted the blinds. The light blinded him momentarily. He shielded his eyes and looked to the dusty road outside his window.

The dust had clouded behind a number of endorsed vans that drove towards his house. He wondered if he was still asleep or in *a game within a game*. The road was never usually that dusty; although his mother had never driven that fast along it. Chad lost interest. He closed the blinds and resolved to think no more of it.

He was stung by the frantic knocking at his front door. He was sure that whoever was knocking had seen the blinds close. He coaxed himself to plod downstairs and open the door. Chad was ignorant, yes, but rude he was not.

Emma was busy knocking the front door of the modest detached home. The garden was overgrown. The rickety fence and gate needed steadying and painting. The cameraman behind her had meandered exceptionally along the rugged path to the front door with the bulky Canon video camera atop his shoulder like a parrot.

Emma's trouser suit was a heavenly bright red colour. Emma heard the stairs creak and sensed that the boy she had seen in the window was about to answer her relentless knocking. She quickly and seductively brushed her hair with her fingertips and admired her reflection in the camera lens beside her.

The cameraman counted down in a high-pitched voice that didn't suit his appearance. 'Five, four, three…' His fingers mimed the last two seconds as he mouthed silently, 'two, one'.

The door edged open. Chad peered out like an inquisitive mouse. He drank in the beautiful woman's red attire. She spoke before he had a chance to say anything. 'Hello viewers, can I please introduce you to Chad Aprilsun?'

Chad was dumbfounded. There were more people outside his house, crammed into the overgrown garden—he didn't understand the melee. The beautiful woman continued to talk; the cameraman stood with a wide stance preventing any other person from having the scoop. 'We are here today in Nelson, the borough of Pendle, Lancashire, introducing Chad Aprilsun, the name on everyone's lips. For those of you who do not know, it was Benedict Maven's words at the American conference yesterday that shook the world, claiming that this young man is the world's greatest athlete.'

Chad had opened the door a little wider, more so to get a better view of the reporter than for his own unbecoming fame. She was a beautiful woman who deserved to be seen on screen. Emma was already halfway through her prepared introduction before she truly saw the boy before her, and as the words fell from her mouth, her expression became more puzzled than profound. Chad was still in awe of the beauty at his doorstep and largely unaware that his lazy frame was on display to millions of viewers.

Emma was confident that she could spin this; she could dust him up with a bit of makeup and some baggier black clothing. Perhaps a pinstripe suit would hide his chubbiness, she thought. For now, she was just happy that she was the one who had knocked the blue door before the mob of reporters behind her, who were stuck in the garden's mud. The fact that an overweight boy in boxer shorts had answered, with sleep in his eyes and crumbs on his T-shirt didn't dissuade Emma from speaking enthusiastically again to the nation. 'This is Emma Gardner reporting for Northern News from Lancashire, with Chad Aprilsun—the fastest man in the world.'

Chapter Nineteen

PROMISSUM

It's the little things in life that are the most significant

Andy was tired. There was nothing pleasurable about the early mornings and late nights. They were taking a toll on his body. The morning chill had seeped beneath his overalls and scratched infuriatingly at his skin. He trudged into the small cabin that was full of unwashed men.

A man Andy had never seen before was busy shuffling a deck of cards. The building trade was like that sometimes. The man had been subcontracted to the site while Andy had been away. The nameless man with hands like shovels offered one to Andy and spoke in a heavy Brooklyn accent. 'The name's Sage—Andy isn't it? What's it like out there?'

Sage knew the answer to his questions.

Andy humoured him. 'Yes, it's Andy, nice to meet you—and yes, it's damn cold. I suppose you wouldn't know, being shacked up in here dealing reds and blacks,' he said, laughing, and shook the outstretched hand of the dealer.

Andy's ice-cold hand made the subcontractor shudder. 'Deal me in and I'll get the coffee,' said Andy.

Andy cupped his hands and blew into them in a desperate attempt to warm his fingers. He thought of Elisha, who would soon be fraternising with Benedict. Jealousy took its first jab since the fire and

Benedict's introduction. He vividly remembered Elisha's tears beside Saint James, and Paul's heartfelt request.

Andy had been the second bearer beside Paul when Evelyn Bryson was finally reunited with her daughter Cadence—laid to rest at the quaint churchyard of Saint James. Andy and Paul linked their arms and stood shoulder to shoulder like brothers as they lifted the elm coffin with four others. It was symbolic, their union. The changing of Elisha's guard.

After hymns and a heartfelt eulogy, prepared but not delivered by Elisha, the small gathering had converged upon a small pub named the Good Morning Dancer. Most of Evelyn's generation were sharing summertime stories and sipping sherry.

Elisha was offering pleasantries to the members of the congregation who had continued to the wake. She was overwhelmed by colleagues, church acolytes and wise old well-wishers. Her popularity allowed Paul and Andy to steal a quiet corner of the bar beside the buffet.

Paul looked across to his sister. She was the focus of the cluster around her. He raised a glass to his sister's partner and spoke. 'I'm going back tomorrow morning, but I can't bring myself to tell her—not like this.' Paul paused, overcome with guilt at choosing his country over his sister, he looked intently at the man before him and was clear in his instruction. 'She's going to need you more than ever now—look after her, protect her.'

Andy had only met Paul a handful of times but had seen Elisha's eyes light up whenever one of Paul's letters had been delivered. Paul was not the most articulate, but it was his news and not the grammar that Elisha craved.

Andy allowed Paul's words to resonate before he tapped their whiskey glasses together and assured the would-be soldier, 'I'll look after her, don't you worry.'

And, for the second time that day, Paul placed his hand upon Andy's shoulder in an act of assurance. 'I know you will.'

Benedict's hands lathered his hair as chunks of the pungent blue foam fell to the shower floor, disintegrating down the plughole. He felt the water overpower the foam until his hair was no longer engulfed by the chemical dye. He stepped out of the shower and stretched to reach a pure-white towel. He wrapped it elegantly around his waist and stood in front of an oversized bathroom mirror. He pulled a second towel from the chrome rail and ruffled his hair with it. After a few seconds, he dropped the towel to the sink and lifted his head to the reflection before him. His transformation was complete; his hair was blonde and fluffy.

Benedict casually stepped from his car, a vintage English TVR. Its small exterior was plain but deliberate. Its curves becoming of a Bond girl. Its colour was a deep racing green. Benedict's blue denim jeans looked like they had been hand-stitched onto him. His athletic frame was still apparent despite the denim. His tweed jacket was brown herringbone. It oozed class and allowed the white shirt beneath it to peek through. Brown leather Chelsea boots completed his outfit.

The day was beautiful and blessed with sunshine. He looked up at the sun, squinting at its splendour. He reached to his inside jacket pocket and pulled out a pair of Dolce and Gabbana sunglasses. He slipped them onto the bridge of his nose and glanced back towards his sports car, admiring its beauty. The TVR returned the favour by allowing Benedict's reflection to grace the driver's window. Benedict was still metres from Elisha's front door when it opened, revealing an excitable lady. She had been waiting for him. The gorgeous brunette stepped out into the dreamy day and allowed her red dress to shimmer in the sunlight. Her floppy hat shielded her face from the sunshine but allowed her hair to flitter on the light breeze.

Elisha held a lottery ticket aloft and shook it back and forth in a melodramatic manner. She smiled at Benedict and shouted to him, even though he was close by, 'I've got my ticket—I hope you know what you're talking about, mister.'

Benedict chuckled and prompted her to keep talking with a subtle movement of his eyes.

'What's with the hair?'

Benedict struck a pose. 'The price of fame, dear.'

Elisha laughed and walked towards him. She held the lottery ticket above his head; it cast a shadow over his blonde hair. Benedict reached for it and took it out of her hands. Elisha enjoyed the moment that their fingertips met and let the ticket slide into his manly hand. He looked at it briefly before folding it into the inside pocket of his jacket. Elisha's hand hovered in the air, her fingertips still tingling. She looked at Benedict, dumbfounded. 'And what do you think you are doing, Mr Maven?'

'I'm looking after it for you, today is going to be an exciting day,' he said, reaching for her hand, which was still in the air. 'And I am currently America's hot topic, so less of the Mr Maven.'

'An exciting day? Well, you'd better tell me today's winners because you just stole my jackpot.'

'Today is my day off, and anyway, I am your jackpot.' Benedict teased.

Elisha interrupted his smug demeanour. 'I think you'll find that you are the real winner here.' She paused, posed and let the image settle within Benedict's thoughts. She broke his daydream. 'Let's go gambling, lucky boy.'

Elisha stood and admired the statue of Promissum at Harrington Park racecourse. The shining bronze racehorse radiated the Harrington prestige, and distorted Elisha's red dress and Benedict's blonde hair. Beyond the striding horse sat the ivy-covered clubhouse.

Its pillars and church-style windows were wrapped in the greenest of leaves. Benedict continued to ogle the girl in the red dress and the way it contoured her slender legs and hips. But it was her disposition that made her the prettiest at the track. Benedict knew that. She sensed his eyes upon her and enjoyed it immensely.

The statue was a crowd-pleaser; it drew further dresses and hats from all directions. Benedict stepped towards Elisha as she admired the clubhouse. A Romeo and Juliet pastiche. She drew a breath at its idealistic beauty. 'It looks amazing—like a palace.'

'Fit for a princess,' responded Benedict.

Elisha enjoyed his compliment and blushed as brightly as the red flowers that circled the park grounds.

The estate owner, Harrington Junior, demanded that only three colours be used—red, white and blue. He was a patriot. Elisha watched him puff on his pipe while he stood alone, surveying his grounds from the comfort of his balcony. She saw his wealth and esteem from a distance.

Harrington Junior was a fastidious man. He dressed only in tweed suits, walked with a limp, with an ebony walking stick lodged under his arm. He was a particular but peculiar man who oozed arrogance. He had chosen from a young age to embrace the pain that shot through his knee rather than disgrace his self-portrayal by relying on a stick. His childhood had consisted of polished oak, elegant shoes and the heavy stench of tobacco. It was a pity that throughout his childhood he had never experienced the hard work that those less fortunate had. In some ways, he had never experienced life.

Junior's cheery old fellows bathed in the stench of his rich tobacco and egotistical importance. They dined lavishly, taking advantage of his kindness. After all, friends were all he wanted. His pipe rarely left his lips and his butler rarely left his side. He was truly his father's son.

Elisha watched the man and imagined how wonderful his life had been. She felt strangely jealous of him, unaware of the encroaching crowd that threatened to burst her bubble. Soon she was surrounded by them as they squeezed around her, posing for photographs against the statue. Benedict stepped sharply between the rushing bubbles and grasped Elisha's hand before any more people fizzed around her. The first thing she felt was his warmth. She held his fingers tightly and followed his steps as he ducked through the crowd of flamboyant hats. Her heart raced. They followed the steady stream of dresses and suits to the paddock area that effervesced with ostentatious fashion misdemeanours of the colourful kind. Elisha followed the trailing hand. She had forgotten the safety that a simple hand could offer. Benedict's hand reminded her of her dad's.

The oval arena seduced the baying crowd. They were crammed into the upper and lower stands in ill-fitting outfits for special occasions. They cheered the horses that held their dollars.

Charles Durant had the best seat in the house. He had commentated at the racecourse for over forty years. His enchanting tone excited racegoers who relished his words. His voice and pronunciation were evocative of the Harrington prestige, as smooth as Frank Sinatra. Charles enjoyed the spectacle immensely but shied away from celebrity status. He felt uncomfortable in crowded rooms. His listeners would often attribute a face to his chocolate voice but would be astonished when Charles made a rare appearance.

Charles pushed the soft microphone to his top lip and introduced another race in a smooth dramatic fashion.

'Ladies and gentlemen, up next is a personal favourite of mine. A debut for the wonderful Runaway Ray.'

Elisha heard the tail end of the commentator's words. She spun around to face Benedict. 'You hear that? I picked him!'

The jumbled-up horses simmered with excitement at the start line. Jockeys tried desperately to control the energy that threatened to boil over. The horses snorted in the cool air and spun like unchoreographed dancers until they were forced into the starting gate. The gate ripped violently open to the words of Charles Durant. 'And they're off.'

Hooves tore at the turf as they exited the turnstiles in a frenzy of pure horse power. The large hats that surrounded the mad rush fluttered like colourful petals, Elisha's amongst them. Torn betting slips showered her like confetti. Harrington looked on and marvelled at miserable faces, knowing that each torn ticket was an extra bank note for him. Elisha held hers tightly between her polished fingernails and listened to the disappointed capricious comments that circled. She turned to the most popular man in New York and her smile doubled up in his sunglasses. He tipped them slightly, allowing them to slip down the bridge of his nose, and winked.

The grass in front of them was tossed violently into the air by the hooves that ripped it from the soil. The tidal wave of deafening noise rushed past them. Elisha looked for Ray's colours but just saw a blur of chaotic colours.

Ray was jammed at the front. All he had ever known was racing. He had been pushed into it, but had never wanted to follow in his father's footsteps. It was a brutal, unforgiving sport. You were only as good as your last race. He remembered his father; his last memory was watching him racing across the paddock.

The tangy zinc-flavoured metal stung Ray's taste buds. Even now, at the age of three, he remembered the first day when this odd piece of metal was forced behind his teeth. It had stung his interdental region and barely allowed him to close his mouth, let alone breathe. On occasions, he had thought he was going to choke on his tongue. Soon his gums had hardened, and the foreign object was no longer an irritation—unless it was yanked harshly by the reins.

He was scared by the noise that surrounded him. It was like trampling thunder. His nostrils flared wildly as he sucked at the fuel in the moist air. His eyes were a deep shade of coffee that marbled and reflected his competitors. Despite Ray's size and supremacy, his master was small and weak; he was scrunched into his stirrups and whipped callously at Ray's rump. Ray galloped as fast as his legs would allow. He often wondered why they hit him the way they did, especially today as he led the field.

Elisha looked on and saw her horse out in front. His colours reminded her of her cube, and that was entirely the reason for her flutter.

The crowds above Elisha and Benedict jostled to improve their view. Binoculars hung around the necks of those too far from the action and too upper class for common interaction. Elisha enjoyed herself trackside, amongst the fizz of the plebeian.

The speakers that surrounded the arena carried Charles's voice. 'And they are on the far stretch.'

Elisha focused on Ray's colours. Ray focused on the finish line, Charles on the pack, and Benedict on Elisha. Ray struggled for breath, gasping at every crack that stung his hind.

'He's winning!' shouted Elisha, unaware of his pain.

Charles's voice trickled over the crowd. 'Runaway is four lengths ahead of the field. His stride is smooth and strong.'

Ray's legs were burning. The spectators gawped at the lead horse, whose stride was masterful, and they quivered in the nervousness of the finale. The chocolate voice melted over the crowd once again. 'As graceful as Gene Kelly, he dances towards glory. The finish line is in Runaway Ray's sight.'

Charles had commentated on Ray's father's glittering career, which had spanned eight years, and undeniably had a soft spot for Ray. He had followed him intently and his impeccably smooth voice croaked on his final words. 'Go on, my boy.'

Ray was still a furlong from the line, but Charles already knew the outcome.

Elisha looked on as Ray stormed down the stretch. 'He's going to win—he's going to win,' she repeated in the thrill of her excitement, skipping to the beat of her words. Ray stormed the field to his first victory. His lungs stung like frostbite. He gasped for air. He felt the first loving touch to his neck. It was firm, accompanied by kind words. 'Good boy. Good boy.'

He realised his ordeal was over and that he soon would dine on sugar beet. His favourite.

Elisha spun like a ballerina into the arms of her danzatore. 'He won!' she screamed.

Benedict's shoulder brushed against her flushed cheek and, for the first time, things happened naturally for Benedict. Elisha had stripped him bare. He was fragile in her presence. He felt alive.

'I won!' she screamed again.

Benedict lifted his glasses from his face and held them between his fingertips. Elisha stepped back from her embrace. Benedict could not help but stare at her smile and her soft lips. Elisha stared at his blue eyes.

'You knew he'd win, didn't you?'

'I did, but you chose him.'

'I did, didn't I? I'm so happy,' bragged Elisha.

For the first time, Benedict was jealous. He had never experienced the joy of anticipation and glory—the feeling of chance.

'This is the first time I've won anything, you know. Just imagine, you could feel like this all the time, you could sleep in a bed full of money.'

'I could—but money doesn't always bring happiness, believe me. It's the little things in life that are the most significant.'

His words consumed her. Andy hadn't even crossed her mind.

Benedict's car rumbled onto Elisha's street as the evening began to descend into darkness. The crisp rasp of the TVR's engine purred to a stop. Benedict looked at Elisha despondently. 'Well, here we are.'

'We sure are,' replied Elisha in a downhearted tone. Their eyes connected like lost stars. Elisha felt both excitement and resentment in that moment. She continued purposefully. 'I'd better go in.'

Benedict understood her tone and persevered. 'I guess so, you haven't got long until your big draw.'

He moseyed from his driver's seat to the passenger door. He opened it and reached down to help Elisha out of the low sports car. He pulled her softly into a standing position, holding just her fingers. She felt his thumb on the top of her hand and her body instinctively trembled as they leant towards each other momentarily. Elisha adored his chivalrousness but looked to the front door of Andy's home, reluctantly indicating that she had to leave. She wriggled her hand from Benedict's hold until their fingertips separated. In a sleight of hand, Benedict had given the lottery ticket back to her. She realised his trick and smiled. She watched him walk backwards, away from her, before she turned slowly. Her red dress waved as she strolled away from him. She looked over her shoulder and held the ticket up. He was watching.

'Wish me luck.'

'Good luck.' Benedict paused and drew Elisha to the last of his words. 'Good evening.'

Chapter Twenty

HOPE

He answered devoid of emotion

Rosetta Henderson was originally from San Francisco. She had been a clever young girl. Her first trip to Alcatraz had seen her fire a total of thirteen questions at the ageing curator, Phillip, in her soft voice. Phillip could only answer twelve with wholehearted confidence.

'Did they have hot showers?'

'No, darling, it was cold showers for cold-hearted people,' Phillip answered quickly.

The question had never been asked before. That night he spent hours doubting his answer and searched through the archives for clarity. He chuckled as he wrote the answer into his repertoire and muttered it to himself, '*Prisoners were given hot water showers to make the sting of the San Francisco sea seem even more severe, should any inmates try to escape and swim for shore from the island.*'

Rosetta had questioned her way to straight-A grades. A teacher's nightmare, a teacher's dream. Her heart eventually led her to Chicago, to pursue a love affair with a news anchor and Sunday golfer, Garrett. It had not worked out, but they had remained friends. The city was her new love. She craved its chaos.

Her eyes were as wide as the Golden Gate Bridge. Her soul was as deep as the Gulf of the Farallones. The first time that she saw her veneer smile on a billboard, she felt embarrassed by the fame.

Queasy. It was, however, a smile that lent itself to several charities that she was proud to be a patron of. She blushed when strangers recognised her, but she spoke to them as if she had known them for years. She was that type of person. Better than most.

Jennifer and Ralph had become close, in a father-and-daughter way. Ralph had introduced her to a career's worth of contacts and sources. Jennifer had introduced him to the internet. They walked into the conference together. The hotel was only slightly less grand than the one where they had first met. It looked like a slice of heaven in gold and white.

Benedict sipped from a glass of water. Louis Fitzgerald was a glaring omission. He had conferred with Benedict privately and already knew the content of the conference. A projector screen to Benedict's left was the focal point of the stage. Jennifer and Ralph arrived later than the majority; it meant that both remained standing as the projector hummed into life.

Rosetta was camouflaged by a backdrop of people. The camera zoomed in as if it were sucked in by her voice. She was standing outside the entrance of a traditional theatre. Thousands of lottery winners were standing on the sidewalk behind her—those who had taken Benedict's words as truth a week earlier had been rewarded. They were not quite jumping for joy. Their congregation was more of a publicity stunt as opposed to a public stunned. The lottery tickets they held in their hands had already been processed but had been returned to their owners as a sentimental gesture. That was all they were worth. Rosetta had personally convinced them to wave their tickets high above their heads during her transmission. The majority obliged.

Rosetta held the microphone in her left hand and a single note in her right. She lifted it into view and spoke. 'And here it is, the lottery jackpot. One dollar. I am outside the Chicago Theatre surrounded by these lucky Chicagoans—where another day is just another dollar. Rosetta Henderson, Channel Three News, Chicago, Illinois.'

Rosetta Henderson's broadcast had been seen across America. Her affiliation with renowned charities had meant that, of all the lottery reports, hers had obtained the most viewers.

It played out on the projector as a gentle reminder to those who were present that Benedict's prediction had been correct. Most of the reporters at the conference had already seen the broadcast. Some thought it was poor journalism. Some thought it was succinct and a success. It was the perfect introduction to a less sceptical room. Some still doubted Benedict's sincerity.

One of the doubters nudged his colleague and, as the transmission ended, he broke the silence. 'OK, so what did I have for breakfast, Superman?' Robert was proud of his question and winked at his colleagues who were semi-circled around him.

He was thirty-five years old. A single man. A handsome man. A narcissist. He had a series of failed relationships behind him and lacked a sense of self. He often pretended to be someone he wasn't. He would buy entire outfits as worn by mannequins in store windows and refused to let the truth get in the way of a good story.

Bobby, as he was known, had tried desperately to coax a cluster of his colleagues to stay in the pub the night before. He had bought a round of vodka shots, but it only served to scrunch faces and sting throats. The group filtered away slowly after that. Most were tired after work, but Bobby liked beer and soon he was drinking alone. He eventually settled for a cab and a cheeseburger before he collapsed into an unmade bed.

His apartment was industrial and lacked warmth. He woke up with a headache and regretted the vodka that burnt his heart. He slipped out of bed and stood facing a full-length mirror; he pinched a chub of fat on his stomach and held it between his fingers. He looked intently at the ageing podgy man before him. He sighed.

He cupped some cold tap water in his hand before sipping it and then splashing it onto his forehead. The kitchen was glossy; the taps were chrome. He had managed to wriggle into yesterday's suit and a pair of blood-red brogues. His tie hung loosely around his shirt collar and his headache had progressed to a thump. The taste of candy cereal collided with the toothpaste on his teeth, causing him to eat his breakfast in slow motion. He took a red felt pen from a glossy kitchen drawer and proceeded to scribble onto a shred of paper. He didn't feel an ounce of guilt. He scrunched the paper into the palm of his hand and then dropped it into his blazer pocket. As he stepped out from his apartment, he fiddled with his tie. The morning air was revivifying.

Benedict calmly sipped at his glass of water and cleared his throat. 'Well, Bobby. You woke up all alone, a little bit worse for wear this morning. Caught a glimpse of yourself in the mirror and realised you are not the spring chicken you used to be. You hastily and scruffily fixed your tie. Then, with a headache in one hand and a spoonful of sugary stars in the other, you planned your next make-believe story. After you bow-tied your brogues and picked up an empty briefcase, you scribbled onto a piece of paper and crumpled it up into your pocket.'

It all seemed too much for Robert. He felt crowded. His skin tightened. The semi-circle around him began to chuckle. He looked down at the briefcase beside his feet. Benedict continued to expose him. 'How is Lucy, anyway? The note is still crumpled in your right jacket pocket. The same scribble you displayed to your friends earlier this morning.'

His colleagues recalled Robert's speech earlier that day.

'Well, if you've got it, you've got it, boys. Didn't get much sleep, if you know what I mean.'

He winked and smirked and fiddled with his tie. He reached into his blazer pocket and produced a crumpled piece of paper. He unfolded it for his colleagues to see; on it, penned in red felt, was a name, a number and some kisses.

Benedict interrupted those who were lost in the flashback. 'Was that about right, Bobby?'

An incandescent reporter interrupted the shenanigans. 'Enough about Bobby, Lucy and his lucky stars—if you have this power, what will you do with it? Can you cure cancer?'

Benedict paused before speaking. 'No, I cannot cure cancer,' he declared.

The room murmured in disbelief. The simple 'no' had condemned the room to silence.

A reporter snapped loudly in despair, 'No? Is there ever going to be a cure?'

Benedict felt the room deflate and spoke softly, apologetically. 'No. There's treatment, as you are all aware, but there is no cure— and never will be—I'm sorry.'

The audience's dejection bathed the room in misery, until a confident female chose to seize the moment. Her mother had died three years earlier from lung cancer. She thought of her mother and spoke in anger. 'I guess that wasn't the answer we were all searching for—so what *are you* going to do?'

She repeated her question in a more direct and aggressive manner. 'What are you going to do, Benedict Maven, to change this world and make it a better place?'

Benedict allowed the entire room to focus on the question posed to him; he was unfazed by her tone. His answer was devoid of emotion. 'Capital punishment.'

Chapter Twenty-One

EIGHTH

He began to rewrite history

Cass Gilbert, put simply, was an architectural genius of the early twentieth century. He had been given the keys to the city in some respects, in the form of an infinite bundle of American dollars and permission to manifest an overindulgence; he obliged. Gilbert considered it not only an opportunity to showcase his talent but to make a statement—a declaration to the world.

He sourced marble from the Vermont and Montarrenti quarries, and the Supreme Court was dressed from head to toe, giving the building an instant and impressive air of grandeur. The courtroom itself was sumptuously decorated.

Mr Stone, the twelfth Chief Justice, accused Gilbert of being bombastically pretentious. Gilbert was offended by Stone's lack of innovated opinion; the ivory buff and golden marble was pompous and polished, but Stone had failed to see the significance of such a building—after all, it was the heart of America.

The current Chief Justice of the United States sat surrounded by the eight associate justices of the Supreme Court. There was an unspoken mutual respect. There was unspoken competition. The justices sat with an upright arrogance. A posture perfected with practice. The courtroom was a cacophony of mutterings and coughs and shuffling feet. At the centre of the proceedings sat the most powerful man in the world, Randolph James Junior. He reflected on his father's words during the obligatory greetings.

The President's father, Randolph Senior, had attained the same high office himself at the tender age of thirty-seven, as a result of strings pulled by a Mr Claiborne. He would preside until he surrendered the office in 1969; now he was unofficially his son's chief adviser.

Randolph Senior's wife had never once wandered into her husband's political affairs; she would occasionally accompany him to destinations and dinner parties, but he had been ambivalent as to her presence. He was a serial adulterer and rarely slept alone. During the last few years of his presidency, he began to meticulously plot his son's path to power with handshakes, endorsements and commendations spanning thirty years.

Randolph Senior loved the old cowboy and Indian films. He considered Gary Cooper to be a close friend and was part of the congregation that laid him to rest at the Sacred Hearts cemetery in 1961. The cowboy influenced him enough to retire to a ranch out west with his wife, Darcy, who he still called Tulip. Randolph Junior was a frequent visitor, drawn to the bucolic setting, his mother's cooking and his father's wisdom.

Father and son often enjoyed rambling walks at the eighty-acre ranch. They would occasionally fish, but they would mainly walk and talk. Randolph Senior had learnt long ago that political conversation was best observed in large open spaces with only those you can sincerely trust.

Randolph Junior was an only child. His father had sworn to produce a son the moment he met Darcy Teulon, the daughter of a Bloomington baker, who worked part-time at the family shop. She was usually coated with a dusting of flour and smelt of warm bread. She had met her childhood sweetheart at the annual Bloomington fete. He had bought one of her butterscotch cupcakes and marvelled at its maker. It tasted divine. A hint of lemon.

Junior had followed a few years later, just as his father's political path was being paved. The moment Randolph Senior took office he swore that his son would be a successor to the throne. By the time Junior had adhered to the thirty-year plan, he had been involved in numerous scandals. The stories had been spun gloriously by his advisers—two Yale spin doctors, graduates with first-class honours in politics, wit and dirty tactics.

They discredited credible sources, bribed busty blondes and mangled mobile phones. Incrimination swiftly evaporated into speculation. Edward Vincent and Albert Eli III had dovetailed magically for the Yale debate team. Both actively enjoyed muddying stories, enough that the piranha of press was constantly suppressed in dirty estuaries while the President swam in open water.

His father had told him that the impending G8 summit was merely a political stunt, stretched out over a few days. He had told him categorically that no one there sought world peace and convinced him that self-preservation and profit were in fact the prize.

He briefed him, 'Son, they will converse lightly, politely in politics through translators and headsets—such stagnant conversation never really attains anything—it's the only time that political debate can fail marvellously but each leader can leave the room smiling. It will undoubtedly play out to a stalemate.'

Randolph James Junior walked into the conference room and all eyes zoomed to him. He was undoubtedly the draw of the big eight and, as he took to his seat, surrounded by an arc of seven of the most powerful men in the world, he remembered his father's words; they settled his nerves.

'Gary Cooper once said that naturalness was a hard thing to talk about, but that it boiled down to a simple fact, you find out what people expect of your type of character and then you give them what they want. That way an actor never seems unnatural or affected, no matter what role he plays.'

Junior was a man, who, like his father, often enjoyed extra-marital activity. He had been married for nearly five years. It was a marriage built on sand. His wife, Zander, was the daughter of a corporate businessman. Needless to say, the corporation and the campaign were successful.

Shisa was drawn to his power. She had watched him enter the large room and, after a day of discussion, had watched him leave. She followed him to his suite and helped him out of his grey suit; she loosened the red tie from his neck and slipped it provocatively over his head before settling her dainty hands onto his silver hair. Her English was practised, seductive. 'Welcome to Okinawa, Mr President.'

Randolph Junior greeted his father with an affable handshake and his mother with an obligatory hug. Zander hovered in the background before offering a couple of kisses to her in-laws. Junior's mother fell back into her role. 'I'm making cupcakes, darling.' He was still his mother's son.

His father pulled him away from the conversation by answering for him. 'Yes, darling, that would be great—why doesn't Zander give you a hand? We'll be back for tea and butterscotch shortly.'

He threw a hand over his son's shoulder and ushered him out of the front door. They continued to walk until he could be sure they were completely alone. 'How was the 26th G8 summit, son?' He laughed at his loaded question.

'Oh, Dad, you should have seen them truckling to each other, to see grown men, national leaders acting like obsequious teenagers—I couldn't bear it.'

'And what of Benedict Maven and the Eighth Amendment?'

'It was venomously denied by all seven men. I guess they are well aware of the fragility and corruption of their own nations—and didn't want an American man controlling their judicial system.'

'And what of Benedict—can we trust him?'

'I believe so.'

Randolph Junior had in fact tried too hard to please. His counterparts at the summit were weary of his conniving kindness. He had spoken passionately and eloquently about Mr Benedict Maven, the quest for truth and judgement, the Eighth Amendment and the power of capital punishment, but they had unanimously refused to wilt to his inspired speech. They all readily feared the oath of one man. An American man. It further empowered the President of the United States in what was already an unrivalled and powerful position. They doubted Randolph's sincerity and his humility. They also feared such a powerful weapon—to legally sentence people to death was a dangerous prospect. A threat to their nations. A threat to the world.

The President stood to the crescendo of shuffling chairs, feet and suits. 'Chief Justice,' he announced.

His words were enough to start proceedings. The Chief Justice fiddled with his tie momentarily then addressed the courtroom with customary aplomb. 'Mr Maven has assured and proven to the President and the American nation that he knows everything—this feat, however unbelievable as it may sound, is why we are here today. With his assurance that all the evidence he provides is precise and truthful, two thirds of both Houses of Congress have agreed to amend the Eighth Amendment.'

Silence filled the courtroom. The Chief Justice cleared his throat and lowered the volume of his deep voice. It was an important statement. A statement that would echo throughout the world. 'We have amended the Eighth Amendment as follows. Comparable capital punishment is a statement implying that the condemned can be tried for a sequence of events that cannot be undone, and sentenced to endure suffering until death as punishment for their crimes.'

As the Chief Justice spoke, a gowned man retrieved a dusty book from a secure cabinet. The man was old and appeared to be a part of the Supreme Court furniture. His wrinkly hands carefully placed the encyclopaedic book onto a large table and carefully brushed the cover. Specks of dust fell from the cover onto the table; the book had lain undisturbed for many years. The man had completed his job. He stepped backwards slightly, allowing another gowned man, a younger version of himself, to step forward and take up his role in the proceedings.

The younger man tentatively held a gold-plated quill in his right hand. In his left hand, he held a small gold-plated inkpot. He carefully took his seat after placing the inkpot beside the book. He blew at the specks of dust that had failed to retreat on the first occasion. The scrupulous scribe opened the book before him and dipped his quill delicately into the inkpot by his side. He meticulously blotted the now-inked quill into a white handkerchief he had drawn from his gown's pocket. The black ink blotched and blobbed onto the white cotton before it was introduced to the book with wonderful calligraphic lettering.

The Chief Justice sensed the young man's nervousness, but there was no need for him to fluster; the scribe's right hand was as steady as a rock. And with it, he began to rewrite history.

Chapter Twenty-Two

SIN

Rise unto the Lord

The high-rise buildings that peered over the proceedings shimmered in the sunlight and the spectacle. The crowd's jeers battled and contorted with the breeze that whistled overhead. The carnival atmosphere suited those who had lost loved ones; it was a time for closure. Retribution. Capital punishment.

The gallows structure was a modern concrete construction that blended effortlessly with its surroundings. The modern masterpiece was a matte grey; its design was based on the mathematics symbol of pi.

The vertical beams were strong. Sharp. Square. The horizontal beam was heavy and curled just a hair to the sky at either end. Etched perfectly on the horizontal beam were just four words. A palindrome would have been better suited to the symmetry, but instead it read *Rise unto the Lord*. It had been etched by a Frenchman who practised calligraphy. He was proud of his work; upon its completion, he pronounced the words in his native tongue, '*S'élever au Seigneur.*'

It was as elegant in its design as it was efficient in delivering death. Those sentenced would suffer unimaginably for a little over three seconds. The crowd waited with bated breath. They all stretched their necks to gain a greater vantage. It was somewhat symbolic, like a sea of soldiers they stood. Tall. Judgemental.

Four braided ropes drooped from the ten-feet-tall structure. They danced hauntingly in the breeze. Beneath them lay a clear glass platform. Concrete steps on either side of the platform resembled bookends. The entire structure appeared to float. The crowd were captivated by it. They believed in its concept. The three condemned people were presented. Each was dressed in a white gown, their hands clasped together in a contraption that heavily restricted their movement. Each guilty soul was accompanied by their own police officer for their final steps on the earth.

Onlookers chanted in chorus as the group trudged towards the structure. The words caught more voices. The chanting was deafening. It rumbled on as the condemned were ushered to their respective braided rope. One was spare on this day. The accompanying police officers hooked the ropes over the guilty subjects' heads. They were tightened in unison. The police officers left the stage—leaving three helpless souls bound to the new structure by old rope. A tannoy announcement prompted the crowd to listen.

'Mortimer Diaz, you are sentenced for the murder of Daniel Ford on February 2, 1997—Bethany Woods, you are sentenced for the murder of Keisha Woods on February 2, 1997—Jonas Gomez, you are sentenced for the murder of Fernando Hudson Junior on February 2, 1997. As according to the Eighth Amendment, I hereby sentence you all to death by hanging. May the Lord have mercy on your souls.'

Chapter Twenty-Three

ABSOLUTION

Their soft lips stung at the piquancy of the perfume

The day had begun like any other. Daniel rushed frantically between his two children who were waiting patiently for their morning milk. He slid glasses of milk across the breakfast counter like a barman delivering scotch. The milk swished in the glass. His children smiled in unison. 'Quickly, children,' he yapped as the iron scorched his creased white shirt, 'Daddy's in a rush.'

Five-year-old Thomas was the energetic type. He would run rings around his dad, and much of it was his dad's fault—too many sugary treats. After all, he was his father's little football star and his mommy's little sugar puff. Rose, on the other hand, was her mother's princess, a sweet rose beneath blonde curls.

Rose was captivated by her brother's bubble-blowing prowess. Milk splashed over his face. Her laugh was infectious, but Daniel was immune to its contagion and had failed to see the importance of the little things in life over the past weeks. He was irritable and impassive, never more so than this morning. He thought about the myriad of leaflets his witness care officer had given him and cursed the whereabouts of his wife. He would be glad when this day was over and he could get back to normality.

The children wandered into the living room, glasses in hand. Rose sat on the sofa and was soon immersed in her favourite cartoon. She rested her milk upon the coffee table beside her; she had forgotten its creaminess, courtesy of animation. Thomas gulped the rest of his.

Thomas spoke over his shoulder to his dad, who was ironing frustratedly. 'What are you doing, Dad?'

Rose copied her brother, 'Yeah, what are you doing, Dad?'

They both giggled.

Daniel needed his children's playfulness more than he ever could have imagined and allowed himself finally to marvel at them. He wished for their carefree attitude today of all days. He indulged them. 'Daddy is ironing his suit for later.'

'Why?' questioned Thomas.

Daniel spoke in a more serious tone to his children. 'So Daddy looks smart for court.'

Thomas continued to question his dad. 'Why?'

Daniel felt the pressure under the scrutiny of his children's questioning. He chose to educate them. 'So Daddy can tell the important people what I saw the nasty man do.'

Thomas and Rose stood on the sofa facing their dad with their backs to the cartoon.

'And we all know what happens to nasty people don't we?'

Thomas and Rose proudly answered in harmony. 'They get taken away.'

'Yes, that's right. They go where all the other nasty people go, and where's that?'

'To the penitentiary.'

He smiled. He was a proud father and soon he was joined by his proud wife who tiptoed down the stairs after eavesdropping on the conversation. He resented his morning moodiness.

'Come on, kids, enough of the inquisition,' she announced. She threw a smile to her husband and then darted the same beam to the two sofa-riding children. 'He'll have enough of that later.'

'Tell me about it,' Daniel sighed.

'You'll be fine, darling,' Chloe reassured his nervousness, kissed him on his cheek and whispered into his ear, 'Just tell them what you saw.'

'Easier said than done, I guess.'

Thomas and Rose listened intently to their mother and father without understanding the subtleness of adult sarcasm. They were inquisitive types. The cartoon had long since become a background noise and Chloe instructed them, 'Come on, Cagney and Lacey, get your shoes on—we've got to go and visit Nanna.'

She looked to her husband and offered warming words. 'It'll be OK, I promise. Call me when you can.'

She kissed her husband's lips—he needed it and she knew that. 'Well done, children. Don't forget to say goodbye to Daddy.'

They rushed to their daddy's arms. Their tender cheeks squished softly against his freshly shaven face. Their olfactory senses were overloaded with the spiciness of his cologne. It sunk deep into their hair. They would smell their dad's fragrance for the rest of the day.

Daniel spoke from amongst the adornment of children. 'Be a good boy and girl for Mom today, and I'll see you later, OK?'

They kissed his cheeks; their soft lips stung at the piquancy of the perfume. Rose rubbed her lips with the back of her hand, ridding them of the sting and bitterness.

'And what's your job today?' Daniel said to his son.

It was a father-and-son moment. Thomas looked into his dad's blue eyes, and answered the question that he had been asked so many times before. 'To look after the girls.' There was a seriousness to his delivery. The boy spun away from his father and took hold of his mother's and sister's hands.

A Cadillac rumbled patiently down the street. The considerable surface area of the thick, out-of-proportion tyres gripped the tarmac like bubble-gum.

Mortimer *Mickey* Diaz was alert and propped himself up in the back seat of the Cadillac. He was unaccustomed to his straight back posture. He scanned the surroundings, looking for the red door with a silver lion's head. He fidgeted with the waistband of his trousers and was visibly nervous. The driver and front-seat passenger looked over their shoulders towards him, annoyed at his agitation.

Marcelo exuded calmness. He nudged the driver beside him. 'There it is,' he declared. His voice was soft and calculated.

Mickey watched the interaction between the front-seat occupants but had barely heard Marcelo speak. Beyond Marcelo, Mickey could see the red door shining like a beacon. His stomach sank to the footwell as the vehicle began to slow. Pepe nudged the brake pedal and they edged to a stop, two houses from the lion.

Pepe adjusted the rear-view mirror until it revealed Mickey's inquisitive eyes peering from the back seat. He spoke clearly. 'You know what you gotta do, Mickey.'

Mickey nodded.

Marcelo abhorred Mickey's nervousness and barked at the back-seated man who had sunk slightly from a perfect posture. 'Don't fuck this up, it's important.' Marcelo threatened him again. 'Daddy T is watching.'

Mickey fumbled at the handle of the Cadillac and repeated Marcelo's words in his head.

The red door and the lion's head shone brightly. It was a beautiful day. Mickey scanned left and right as the sunshine landed onto his black vest. Mickey pulled at the lion's head. It crashed sharply. Daniel was startled by the noise. He rushed to the door, dressed in his freshly pressed attire. The door creaked open.

A wiry black man stepped over the threshold. Uninvited. He pushed the immaculately dressed man to the chest and pointed a pistol to his head. Daniel was frozen by fear. He battled the reality of the moment and looked at the flutings on the inside of the barrel. He was hypnotised. Breathless. Crowning the pistol were two of the whitest eyes he had ever seen. He fixed upon their evil but there was no salvation. Mickey's white eyes barely fluttered as he callously squeezed the trigger. Daniel's body stiffened as death and gravity sucked him to the living room floor. Blood spouted from his decimated forehead onto the carpet. Mickey stood over his victim for a mere second or two and then walked briskly back to Marcelo, Pepe and the purring Cadillac.

The prosecution witness was dead. An aftermath of adrenaline coursed through Mickey's body. It caused his skin to tingle in the frenzy of the occasion. It was his first hit. He jumped behind the duo into the plush interior of the Cadillac and obligatory gangland infamy. The Cadillac rumbled along the street. The sun arced across its pearlescent crimson shell.

The pool of blood sunk into the carpet like treacle. Atop the coffee table were the remnants of Rose's morning milk. Speckles of blood had seeped into the velvety white liquid, causing it to emulsify into the palest of pinks. It was Rose's favourite colour.

Chapter Twenty-Four

MERCY

The orange flavour tickled her taste buds

Bethany Woods had become a daughter too late and a mother too soon. Her childhood had made Oliver Twist's seem plentiful. Her mother had overdosed when she was only three years into her life. For thirteen hours thereafter, she crawled around the crammed room—her mother's lifeless body watched over her, slumped in a soiled armchair.

It was a neighbour in the flat below that had first heard Bethany crying. She knew that the flat above hers was never usually quiet enough for a child's cries to be heard. Peggy decided to investigate the sound coming from the den at the top of the communal stairs.

Peggy was not a strong woman. She was a frail widow, but the door opened with a gentle push. The lock bore the scars of previous break-ins by undesirable people. Peggy lifted her hand to cover her nose; the room was decaying before her. A sobbing child was huddled beside a ghastly figure in the corner armchair. The neighbour was too ashamed to cry. She stretched out her arms and stepped towards the infant. 'Come here, my darling.'

Bethany did not respond but Peggy pulled her into her cocoon, blinding her from the colourless body on the chair. Froth had bubbled on her mother's mouth and the saliva was the only thing that shone on her grey, grainy face.

Bethany was eight years old when she was officially adopted, but the scars of her childhood manifested to destroy the transition to her teens. It was enough that her legal guardians, Jeremy and Lucy-May, had to relinquish their parental rights and allow social services to support Bethany as she wandered in and out of the youth correctional system.

The first time Bethany sold her body was to an overweight businessman; she was sixteen. She cost him twenty dollars. She felt no remorse, no regret, no worth.

Bethany loved her own daughter with a concerning infatuation. It was fuelled by her paranoia and recreational drug use. It was not a mother and daughter love. In contrast, Keisha adored her mother and the social worker that visited her weekly. Keisha was always showing off her array of dolls to the pleasant lady named Delores, who always brought a clipboard and cheerful conversation. She saw the best in everyone. Delores's visits were becoming more and more frequent.

Keisha told Delores that her favourite colours were pink and purple, and presented her with a doll, while Bethany settled her nerves in the kitchen with a cigarette. Delores looked at the doll that was missing hair and had looping eyelashes above its powder-blue eyeshadow—it was truly ghastly. The doll blinked as Delores handed it back to the sweet young girl. Keisha sat it beside her on the living room floor and marvelled at its eyes. They shone like marbles.

Delores walked into the kitchen and leant a steady hand onto Bethany's thin, bony shoulder. Cigarette smoke swam into the living room. She emerged from the kitchen twenty minutes later. Keisha was still lost in her own imagination. Delores interrupted her with a ruffle of her wavy hair. Keisha looked up to the pleasant lady with the clipboard and felt the words fall upon her.

'I'll see you soon, my little sugar cube.'

Bethany watched Delores's goodbye from the kitchen and then lit another cigarette to calm her nerves. She watched over a series of splashes that appeared in a glass of water. They rippled like raindrops in a puddle. Thirty-two white tablets sank slowly beneath the ripples and began to fizz towards the surface. Bethany added a dash of orange cordial and stirred the liquid. Bethany's black-nail-varnished fingertips gripped the glass and lifted it calmly from the counter.

Keisha played innocently on the living room floor as her mother sat down on the shabby sofa behind her. Bethany took a deep breath before addressing her daughter quietly. 'Keisha, come to Mommy, darling.'

Keisha dropped her doll and it bounced onto the floor. She scrambled to her mother's request and landed her elbows onto her lap. Bethany spoke again, 'Drink this, princess, and you and your dolls can have some sweeties.'

Keisha sipped the drink with her mother's help. Bethany's hands lifted the glass gently, allowing Keisha to gulp it courtesy of gravity. Bethany took the empty glass and put it to rest beside her feet. She reached into her pocket and handed Keisha a packet of lollipops, as promised, to the polite and spritely girl.

'Thank you, Mommy.'

Keisha jumped back to her circle of dolls. She excitedly placed a lolly beside each one before setting one down in a space for herself. She took her seat. Knees crossed and back arched. She sucked at her lolly and her bright hazel eyes wandered around the dolls in turn. The orange flavour tickled her taste buds. Bethany watched from a distance and whispered, 'I won't let anyone take you away from me.' Keisha began to cough.

Chapter Twenty-Five

JUDGEMENT

The wandering chocolate coated his lips

Jonas Gomez crammed his podgy frame into his beaten-up Buick Nova. The engine rumbled as he cruised a suburban street filled with colourful cars and gardens of deepest green. Jonas anxiously scratched at an itch on the inside of his leg. He was fidgeting while monitoring the sidewalk, the car tyres occasionally prodding the kerb. He slobbered over an ice-cream cone in his hand; he had perfected the art of eating and driving.

The afternoon sun rebounded off the battered exterior of the Buick and threatened to melt Jonas's treat. The temperamental air conditioning cooled the grotesque man, goose-pimpling his thick greasy skin. The orange car was ambling along nicely until he jabbed at the brake pedal. The car stuttered momentarily before it continued edging forward at walking speed.

Fernando was seven years old. He was slightly smaller than most children his age, but what he lacked in height he made up for in tenderness. The Spiderman rucksack perched upon his back was the epitome of cuteness, bumping merrily up and down as the boy walked in time with the slowing car beside him.

Jonas spoke in a calculated, almost comic-book voice.

'Cool rucksack, Spiderman.'

The boy enjoyed the playfulness and turned towards the

compliment. Fernando had inherited his politeness from his mother. He courteously replied, 'Thank you, sir,' and puffed out his cheeks. The sunshine had zapped his sprightliness.

His mother had taught him the error of his wandering father's ways and the boy truly was a little gem. Fernando's chestnut eyes were drawn to the drippy, silky sauce that had trickled onto the strange man's hand.

Jonas teased the little boy's appetite, holding the squelching cone aloft. 'Do you like ice cream, Spiderman?'

Fernando nodded excitedly at being compared to a superhero and the promise of frozen flavour. The man continued to tempt him. 'I've got all the ice cream you can eat at my house. Do you want some?'

The little boy responded entirely in his mother's words as he battled his cravings. 'I'm not supposed to talk to strangers.'

Jonas sensed weakness. 'I'm not a stranger, I know your mom. I can take you home afterwards—plus it's chocolate.'

The word *chocolate* was enough to persuade Fernando, not that he needed much convincing. Children love ice cream. Jonas scanned the street before inviting the little boy to sit beside him with a casual flick of his four fingers.

'You can sit in the front like a big boy if you want.'

Fernando edged around the front of the purring Buick and the passenger door swung open. The boy nudged the rucksack off his shoulders and clambered inside the car. He placed the bag between his feet and was instantly dwarfed by the large interior. His eyes wandered around the dials on the dashboard.

'Seatbelt on, please,' instructed Jonas.

The boy obeyed the instruction and then began to display his conversational skills to the stranger.

'My name's Fernando, what is yours?'

'Nice to meet you, Fernando, I'm Jonas.'

'My mom told me that I'm not allowed in the front seat.'

'Well, it can be our little secret—can you keep a secret?'

Fernando replied unfalteringly, hypnotised by the melting, drippy mess. 'Yes.'

Jonas saw his stare. 'Here you go, Fernando.'

Jonas handed Fernando the half-eaten ice cream and licked the remainder from his tacky fingers. Jonas was captivated by Fernando's tongue as he devoured the sweet treat over the short journey from pick-up to home. Fernando savoured the flavour and only wanted more. Jonas knew that a half-eaten ice cream wasn't enough—it would only heighten Fernando's desire.

'You want some more, Fernando?'

'Yes please.'

'OK, follow me. I have as much as you can eat inside.'

Jonas pushed himself out of the worn, distorted seat and fumbled with his jeans that sagged beneath his potbellied frame. Fernando sprung from the crisp, unused seat and wandered after Jonas and the promise of ice cream. He followed him into the house and was gestured to sit down in the living room. He scanned the room and began to question his surroundings. The host quickly rummaged through his fridge freezer and swiftly returned to his guest with the biggest bowl of ice cream the boy had ever seen. It was the ideal distraction.

'There you go, Spiderman, I did promise, with an extra helping of chocolate sauce.'

Fernando's eyes were hypnotised by the swirling chocolate and he instantly forgot the strangeness of the room. He held the bowl in his hand and took a large spoonful. He shovelled the cold treat into his mouth just as the chocolate sauce overflowed the spoon. The wandering chocolate coated his lips.

Their eyes met properly for the first time. Fernando giggled at the chubby man, who smiled back. Jonas couldn't help but ruffle Fernando's hair in his moment of ecstasy. The boy's soft hair tickled his fingers. Fernando took another enormous spoonful as Jonas spoke.

'You want to play and eat some more upstairs, Spiderman?'

Fernando was too busy in his euphoria to reply and just nodded. Jonas offered one hand to Fernando and took control of the bowl and spoon in his other. Fernando didn't hesitate and grabbed the fat-fingered man's open hand. Fernando's small hand curled into Jonas's. The hunter relished its softness and carefully stepped onto the staircase. Fernando followed. Jonas spoke softly to the boy in a tone that was the antithesis of his character. 'Shall we go and play a game, Fernando?' Jonas unbuttoned his jeans.

Bethany barely opened her eyes—she couldn't muster the strength to lift her lids. She wanted it to be over quickly.

She had watched the first hanging in Washington on television and decided to end her own life. She didn't want to die kicking violently at thin air like the lady in white. It was her bare feet that had truly startled her, how her toes curled and contorted moments before her last breath. She couldn't banish the horrifying thoughts from her head and dropped some pills into a glass. Days later she had woken in a guarded hospital bed—Benedict wouldn't allow her the easy way out and had alerted authorities to her suicide attempt.

Jonas and Mickey hadn't entertained suicide, but the eerie clunk of the hydraulic platform startled both men. The gathering gasped in delight.

Bethany was the first to feel the rope tighten. The vein that ran from her neck to her temple bulged at the pressure. Mickey watched Bethany's toes stretch slowly, frantically trying to remain grounded. Beyond Bethany was the flat-footed, obese Buick owner. Mickey felt no remorse for the family that he had destroyed. It was his sacrifice, in honour of the gang's mark. The promise of martyrdom awaited him.

Bethany mustered every sinew of strength to elongate her already extended five-foot frame. She was as slender as a ballerina—en pointe. The structure tugged her towards the sky. Her calf muscles tightened as her toes floated slowly from the glass—entrechat.

Jonas could barely look to his left because of his rigid, flabby frame. He didn't want to anyway. Mickey couldn't help but look to the flailing damsel beside him. Jonas scrunched his eyes tightly. He was only slightly taller than the girl. The strands of the rope creaked at his weight but lifted him unsympathetically. His feet kicked out immediately, searching for the solid glass. His panic caused him to sway.

Mickey's lanky frame had afforded him another minute on the earth. His feet were still planted firmly on the glass. The people beside him were being emptied of life. It was at this precise moment that he wished he had chosen a different path. The reality of death had weakened him. He was scared. Bethany's toes curled horribly as the final breath left her body. Jonas's vocal cord snapped courtesy of the weight tugging at it. His wallow was audible, screeching horribly, piercing the crowd with a nightmarish execution of sound. The viewers continued to suckle on the entertainment of death.

Mickey remained. Steadfast. Jonas's scream had turned the gang man's belly. The involuntary tumble was uncontrollable. The subtle creak of taut rope preceded the man's 'Rise unto the Lord'.

The last of the murderers closed his eyes.

Chapter Twenty-Six

SUPREMACY

We must encounter evil, but we must not endure it

The room was vast. Too big for one man and yet too small for his ego. Benedict had been summoned to enter. The door was opened politely by a man wearing a headset. A man named Gerry. A colossal figure who spent his days walking along marble hallways dressed in a tight-fitting black suit. Gerry rarely spoke. He listened to men far smaller than him in size, but far bigger in stature. The biggest and strongest man in the White House was in reality one of the weakest.

Benedict edged through the door's opening, nodded to Gerry and looked to the desk at the far end of the wide room. Gerry enjoyed the moment that afforded him the opportunity to speak. 'Sir— Benedict Maven.'

The man behind the desk was marvelling at his own achievements. The President wasn't one for introductions and instead he focused on the walls, cluttered with accolades and pictures of handshakes with famous people. He spoke without looking at the man at whom his words were aimed. 'Are you a religious man, Mr Maven?'

Gerry closed the door. It was the only sound that followed the question. The President spoke again, as if the question had been rhetorical. 'Well, I am a man of faith and a man of science.'

A Bible and an ammonite fossil paperweight were the focus of Benedict's attention; both items lay, unassuming in their contradiction, on the President's desk. The President, now standing, continued his lecture. 'I remember the day I swore an oath to this country.' He recited the oath, imprecisely; he was revelling in the sound of his own voice. 'And I swore that I would faithfully execute the office of president, to preserve, protect and defend the constitution of this country.'

Benedict chipped in, intentionally upsetting the President's flow. 'I guess God is there for when Google isn't.'

The President chuckled. 'Indeed, Mr Maven, great minds think alike.' He turned away from the decorated wall and allowed Benedict the courtesy of his attention. It didn't last long; he had seen Benedict before and couldn't bear to look at a man more handsome than himself. He looked back to the wall and, in particular, a framed blueprint.

'That is what we created, Mr Maven, in order to faithfully execute the tyranny, the evil that threatens our land.'

The President's words were unnecessary because Benedict had been the pioneer of its conception. The blueprint showed the structure—bold, loud, in sharp lines—with a map of America shadowed behind it, which plotted the four locations that perfectly dissected the land of opportunity. It was as financially sound as it was formidably set.

Each structure was identical. The glass, the beams and the steps were all engineered at a secluded unit in Washington. The President had watched eight artic lorries with eight overweight drivers leave the yard in tandem. The first two spent a large part of their journey on Interstate 90, eastbound, destination Minneapolis.

The structure was in place twelve days later. It complemented Lakewood Cemetery beautifully. The glass and heavy pillars were sympathetic to the manicured lawns and rows of poppies. The structure drew untold attention, enough that the first public execution saw the Minneapolis Police join forces with the Saint Paul

PD, in an attempt to steady the protest of religious people who had flocked to the city. On the first day, eight people dressed in white were hanged for crimes of murder. Thirteen people were arrested for disrupting the peace. The courts would later deem the offences unconstitutional.

The President began to pace and continued to preach. 'I'm taking Air Force One to San Jose this week, the Plaza de César Chávez. A few of the locals need reminding as to what this blueprint has done for our country and need to forget the fountains that my creation has replaced. The disapproving locals will soon forget those silly sprinklers when their pockets are lined by buying crowds. Public trial naturally brings with it public trade.' He cleared his throat and spoke again. 'You're more than welcome to join me, Mr Maven. I have been reliably informed that the Cathedral Basilica of St Joseph is quite a sight. It will allow us some time to discuss our next venture.'

Benedict replied politely without committing to an answer, and then massaged the President's ego to prevent him asking again. 'Thank you. The New York structure is quite stunning, the glass allows the frame to levitate.'

It worked; the President forgot about his invitation to Benedict. 'Heavenly, isn't it—it's slightly tilted, you know, the glass, enough that the damned can see themselves in their final moments.' He continued to elaborate. 'I'm also told that its reflection allows those hung in Houston to also see the Hermann Park Monument before they succumb to the afterlife—the bronzed equestrian of Texan independence, General Sam atop his horse Saracen. It pleases me to know that an American hero is the last man they see. Much like us, Mr Maven—we are the evolution of America.'

The President looked at Benedict and then turned back to the blueprint. There was white handwriting scribbled beneath the architectural drawing; the President pointed at it.

'I chose those words, you know—a lot of people think that it's from a religious passage, but they are indeed my own.' He sounded them aloud egotistically. 'Rise unto the Lord. And you will accept thy Judgement.'

The door opened as the President spoke the last word of his quote. Gerry peeked in and spoke without invitation from his master. 'Sir.'

The President, who had been hypnotised by his own importance and anecdotes, was startled. Benedict hadn't flinched. He knew that Gerry was about to inform the President that a Secret Service officer had just taken out a madman outside the White House perimeter fence.

Mr Probert Kettering had just been fired from his municipal job and was recently divorced. His ex-wife had relocated to Europe with the children and, in essence, his whole family had left him. His grievances had transformed into a mental instability. He had taken a Colt Eagle to 1600 Pennsylvania Avenue and had begun shooting. He shot at nothing and no one in particular. He was hoping to be gunned down on prime-time news.

The shots could barely be heard from inside the White House and, instead of causing uproar, he had only succeeded in frightening the gardener. Probert had released two shots into thin air and been taken down by a sharp-shooting Secret Service rookie, Regis Spieth. Probert would be later sentenced to three years' imprisonment. The story would only serve to frustrate the President, who had little time for madmen and the sensationalised headlines that would follow.

Benedict also knew that Gerry would be castigated later that evening for interrupting the President and not gently tapping at the heavy door before being invited to enter. The President watched Gerry as he muttered through his message and made a mental note to discipline him. Benedict had taken advantage of the moment and edged towards the door. The President was still frowning at Gerry's rudeness but had followed Benedict's movement. He shook his hand firmly, and spoke confidently, not knowing that it would be the last time they would be alone. 'We will recommence this discussion, Mr Maven. Please excuse Gerry.'

The President gently gestured for Benedict to leave the room and then eloquently delivered his finale. 'Remember, in this life, we must encounter evil, but we must not endure it.'

The President's words were dropped to the polished floor of Benedict's penthouse suite. He had been allocated the suite by the President's Chief of Staff on his arrival in Washington DC. Despite the extravagant furniture and decoration, Benedict sat on the Ercol rocking chair beside the panoramic window. He carefully and meticulously inspected the silver cross in his hand. He stood up and walked to the expansive window that surveyed Washington's horizon as the now-empty chair rocked in tandem with his steps. He looked over the bright lights of the city, casting his stare in the direction of New York, his smile as wide as the skyline.

Elisha was sitting two hundred miles to the north and concentrating intensely on the jumbled Rubik's cube between her fingertips. Andy was sitting opposite her, fixated on a larger cube, watching the New York Yankees and Chicago White Sox. Elisha twisted the chaotic cube until the colours began to group together. They were almost in their respective groups. Elisha's bright brown eyes widened at the prospect of completion. She twisted at the last of the algorithms and the gift from her dad was whole. She rotated the cube, just to be sure. There were no breaks in colour. She held it aloft, crying in excitement.

She looked to the stars outside through the bay window. 'I've done it, it's complete—it's finally complete. I told you I would.'

Andy looked towards her, bemused by her silly talk, and muttered, 'Well done, darling.'

Chapter Twenty-Seven

STRATAGEM

Enemies yesterday, comrades today

The roar of Friday night football resounded around Andy's living room and echoed throughout the neighbourhood. Elisha had long since waved goodbye to Andy and Benedict before trotting away in heels, wearing a smile and French-plaited hair. Andy and Benedict had watched her walk away. Andy was no great host; Elisha knew his faults and had prepared a coffee table full of snacks for the 'football fans'. All Andy had to do was to offer Benedict a beer now and again. It was the quintessential *boys' night in.*

Elisha and her plait descended on a swanky retreat in the company of her female work colleagues for an equally typical *girls' night out.* The girls enjoyed their reserved seating at The Mulberry and were front row at the cabaret. They listened to soulful music, ate lobster and talked long into the night.

Andy quizzed Benedict at every stage of the game, but Benedict refused to engage in the predictability of predictions and allowed the game to play out as destiny had planned. He watched Andy's elation and despair at every instance and revelled perversely in it.

Across America, perched on their seats, football fans drank in the theatre of the night and of the game. The New York Giants versus the Chicago Bears. Eventually, Andy realised that the rudimental questions he was relentlessly throwing at Benedict were being dropped intentionally like a flailing running back. Andy was a Giants fan. Benedict was ambivalent, but he enjoyed the highs and lows that were etched on the faces of mere mortal players and fans. It reminded him of what the world didn't know.

The Giants quarterback, Jordan Jacob, called the play, 'Sophia Grace,' in a husky voice, as a flurry of receivers tiptoed in anticipation behind him.

The football sprang backwards between a burly man's legs and straight into Jacob's gloved hands. Blockers wearing the same jerseys arced around him with military precision, protecting their most valuable player. Jacob feinted to his left and then jolted to his right before arrowing the ball high into the New York sky. It soared like a falcon as Bears and Giants danced beneath it in defence and attack.

Eden Zach, the darling of New York City, was an athletic, charismatic character who had spent the early part of his teenage years sprinting the track. His speed had earned him a football trial, and the rest was history. His Nike contract was worth far too much for this humble man and, after treating his family and friends to his wages, he would often make charitable donations without any real acclaim.

His Nike footwear glided along the turf like ice on ice; his strides were long and graceful and landed him into the touchdown zone. Eden leapt off his last stride and stretched his left arm high. The laced ball, still watched by Jacob, hit Eden's left hand as his body defied gravity and arced in mid-flight—it rocked in his hand before settling; the stadium erupted as Eden twisted his two-hundred-and-ten-pound body before it crashed to the ground, his left hand still with its palm to the moon. The ball wobbled momentarily but remained safely in his hand. Touchdown Giants.

Beer erupted from the bottle Andy held tightly in his right hand. Benedict snapped a tea towel from the radiator beside his seat and slipped it with Jacob's precision into the spilt beer's path, absorbing it instantly before it even reached the floor. Andy spun his attention from the television to the beer he had just spilt and threw his left hand over the bottle's top to prevent more spillage. Beer frothed between his fingertips. It was sticky. He felt the tea towel at his feet and looked at Benedict across the room.

'Nice throw,' he quipped, before they both laughed.

The sound of celebration burst from the television. A cheer could be heard from the surrounding houses; this was a Giants suburb. Benedict focused on the colour that graced the enlarged television screen before him. The letters and digits were illuminated in bright yellow, 'NEW YORK GIANTS 13 – CHICAGO BEARS 0'.

'Touchdown Giants!' echoed from the commentator's lips as the replay showed Benedict what he had already seen twice. The time on the television read 18:44, Friday, August 24. Andy watched the touchdown play out again in slow motion. He studied the ball that spun like a gyro from every angle imaginable. He watched Jacob's hand hook and loop the spinning ball. He slurped at his beer, picked up the tea towel and licked his fingers.

Randolph James Senior was sworn in as President on November 22, 1963, while aboard Air Force One on a runway in Dallas. One hundred and twenty-eight minutes after the assassination of his predecessor.

Darcy and Junior were at his side when he took the oath, crammed into a plush plane full of panicked people. It was a situation full of storm and sorrow and, in all the hurly-burly, no one could find a Bible for the Vice President to place his left hand upon. Darcy didn't do much talking when her husband was set amongst the elite of the nation. It was in these moments that she was the doting housewife and merely an onlooker, but nervously, on this day, she offered her timid voice to no one in particular. 'I have a Bible, I take it with me everywhere that I go.'

She reached into her handbag and revealed a miniature Bible. Before she had even fully removed it from the bag, a lady in bloodstained clothing snatched it gratefully from her. It was an image that Darcy would never forget.

The first night that Randolph Senior, Junior and Darcy spent at the White House was six days after that fateful but triumphant day. Junior was nearly nine years old and full of zest; he spent most of the night gawping at the grandeur of it all. Randolph Senior spoke to his wife while his son explored. 'Bittersweet, that day on the plane.'

Darcy's voice bloomed when she was not in the company of her husband's entourage. 'My grandmother gave me that Bible, God rest her soul.'

Randolph enjoyed the sound of his wife's voice. 'Lucky that you had it, my darling.'

She spoke again. 'Oh, Randolph, to see his wife there, in bloodstained clothes…it was truly awful.'

'I know.'

'What if something like that happened to you?'

'It won't. Come on now, dear—this is our night, me, you and Junior.'

He took her tightly in his arms and landed a kiss onto her forehead. 'I love you, Tulip,' he murmured, and then shouted over her shoulder to his son. The President's voice echoed in the halls. 'Junior, come in here, son.'

Randolph Senior went over to the record player; he allowed the needle to fall and watched the record spin before a song crackled into life. Junior rushed from room to room, following his father's words and the hum of Italian music. He ran into his father's arms, colliding awkwardly with a padded leather book that his father held.

'What's that, Dad?'

'A picture book from before your time, son.' He pulled Junior onto his lap; Darcy perched on the arm of their chair. Randolph

Senior opened the book and began to look through the pictures of yesteryear—the wedding of Randolph James and Darcy Teulon. It was a sentimental moment of reflection. A moment that caused Randolph Senior to remember the times that he had been unfaithful to his wife. He vowed internally not to deviate again. It was a promise he would not keep.

The last photo revealed a muddled group of people. The photographer had climbed up a wooden ladder to capture the entire congregation. There was no order to it; friends and family were intertwined like a paper chain, smiling helplessly at the man off camera, perched on a ladder. Randolph was a fair distance from his wife in the photo, huddled beside a dashing man named Daley. Junior scanned the crowd in the photo.

'Which one are you, Dad?'

'That's me, son, the man in the blue suit—and that's your mother, smiling, in that divine white dress.'

He looked up to his wife, balanced on the chair's arm beside them. He leaned towards her and landed a kiss onto her plump lips. He bumped his son playfully off his knee and jumped to his feet. He placed the photo album onto the warm cushion and took his blushing bride's hand. He pulled her to her feet and swivelled her towards an open floor. The music intensified as Randolph Senior fiddled with the record player's volume. Junior took his mother's place on the arm of the chair. He watched his mother and father fall into each other's eyes and swoon like ice skaters around the floor before him. His father pirouetted and caught a glance of his son; he threw words to him during his dance with Darcy.

'And who would have thought that the man in the blue suit would end up here?'

Big Daddy T embraced his nephew, who was sitting beside him in his plush Mustang interior. He had sworn to look after him ever since the boy's father was murdered in a gang turf war, nearly fifteen years ago. He loved him like a son. Durrell loved him like a father. They both loved the New York Giants.

The Mustang stopped outside the grand entrance to St Phillips Church as the radio played. An excitable commentator decorated the airwaves with his wild words. 'What a take by wide receiver Eden Zach. The twenty-three-year-old twinkle-toed receiver from Brooklyn has set this game alight. The Giants lead thirteen to zero.'

Big Daddy slowly climbed the concrete steps to the arched doorway and envied his nephew who skipped towards the top. The Mustang driver hurried up the steps past them both and opened the door to the church. Daddy T finally arrived at the top of the steps as the huge door glided open. It made him look small and insignificant, something that never usually happened.

The church was overcrowded with egos. The congregation turned to the doorway and acknowledged their leader. The significant one. This once-almighty place had been built on love, forgiveness and life's values. From the stained-glass windows to the walnut pews, this church had it all, but as with everything, times change. People change. Places change. Each pew was filled with a different colour. The scene was deceivingly beautiful. Big Daddy T stood in front of the altar and shouted, 'Hey!'

His voice was grainy; it echoed chillingly down the aisle. His name described him perfectly; he was big in every sense of the word. He was six feet four, three hundred pounds; his three-quarter-length black leather jacket hid his heavy frame. A weighted gold necklace rested on the outer lapel of his jacket, a gold, diamond-encrusted 'T' hung down. Some might have been fooled into thinking this was a religious cross, but T wasn't religious in any way.

T placed his hands on the altar and preached to his congregation. 'Remember this day, the day we seek vengeance for our lost brothers and sons—the Brooklyn Baysides—the LA Angels—the Mississippi

Mohawks—the Vegas Vagabonds—the Washington Warriors—the Texas Sunshines. We are all here together in the St Phillips Church of New York City, drawn together for our greatest hit. We know that over five thousand of our brothers have been slain to the testimony of a man named Benedict. Radical times are upon us and this is our time to fight back—fight back against the injustice which is threatening our legacy and existence. America, my friends, is no longer our playground. Today we are one. Today we claim back America.'

Chapter Twenty-Eight

DIVINITY

It steadied the orphaned girl's heart

The end of summer was officially lit with glorious sunshine. It was decidedly out of season for Labor Day and was almost certainly the fault of the bashful weathermen on morning television, who had only predicted a mild morning and not a searing heat.

Atop the canopy of black cherry trees, high above Cherry Tree Lake, sat a Mississippi Kite. His soft silvery cloak basked in the purest of azure skies.

Each morning, the kite watched as the sun rose and the moon settled, marvelling at the transition, waiting patiently for the feathery mist upon the lake's surface to be whisked away by a waking day. He never tired of the place. Its beauty defied the boredom of recurrence. Today, the sunshine accentuated the allure.

There was a faultless silence that surrounded the lake. The air was delicately blessed with the wintergreen scent of birch. Elisha whispered to the man beside her, respectful of the tranquillity. 'It's perfect.'

The silver spectator was a native attraction, often seen in photographs surveying the skyline. He looked to the land below and studied the subtle movement. His glassy eyes zoomed in as the beautiful, tittering pair approached the water's edge.

Benedict offered his hand to Elisha as they stepped gently onto the rickety wooden walkway. It creaked with his words, 'Your boat awaits, madam.'

Andy wiped the sweat from his forehead. Labor Day wasn't a celebratory day for him, and the industry continued regardless of his discomfort. Time was money for the property tycoons of tomorrow.

His mouth was dry and his skin was reddened. It was the hottest September day since seventy-five, but despite the heat, Andy heaved a pipe onto his bare shoulder and ambled towards the skeleton frame of a building. Andy landed the awkward bar onto the pyramid pile of piping that he had amassed, but the stifling warmth was sapping and caused him to pause and take a heavy breath. A voice of reason echoed from the edge of the forecourt. 'It's too damn warm. I'll deal, you get the water.'

Andy didn't argue with Sage. He retreated to the shelter of the cool, air-conditioned cabin and settled in for some well-deserved rest. Immediately, his prickly skin was appeased by the sudden change in temperature.

Andy shouted to his friend. 'It's supposed to be eighty! Hundred and five they said on the radio!'

'Chucky reckons it's one of those Indian summers!' yelled Sage.

Andy bit back in jest. 'What the fuck does Chucky know?'

Elisha stepped tentatively onto the moored oak rowing boat, assisted by the firm gentleness of Benedict's hand. The small boat swayed gently but soon stabilised itself courtesy of Elisha's prowess.

'Your turn,' she instructed.

Benedict took a timid step towards the boat's edge. She smirked at his careful plodding and continued, 'Come and join me. I'll keep you safe, I promise.'

Benedict landed his foot onto the hull of the boat, reluctant to allow his remaining foot to leave the comfort of the creaky old pier.

The boat rocked. Elisha watched his arms flail as he lunged his remaining foot from the pier, prompting her to react and embrace his unbalance. She wrapped her arms around his back and her face nudged softly into his chest. The boat rocked wildly from side to side and yet all she felt was the warmth of the stumbling man's racing heart as the boat slowly steadied. She steered herself away from the moment and looked up at him. 'And now we're even.'

Benedict laughed and softened the fluttering of hearts. 'It's not quite a burning building.'

Andy sat amongst the cold air. Sage shouted from across the round table, interrupting his thoughts, 'Your turn!'

Andy was jolted by the booming voice and hurriedly checked the cards in his hand. He threw one to Sage and slipped back into his thoughts of Elisha.

'There's nobody here.' Elisha's words echoed in the emptiness. Benedict smiled wickedly at her from the comfort of the boat's seating. 'But I guess that's the reason you brought me,' she continued.

Benedict pointed to the tree-top observer. 'You could say that— but contrary to what you think, we are not alone.'

Elisha beamed at the bird's balance and then offered a rhetorical jibe. 'I hope you know what you're doing, mister.'

The oak vessel left the safety of the pier, as Benedict cast it out onto the lake with a strong stroke, and skimmed across the water's surface, scattering the chirping yellow-breasted warblers from the lake's surface to the sky.

Elisha watched the birds dance around them until her gaze was stolen by the man opposite her. His shirt caressed his frame. His beauty was undeniable. She took the opportunity to peer deeply into his soul. 'When did you realise you knew everything?'

Benedict mocked her sentiment. 'A serious question for once.'

'I've fooled you so far—I'm a serious kind of girl, you know,' she said, smiling.

'I guess you have…the moment I was beyond the buzzing confusion of the world.'

Elisha giggled. 'I'm *still* confused by it.'

Benedict shared her light-heartedness. 'It is a wondrous, almost overwhelming place this world—but the answer to your serious question is when I was a baby.'

'So, what was it like growing up—knowing everything and not being able to confidently board a boat?'

Benedict smirked. 'I'm a yacht man and physics was never really my thing.'

'Seriously, I bet everyone wanted to be your friend?'

'Not exactly—it was a truth I knew I could never share.'

Elisha understood. 'Children and secrets.'

'Exactly. I just knew I couldn't trust anyone—and in the end I was just another outsider.'

Elisha felt Benedict's subtle sadness and quipped, 'My mother always warned me it was the quiet ones that I needed to watch.'

'Smart woman, your mother.'

'She was—she always promised me that I'd become a princess in a modern-day fairy tale…'

Benedict lay the oars at his side and stood up precariously. The boat bobbed in the calm waters causing Benedict to comically embrace his imbalance. Elisha watched in hysterics. Upon steadying himself, he looked intently at the chuckling girl before him and cleared his throat. 'Once upon a time, in a faraway land, a knight witnessed flames on the horizon. Sensing a damsel in distress, he fought the dragon's breath, saved her from her crumbling castle and they lived—'

'Happily ever after?' Elisha's tone was sarcastic, and she diverted to an angry retort about a recent local tragedy. 'So why didn't you save that woman and her child? Why didn't you save my parents?'

She looked sternly at the man before her, annoyed at the content and sentiment of her own questions. Benedict took his seat and replied softly. 'I can't save everyone.'

Elisha was drawn to the resignation in his eyes. He was clearly buckled by the four deaths she had just thrown at him. She watched his heart ache before her and chose a delicate tone to lift him. 'So why me? Why now?'

He paused for a second, 'I cannot explain why I was there that evening; I have thought about it every day since and questioned why my footsteps led me to you—I guess some things are just meant to be.'

His sincerity was plain to see. The girl before him felt his inadequacy. 'Could I ask you something, Benedict?'

'Yes, they were together,' he answered.

Elisha covered her lips. Her hand trembled as her eyes welled with tears. 'I know it's silly, but I've always wished that they were.'

'They were one.'

He allowed her to fully appreciate his revelation. The ache in her soul had been quelled by his simple words.

'And Paul?' she questioned, amongst staggered breaths.

'Yes, he will be fine.'

'Promise?'

'Yes, I promise.'

Elisha settled as a warmth flooded over her. For the first time she had truly indulged Benedict's gift and the two questions she had agonised over had finally been answered. A burden had been lifted and she felt the need to question him further. 'What about your family?'

'I couldn't save them,' he said dejectedly.

'Save them—what do you mean?'

'We were travelling to the beach, March 1976—I can remember

the sound of the wooden pier creaking beneath my parents' feet, the fairground music and families laughing…'

Benedict tottered hand in hand with his mother and father, listening intently to the rickety old pier that creaked with each step they took, but his impressionable mind was soon overcome by the heavenly jewellery-box-like music that echoed around the bright lights of the fairground. He sniffed at the sizzling, smoky sausages and heard the stage voice that sold their flavour. 'Step right up, get the best hotdogs in America!'

The words and delicious meaty smell wafted towards him but before he had chance to savour the smokiness, the scent of sweet caramelised candyfloss took over.

Benedict's eyes darted from child to child as he stared at their sugary fingertips, the last licky remnants of devoured doughnuts. The fairground fascinated him and soon he was charmed by his dad who trotted across with puppet-pink candyfloss that preyed on young eyes. His mother took the stick from her husband and knelt before her son. The scent of her perfume blanketed his face. It was his favourite. Rose and jasmine. She pulled at the soft sugar that tore like cotton wool, and he tasted the sweetness for the very first time. His taste buds relished the flavour and his mother could not resist pinching some for herself.

Benedict's father held him snugly as they rode a horse, bobbing up and down in time to the music. With every revolution of the carousel, Benedict's mother wore a new grin and snapped a new photograph. The bouncing boy chuckled at her array of brightening smiles and cartoon expressions every time she spun into view. She always knew how to make him laugh.

'Darling Bay Park is just a memory that never happened,' said Benedict.

'What do you mean?'

'My parents were killed on our way to the park.'

Elisha was crushed. 'I'm so sorry, Benedict.'

The boy from the story replied tenderly, 'Don't be sorry, I know they are happy.'

Elisha dared to ask the question, 'So what happens to us when we die?'

Benedict allowed himself a moment to settle before he answered. 'We get to relive the best moments of our lives over and over again.'

It steadied the orphaned girl's heart and struck her again with a moment of divine breathlessness. She recognised their commonality and decided not to dwell on their losses or the afterlife. She steered the conversation back to carefree times. The shore was almost upon them.

'Did you see this in your mind—us?'

'Not really, it's strange with you.'

'Strange? Is that a good thing?'

'Most definitely is. It's natural.'

'So, do you see everything playing out beforehand? When you pass people in the street, do you know what they are thinking or what they are going to do next—people's futures?'

'If I focus on them, yes, but it was too much for a child to bear. It was difficult for me growing up. I was overloaded with people's problems, hearing a million voices in my head.'

Elisha felt his isolation and chose a flirtatious response. 'Indulge me. Focus your gift entirely upon me. What do you see happening next?' She fluttered her eyelashes.

'I couldn't possibly say—what do you see?'

'I see a lonely boy who misses his mom and dad.'

The emotion in their eyes reflected a mutual understanding. He croaked a response. 'I guess I'm not the only one who knows everything.'

Elisha was captivated by his lips. It had all been too much. They leaned closer. Their lips met in a deep kiss. Elisha pulled away.

'I shouldn't have done that. I'm sorry.'

Chapter Twenty-Nine

AVOWAL

He was delirious in his exhilaration but overwhelmed at the end of his quest

Andy sipped at his beer. The television murmured above Elisha's clattering in the kitchen. He was oblivious to the thoughts that rattled around her mind; his attention was completely focused on the box. Andy gulped at the bitterness of his ice-cold beer; Elisha sipped at the sweetness of her lemon-infused tea. They were separate entities.

Elisha thought of Benedict, his parents and how he had opened up to her. She contemplated the kiss, the awkwardness thereafter and her solitary journey home. She was choked with emotion. She steadied herself and concentrated on the mundane task before her and wiped the scent of the rose dishwater from the evening's china. She tried to stifle her wandering mind.

Andy sipped the last remnants from his bottle and shouted from the living room, 'Another cold one, darling.' It jolted her momentarily.

Dr James sipped at his tepid cup of tea and scribbled furiously on his blackboard. Mrs James would always bring her husband a cup of tea when he was absorbed in his extra-curricular research. He struggled to concentrate without it. The chalk pounded against the board as more numbers and letters appeared. Several equations overlapped each other—the blackboard was a black and white puzzle.

Dr James stood back and stared at his latest scribble, musing over this muddle of maths and physics. He laid the chalk to rest in its tray. It rolled back and forth for a few seconds before settling. Worn out.

The physician sat on a sturdy, vintage desk chair. He slid his hand over the desktop. The wood was etched with a million grains. His hand continued along the desk until it met a slightly crumpled scrap of paper precariously balanced on the desk's edge. He unfolded it and flattened it on the desktop with the side of his hand. He looked briefly at it, as if he had seen it before. He had—countless times, but this glance superseded all the others. Dr James reached for a pencil and aggressively pressed the nib onto the creased paper and allowed the lead to flow. His mind was euphoric. He was on the cusp of a remarkable dream.

A firm, sharp knock on the front door startled Andy. He hopped to his feet and set down his empty bottle. Elisha had yet to deliver another one. She hadn't heard the door amongst the clattering of the dishes and blaring television. Andy didn't interrupt her and ambled to the door. He sluggishly pulled it open to reveal two uniformed men. He was confused but naturally polite. 'Officers…'

Elisha felt the draught rid the house of its warmth. She looked at the goose pimples that adorned her skin and peeked towards the doorway. 'Who is it, dear?' she asked.

Andy failed to hear her. The officers had his undivided attention. He sensed their seriousness and felt the cold evening air encapsulate him. Elisha raised her voice and briskly walked towards the doorway beyond the living room. 'Who is it, dear?' she asked again.

Andy heard her this time and turned to face her. 'Elisha…' he said blankly. The colour had been stolen from his face.

Panic coursed through her veins. An indistinct weight sank to the pit of her stomach. It caused her words to bumble in stilted cadence. 'No, not Paul—please. No, no, please.'

Elisha was overwhelmed by a barrage of horrible thoughts. Andy tried to calm her. 'No, darling, it's not Paul.' But Elisha was wallowing like a war widow. Beyond reason. Andy shouted at her angrily, 'It's not Paul!'

A police officer interrupted, glancing at his watch before he spoke. 'As I said, Andrew John Birchill, I am arresting you for the murder of Julia Marsden contrary to the Eighth Amendment. The time is now 6.21 p.m. on Tuesday, September 4, 2001.'

Elisha scowled. Confused, angry and horrified all in one moment. She processed the robotic delivery and repeated the stranger's name in a high-pitched voice. 'Julia Marsden—who's Julia Marsden?'

The police officer interrupted her confusion and issued Mr Birchill with his Miranda Eighth. 'You have the right to remain silent. Anything you say can and will be used in a court of law. The content of your affidavit will serve as a dying declaration. It will not detract from your punishment but will absolve you from sin and bring others to justice.'

The words stabbed Andy in his solar plexus. Elisha reached out to the officer's arm which had moved to her partner's shoulder. The officer shrugged her away.

The other officer spoke for the first time and stepped in front of Elisha, blocking her. 'You need to come with us, Mr Birchill.' He nudged Andy out through the door, causing Andy to sway slightly.

Andy threw a zombified stare at Elisha. His hands had been drawn together at the small of his back and the robotic officer snapped handcuffs around his wrists. The cold steel gnawed at his wrist bones. Andy thought of Benedict.

Elisha was incensed but could see that the situation before her could not be undone. She tried to remain pragmatic and sucked in the emotions that threatened to erupt. 'I'll call Benedict—this has to be some sort of mistake.'

The pencil fell out of Dr James's gifted hands and spun off the desk. He looked over his thin-rimmed glasses towards the blackboard. He closed his eyes and slowed his breathing. He was delirious in his exhilaration but overwhelmed at the end of his quest. It caused his body to fizz. Decades in dreary rooms had culminated in a single solitary moment. He rested his hands upon the desk, unaware that he was now standing. His gifted mind was blank. The teacup on the desk brought him back into the world.

'Roselyn!' he shouted and ran as quickly as his ageing bones could carry him. His excitement caused his hands to fumble at the door. 'Roselyn! Roselyn!' he shouted repeatedly as he groped the handle in the most awkward of ways, like a toddler. The door swung inwards, crashing loudly against the wall. 'Roselyn, you will not believe it!'

Mrs James headed out of the kitchen to investigate the rattling and crashing of the door and the faint echoes of her name.

'Believe what, dear?'

Her husband was panting. He caught his breath.

'That I know everything.'

Chapter Thirty

TESTAMENT

Nothing but the truth, so help me God

Andy's reflection in the wall of mirrored glass revealed a broken man. The remaining three walls in the stark room were white. The floor was grey and gummy. There was no skirting board; the thick vinyl floor rose four inches up the wall, finished off with a thin trim—for hygiene. He sat at a square table with two empty chairs opposite. A digital clock hung on the wall behind him. He could see its reflection. The block capitals and numbers displayed: 'WEDNESDAY – SEPTEMBER 5 – 12:00'. He could sense that people beyond the glass were watching him.

His every move was in fact being noted; his non-verbal communications were being nibbled at by the psychologist. Dr Yang devoured Andy's mannerisms and scribbled illegible words onto a pad with a beaten-up biro. The pen belied his professional status.

Andy was worn out. He thought of his mother.

Warren was a dashing fellow. He often wore patterned shirts and had a penchant for a gilet. He had two children whom he loved dearly and an ex-wife that he didn't. He had joint custody of his children and that suited him perfectly. The children were better off for it— their parents' relationship had become increasingly destructive before the inevitable separation.

Warren met Andy's mother on a business trip. She had wandered into a coffee shop and took a second glance at the man in the gilet cradling a coffee cup. They talked long enough for his latte to cool. Warren was from Nassau-Suffolk county—The Island, commonly known as Long Island.

He met Andrew on a Sunday and tried desperately to be his friend instead of his father. Perhaps he tried too hard, but whatever the day, Andy was not amenable to his charm or hot chocolate. He was a pretty difficult teenager.

A few years later, Andy had, under the instruction of his mother, shook Warren's hand before he left home to pursue his career—his independence. Andy returned a handful of times, but it was quite often under obligation as opposed to desire.

Warren's children loved the beach, and the draw of the shore convinced Marilyn to follow Warren to a detached beach house. She wanted a calmer life, one where she could watch Warren's children run freely from afar instead of darting after them in a city of corners and alleys.

Andy spent a couple of Christmases there, but the place was far too quiet for him. He began to dwell on things he would have preferred not to, and Warren grated on him. He was too nice. But Andy was clever enough to know that his mother had found happiness. He was caught between being disappointed and thankful. The feeling suffocated him, and Andy knew that he could not keep visiting the sandy house.

The following year he opted to work. He left long before his mother's new family sat down to Christmas dinner. Warren had prepared it. Marilyn complimented him on his culinary skills. Even the children cleared their plates.

Benedict looked at Andy through the glass. Dr Yang had left. In his place were a plethora of government officials and the Chief Justice of the Supreme Court. The Chief Justice jotted purposefully upon lined Liberty Justice Hall headed paper. His pen was more becoming of his position—a black and gold Montegrappa. He questioned Benedict. 'Considering your recent disclosure yesterday afternoon, could you please testify against the accused?'

'Yes. It was 18:44 on Friday, August 24, 2001, when Andrew John Birchill violently pushed Julia Marsden into the path of the Metro-North oncoming train. It resulted in Julia's instant decapitation. I can confirm that the person sitting alone in the room opposite me is Andrew John Birchill. Andrew John Birchill is responsible for the murder of Julia Marsden. I swear the evidence I have given is the truth, the whole truth and nothing but the truth, so help me God.'

The Chief Justice addressed those around him. 'I hereby sentence Andrew John Birchill to death by hanging, in accordance with the Eighth Amendment. It is now 12:05 on Wednesday, September 5, 2001. I award three days' grace for both the victim's family and the prisoner. Andrew John Birchill—you will be hanged for your crime on Saturday, September 8, 2001.'

The Chief Justice finalised the proceedings with an occasional sweep of his pen before offering it to the government officials either side of Benedict. They endorsed the declaration of death.

Benedict was the last to approach. He held the letter briefly before carefully placing it back onto the table. He grasped the thick black and gold pen. The nib scraped over the textured paper and it was complete. The simple strokes of the ornate pen had condemned a man to death.

The paved forecourt of the State Capitol building in Albany, New York, was lined with protestors and police. Benedict arrived in style. He leapt from his Presidential Phantom to a cacophony of jeers and people holding banners. Benedict's gift had drawn the protestors in droves for all the wrong reasons. None of them took photographs, none of them admired him. Instead, they blamed him for their heartache and called *him* the murderer.

The desperado walked towards the Neo-Renaissance building escorted by two sheriffs, who had been drafted in when the activists increased in both number and confidence. The other county sheriffs were jostling with the pushing protestors. The three men walked in the shadow of the six-storey building, the outer two spires of which were lined with burnt-orange tiles. The building could best be described as a fairy-tale citadel. The small-minded protestors, in the shadow of their ignorance of history, failed to recognise the grandeur of the Romanesque Revival architecture. Instead they focused on the man that ridiculed them, who sought to devastate their race.

Benedict gestured simply to the two sheriffs who had relished their moments in the man's company. The duo understood his request and allowed Benedict to walk alone, despite their earlier briefing stating otherwise.

The protestors jostled behind the thin blue line as Benedict strolled towards the building's entrance. He acknowledged the fairy-tale view and thought of Elisha, who had been desperately trying to contact him since Andy's arrest the night before. When he reached the portico at the building's centre, he turned and faced the plebeian in dictatorship style, in a final act of insolence. The noise from outside was quelled upon his entry into the grand hall.

Benedict sat calmly at a pew surrounded by a walnut stall; the surface was a mottled tiger skin of deep chocolate colour. He was overlooked by a congress of political leaders, who sat behind an ornately carved seventeenth-century bench, each with their own specific role, each with their own agenda. The TV cameras zoomed in. All eyes were fixed upon him—wide-eyed, like a parliament of owls. The wisest of owls leaned forward and spoke. 'In this current economic climate, I believe that our education and the health system are pivotal to the restoration and progression of America.'

Benedict nodded in acknowledgement. He remained silent; he chose not to respond to the meaningless statement. The owl paused and, before the silence became uncomfortable, another owl flew into the melee. 'So, much like the Chad Aprilsun prodigy you have promised us, who we are led to believe has recently broken the hundred-metre regional record, can you identify the future leaders of our nation?'

Benedict spoke, addressing the nation. 'Chad Aprilsun was a message of hope for millions of Americans—that ordinary people can be powerful beyond measure.' He paused. 'My uncovering of future leaders will only place a pressure upon them and leave them vulnerable to outside influences. The less we know about the consequences of our decisions, the more likely we are to make the correct ones.'

Mr Wright, yet another owl, stood and responded angrily. 'So, the eradication of the black race is the correct decision, is it, Mr Maven?'

Benedict replied immediately. 'No.'

'Then, can you tell me why, Mr Maven, since the introduction of the new Eighth Amendment, eighty-three per cent of the condemned sentenced to death by hanging have been black?'

Benedict offered Mr Wright a question. 'But is there rationale for murder?'

Mr Wright threw a slurry of snappy words at Benedict. 'Social preclusion. Poverty. Discrimination. Education. Racism. Need I continue?'

'But isn't murder a primitive act? The human mind has evolved beyond limit and can act beyond its own consciousness. We are a race perfectly equipped not to kill. Put simply, there are differences in people but people are not different.'

Mr Wright poked at Benedict's insolence with a loaded question. 'But aren't we all ethnocentric by definition?'

Benedict jostled in his seat before he spoke with precision. 'Not all of us. One day, humanity will be defined by the purity of innocent children.'

Soft mumblings reverberated around the room and echoed from televisions throughout America. Protestors outside the Supreme Court jostled the barrier of police officers, courtesy of Benedict's scathing truth.

A decorated owl stood to attention inside the courtroom. War medals hung like feathers from his flawless uniform. He was a war hero; he was not forged from favours and gifts like the others. They had never experienced the consequence of combat; they had never smelt the stench of death—they had only savoured the sweetness of champagne and canapés. They were a disgrace to the office, a disgrace to this veteran—a disgrace to America.

His grating voice cut through the murmurs offered up by the hypocrites. 'Evidence shows, Mr Maven, that China, Russia and Korea are currently in the possession of nuclear warheads. Can you confirm this? Is our nation safe from these superpowers?'

Benedict responded swiftly. 'Colonel Reeves—my words would instil fear and judgement within the countries in question. People would act unnaturally to what I would say.'

It wasn't the answer the veteran had hoped for, but he understood Benedict's words entirely. He knew first-hand the casualties of war. He had lost many friends. Mr Donovan stood sharply. He had been appointed by the current president on neither merit nor sacrifice. He barked, 'We need to know all intelligence linked to terrorism against our great country. We need to know who or what threatens our national security and how they plan to infiltrate us. If you know the answers, you are required—no, no, excuse me—you are ordered to tell your president.'

Benedict stood and dismissed him abruptly. 'I am a patriot, Mr Donovan.' He centred his attention on the colonel. 'At present, the world we know is balanced; for every action there are reactions, and any pre-emptive attacks would upset this balance and threaten the lives of millions of people you or I have never met. The not-knowing of one's destiny is liberating—if everyone knew the events of tomorrow, their lives and actions would be overcome with worry, influencing everything they do.'

The huge oak doors to the hall swung open and a senior police official hastily entered the hall, whispering to yet another official, who nodded nervously in acknowledgement. Mr Donavan responded in haste, in an attempt to belittle Benedict's claims, totally oblivious to the uprising outside. 'You could be the leader of this nation, the leader of all nations, the power to rule the world—and you say no?'

Benedict stood sharply. 'It is something everyone desires but no one really wants. Enlightenment is something that all of us possess, but the moral responsibility to condone pain and suffering for righteousness to prevail is a paradox that few understand—it is true that I know everything, but it is precisely this that haunts me.'

The chairperson stood anxiously and halted the questioning. 'Unfortunately, we have a situation outside that requires us to cut short these proceedings—so, Mr Maven, will you be gracing us with your presence for the next conference?'

'No, sir, this will be my last public engagement.'

Benedict's words were interrupted by an intruder who yelled, 'WHO KILLED JFK?' before he was taken to the ground by a police officer.

Eyes darted from the restrained questioner to Benedict. The room was awash with silence. Benedict looked directly at the camera, broadcasting to America. 'It was a man in a blue suit.'

There was a sharp whoosh and the hall was bathed in darkness. The power had been cut.

Chapter Thirty-One

SANCTION

I hereby authorise the capture or death of Benedict Maven

Randolph James Senior always enjoyed his son's visits. The fact that his son was the current President of the United States allowed him to revel in the company of untouchable power. The retired president's life was much simpler now. He enjoyed carving chess pieces in alabaster and he was a coffee connoisseur. On the desk in his study sat a model car and a photograph of his wedding day displayed in an ornate gold frame.

The Delahaye 135 threatened to steal the day. A day that belonged to the bride and groom—Mr Randolph James and Miss Darcy Teulon. The sports car stretched and shimmered in the midday Sunday sun. Its body was curvaceous and coruscating. It was a deep ruby red, like a rich French wine. The congregation were torn between the bride and the automobile.

Randolph's uncle William was already drunk. He had no children, no wife and no desire for either. He did, however, have a collection of wealthy friends with whom he often shared a tipple of whiskey. It was his merriment and his intellect that endeared him to them. His friends had made their money in oil, and with this fortune came a power which they craved more than crude. The mayor of Indianapolis, a life-long friend of William, was often seen sipping bourbon and colluding with 'the oilers', as they were known in Bloomington, Indiana, whenever they swooped in. The oilers had needed a small pond where they could flourish as big fish and had decided to relocate to a place where they could be almighty.

On this particular day, they had all converged on the wedding. The leader of the pack, Mr Daley Claiborne, hailed from North Louisiana. He had been privy to the discovery of the Haynesville field at Claiborne Parish; his new-found fame and fortune preceded him whenever he arrived in Bloomington. He was a man who dined on fine wine and fancy conversation. He was motivated by power and politics; he had contacts in the White House but had the reputation of a crook. His money often afforded him a second chance.

The convertible that carried Darcy to her wedding belonged to Mr Claiborne. He had been impressed from the moment that he met the groom with a warm handshake. Randolph was a handsome man, blessed with business acumen and eloquent conversation. Daley revelled in his scrutiny of current affairs. He stole Randolph away from his bride on more than one occasion that day; it was a theme that would blight their marriage.

Daley's suit was tailored and lavishly lined with silk. His pocket watch was silver. Randolph was captivated by the tall man's appearance and persona. Daley told him of his recent investment in the Indianapolis racetrack; he also told him of the importance of a Republican America. The sun had just begun its descent beyond the manor house and the Bloomington skyline when Daley's conniving truly began.

'Thank you kindly, sir, for allowing us your sports car for the day.'

'Ah, the Delahaye—only two thousand ever built, you know—four-speed, with a top speed just a shade under one hundred and twenty kilometres per hour. It's a work of art.'

'Yes, sir, she sure is.' Daley nodded in the direction of the bride, who was busy dealing with countless compliments. 'It looks like you've got yourself a little beauty of your own there, son.'

The crowd had, by now, trampled the lawn flat. They were like cogs, turning methodically in circles of conversation. Daley continued to politely probe Randolph—grooming the groom. 'So, what are your aspirations, son?'

'Well, I've just taken a job at the Indianapolis Legislative Council.'

'Indeed you have son, your uncle Bill informed me.'

'Yes, I've got big plans for this place.'

'I guess you have, son. Did you know that this place is a lot like Washington? Even the roads are laid out the same.'

A man on a ladder interrupted their conversation and shouted to the crowd, 'Ladies and gentlemen, can I have your smiles?'

Darcy quickly looked for her husband in the shifting crowd that was shuffling into a semi-circle; she spotted his blue suit and saw that he was engrossed in conversation with a tall man. She looked back to the man on the ladder who held a camera high above the arc of people; she smiled just before it flashed.

Randolph James Junior walked through a room embellished with paintings of remembered men by forgotten artists. The portraits were set in gilded frames that complemented the waxy oil colours and the amour-propre of such presidents. Side tables were dotted symmetrically throughout the wide halls and wider rooms. The table lamps were plentiful and together they spread a dim, soothing light.

Eight officials, some more important than others, sat in silence upon high-backed leather chairs around a vast mahogany table, surrounded by pale-lemon ornate moulded walls, awaiting their president. Two bold-yellow chandeliers hung above the oval table; at its centre sat an untouched jug of water and some glasses. The empty chair, in the middle, was taller than the rest, not significantly so, but enough to suggest it belonged to Junior. The President had yet to enter the room in which the atmosphere was bubbling with egotistical importance. The Chief of Staff sipped a glass of water impatiently. A Federal Bureau officer and the Secretary of Defence held a conversation about their weekend jaunts. Both perched forward on their seats in order to hear each other's whispers about extra-marital activity.

All stood immediately as the President entered the room. He demanded the room's attention, much like his father decades ago. He peered sharply at the Rolex clock on the wall; the date read 'Thu – Sept 6 – 2001'.

There was a shuffling of suits as all took their seats once more; the President, however, stood with his hands perched upon the back rest of his chair. He spoke harshly. 'This man knows too much—too many of our secrets, and the consequences of shared secrets threaten this office, this country and my presidency. When was he last seen and what were his last known movements?'

The Chief of Staff stood and addressed the President. 'September fifth, twelve hundred hours, Liberty Justice Hall. Mr Maven testified against the following persons—David Sparks, Marcin Byowski, Andrew Birchill and Denzel White. Thirteen hundred hours, he left Liberty Justice Hall in a Presidential Phantom. Fourteen hundred hours, he arrived at the State Capitol building. Fifteen hundred hours the inquiry commenced. For the next hour, Mr President, you witnessed Benedict Maven answering questions in relation to the evolution of America. Mr President, you saw what happened when he began the story of the man in the blue suit.'

The most powerful man in the world put his head in his hands. 'DAMNED BLUE SUIT!' he blasted, still standing by his seat. He looked up slowly, hopelessly. 'What about the cameras on Washington Avenue.'

'Nothing, sir—it's as if he has just vanished,' said the Chief of Staff. He wished he hadn't.

The President grabbed his glass of water, spilling some over his hand, and fired his response. 'One man doesn't just disappear from a conference viewed by sixty million people!' He hurled the glass at a projector screen bearing Benedict's image.

The officials gasped. The quandary washed over them as the water dripped from Benedict's face. The President leant over the top of his seat and looked down at the table that reflected Benedict's image. 'Someone, please tell me something.'

A surveillance officer spoke succinctly. 'Mr President, it appears that we're not the only ones chasing him.'

The President was intrigued. 'Continue, son.'

The President's softened tone fuelled his confidence.

'Yes sir, thank you, sir. Agent Smith has been undercover within the New York gang, the Baysides, for three years. During this time, he has witnessed first-hand the arrests of Rio Lopez, Santana Lopez and Ahmir Vasquez for first-degree murder as a result of Mr Maven's testimonies. All were subsequently hanged for these crimes and Smith has confirmed that these same three men were the subject of murder investigations by this office. I have also been informed that an underground meeting has taken place recently involving rival gangs across America, discussing the elimination of Mr Maven. I guess that it's not just our secrets that are too important to be told.'

Colour flooded back to the President's face. His response was glittered in hope and promise. 'Thank you, son.'

He paced about the room, allowing the silence to stir before speaking again. 'I have not come to this decision lightly, but I must act now to prevent severe problems arising that will have a detrimental effect upon our nation. I hereby authorise the capture or death of Benedict Maven by us or, preferably, them.'

Chapter Thirty-Two

PURPOSE

It served a purpose—to kill those who have killed

The early morning was as eerie as it was silent. Benedict's footsteps landed crisply on the glass floor. He gently caressed the sharp square beams, stopping at the final braided rope. It hung peacefully, poetically, like the engineer's blueprint. He stood beneath the dangling rope and was drawn to its texture. It was rough but not nearly rough enough. He twisted it between his fingers. He looked to the immortal words above his head. *Rise unto the Lord.* He contemplated the words before releasing the rope. It swayed at the mercy of its motion like a settling pendulum.

Four people dressed in white gowns stood beneath the four words. Andy was one of the quartet. He was still, frozen by the spectacle. The coarse rope gripped his neck, pinching at his skin. His sockless feet rested flat upon the crystal-clear glass platform. He couldn't help but look at his toes. He couldn't bring himself to look at the crowd that roared, blurring the thoughts of death.

The stage was no longer a public attraction. No longer controversial. It served a purpose—to kill those who have killed. Amidst the onlookers stood Benedict. His presence went unnoticed. Elisha scrambled through the crowd, jostling towards the platform, towards Andy.

A voice echoed loudly over the tannoy, prompting Elisha to charge forward. The strong voice declared, 'I hereby commit you all to death by hanging; may the Lord have mercy on your souls.'

Denzel's soulful voice sang *Silent Night* with a tenderness unbecoming of the situation—his mother's favourite melody. It was a rendition fit for church. Its innocence troubled the congregation. Andy felt the croaky voice sting his heart and scanned the horizon looking for his saviour, but Benedict did not appear.

An abandoned New Jersey hangar sheltered a cauldron of gang members, all with one purpose. One target. The united front was divided into factions, each distinguishable by their gang colours and clothing. Big Daddy T was the kingpin. He was a callous individual who lacked remorse.

Music reverberated from the corrugated stainless-steel roofing of the industrial dome. Pool balls cracked together over plush neon-purple felt. Empty beer bottles were strewn over every surface.

The faint jangle of a mobile phone was largely drowned out by the surrounding chatter. Big Daddy T grasped his phone; his sovereign-ring-covered fingers engulfed it as he pressed it against his ear. His free hand gripped his maple pool cue. The conversation was short. He addressed the room. His deep voice echoed around the metal walls. 'HEY!'

They spun like tops to the big man's roar.

'We've found him—New York Square—Benedict is mine,' T proclaimed aloft. Rapturous cheers filled the hangar and soon the rumble of departing muscle cars echoed down the runway.

Seamore Smith hopped into the back seat of Lacey and Lamar's Cadillac. He had spent his last two Christmases with the pair from the Bronx. The three had become inseparable. Agent Smith had infiltrated the gang during a sting operation, three years before. It was his first assignment. He had been recruited for his skill in deception and his lack of family. Since his introduction to the underworld, Seamore had witnessed five gang-related murders. His life was entangled in a friendship with the Bronx Brothers and his fictional legend. The Brothers vouched for him. The Bureau's psychologist documented Agent Smith's detachment. You couldn't make an omelette without breaking eggs. The Bureau knew that.

Since the President's order, Seamore's goal had changed significantly. To his relief, Agent Smith was no longer required to report on the gang. He was now solely being used as America's best chance to locate its most wanted man. He tapped at his mobile phone. *Benedict Maven. New York Square.*

Deen was tired. He had slept on the sofa the night before, owing to a trivial argument with his wife and a stubbornness he could not shake. The shifts were tiresome; the three-days-on, three-days-off pattern was conducive to family life, but the constant drone of emotional goodbyes was tiring. He was privy to all last-gasp conversations centring on the majesty of love, time and the travesty of impending doom.

The holding centre was minimalist, allowing no glimmer of luxury for the soon-to-be departed. There were no windows, but doors were plentiful. The father of two wandered to the first of seven checkpoints and set his chin upon the retinal scanner. The laser passed over his glassy eyes and the door beeped into submission. Deen leaned through and approached the second point. It was a drawn-out process; no person could breach such security or enter unannounced. He was glad it was the last day of his shifts and the promise of three days off spurred him on to the next heavy-set door.

The three-day shift patterns aligned nicely to fit the last three days of those doomed to hang. It was the continuity that defied time. No clocks lined the walls and those who lay stagnant within knew not whether it was dark or light outside.

Andy was dejected. Famished by false promise. Elisha looked up to the glassy-eyed security guard and shuffled into her seat opposite her wilting man. Thick transparent glass separated them, and the tired guard prepared himself for more doomed conversation and tearful proclamations. The holding centre monitored all conversations between the sinful and the saintly—an appendix added to the policy under the orders of the FBI and the President. The last conversations of the condemned could unearth all manner of secrets.

Andy barely looked up at Elisha, but he could see the resignation on her face. He muttered a solitary word, 'Time?'

Elisha shook her head in distress but didn't address his daily request, saying instead, 'I still can't find him anywhere.'

Andy slumped further within himself and closed his eyes. His left hand rested upon his forehead.

Elisha tried to stir him back into her world. 'He'll be there—he would never let anyone hurt you. I'll try again this afternoon.' She had battled Andy's despair for days.

Andy struck back at her naivety. 'Don't you get it? Benedict testified against me. Elisha—he was with me that day. It was the Giants game. Why hasn't he told them that it's all a mistake—where the fuck is he?' A realisation overwhelmed him and he snapped. 'It's so he can have you to himself, isn't it? I knew there was something going on!' He jumped from his seat and slammed the thick glass with his fist. His anger enveloped him. He struck the glass again and heard a dull echo completely absorb his power.

'Sit down or you are in solitary,' warned Deen, who was keeping an eye on the unfolding drama. He had seen it before. His tiredness made him less reasonable than normal; often he would allow such outbursts to run their own course, knowing that the detained could cause no harm to themselves, any officer, or the glass itself. Today his mood did not care for it and he toyed with a series of red buttons set upon his desk.

Andy's anger was unabating and he began to hammer on the glass like a frenzied caged gorilla. Elisha stumbled backwards in her rush to stand up. She was overwhelmed but not frightened.

'Andrew, please,' she tried to reason with the animal behind the glass.

Deen's weary eyes zoomed upon their target and he reached to button three, the corresponding number above Andy's seat. He pressed it and, within seconds, two burly guards tackled the beast who was now shouting unintelligibly. Before Andy could acknowledge the presence of the duo, he felt a sharp sting at the back of his neck and succumbed instantly to a numbing sensation. The sedative temporarily toppled him into paralysis. The two guards caught the tranquilised animal as he fell and dragged him away from the glass and the helpless spectator.

'Andrew—Andrew!' Elisha shouted, but no one acknowledged her.

The trio disappeared from view. She shouted again. 'ANDREW!' but her voice was absorbed by the glass and the emptiness behind it.

Deen was thankful that his three days of surveillance at pod number three had concluded. He watched Elisha retreat, her hands clasped over her mouth to soothe her breathlessness. She looked up to the guard and, with sudden energy, viciously spat, 'I hope you are happy!'

Deen had been taught not to engage with those he snooped upon. He edged from his seat, still undone by his slumber and lethargy. He looked to the beautiful woman who had decorated his working week. He calmly addressed her unbecoming outburst. 'Sow the wind—reap the whirlwind.'

It was a typically cold November. Andy scrunched his small hands into his trouser pockets and said goodbye to his friend Matthew. He envied the fact that his friend's house was closer to the school than his. Although it did make the journey to and from the educational establishment a more enjoyable one. Andy felt his body ache in the cold, but he continued to walk briskly.

He opened the door to his house and savoured the moment when the warmth embraced him. He dropped his satchel and was ready to settle in front of the television. His mother would be home in an hour or so. He leapt into his favourite seat and snuggled between some tatty scatter cushions. While arranging them he saw a welcome sight by the stairs. His dad's boots. They were as worn as the cushions. Dried mud and concrete clung to them. Andy shouted, 'Dad?' in an elated puzzlement. He scurried up the stairs.

He shouted again cheerfully, 'Dad!' He pushed open the bathroom door, expecting his father to be relaxing in a hot bath; he could always be found there after weeks away in builders' digs. The door swung open. The bathtub was empty.

'Dad?' he shouted again, confused. He turned to his parents' bedroom and pushed open the door. His father's eyes were locked upon him. Unblinking. Andy walked slowly towards him. The wooden beam was strong and held his dad's weight effortlessly. A contorted rope squeezed at his neck and creaked as it swayed ever so slightly.

'*Dad…*' he said, his voice trembling.

He reached out and touched his dad's bare feet. They were as cold as the day outside. Andy was scared. He looked up and only then realised that his dad's eyes were still looking at the bedroom door.

The front door swung open, hitting the living room wall hard. The blow left a handle-shaped scar in the wall. It would never be fixed. Marilyn was frantic, shouting even louder than her son. 'JOHN!'

John didn't reply. Andy remained silent. Marilyn took the stairs two at a time. She too flew into the bathroom. John's favourite room. She threw back the shower curtain and spun round to see her bedroom door was wide open. She rushed towards it.

Her hands covered her mouth before the scream had reached its crescendo, causing it to wilt into more of a yelp than a shriek. Andy cowered. The sound of it was awful, like a dying wolf. She rushed to Andy and hugged him like she had never hugged him before. Andy turned his head away from her shoulder to look once again at his dad, whose eyes seemed wider now, as if he too had heard his wife's painful scream. She pulled him back into her shoulder and looked up at her husband. She was numb, overwhelmed and trembling.

Andy was back in his favourite chair. His mother was perched beside him. She wasn't making much sense. Andy had been squeezed several times by her and been told four times that she loved him. Andy noticed the scarred wall beside the door. His mother told him not to worry when he pointed it out to her. She dismissed it. She was busy dealing with death.

Two police officers stooped as they came through the front door respectfully removing their peaked hats. Marilyn squeezed her son again and kissed the crown of his head. Andy couldn't remember the walk home from school.

Benedict watched, camouflaged by the crowd. Andy's feet dangled, motionless, beside three other pairs of feet. The crowd's baying chants had slipped to a daydream of silence. Death wasn't always a spectacle.

Benedict immersed himself in the gloom that surrounded him, his eyes as blue as the heavens. He contemplated society. Knowing the spiral was downward—knowing nothing would revolutionise its weakness. He watched Elisha stumble through the hordes of sorrow that were beginning to leave. Her grief was palpable.

She felt Benedict's presence. She spotted him watching her. Her skin trembled. Her heart thumped in anger as she sobbed into her hands. She summoned the strength to shout, 'Who are you to decide who lives and who dies? I know you were with him!'

Benedict retreated into the crowd. Elisha watched him disappear and tried to shove past the people that separated them. Her efforts were cut short by an overwhelming roar of vehicles. A spectrum of muscle cars zoned in and zoomed upon New York Square, causing instant chaos.

Big Daddy T's crusade had begun. The cacophony of powerful engines echoed through the city streets. They screeched and screamed in different directions like wild fireworks. Enthusiasm was their downfall. The colourful army was uncoordinated and disjointed.

Benedict had retreated patiently to the entrance of a narrow alley. He watched his enemies split wildly in a kaleidoscope of colour, some of them in his direction, before he darted into the alley's shadows.

The lead vehicle overshot the alley's entrance. Big Daddy T commanded his driver, 'BACK UP—BACK UP—THERE HE IS.'

The driver crunched the car into reverse, flooring the accelerator. The wheels spun violently as thick rubber tarnished the tarmac and smoke bellowed forwards. The rear passenger, T's nephew, saw his opportunity to impress his uncle and soared from the moving vehicle to give chase.

The alley was a mess of rubbish bags, bins and putrid puddles, but Benedict negotiated it like a free runner. His pursuer was less graceful but his spirit was commendable. The sound of footsteps ricocheted loudly down the alley. Durrell withdrew the Glock that was tucked into the waistband of his jeans. In a fluid motion he cocked the action, loading a round into the chamber.

Benedict had increased the gap significantly. Durrell jerked the trigger in panic, sending rounds bumping, bouncing and buckling through the alleyway. The sound rebounded against the damp walls, exiting at each end of the alley. Benedict darted between the wave of sound and rounds, spinning into a nook. Durrell was rejuvenated by his gunshots and a burst of adrenaline coursed through his body. He ran towards the nook that hid Benedict.

Benedict jumped out in front of his unsuspecting pursuer. Durrell was wide-eyed; he was no longer the hunter but the hunted. In his quest for savagery he had failed to contemplate that he had always been the prey. They all were. No words were exchanged, Durrell didn't have the opportunity to scream. Benedict landed a ferocious blow that sent Durrell into a tailspin, causing his neck vertebrae to snap like a twig and rip through his trachea with ease. The fissure caused Durrell to squeal uncontrollably, a sound heightened by the alley's acoustic qualities. Daddy T heard it and recognised the tragedy from inside his car at the head of the alley. He saw Benedict standing over his nephew and roared loud enough to drown out the Mustang's engine, 'DURRELL!'

Benedict began to run towards the roaring man in the Mustang blocking his exit as a red Dodge Charger snarled into the alley behind him. The car, true to its name, charged between the narrow walls, tossing litter into the air. The puddled water was ripped from the stagnant pools and splashed high against the walls. Daddy T watched the situation unfold in front of his evil eyes and shrieked at his driver, 'Out. We've got him caged!'

The passenger door swung open and the alley was graced with the formidable frame of Daddy T. Benedict was trapped between the red Dodge, the Mustang and the massive man. He ran at the man and his driver. The Dodge Charger followed, gobbling up the alley's contents with its heavy grille. The animals inside the chasing car readied their weapons.

Daddy T ripped dual sub-machine guns from his bulging waistband. The Dodge's occupants watched Benedict frantically sprinting away from them and towards T's arsenal of firepower and vengeance. They focused on Benedict, hovering their weapons out of their respective windows and shot like madmen.

Daddy T yanked at the triggers; both instantaneously kicked softly in his oversized hands. His entourage followed suit, convinced that they would be the ones to end Benedict's reign. The rounds spun down the alley, but the man coolly bobbed between the bullets.

The windscreen of the Dodge was first to bear the brunt of Daddy T's misplaced shots. The friendly fire tore through the vehicle's interior, instantly staining it red. The driver's body shuddered brutally with every bullet that pierced his skin. His eyes widened before his body slumped over the steering wheel.

Daddy T and his driver had been intermittently struck by a flurry of staggered bullets. Each hollow pointed round crushed through their bodies, buckling them almost instantly. The entry wounds rippled on their skin, splintering through their mass and exiting brutally. T was the last to fall.

The freewheeling Dodge swerved violently to its left and was thrown uncontrollably into the air. The passengers were at the mercy of the vehicle's uninterrupted motion. One dead, one living. Gravity ripped it from its flight causing it to land horribly without any compromise. The deceased driver was thrown through the peppered windscreen, saving him from the car's cruel cartwheel. The Charger tumbled end over end—its passenger was contorted pitilessly with each rotation.

The vehicle and passenger soon became unrecognisable. Mangled, creased and separated. The vehicle finally rocked to a stop. Benedict strolled purposely towards the departed T. He mercilessly stepped over him and exited the alley.

The street beyond was bustling and had absorbed the sound of the car crash and misplaced gunfire. A neon green light purred and buzzed from across the street. A line of lime green edged a modern low-rise building. Benedict was drawn to its hum. As he approached it, he could see the word *Porsche* emblazoned on a window beneath the soothing light. Beyond the showroom glass was the epitome of German automotive engineering. Three beauties seduced Benedict's eyes. Three Stuttgart stallions.

He strolled across the street and entered the showroom through its open door. The place was bereft of customers. The salesmen were oblivious to his entrance and missed the chance to welcome him. He chose the middle vehicle of the three and opened the aerodynamic black door. His fingerprints smudged onto its glossy, glass-like finish. Benedict's image in the door's mirrored finish slid out of his view as he entered the 911 GT. He stepped confidently into the driver's footwell and settled into the luxurious, soft-cherry bucket seat. He buckled up and snapped the racing harness tight. The Porsche's keys dangled invitingly in the ignition.

Agent Six, a rookie Secret Service Agent, drove patiently in his black SUV. Low in experience but high in enthusiasm, he patrolled his designated sector. He drove unsuspectingly towards the Porsche's showroom, searching for the man upon whom his children had bestowed superhero status.

The showroom window smashed into a million pieces before him, decorating the street like brittle caramel. Benedict's newly acquired 911 landed onto the street in fantastic fashion. His right foot pushed hard on the accelerator and began to gobble up the street. The showroom staff were stunned. Helpless.

Agent Six frantically reported this spectacular development to his fellow agents. 'Subject has stolen a black Porsche. Northbound Sixth Avenue—West Twenty-Third.'

The Porsche's stability equalled that of a race car. The city street pushed up at the thick tread of the tyres as the gravitational pull and horsepower pushed down, sandwiching the car to the tarmac. More black Secret Service vehicles emerged like ninjas onto the city streets, uniting on the Porsche's tail behind Agent Six. He welcomed their arrival. Benedict slipped in and out of traffic, cheetah-like. He raced through a red light, narrowly missing vehicles looming from both sides. His reactions matched those of a fighter pilot. Agent Six followed closely behind. He winced as crossing vehicles zoomed past his SUV. His vehicle was powerful but cumbersome and was no match for Benedict's German masterpiece. Benedict dipped the accelerator pedal and whooshed past pedestrians and street artists, who spun like tops. His peripheral vision was a horizontal blur of colour.

Agent Six flitted through the traffic like a dog after a ball, barking over his headset, 'Eastbound, Thirty-Third, he's getting away.' He grew in confidence, thriving on this real-life mission.

Agent Four joined the chase, screeching from a side street, and arced in front of Agent Six, taking the lead. Agent Six was annoyed but also slightly relieved. He fell back into the formation of identical SUVs. Agent Four was just three car lengths away from Benedict. He could hear the Porsche's growl.

Agent Four shifted his vehicle sharply to the left. Benedict witnessed the tactical move. He was the embodiment of composure. Calm. Tranquil. He twitched the Porsche to the right then swung harshly to the left. White smoke billowed from the screeching tyres and wafted over the rear diffuser. The rear quarter of Benedict's Porsche slammed heavily into a red five-door station wagon travelling in the opposite direction. The red car spun anticlockwise. Benedict's vehicle followed suit and they spun in unison.

Agent Four's gloved hands pushed against the steering wheel as he used every ounce of his strength to stamp on the brake pedal to avoid the two revolving cars before him. The unforgiving wheels locked, squealing like a dying animal. The two vehicles twisted and turned and allowed Agent Four's SUV to pass through the gap between them as if it were choreographed.

Benedict wrestled with the Porsche's disobedience and quickly regained its trust and traction, accelerating hard once again to combat the spin. Benedict zoomed away from the rumpus. The rear quarter of his sports car was crumpled; red paint scarred the Porsche's black finish. The station wagon finally screeched to a stop. It rested on the sidewalk, whining and whistling, just before the bridge, its occupants shell-shocked but apparently otherwise unharmed.

Agent Four's dramatic stamp on the brake pedal had only served to stiffen his body. His vehicle had slammed hard against a hooped red-and-white water bucket, which protected industrial machinery at the side of the road. Its contents exploded into the air; water showered Agent Four's crushed vehicle as well as fleeing pedestrians.

Agent Six yelled, 'He's just rammed an oncoming vehicle and Agent Four is down, I repeat, Agent Four is down!'

Benedict's supple sports car was damaged but undeterred. The mechanics of his vehicle were still flawless beneath a dented shell. It left the falling water in its wake.

The chase was relentless. Agent Two spun his SUV quickly with a heavy handbrake turn, avoiding any imminent collisions. He was fuelled by Agent Six's words and darted through slowing and stopping traffic to pursue the Porsche. Agent Six followed closely behind. Agent Two took over the commentary. 'Southbound Second—we need to take him out before he kills someone.'

The brake lights of the Porsche illuminated briefly as it approached a stationary vehicle at a red light. The old brick buildings to Benedict's right and left concealed the Secret Service vehicles converging on the crossroad. Agents Two and Six were close behind him, close enough to smell the dispelled fuel and burning tyres as the fumes swept over their bonnets as Benedict accelerated. The rear of the Porsche descended into the tarmac; the tyres gripped the road like industrial magnets. He darted through red lights and confronted the opposing traffic. Agent Two barked, 'Target heading West on Houston Street.'

Agents Two and Six buckled under the fearlessness of the daredevil's death-defying stunts. They both skidded to a stop, marvelling at Benedict's driving skill. The Porsche was at the height of its dance and skated through the oncoming traffic with grace and poise. Benedict disappeared from their view. His movement was beyond transmission.

The New York Police Department was busy dealing with the carnage. Concerned onlookers jammed the emergency telephone lines with varied fantastical reports of a car chase through Manhattan. The sound of sirens starting up in the underground car park began echoing through the city streets. A flurry of police cars emerged in columns and lines, herding towards Benedict's location. To protect, to serve.

Stacey Corgier possessed the virtue of patience. His surname and his service had afforded him the nickname 'Old Codge'. He was assigned the lead role in a rolling despatch of nine—a plot hatched hastily as the intel reports relayed Benedict's location: Brooklyn Bridge.

Five thousand feet above Old Codge and New York City, skyscrapers and vehicles resembled childlike drawings. A solitary helicopter suckled on the advantage of vantage. Its pilot wore a highly decorated uniform that was a testament to his service for America's freedom. The freedom that Benedict threatened.

A silver-and-black striped Shelby roared at street level, screeching down Theatre Alley. The gang member driving it was tense, edgy, his intent fuelled by rage—he wanted to kill the man that had killed fellow members of his brotherhood. His right hand tugged at the handbrake, his left at the steering wheel. The Shelby's chassis absorbed the torque as it manoeuvred from an alley ordinarily unfit for vehicles. He emerged in Benedict's rear-view mirror. The infiltrator had flummoxed the three banks of three police units but the lead central car remained professional. Codge calmly announced the development and awaited instruction. 'Silver Shelby has undercut our formation at Park Row and is in active pursuit of our target.'

Agents Two and Six whizzed through the stagnant traffic. The hustle and bustle of Manhattan was being diverted and directed by cops, yet the agents bundled their way through with bullying moves and belligerent radio transmissions. Their determination had landed them at the heart of the action but they were mere spectators. Codge's sequenced formation was in position and the agents were forced to observe, parallel to each other at the base of the nine-pack. Three waves of identical police cars blocked their path to Benedict— it would have caused chaos to intervene in an unfolding plan. The bridge was beckoning.

The helicopter above was prancing like a gypsy pony. The Shelby was on the tail of the Porsche. Both felonious vehicles were being squeezed between the forces of law and order, who were loaded up behind and planted a mile or so in front. The helicopter pilot had the best view of Roebling's limestone-granite towers. 'I'm currently above Brooklyn Bridge, East River, following the subject. I still have a confirmed sighting, maintaining visual. Subject heading towards the interstate. I-278. I repeat, I-278.'

Benedict purred merrily along the empty road. The chopper lowered its nose and coasted high above him. The pilot saw a series of Brooklyn units in the distance and announced it concisely. 'Unit has entered sterile area, road block approximately one mile ahead. All officers involved maintain visual.'

The interstate was obstructed by a multitude of blue and red flashing lights—a Brooklyn standoff. Police vehicles were parked, fanned out in a specified formation that spanned all three lanes, forming a wall of metal and officers—a barrier of weaponry poised and pointing.

Benedict pressed his foot to the floor; the Porsche growled violently as the engine roared into action. His pursuers watched on as the sports car shrank beneath the dust it tossed from its diffuser. The barricade gasped collectively as the black asteroid hurtled towards them. Benedict stamped on the brakes. The front wheels dug into the tarmac and were soon relieved as Benedict yanked at the handbrake, causing the Porsche to flick into a spin, spitting thick smoke into the air. The rear tyres gained instant traction and launched the car away from the mouth of the barricade towards the oncoming predators.

The Shelby driver was blinded by his rage and the friction smoke. He turned sharply towards Benedict's path in a last-ditch attempt to complete the mission. His high-speed manoeuvre caused his vehicle to derail like a runaway train, popping up off the road and twisting to its left. The gangland car tumbled like a cast die, indiscriminately bounding off the barrier of police cars and clambering cops.

The helicopter pilot yanked at the stick and stamped on the rudder to follow the madness below; instead, it shot past, submitting wildly to the extreme forces placed upon it. The long, swooping arc was hopeless against the Porsche's nimbleness. 'Reporting collision at roadblock—silver muscle car—units converging on target, black vehicle has spun, repeat, black vehicle has spun, visibility low, approach with caution.'

The first line began to sway back and forth, daunted by the impending tragedy ahead. They buckled in turn to human instinct, sensing a head-on collision with the advancing Porsche. The vehicles veered right and left without any consideration for their colleagues. Benedict seized the moment of panic and zipped between Codge and his wingmen. The agents looked on in bewilderment but the second line of marked cars before them was steadfast. They slowed slightly and joined together, eager to pin the Porsche in.

Benedict watched the second string of rampaging cars and dashed towards the tightening group. He was stony-faced, undeterred by the tidal wave of government men approaching. Benedict gripped the seatbelt and tugged it downwards. His car's agility was soon undone, colliding heavily with the middle of the second wave of police cars, head-on. The bonnet crunched and contorted but the wheels were unbuckled by the perfectness of opposing force. The vehicles rested momentarily, fused to the front of one another. His windscreen had fractured but remained in situ. Benedict took a deep breath and rocked within his seat to reinvigorate himself. He peered through the webbed windscreen and saw that the man before him was unconscious.

The third wave swept towards the stationary car. There was little time for sentiment. The twisting helicopter announced the butchery. 'Collision with second line, I repeat, head-on collision with second line. Officers approach—target is blocked—stationary.'

Benedict floored the accelerator, pushing the car before him backwards and then abruptly ragged his vehicle into reverse. His Porsche smashed into the rear of two vehicles that had overshot the crash. The momentum kicked him forward; he snatched the car into forward motion and it spun into wicked speed. The third string of vehicles rampaged towards the failing Porsche. Benedict was like a crazed convict; he smashed between two of the bloodthirsty vehicles. All three vehicles screeched and squealed at the pain of parting paintwork, a vicious howl of metal on metal as the two adrenaline-drunk police cars turned inwards. The two rookie drivers looked over their shoulders as the Porsche wrestled between them. Then they looked at each other, undone by the audacity of his escape and the failure of their attempt to stop him.

Agents Two and Six saw the beaten-up sports car fizzing towards them and a trio of police cars shuffling beyond it, trying to turn amongst a muddle of chaos. Agent Two piped up after witnessing the hopelessness of local law enforcement. 'Six, bank on my shoulder, we'll ram him into the bridge.'

Agent Six fell into position, neatly shadowing his partner as they prepared to flank the Porsche. Benedict spotted the subtle movement before him and edged towards the bridge's columns. The agents offered him an open space alongside the barrier. A booby trap planted. He drove towards the gap. Benedict turned sharply into the bridge, scraping the entire front end like a sword sharpener. Sparks decorated the dissipating front end of the Porsche. The impact at speed caused it to stick and slide along the barrier at an angle. The pilot chipped in, 'Target has crashed into the bridge, repeat, target has crashed.'

The Porsche was slowing, owing to the force of immovable metal upon it. The agents darted towards the target, tempted by its frailty and their ascendancy of speed. Benedict was calm and awaited his fate. Both agents floored the accelerator, wanting to destroy the staggering outlaw. Benedict slammed the vehicle into reverse and yanked against the volition of the steering wheel. He stamped on the accelerator and jolted across the path of his attackers. He braced for impact. Agent Two slammed into the front edge of the Porsche, sending it into a wild reverse spin beyond the duo.

The Porsche clunked in agony for a second but was soon ready to play again. Its front end was almost completely tattered but its engine was glugging, thirsty for more adrenaline. Benedict's body bounced back and forth as the car jerked into forward motion. He looked at the bedlam in the rear-view mirror as the agents snaked to a stop. They watched the Porsche disappear from their view and looked up to the heavens and the swirling helicopter.

'The target has eluded the marked and unmarked vehicles and is alighting the open end of Brooklyn Bridge, visibility poor at this time, significant distance from the target.' The pilot dipped the helicopter's nose and dived through the city air, towards the fleeing vehicle. He looked back at the mess on the bridge. The view was exceptional, playing out almost in slow motion. He was drawn to it, watching the sluggish movement of cars and cops. Benedict raced towards Manhattan's level ground. Each adjoining road was jammed with vehicles and cops who were busily keeping the jostling crowds at bay.

All routes were blocked. Benedict struck the brake pedal causing the vehicle to jolt severely as the speed was sucked from it. The sports car edged to a rolling speed at the tip of the Brooklyn Promenade. He popped the Porsche into neutral and slid into the passenger seat before stepping out of the car. The ambling vehicle gasped at the release and Benedict watched as the beaten-up Porsche coasted down the road.

His escape was covered by the plodding car and a slender hop over the metal barrier beside him. The drop sent a shock through Benedict's body but he dismissed the momentary pain. He walked casually beneath the road as the Porsche gained momentum above him. The helicopter pilot failed to see Benedict's dismount courtesy of the colour and the chaos. 'The target is approaching Manhattan base. Any available unit in vicinity. I repeat target vehicle is approaching Manhattan base.'

A young cop amongst the pandemonium looked up to the bridge and cried out, 'Target in sight! Centre Street. Two hundred metres.'

Benedict jumped a concrete barrier while cops watched the rolling decoy and landed onto a road jammed with slow-moving vehicles, backed up by all the city drama. The young cop drew his gun and prepared to shoot. He zoned in upon the gliding Porsche which was veering madly to its left but chose not to fire. His transmission was feverish. 'Porsche is unoccupied, I repeat, Porsche is unoccupied.'

The car broke through a road sign in a manner that did not compare to the suffering it had sustained upon the bridge. The young cop left his post and gave chase to clear the target vehicle. He watched the car crash into the concrete barrier and grind to a halt.

The cop was twenty years young and fresh from the academy. His enthusiasm was infectious but his radio manner was panicked. 'Vehicle is clear, vehicle is clear! Suspect is on foot. I have no visual, repeat, I have no visual, suspect is on foot.'

Benedict filtered into the city's carnage and sauntered to a yellow cab amongst a sea of yellow cabs. The car was staggering, pinned between beeping horns and impatience. Benedict flicked out his hand to the unsuspecting taxi driver, who, with a rolling hand in return, offered an invitation to a cloak of invisibility. Benedict capered to the cab, and as he landed his body casually into the car, said, 'Liberty and West.'

'Business or pleasure?' enquired the driver.

'Pleasure.'

The taxi driver looked over his shoulder. 'It's bedlam—some sort of Hollywood drama on the bridge, could be a while, sir.'

Benedict was unfazed by his honesty and replied wearily. 'I've got all the time in the world, sir.'

The driver sensed his passenger's need for solace and replied softly, 'Those towers are something to behold.'

Chapter Thirty-Three

REQUIEM

Where is Benedict Maven?

The log cabin that overlooked the Four Corners village was only one slice of the bitter divorce-settlement pie. A pie made of estates, assets and chattels—the many segments that both parties wished to devour. The cabin's value was insignificant to both of the already-wealthy parties—but wealth breeds greed and it was a matter of principle.

It had once been a secluded retreat for the Brooks-Parker family, who enjoyed hiking, fishing and campfires. It was Bernhard's infidelity with an investments officer named Aaron that had been their undoing. The cabin had lain empty for nearly a year and had been nibbled at by the elements during the lengthy divorce proceedings. It had last been visited, and left unlocked, by an aloof valuer named Christoph.

Benedict drove his cactus-green Jeep Renegade as far as the trail would allow and parked it amongst a jungle of trees and bushes. They snagged at the paintwork but cloaked it with invisibility. Benedict tugged at his leather kitbag as he leapt from the elevated driver's seat to the rocky path. His mustard Danner boots softened the landing.

The Adirondack Park, in the north-east of New York state, was where Central Park longed to be. Benedict sucked at the air and looked up to a sky as blue as a robin's egg. He was incommunicado.

Cut off from the city. Cut off from civilisation. He began to walk the path beyond the trail that had submitted to his Jeep. It was lined with yellow birch trees and revealed a monumental parish of greenery. It was quite the fairy tale. This place. This hideout.

A narrow opening between the trees drew Benedict's footsteps towards it. It meandered to a shadowy glade beneath guarded branches. Benedict ducked beneath them and allowed his leather kitbag to drop behind his body as he squeezed through the last of the nettles. He accepted the occasional sting as if he owed it to the place and felt his skin bubble and burn for a moment. He ignored the urge to scratch as he came upon a breathtaking vista—the mountains of Speculator and Oak set above Lake Pleasant. The panorama stretched for miles. As did the silence.

The cabin creaked from disuse as opposed to poor craftsmanship. It smelt of mildew, like damp books. Benedict set about revitalising the forgotten place and sparked up the log fire with gathered birch bark and flint. The resulting burning cluster cast a warmth and amber light into each corner of the small cabin.

Benedict watched a pot of water boil atop the fire, disproving the pithy proverb. He took a tin mug from his bag and emptied the boiled water into it; he stirred in some coffee granules from a jar that had been left in a cupboard and headed to the lean-to viewpoint beside the cabin. His mind and his body were cleansed by the colour and the cold of the mountain lake. The autumn dusk was a backdrop for a suffusion of evening colour. A forest of kiwi-green and pineapple-yellow, intermittently pierced with trees coloured pomegranate-red. The sky rested and reflected upon a lake of blueberry-blue. Benedict ate up the view. It was primitive this tranquillity. This place. It soothed his soul—he thought of Elisha.

Julia Marsden was twenty years young the day she died. A bubbly, vivacious young lady tormented by her alter ego. An alter ego riddled with inner anguish and depravity—the devil on her young shoulders. Julia had lived a pretty reclusive life. She functioned within society but had always been on the periphery of inclusion. She had no family. No friends.

The railway lines and bunkhouses were a children's playground by day. Julia was serenaded by chirping starlings in the trees overhead. The sun barely lit the evening as Julia delved into the darkness of her troubled mind.

Doug had filled his mug with simple instant coffee at Pennsylvania Station. The freight-train driver cared only for the heat that it drove into his cold, aching old bones. With one sharp yank, the horn echoed around the station and jolted the train into imminent departure. The platform stunk of oil. Above the stench a digital clock hung from the station's promenade. It read '18:40 – Friday – August 24'.

The klaxon carried for a mile on the breeze and echoed past Julia into the trees. The starlings rustled their feathers, but they were accustomed to the regular noise. Julia's stroll amongst the starlings had been an impromptu decision—her depression had strangled her into submission.

Doug's eyes had been slowly clouding with age and for the last fifteen years his bones had begun to fuse together. His sacroiliac sting was only suppressed by the concoction of glucocorticoids, anti-inflammatories and his love of anything railway.

Julia saw the train approaching; she fought every human instinct she had and walked towards the track. Her instinct tried to tug her away but she ploughed on as if she were walking through mud. The train didn't divert as she stepped into its path.

The train was undeterred and it dismissed her by ruthlessly crushing her timid body. It continued to follow its course to Franklin Street Station. The only sign of the destruction it had caused was a blotch of scarlet-red on its bumper plate, but all in all the death of

Julia Marsden went largely unnoticed by the juggernaut.

For the first thirteen hours of her death, Julia Marsden was referred to as Jane Doe. She had been found beside the railway track, torn and scattered like shark bait. Her shattered teeth would later identify her otherwise unidentifiable body.

Benedict had allowed the afternoon fire to fizzle out and slept long into the tenth night of September. His body was tired. His days had been spent gathering wood, hiking mountain trails and scaling Oak Mountain. It was an ascetic existence that palliated the burden of his guilt.

When he woke at around midnight, fully clothed, he wandered outside to the viewpoint. He sparked a fire in the pit at the lean-to's outermost edge and watched the draught from beneath the rock face send the flames into a tamed frenzy. They threw back a welcome warmth into the small enclosure and he looked out to the panther-black sky. It was a moonless night.

One thousand nine hundred and five beguiling stars filled the sky. He didn't count them; instead he goggled at them for hours, purposely forgetting the reason they shone. Fortunately, they were simple to behold—they defied any reasoning and you didn't have to be Einstein to see them.

At just after 6.00 a.m. sunlight ascended upon the scene. It defined life. Creation. Existence. The fire before him had calmed and was crackling as if it were wilting at the rise of a greater power. A swathe of salmon-pink began to colour the daylight. Lake Pleasant mirrored its beauty, rippling in the morning breeze, scattering its colour. The warm morning air had blotted a layer of stratus clouds. It caused the heavens to haze into a hue of heliotrope.

'Who are you to decide who lives and who dies? You don't know what it's like to kill someone, you just sit there and turn your thumb.'

Elisha's angry voice woke Benedict. Her tone resounded in Benedict's head like tinnitus. He tried to plump the rigid lumpy pillows that aggravated him. He pulled them over his ears, blanketing his thoughts. The wooden bedframe creaked as he corkscrewed his thick weighty duvet, before throwing it off himself and down onto the bold-patterned carpet. This room was a million miles from the retreat up country. Benedict looked up at the motel room ceiling. There was a strong smell of damp.

Benedict's toes landed on the duvet that now lined the floor. He stumbled regrettably to the television opposite his bed. It was positively retro, with a hooped aerial sticking up awkwardly from its top. He pushed at the protruding button and was greeted with devastation. New York buried beneath a blanket of grey dust.

A voice narrated the sorry scene. 'It's been just over two weeks since the towers fell, and people are still searching for survivors, still searching for loved ones. New Yorkers haven't given up hope.'

The reporter paused, noticing a firefighter walking alone in the street, covered in the same grey dust that blanketed the city. He carried a wrecking bar over his shoulder as he trudged down the street.

The reporter bobbed across the street towards him, with the cameraman following close behind. 'Thank you for all you are doing at this terrible time. Could you give us your thoughts on the rescue attempts? Are there any more survivors?'

The camera zoomed in on the face of the firefighter. He removed his hat with his gloved hand. He shook his head in despondency. 'We're still excavating at the South Tower. We have search dogs at the scene helping us with the location of possible survivors.'

He shook his head in frustration. 'Where is Benedict when you need him? He knew this was going to happen and did nothing about it.' Sadness had consumed him. He walked away from the reporter, shaking his head in anger. The reporter jumped on the occasion. 'As you can see, tensions are running high here today. People are extremely angry. And the question is, where is Benedict Maven?'

Benedict pulled his baseball cap down further until it was almost covering his eyes, as he reflected on the devastation before him. New York City was a shell of the bustling city it used to be. The dust still polluted the air. Benedict coughed as it clung to the back of his throat. He walked past a thousand heartfelt handwritten notes. He paused to look at one, but he had read them all in a heartbeat. He felt the myriad of losses and the occasional miracle.

A widow looked down over Ground Zero and held her six-year-old son's hand tightly. His dad had been his hero. The madness around the little boy confused him. He tugged at his mother's hand and demanded her wandering attention. He asked simply, 'Mom, where's Daddy?'

Benedict threw his cap across the motel room and snatched at a set of hair clippers that sat by the sink. His return to New York City had stifled his heart. He thought of the tranquil place in the mountains that he had left behind. He roughly brushed his left hand through his hair, followed quickly with the powered clippers in his right. Each pass felled further clumps of hair onto his neck, shoulders and the sink. He steadied himself before stepping into the cramped shower cubicle. The cold water was refreshing. It cleansed his face of the dust.

The telephone rang briefly and an automated message played. 'Welcome to the Sunset Motel. It is 12.30 p.m. on Friday, September 28. You have reached room three-zero-three, please leave a message.'

A commanding voice replied, 'This message is for the attention of Maverick James. I was informed that you were due to commence service within the next two months. Considering recent events, your service will be effective immediately. Report for duty at Camp Alpha on Monday, October 1, at zero eight hundred hours, to commence Marine Corps training. Help protect this nation from the tyranny that threatens it—*Semper Fidelis.*'

Chapter Thirty-Four

PASSAGE

He was a forgotten soul

The caramel-coloured sofa was oddly positioned within the miserable room. It wasn't sweet to sit in, nor was it delicious to look at. It was falling apart. The metal springs had spiralled wildly out of control and caused the sponge to bubble from the torn fabric like honeycomb.

Billy had been sleeping amongst the contorted mess that dug horribly into his back for the past three weeks. However, for Billy, it was a haven, a welcome change from the cold ground of the unsympathetic streets. Warmth—it was the second most important thing in Billy's life. By now, the smell of the room had seeped into his clothes. He no longer noticed the stench of rotten faeces and rats. Billy enjoyed the rats' company when his highs had become lows. He would sit there in silence, listening to the tiny paws that scurried under the floorboards, listening for snuffles from their pink noses. Before long they had become accustomed to Billy's presence and often surprised him as they scuttled to his feet for their treats of seldom-pocketed scraps.

The harsh streets had battered Billy into submission, but his heroin habit drove his desire when the cold mornings stung the tips of his ears and the bottom of his belly—it was a discomfort he would endure for his ultimate high. Billy stumbled through the mess, leaving his friends, and forced his way out from his den of iniquity. The ice-cold air spat unceremoniously at his face but, for now at least, his ears were warm. Soon his hat would double as a charity bowl, treasuring any offering of kindness.

Benedict's hands rummaged through the silky mud that coated the front of his body in a blackened gummy mess. He smelt garlic. It spiralled towards him on the breath of the drill sergeant, Major John E. Gray. Gray was a Texan. Kind. Nurturing. It was his father who had introduced him to biltong. Since then, he had never been anywhere without it. He loved the smoky garlic flavour.

Fittingly, Major Gray was nicknamed 'the gentle giant'. He was a fine specimen of a human being—in his prime, his hair had been jet-black, his body proportioned like a bull, with a thirty-two-inch waist. He could run the hundred in under eleven seconds and was ruthlessly kind. Gray wasn't the type that needed to shout to gain respect, nor bark orders to prepare recruits for war. He exuded charisma. He inspired recruits. He took the time to get to know them. He recognised the sacrifice they and their family had undertaken—to protect and hold the oath of the United States of America. For some of the recruits, he was the father they never had; for others, he was the father they wished they had.

Billy felt a tickle in his foot, but not in a good way. It was pale and blotchy, as taut as leather, and on the verge of splitting like a bursting balloon. A needle dangled from the top of his foot. A tourniquet was strapped tightly around his calf, causing the skin below it to swell with a tinge of blue and above it a tinge of red. Billy felt the heroin course through his buckled veins. The sensation caused his toes to curl.

Benedict watched the thick muddy water as it swirled into the gurgling plughole. He cupped the running tap water in his hands and tossed it over his face, ridding it of the chocolaty mess. The water soothed his sensitive skin and allowed him to view himself for the first time in over forty-eight hours. He took hold of the dog tags that dangled from his neck and looked at the engraving. *Maverick James – 110383.*

Gray's voice was smooth. It echoed inside the barracks. 'Well done today, soldiers, I'm proud of you all. We need to tighten up on our six. Remember, the man behind you, the man in the dirt beside you—he is your best friend. Endeavour to keep him safe. We have a busy day tomorrow, so freshen up. Get some food and get an early night. Lights out twenty-one hundred—goodnight, men.'

A chorus of men returned fire. 'Goodnight, sir.'

Gray had been formally introduced to the President as Captain John Edward Gray. Gray's hand dwarfed that of the President as they shook hands. The President's hand was rougher than the marine would have expected; after all, he was the man who penned orders— he didn't fulfil them.

The President's compliments and condolences were heartfelt. He knew the captain had lost men that day—if it hadn't been for this man's heroics, they would have certainly lost more.

Standing beside the President was a tall man who spoke with an acquired elegance. Gray wondered who he was. Daley Claiborne was in fact the President's puppeteer. He had been on the President's shoulder and in the President's ear for the duration of his tenure, and the election campaign before that. Claiborne had single-handedly paved the President's pathway to and through politics since they had first met on Randolph's wedding day.

Claiborne took hold of Gray's hand and shook it firmly. He offered some words to the medal's recipient. 'Babe Ruth...now he was an American hero—an incorrigible man who could hit the ball to the sky with a forty-ounce bat.' He gave Gray a waggish wink and delivered his second sentence in a softer, more sincere tone. 'Remember, son, it is the darkness that defines us, not the light.'

Later that evening, at the Blue Paradise Motel, overlooking the Anacostia River, Gray inspected his medal. It was here, away from the hundreds of eyes, that he truly appreciated its craftsmanship. He sat contented, on a creaky motel bed, leaving his lavish reserved hotel room unoccupied.

His fingers gently held the Medal of Honor—America's highest military accolade. It was awarded for personal acts of valour above and beyond the call of duty. At the centre of the medal's star was Minerva—the Roman Goddess of wisdom and war.

Perspiration drenched his face. He wiped it away with his fingers. His combat clothing was horribly uncomfortable. Mosquitoes buzzed around him and stuck to his bare skin. They were unrelenting. He detested the Rung Sac forest of Ho Chi Minh City. The stench of it. The bloodsucking parasites. Even the remarkable views disgusted him. It had been Gray's unit's home for two years and became aptly known as the Forest of Assassins. The tour had taken its toll on his men, both mentally and physically.

An early morning reconnaissance mission in the A Shau Valley along the border of Laos saw Gray's unit trudge through the awe-inspiring gorge. It was as impressive as it was deadly. They were on high alert. Gray saw nothing but shards of green grass, up to and beyond his eyes. The thick, ten-foot-high blades of elephant grass carpeted the mile-wide valley, sucking the air from the stifled path.

Gray looked to his unit—they were boys in men's uniforms, young and undeserving of impending doom. He trudged on confidently, a beacon for the boys that followed him. A column of grass had been bent and buckled, revealing a subtle clearing. It allowed a cool breeze to filter through and wash over their sweaty faces. His unit was flanked on each side by two strings of densely forested mountains as high as low clouds. The scenery suffocated all American soldiers. Gray took short sharp breaths. He was composed. He was in command.

Private Cruise and his heavy-gunner partner Donaldson had it much harder than most. Cruise carried a Browning M2 heavy machine gun over his shoulder, while Donaldson carried the tripod. They were the support-gunner duo—when events turned sour. The weapon weighed a staggering fifty-eight kilograms—strictly a two-person weapon, fired from a solid surface. Cruise stole a moment to bask in the sweetness of his canteen as he poured copious amounts of water over his face.

Without care or consequence, gunfire tore through the centre of the valley of terror and caused Gray's unit to fizz in all directions, diving and scurrying for cover. A horde of Vietcong had burrowed into the darkened corners of the undergrowth, like vampires intent on drawing blood. Gallons of muck and water spun into the air as a flurry of grenades exploded in sequence. Gray witnessed his soldiers spinning into the air. He shouted frantically, 'RETREAT TO PAPA THREE, RETREAT TO PAPA THREE!'

His unit of twenty-two had already been tumbled down to thirteen. Six had been killed instantly by gunfire and grenades. Three were lying in flattened elephant grass that was turning a dirty red colour as they were drained of life. Gray saw one of his unit succumbing to the afterlife, but could not dwell on its sadness, as a plague of flames grew around his disjointed unit.

Ferocious foes relished the gore, scampering like children towards a downed enemy. Bullets ripped through the blue sky. The thirteen remaining soldiers crawled in the direction of their last checkpoint, Papa Three—the crest of the gorge. Their sole purpose was to survive. By now, a wall of fire had risen beyond the American troops. Smoke clogged their lungs and clouded their vision. They were frightened. Human.

Trapped, the American soldiers settled into the sludge beneath the burning fields, engulfed by fear, surrounded by fire. Corporal Gray scanned the horizon of thick grass and frenzied flames that stretched to the sky. He surveyed the movement and plotted the path of impending attack. His unit had clustered together, penned in and pinned down. He sank into the mud and took shelter from the blistering heat. His pupils were fixed—full of fire. His desperate unit looked towards him through the suffocating smoke.

Gray crawled through the mud and came upon a fallen soldier. It was Private Cruise. The sediment had failed to drink the blood from his body, instead choosing to pool on its surface. He was nineteen years old. Gray barely glanced at him. Death was not a spectacle. The boy's beautiful face had been torn open by flames and shrapnel. He took comfort in the boy's quick passing. He tore Cruise's shirt from his body and looped it around his left forearm. He shielded himself from the flames by dousing himself in the sludge, and heaved Cruise's muddied and bloodied Browning to his chest. The tripod lay tangled in the swamp beside Donaldson's mangled body. The tossed grenade had separated the inseparable pair.

Gray cradled the weapon, using his forearm as a brace. He barely had time to breathe. The wall of flames imprisoned his soldiers in a firestorm of certain death. He trudged forward. The only way out was through the enemy. Through the flames. There was no backing down. The heat caused his skin to tauten like leather. He shielded his face and took a leap of faith.

Fire swept over his body, immediately stripping his head of its hair. The intense heat began to melt the mud and caused the sludge to run like treacle to his boots. His skin, however, remained cool, like the ice cream in a baked Alaska. He was a walking ball of flames. The enemy saw him. They watched the American soldier burn. It was the chance that he needed. He yanked at the large action that fed a round into the chamber. His finger snatched at the heavy trigger and the weapon kicked into life, buckling his body, sinking his boots into the mud, but the huge man stood strong, tussling with the weapon that chewed up and spat out .50 calibre rounds. His body was battered by the power. He tamed the beast while fanning his body left and right, causing the spent rounds to flatten a wall of grass in front of him.

The enormous rounds bounded into the trees, sparing little remorse. The enemy hoped the trees would provide protection, but it was fruitless. The sheer magnitude of the round was an unstoppable force. The enemy quite literally separated. Flesh and bone fell like damaged pieces of a bloodied jigsaw to the ground. Their screams were silent amongst the chaos of blood and uprooted vegetation. Bullets tore at the embankment while mud blasted into the air. The last to fall had watched his friends disintegrate in the most grotesque of ways.

The weapon clunked empty. Gray had failed to hear the final shots that echoed in the valley—his eardrums had perforated. His eyes tried desperately to rid themselves of kaleidoscopic vision. He could smell his own burnt flesh. He dropped his weapon to the ground and collapsed into the swampy water.

Benedict opened his eyes. His body was contorted amongst the cotton sheets of his steel-framed bed. The rising sun coloured his skin the deepest orange. He shuffled himself into a seated position on the side of his bed, surrounded by sleeping soldiers. Beneath his pillow lay a metal cross. He unravelled a ball-chained necklace and fed it through the hole at the top of the cross. Carefully, he looped it over his head. It fell tenderly against his dog tags. Then, in the silence of the barracks, he recalled Billy's last breath.

Billy's disappearance had gone unnoticed. Sadly, not a single person paid their respects at his passing. He was a forgotten soul. He was just twenty-six years old. He died alone on his caramel sofa. It was three weeks before the police were notified of a partially eaten, decomposing body. Between barfed breaths the police officers showed a distinct lack of sadness; you couldn't blame them—the stench was horrible. It coated the back of their throats. To them, he was just another homeless junkie. They peeled Billy's St Christopher pendant from around his neck and slipped it into an evidence bag.

Chapter Thirty-Five

CONTEMPLATION

Falling hopelessly in love like a couple of seahorses

Elisha had never met Andy's mother. She had asked many times, but it had never materialised. Eventually, Elisha realised that it was entirely intentional. Andy had rocketed through a story about his father dying when he was a child and said that he had never seen eye to eye with his mother's new partner. That was an untruth—his mother's partner was a divorcee, a doting father and a pleasant old chap. But Elisha had no reason to disbelieve him and accepted the story willingly. The story, in fact, fuelled their relationship, and both blossomed in one another's undivided attention, falling hopelessly in love like a couple of seahorses.

Two years after they had first met unromantically in the local supermarket, where they had shared an introduction beside the apples, he finally told her the truth about his father. Elisha had prepared a delicious steak meal and they were sharing a few bottles of red. Andy had drunk six glasses.

The conversation had floated to the concept of parenthood. Elisha told him of her desire to be a mother, but Andy hadn't quite shared her enthusiasm. Elisha prodded him with a flurry of questions relating to his indifference. He was bordering on being annoyed when a sudden surge of emotion overwhelmed him. It was enough to take his breath away, and before he knew it, the words had fallen unintentionally from his lips. 'My father hung himself.'

Andy never spoke of it; he rarely elaborated upon answering questions and had absorbed the image deep into his soul, concealing his anguish. He was far from a flamboyant man and it helped his cause. Andy was a chivalrous man who always preferred to ask rather than answer. From the outset, he seemed like the easiest person to judge and the most likely person to blend in. He couldn't paint you a picture or write you a poem, but he could build you a shed.

The first time he missed Christmas dinner in Long Island was because of unfinished work in the city. At the time, his mother hadn't thought too much about his fleeting morning visit; she was unhappy, yes, but she understood the times—times that valued profit over people. She was, however, kept busy for the duration of the day, tending to her two stepchildren who were both under the age of ten. It would be the last time Andy would see his mother. They continued to speak occasionally on the phone, but their conversations were stilted. Soon they both stopped dialling and the phones stopped ringing.

It was dark. He was exhausted. His eyes tried frantically to see through the weaved material that had tormented him ever since it had been yanked over his head. It scratched his face, causing him to puff air from his lips to rid the itch of its torture. It smelt of damp. His pupils were often subjected to intermittent flashes of light. It was mentally draining, and the constant disorientation had increased significantly since his capture, but the soldier had somehow managed to maintain his perspective. He offered occasional pockets of information. It was a necessary evil—it was enough to buy him time.

He shivered uncontrollably in the cold clammy room, curling his bare feet. His hands were bound tightly behind his back; he cupped them together—his fingers had started to numb. Today had taken its toll on the soldier. He failed to banish the thoughts of what they would do to him. He thought only of death—oddly, he had accepted death, as long as it was quick. As long as it wasn't publicised. He took the opportunity, at his lowest point since his capture, to rejoice at the possibility of being reunited with his parents. He hadn't thought about his parents for a long time.

The entire head office of Hess Corporation observed a minute's silence in tribute to the loss of one of its employees. The majority of those who honoured the hush barely knew the man. In truth, the sixty seconds of quietude served only to halt conversation.

The tragic death of Mr and Mrs Carter was as untimely as it was unjust. Their son and daughter were at an impressionable age, already questioning their role on this earth; the news further compounded teenage agony. Elisha was nearly fifteen and Paul was approaching his seventeenth birthday when they were told of Hugo, and how he had contrived to take their parents. It was their grandmother, Mrs Carter's mother, who had sat them down and told them of the tragedy.

Before she could finish her prepared speech, her grandchildren had stood up and stormed around the room in search of air. Maddened. Muddled. Their grandmother's words had clogged their young lungs and its truth began to suffocate them slowly like asbestos.

Arabic conversations stifled his sorrow. Thoughts of his sister had invigorated him. He counted three voices. Three men. He saw black. He listened for important phrases. Important words. He recalled the words of his shouting sergeant at Marine Corps training—he wished he had listened more carefully to them. '*If you are captured, which some of you will be, this information will become vital in your survival…believe me.*'

He had failed to unjumble the muddled words of Arabic conversations throughout his captivity, yet infuriatingly, even in this precarious position, he thought only of the blonde he had met at the barracks, the same blonde that occupied his mind during the 'Arabic translations and phrases' training.

Two sharp knocks at the door stole the beautiful girl from his mind. His captors' peculiar chatter ceased as the noise echoed around the cold damp walls. The soldier thought of horrible things as he rode a rollercoaster of emotion—it chilled him to his core. It was the first time today he had heard the door being knocked—oddly, he had become accustomed to the three strangers that spoke in gibberish.

A croaky voice in front of him shouted, '*As-salamu alaykum.*'
Hello or welcome, he thought.

There was a pause. He was jolted by a loud voice that shouted, 'Kasim?'

A muffled voice replied from behind the door. '*Shay.*'

Tea, he thought. They drank copious amounts of tea.

He turned his ears to the door that screeched slowly open. He shuffled in his seat, manipulating the material to see something— anything—of benefit. He saw the back of a blurred figure a few feet away. The door crashed open, a single shot whizzed over his head, fracturing just behind him. A wet and warm liquid spattered over his tangled hands. He wriggled like a madman, knowing it was blood. He couldn't feel any pain but was conscious that he was too cold to feel anything. He scrambled, desperately attempting to defy the gunshot. It caused him to fall onto the clammy ground, and he began shouting uncontrollably. 'Help, HELP!'

He curled into a blundering ball, hoping that it would be quick and painless. The darkness had turned entirely to black. His body was shutting down but his hearing had mellowed—a constant echo began to drown his mind. He screamed again in frenzied panic. 'HELP! HELP!'

A single touch to his shoulder caused his curled-up body to spark into motion. His heart drummed in his chest. He heard a voice murmur overhead. His panic caused the words to jumble incoherently. To his astonishment his arms had been cut free. He ripped the sack over his head, tossing it to the ground, where it landed in a pool of blood. He reached out to the man that stood over him. His eyes batted with the light-blindness but he saw the badge—the stars and stripes. An American soldier appeared through his hazy vision. A voice said, 'I'm American, steady yourself, soldier.'

He rubbed his face, incredulous. 'You're a marine?' he gasped.

'Yes—now stay low and follow me.'

He felt a heavy shove to his shoulder as the soldier pushed him towards the draught at the end of the room.

'Who are you?' he questioned.

The soldier wrenched him under his cover.

'I'm Maverick.'

Chapter Thirty-Six

HOMECOMING

The last of the letters was handwritten in a stretched but neat scrawl

Huge crowds shuffled to the runway's outermost edge. Chains of security personnel stood beside a low-rise barrier that allowed the Hercules plane to roll into position. The doors were opened, allowing the passengers to descend safely onto American soil.

Banners coloured the airport. American flags were waved frantically by the waiting crowd. There was a chorus of cheering. It was the sound of families and friends welcoming back their camouflage-clad loved ones. Stars and stripes decorated the day.

The troops ambled down the metal staircase and lined up on the tarmac. They obeyed the command to fall in. A heavily decorated colonel shouted inaudible words. Each regiment marched across the runway towards the crowd. All the segmented troops marched professionally, in time, and to the tune of a trumpet fanfare.

The soldiers marched towards the security barrier and stopped in unison as the colonel shouted another order—to fall out. Some of the troops dropped their bags from their shoulders and dashed towards their families; others walked quite casually, oblivious to the heavy weight of their hearts and shoulders.

Benedict and Paul walked together through the crowds of military and family members. Paul saw Elisha in the distance. He hadn't seen her for over six years. Elisha scanned every face that approached her.

Her body shook with a series of overwhelming emotions.

'There she is!' Paul communicated.

He began to walk with a little more purpose towards the object of his view. Benedict shuffled his footsteps until they fell in time and in line with Paul's.

Paul glanced at Benedict and announced, 'I want you to meet someone, Mav.'

Paul looked at Elisha—tunnel-visioned. Her stomach tumbled and turned. Tears fell from her eyes. Paul held her shoulders and eased her towards him. He squeezed her with unconditional love. The embrace lasted well over a minute. No words spoiled the moment until Paul delivered an invitation.

'Sis, I want you to meet Mav, the man who saved my life.'

Paul turned to introduce his comrade. He had disappeared. Paul spun round and craned his neck, scouring every possible angle in search of him. Paul was blinded by crowds. He shouted anxiously, 'Mav—Mav!'

Elisha was confused; she too started to twist and turn her head looking for someone, without really knowing who she was looking for. People were jostling everywhere, and soon Paul ushered Elisha back into his arms, realising that his attempts to find his friend amongst a frenzy of people were fruitless. Elisha didn't overly mind that Paul's friend had wandered into the crowds. She soaked up Paul's hug and felt a sense of weightlessness overcome her. This soldier was home safely. Her brother was home.

Gratuities and obligatory high fives greeted Paul as he walked with his sister to the airport car park. Soon enough, the crowds of people had dispersed into their own clans and own cars ready to whisk their respective loved ones home and cook them a well-earned, home-cooked meal.

Paul bundled his weary body into the passenger side of Elisha's car. Elisha fumbled with the keys. Her body was still fuelled by a surge of adrenaline. The high began to drain her as it seeped from her body. Elisha sighed. Paul sat with a holdall on his lap and reached across to his sister's leg and patted it, confirming that he was real, that he was on terra firma.

The short journey home was uncomfortably silent; neither had pictured it being this way. Elisha and Paul occasionally began to question each other but found the conversation mysteriously strained. Elisha concentrated on the road. Paul leant his head back; he placed his two hands onto the bag on his lap and closed his eyes. The radio was faintly playing in the background. The sound of the road outside was soothing. A brother and sister were reunited.

Mr and Mrs Carter had arrived on St Croix island on September 13, 1989. Their attendance there was owing to Mr Carter's business acumen. He had persuaded his superior to delay the trip to the US Virgin Island by a few weeks in order for it to coincide nicely with his silver wedding anniversary. It was an easy sell to his bride of twenty-five years.

For the first few days of their stay, Mrs Carter had relaxed alone by the hotel pool and sipped colourful drinks garnished with fancy decorations. Mr Carter had donned a fitted suit to loosely oversee production practices at the Hovensa oil refinery and occasionally offer his opinion or signature. He attended a couple of meetings, but mainly indulged in polite conversation and fancy flutes of bottled water.

By the third day, Mr Carter had hung up his fitted suit, put down his Franklin-Christoph pen and sauntered down to the pool. For the next two days, Mr and Mrs Carter were carefree in their canoodling, holding hands and sipping cocktails gleefully like a couple of newlyweds.

On the seventeenth day of September, both had retired to bed, exhausted by afternoon alcohol. A glass bearing the remnants of dark rum rested on the bed cabinet beside Mr Carter. A nightcap. It was the sound of the glass smashing that woke them.

Paul was awoken from the light sleep that he had melted into. Elisha returned the gesture and patted on Paul's thigh, delivering soft sisterly words. 'Come on, sleepyhead, we're home.'

They shared a smile. Elisha opened the front door and waited for Paul to join her. She gathered a cluster of letters from the welcome mat and watched Paul walk towards her. He carried the holdall on his left shoulder and walked with purpose in her direction. They entered the house together—Andy's house. They were both emotional. They were both tired. 'It's good to be home,' Paul puffed in his tired state. Mind and body.

They entered the living room. Paul dropped his bag onto the floor. He stretched and sighed. Elisha dropped the pile of letters onto the worktop before hugging Paul sneakily, in recognition of his presence. Her words were muffled by the embrace. 'I'm so glad you're back home—I've been so worried about you lately.'

Paul understood each word and looked down to his sister; she felt his head movement and arched backwards to catch his line of sight. 'I'm so sorry,' he said, hugging her.

Elisha began to cry, overcome with the reality that Andy was gone. Her body struggled to cope with the grief and relief that surged simultaneously within her. Paul squeezed her tightly. He too was overcome with conflicting emotions, the guilt of his absence and the solace of his return. He steadied himself with trivial words, 'Don't get upset, marines don't like tears.'

They separated from their seemingly endless hug. Paul walked towards the kitchen. 'Cup of tea, sis?'

He knew that a simple gesture would cut the tension. They both chuckled and it knocked them from their despairing moods. 'I'm so happy that you're back.'

Elisha looked at her brother and drunk in the fact that he was home. Paul stopped, turned to her, and bowed theatrically. 'That's my job, to keep you happy.'

He spun out of his arched bow and entered the kitchen. Elisha gasped at his last movement. She was stifled by his theatrics and questioned him sharply. 'What was that?'

Paul looked at his sister blankly.

She spoke again in a serious tone, 'What did you just do?'

'I just said that's my job—to keep you happy, sis,' mumbled Paul, not understanding her question.

'No, no—before that, you bowed—why?' questioned Elisha and began to walk towards him.

'Just a habit, I guess. Mav used to do it all the time,' said Paul.

'Mav, who's Mav?' Elisha was intent on finding out why her brother had bowed to her. Her voice had increased in pitch and volume.

Paul tried to reassure his sister who appeared to be angry. 'Mav's the guy who saved my life.'

'The one who disappeared earlier on?'

'Yes. I guess he missed his family almost as much as I missed you.' Paul smiled. Elisha didn't. She turned away from her brother and shielded her eyes, attempting to deal with the realisation that her brother's friend was in fact Andy's killer.

'What's wrong, sis?' Paul reached to her with his words and hands.

'It's a long story,' she uttered before crumbling to tears.

Paul wrapped his arms around her just as the kettle boiled. 'Let's have that tea,' he said, sensing heavy conversation.

Elisha gathered her composure and began to tell her brother of Andy's death and how Benedict's testimony had allowed Andy to be hanged in plain view of a thousand people. Paul battled his sister's truth. He replayed every moment they had shared, questioning whether his hero friend could be America's most wanted man. His sister's sadness convinced him. He slammed his cup of tea onto the kitchen worktop and stormed off.

'Where are you going?' Elisha shouted.

'To make a call. I won't be long.'

Paul slammed the front door behind him, allowing his words to catch the draught that swept to Elisha. She was bereft of energy, emotionally shattered. She walked calmly to the kitchen. The pile of letters lay atop the counter and fanned the steam of her mug as she lifted them. She put down her brew and ripped at the seal of the first letter—it was cathartic and compulsory. Nothing important revealed itself, and so she tore its insignificance into pieces.

The last of the letters was handwritten in a stretched but neat scrawl. It stifled her destruction and caused her to open it with more care than the others. A pastel piece of paper, full of the same scrawl, was tucked inside. She unfolded it—it had been folded three times. She took a deep breath.

Chapter Thirty-Seven

PRESCIENCE

Unrequited love

Elisha,

Suckle on wisdom without provocation. Allow temporary empowerment and bask in the silence of contentment.

Nurture an unadorned faithfulness and be an adherent of a utilitarian nature. Eternal light can illuminate the darkest of dominions.

Embrace those around you and be an unfaltering shield against the vile, the ungodly and the immoral.

Purge yourself when troublesome thoughts threaten your spirit, raze all to the ground and begin again more purely.

Believe that there is purpose for pain. Natural selection cares little for creed, colour and compassion. Its fleeting depravity is necessary for the betterment of existence.

Marvel at this beautiful life and surrender to the premise of unrequited love.

Deny vulgar indulgence. Be defined by the people around you and the magnanimous deeds you do.

Savour the pursuit of divinity and the occasional brilliance of people. They will be the preservation of peace and the salvation of life.

Quell the evilness of men or suffer the malevolence of children. Absolute sin will be punished evermore, final breaths immortalised by the weakness of the soul.

Relinquish the burdens of rage and seek out those who are worthy of forgiveness.

Benedict

Chapter Thirty-Eight

BROTHERHOOD

My dearest Aquila, my pearl

The fire spat burning splinters into the dark desert air, crackling with rhythmic frequency. The air was smoky. Paul and Benedict were comforted by the fire's golden glow as the deepest of darkness surrounded them. The temperature had quickly descended below zero, making them lean closer towards the fire.

Benedict had propped his bergen up in the sand, allowing him to sit upright against it. He looked at the starlit sky above and remembered the Four Corners village. It was a memory he would never erase.

He watched over Paul, who cradled a chromatic harmonica in his hands. Paul teased the instrument with his lips, allowing trickling, muffled notes to whine out. A bluesy tune drifted around the flames. Benedict enjoyed the sound. It made him sleepy.

Paul looked at his parents with excitement. The conspicuous object that rested on the sofa's arm was wrapped in bright Christmas paper. It had been wrapped carefully the night before by his mother, while his father drank a glass of milk and peeled an orange. Now he watched dotingly over his son, holding back his tears. Elisha was occupied with her presents and paid little attention to Paul or her emotional father. The doting mother watched over them all.

Paul was oblivious to his audience and began blowing his harmonica like a jamming jazz musician. His puffing and frantic shaking of his head produced a muddle of mismatched chords. It was truly awful but his parents cried out for more, weakened by their laughter and their boy's obvious enjoyment. They stamped out of time, trying to offer a subtle beat to the monstrosity of noise. Paul continued to indulge them with his lack of playing prowess. He enjoyed the madness. Elisha too, began to improvise, tapping a discarded empty box in time with her parents' feet. It was a special moment—the family had lost themselves in the hullabaloo, that eventually resulted in uncontrollable laughter.

Paul mouthed the harmonica's chambers and couldn't help but smile. He recalled the impromptu Christmas Day concert and felt an ache in his stomach—a jitter of happiness combined with sadness.

Opposite him, Benedict gracefully wrote on lined paper, headed 'Elisha'.

Paul dismissed his daydream and observed the writer before him. 'Who's the lucky girl?'

'Ha, no one in particular.'

Paul spoke again, refusing to be discouraged. 'Quite the mystery you are, Mav—there must be someone back home waiting for you?'

Benedict replied in jest, enough to throw Paul away from his prying, 'I'm a free spirit, buddy, most of my time is spent keeping you out of trouble.'

It had the desired effect. 'Ha, that is true.'

Benedict continued to write. Paul looked across at his friend and understood his reluctance to speak about home. Paul felt a poignant twinge in his stomach; he fought it with more hopeful talk.

'Can't believe we're going home, Mav.'

Benedict stopped writing. 'I know, just another hundred klicks across this desert and I reckon we'll be close to Checkpoint Alpha.'

'Only seems like yesterday you broke me out of that shithole.'

Benedict smiled. Sensing Paul's emotional turbulence, he steadied his friend. 'Yeah, it does. Had some close shaves since then, but we made it through.'

Both men thought of those lost, not wanting to revel in their own survival. Benedict spoke profoundly to break the extended silence. 'It was a mission doomed to fail, buddy—the attack on the province.'

Paul nodded. Benedict felt the heaviness of death upon his heart before he spoke in resignation. 'War often dreams of itself.'

Benedict's camouflage jacket stifled his skin. The night air that shimmered over the desert was near freezing. Grains of sand crackled between his teeth. His chest slithered over the sandy gravel that still held the warmth from the midday sun. Benedict pulled himself towards the cabin, taking steady, slow breaths.

Amidst the desert's darkness were two illuminated windows either side of a single wooden door. The cabin's porch was manned by a single figure. The distance and the darkness only allowed Benedict to see the shadow of the patrolling soldier.

Kasim ambled into the cabin, sat on the tatty sofa and rested his eyes; he was tired and cold. He was a father of one. His son was named Jamal and he aspired to become a pilot and further the cause. Both had cheered as the planes crashed into the towers. The young soldier hadn't seen his son for over four months, but he wrote to his wife regularly to monitor his son's progress. Every epistle started the same way—*My dearest Aquila, my pearl.*

Benedict stepped carefully along the creaky boards at the cabin's entrance, holding his Glock pistol, which was equipped with a silencer. He listened to the wind that circled the cabin and the lifeless shrubs. Benedict was careful to choose specific boards to step on—stepping stones to the man that was snoring. He looked down at Kasim. His head was arched across the arm of the tattered sofa, his mouth agape. He was peaceful. Benedict hovered the barrel of his pistol at the forehead of the sleeping man. He gently held Kasim's head with his right hand. It felt clammy. He softly squeezed the trigger. There was a whisper as the chamber exited a 9mm casing. Benedict caught the tumbling case and steadied the slumped soldier.

He crept towards the basement. He switched the pistol to his right hand before knocking twice on the iron-clad door. The knocks jolted the peculiar conversation inside. Benedict listened.

A croaky voice shouted from within. '*As-salamu alaykum.*'

Benedict stood still. The voice shouted again, 'Kasim?'

Benedict called back, '*Shay.*'

A single set of footsteps approached the door. The iron door creaked slowly open. Benedict crashed through the opening and grabbed the lacklustre soldier. He ripped the guard's neck with his left hand and simultaneously raised his pistol. He fired a single shot across the dingy room. The bullet crashed into the man that stood behind Paul, causing his blood to stain the Iraqi flag that hung on the wall. Some of the claret droplets spattered onto Paul's bound hands and orange overalls. The captured guard tried desperately to release himself from Benedict's grip, jolting his body back and forth. Benedict wrestled with the soldier's movements before wrenching him backwards, depriving him of air.

Pauls began to wriggle. His panic caused him to fall from his stool. He began shouting uncontrollably, 'Help, HELP!'

The defenceless man in Benedict's grasp struggled momentarily against the forearm that squeezed his larynx. The last powerless soldier that stood opposite Benedict felt his friend's anguish. The middle-aged soldier was without his weapon. He was at the mercy of the athletic intruder. The podgy soldier delivered his plea in broken English. 'Please, please no shoot, begging you—baby, baby—I have baby.' Benedict saw through his pleading and squeezed the trigger. The begging man's skull fractured and imploded. One remained, still choked into submission by the assassin. His shallow voice failed to transmit his heartache. 'I have five girls.'

Benedict ignored the father's plight and executed him without repentance, and allowed his body to slump to the floor. Benedict unsheathed his knife and leant his hand onto the man who was still shouting, 'HELP, HELP!' in a frenzied panic.

Paul tried to pull away from the hand on his shoulder and cowered to the ground. Benedict settled the hysterical man. 'You're safe, marine, you're safe.'

The truck rumbled along a makeshift desert road, hurling dust into the air. Benedict looked intently at Paul, opposite. Paul was replenished, a far cry from the gaunt figure that had fallen into Benedict's arms during the festive season.

Paul had been reintegrated into the regiment for a week now but was still mentally bogged down by the arduous debrief that had greeted his return to camp. The intelligence officers had interrogated him intensely. Paul knew that they wanted to know everything, even the minutest details, but eventually the trivial information he offered seemed to eclipse his welfare and safe return. It was a grinding mental torture not that dissimilar to his time as a hostage. He wanted it to be over. He told them everything he knew.

Fourteen soldiers were jammed in the truck like sardines in a tin. The noise of the engine was compounded by the constant sound of the canvas cover rippling in the wind. The noise, combined with the constant bouncing upon the uneven road, had long since put an end to moments of chatter and banter. The journey was uncomfortable and the air was thin. It was hard to breathe, especially for Paul. He had not fully healed. He leant his body forward and sucked frantically at the dusty air; his legs trembled. Benedict reached over and steadied his hand on Paul's knee. Benedict propped Paul back against his seat and gestured for him to sit upright and breathe slowly with pronounced breaths and proud posture; Paul mirrored him—he sat back, raised his chest and began to calm himself and slow his heart. Benedict edged back into his own seat and reached up to the canvas strap that dangled behind him. He twisted it, knotting it in his hand with a firm grip.

The truck flipped into a somersault, propelled by an explosion beneath it. A heavy whistle pierced the desert sky as the catalyst sucked at the oxygen in its proximity. The improvised mine had been nestled beneath the sand like a dormant volcano. Sand engulfed the wreckage each time it bounced, flipped and spun like the flick of a runaway coin. The eight-tonne hunk of metal landed head first. A barrage of sand ploughed over the bonnet through the shattered windscreen. Petrol glugged from the ruptured tank and was drawn to sparks from the engine bay. The mound of sand delayed the impending explosion.

The observer and driver were dead. Tangled bodies were being suffocated by a layer of sand that had almost buried them. Blood trickled through the golden sand and pooled in occasional troughs between bodies and cargo. Benedict nudged Paul with a sharp push to his lower back. Paul tumbled out of the vehicle, landed on his side, and skidded down a small crater-like void beside it. An injured soldier pinned inside the truck stretched his arm towards Benedict but made no sound. The soldier's legs were buried beneath sand painted red with blood. The soldier was defenceless against the impending flames, drained of all hope. Benedict overlooked the outstretched hand and mercilessly stepped over his stricken comrade. He crawled from the mangled wreckage.

Benedict shouted at six floored soldiers who had been thrown from the truck. 'ON ME!'

He shouted continuously as he clambered to his feet, trying to rouse them from the desert daze. They began to stir. Benedict kept repeating the simple instruction and then began to violently round up his comrades. He grabbed each burly soldier without consideration and pulled them to their feet. He flung the wounded men into the same hollow where Paul lay.

Benedict followed the last of them to safety and kept shouting relentlessly at them to prevent them returning to the downed truck. 'ON ME, ON ME!'

The truck burst into flames. The remaining men turned and looked at the distorted view of their dying friends through the heat haze. The truck was sandwiched between compacted sand and the torrent of fire revelled in its confines, sending wild, monstrous flames into the desert air. The heat tore through the shell swiftly and spat hot sand towards the survivors like erupting lava.

A trail of bags behind the truck revealed the extent of the cartwheeling. Their position was compromised. Benedict ordered the group to collect the strewn bergens. There was no time to mourn fallen comrades. Eight men marched on. Stupefied. Stranded.

Chapter Thirty-Nine

HONOUR

The cruel man was buried on a Monday

Corporal Philips had served his country wholeheartedly. He was a patriotic, faithful and enthusiastic man. He had an American flag set in the garden of his single-storey home, which he saluted every Sunday on his way to church. John Philips had been a young man when the Vietnam War damaged his hearing for life, but he had since acquired a knack for reading people's lips when they addressed him, and he always had his television turned up to a volume of eighty-six. His wife could hear it from the kitchen but never complained. They were childhood sweethearts. The war had strengthened their bond.

JP had watched on as his friends died agonisingly around him. During the resistance, an American air strike had thrown confusion into the North Vietnam forests. JP ran for cover but was violently hacked down by enemy fire. The two fragmenting bullets that disintegrated his left kneecap had ripped through his skin and bone like a silver spoon through jelly. He had landed amongst fiery leaves, buckled by his injury. He waited impatiently for a Vietcong soldier to end his misery. He eventually passed out as the pain overwhelmed his body, yet the frenzy continued around him.

He lay there for thirty-two hours until all was quiet. Lifeless. He was prodded by an American soldier tasked with locating the dead and the wounded. He coughed as the end of an unknown soldier's rifle dug into his left shoulder. Thereafter, he was hoisted high into a rescue helicopter, but the stench of death and burnt flesh had soaked into his uniform. It stayed with him for the entire journey back to base. He had been bundled onto a stretcher and was unable to enjoy the breathtaking views beneath him—a country torn apart by war.

Corporal Philips strolled into Benedict's classroom and introduced himself to the students. 'Hello children,' he said in his deep voice.

The students were instantly mesmerised by this uniformed man. His presence filled the room. Mrs Newman greeted the medalled veteran with a firm handshake. The corporal saw his name spelt incorrectly upon the blackboard and frowned at Mrs Newman's chalky fingertips. He picked up a piece of chalk and rubbed out the entire name, *Corporal Jonathan Phillips*, and rewrote it in bold capital letters until it resembled the name tag pinned upon his chest. Mrs Newman acknowledged that the corporal had one 'L' in his surname and whispered an apology to him. He laughed gracefully and uttered, 'No worries, ma'am,' in a heavy New York accent.

The corporal then cast his attention to the classroom; each child responded by shuffling into a respectable posture within their chairs. One of the chairs was empty; it grabbed the soldier's attention. He questioned the teacher. 'Got one missing, have we, ma'am?' and turned to watch her reply.

'Yes, sir,' she replied, unconscious of the fact that she had addressed him so professionally. She continued to inform the soldier, 'William Benter is not present—his father passed away, sadly, at the beginning of the week—William is currently being cared for by the state, he should be back soon.'

The corporal responded, 'Oh, that's a shame, everyone needs a father.'

Billy would not be back. His father had been found decomposing in the midday sun of a mall car park. He had collapsed with a bottle of beer in his hand. It had smashed on the ground beside him. His liver had endured a level of alcohol abuse it could no longer take. Billy cried at his dad's funeral. The cruel man was buried on a Monday. Billy was subsequently moved upstate into a foster home.

Corporal Philips slowly edged to the window of the classroom. An American flag decorated the entrance to the school. He drew power from it and shuffled between the desks, humming *Star-Spangled Banner*. His limp was barely noticeable. The military had requested that he conceal his prosthetic leg from those he addressed; they believed it would instantly dissuade them from believing in the price of American freedom. His pride and loyalty ensured he would never disobey this order, despite his role being entirely voluntary. Benedict turned his head as the pensioned soldier paused at the missing boy's desk, and he thought of the five dollar notes he still had in his coat pocket.

The corporal meandered to the front of the class. His intense stare was serious but strangely comforting. He cleared his throat with a habitual cough that reminded him he was still alive and began to lecture the children, and the teacher, about the importance of the United States Army.

Chapter Forty

DESTINY

Covering the remaining men with an offering of death

There was beauty in destruction. Recent missile attacks had broken the city, and its obliteration was fair warning to the hostility of such a place. Benedict walked with purpose through an avenue of disintegrated buildings and upended vehicles. Bloodless corpses lay strewn along their path, infested and overlooked.

He addressed the unit who followed him loosely. 'On my six, men. Stick close.' His unit took formation. Benedict grabbed Paul's shoulder and pulled him into line. 'Behind me!' he ordered.

A frenzy of machine-gun fire unceremoniously interrupted his instruction. Masses of concrete scattered the soldiers, showering them with dust and debris.

Benedict shouted, 'TWO O'CLOCK—TWO O'CLOCK!' and set off in that direction. Paul followed his sprint. Gunfire erupted from both sides of Benedict's men; they were severely outnumbered by a hidden enemy. Benedict dived behind some piled-up vehicles and watched his unit fall in tandem onto the dusty hard ground beside him.

A barrage of lead ripped through the air surrounding them, pinning the group of frightened soldiers to the sand. The concrete walls of the building behind them began to crumble under the fire, reducing stone to sherbet, allowing burnt-orange rusted metal beams to become visible. The beams clanged like church bells with each bullet that ricocheted off them.

The chorus was spoiled by an incongruous note that arced through one soldier's helmet. His head exploded into flesh and matter, covering the remaining men with an offering of death. The helmet crashed to the sand and oscillated slowly for a few moments before lying still. A family photograph, stained red, was taped to its underside. Benedict's unit could only spare their dead friend a momentary glance. Fear engulfed them. A rocket-propelled grenade arced into the sky above them—whistling before exploding. They needed to move.

Butch stood up, fuelled with rage, consumed by grief. He fired his belt-driven M60 machine gun wildly from his hip towards the unseen enemy. Butch's heroism inspired another soldier, Reno, to stand up in the face of adversity. He too shot fiercely back at the oncoming fire. Butch and Reno charged forward, ears stinging with the perpetual noise and madness. Every ounce of fear was expelled from them. They ran beyond Benedict and fired riotously at the enemy position. Butch's finger was clamped on the trigger, causing his weapon to reverberate cruelly against his shoulder, shuddering his footsteps between the falling, dispelled cases. Benedict refused to follow them. The young men were in no man's land.

Butch shouted in a high-pitched voice, 'ON ME, BOYS!'

All but one of the crouched soldiers stood promptly. Paul was the last to stand to his feet but was instantly knocked to the ground by the man beside him. The standing unit ran towards the voice and adjoined Reno and Butch like a chain of men. Butch's frenzy of fire continued as his unit shuffled to temporary cover—a nearby rusted bus.

Paul wrestled with Benedict who refused to release his grip. Benedict pulled at Paul's assault vest and pinned him solidly to the ground.

Butch shouted in the direction of Benedict and Paul, recognising that the unit was not complete. 'MAV, LET'S GO!'

Dust clouded over the ground separating the bus and Benedict. The momentary silence was broken by a sickening whoosh. Benedict arced his body over Paul, covering his head with his hands. A rocket-propelled grenade catapulted into the bus, exploded, and instantly consumed everything in and around it, including Butch and his brave following.

Paul was silenced by Benedict's hand. Benedict didn't dwell on the scene and instead hoisted Paul to his feet. He dragged him into a cove within the ruined building behind them. He held Paul tightly as the dust settled. Paul was almost paralysed with the trauma of it all. He thought of his sister. Benedict thought of Elisha and waited patiently for the cover of darkness.

Chapter Forty-One

PREY

The Secret Service had converged upon their target

The President's image appeared on a huge screen in front of an oblong table. Those dotted around it adjusted their chairs to view the man whom they all ultimately served.

The President focused the entirety of his attention upon the meeting's head, Major Edward Deekan. Randolph had spoken to Ed prior to the meeting and had told him *off the record* that, 'Everything, and I mean *everything* is centred on finding Maven.'

The President instantly regretted his decision to observe the meeting as soon as those at the table sycophantically introduced themselves to him. He didn't suffer fools lightly. He interrupted and tore into them with a flabbergasted fury. 'How can America's most wanted man infiltrate *my* army and serve in a war which *he* created?'

The men shuffled in their seats, each wishing that another would speak. The fact that he was talking to a screen that had been wired up in the White House office only served to further infuriate the President. He wanted to smell the fear he instilled in them and yet all he could smell was Gerry's pungent aftershave.

The President could no longer bear the agony of bumbling men and so he delivered a resigned parting gesture to the major—a fateful and poisoned chalice. 'Ed, don't let me down.' The President immediately tugged the microphone wire from his left lapel and pulled the audio emitter violently away from his tie; it fell to the ground like a tangled yoyo. Randolph pushed himself to stand with an aggressive backward scrape of his chair. The sound of that combined with the unclipped microphone clashed horribly. The watching room winced.

The President then directed his anger at Gerry, who was awkwardly fiddling with the disconnected video camera link. The President roared like a mythical monster. 'GET OUT!'

Paul ushered Elisha into the room, where there was an undertone of aggression. Paul was the reason for the meeting. He had careered into Major Ed's office after several security checks and revealed who Maverick James really was. Soon after, Randolph and Ed had shared a brief phone call riddled with obscenities, and the meeting had been hastily arranged, resulting in the President's appearance on screen rather than in the flesh. The occupants of the room were thankful, given his tempestuous and flamboyant exit.

Paul hadn't properly thought his revelation through, which had resulted in an armed vehicle returning him swiftly to his sister's home, from where they were both escorted to Major Ed's office without further ado. The men stood upon Elisha's entrance. Their uniforms were sharply starched, causing them to stand tall like toy soldiers.

The room had been a cauldron ever since the President had signed off abruptly. Intelligence reports had been scrutinised, analysed and undermined under the watchful eye of the major—all records relating to a soldier named Maverick and a man named Benedict. Elisha's presence had subdued the room like an antidote; two analysts stood to relinquish their seats. Major Ed introduced Paul and Elisha to the think tank. His voice was disconcertingly calming. 'Gentlemen, this is Paul—and Elisha. Both have had sustained contact with the man we seek; they know him better than anyone, albeit by different names, but, it is the person we seek—not his persona.'

The room had already heard Paul's story. Major Ed spoke again, sensing Elisha's nervousness. 'Please be seated, Elisha—can I get you anything?' he offered.

'A glass of water would be great, thank you.' She felt her voice croaking in its dryness.

The major carefully poured ice-cold water from a jug and passed the glass into her nervous hands.

She took a sip before replying to his gesture. 'Thank you.'

'Elisha, can you enlighten us as to how you met the man you know as Benedict Maven?'

Elisha posed her own question before answering. 'Have you seen the letter?'

Major Ed was a charming man with a strong deep voice. Its tone was as charming as a car salesman's but laced with a patronising power not to be questioned or challenged. 'Yes, darling, but as you can understand, we still need to speak with him—you saw what happened on September eleventh, the whole goddamn world saw it!'

His annoyance threatened to overwhelm him, but he settled himself and spoke calmly without weakness. 'Its content has been analysed and there is no DNA or fingerprints upon it apart from your own. Do you believe such preposterous ideologies?'

Elisha had no answer. She was no longer strangled by her anger. Ed prodded her with his exasperating words. Elisha sensed an undertone that muffled her. 'I don't know, I just don't know what to think.'

Ed felt her willingness to participate in the meeting slipping away and threw her a lifeline in the shape of a perfidious apology. 'I'm sorry. Please, darling, can you just talk us through how you met Benedict—where, when and why? As much as you can remember.'

The man had slipped the lock to Elisha's front door effortlessly. It was a practised art, the lock-pick. He was dressed in a dark blue, baggy uniform and whistled his own made-up tune. It was annoying to anyone who met him. His nickname back at the Secret Service office was 'Skeleton Steve', in recognition of the fact that he could open locked doors, as well as a nod to his skinny frame.

Skeleton Steve had a small rucksack with him, made entirely of black leather; in it was a multitude of wires, wire cutters and household tools—it would have looked like a bag full of mess to the untrained eye. Steve reached in and pulled out a singular device. He delighted in holding it.

The contraption was based on a Léon Theremin original mid-forties design. It had been modified by a Sino-American professor, Benson Kao, but it was largely the same design, only on a smaller scale. Theremin had been pre-eminent in the covert-listening-device world ever since he designed the Great Seal bug in 1945. Physicians had studied and tinkered with his bugging designs ever since; it had revolutionised the art of espionage. Dr Kao had altered his idol's concept and created the ChangChang1, a wireless piece as big or as small as a matchbox, depending on how you viewed it. He had named it after his firstborn. The CC1 fitted perfectly into light switches, without interfering with their primary function. The CC1 recorded conversation perfectly and any murmur of interaction.

Steve began to unscrew the light switch fittings of Elisha's home one by one and steadily fixed the CC1 within them. Every room had a light switch. Every room now had a CC1. There were eleven in total. At conversational height. The skeleton whistled all the while.

Paul watched his sister, who had fallen into her storytelling like a true raconteur. It was the subject that spurred her confidence. Paul could see a sparkle in her eyes and expression. He silently began to question why they were there. He had disapproved of the major's condescending attention to his sister. He scanned the oblong table. Not one pair of eyes looked back at him. The room was transfixed by Elisha's story and her smile. Elisha had spoken without interruption and told the story in perfect chronology, reliving those moments with Benedict. She told them everything. Her burning home. Maggie's Diner. The racetrack. Her speech had been recorded by operators in another room, documented as to its content and analysed as to its truthfulness. Its level of detail ensured that there was no requirement to probe her further.

Elisha finally relinquished her voice. She had forgotten that she was speaking aloud to a room full of superior strangers. As soon as the realisation landed upon her, so did the steadying hand of her brother. He had sat beside her throughout. Major Ed decided then that Elisha would benefit from non-intrusive surveillance; it was offered to her as if it were for her protection, although that was not the true intention.

Benedict was troubled. He was perched on a chair in the corner of his motel room, still dressed in his service uniform. He kicked off his desert boots and snapped the top off a bottle of whisky, the widely revered Macallan 1974 Gran Reserva. Its bottle oozed character and charm—single malt. Its smell titillated his taste buds. A gentleman's whisky. Benedict didn't afford it any sacred sentiment; he swigged it from the bottle like a bingeing alcoholic, pausing only to breathe and allow its spirit to seep into his skin.

He sat in silence; the alcohol warmed his heart and steadied his sorrow. He took another gulp every few minutes and felt the sting of the liquor overcome his blood. He fell drunkenly back into his chair; the empty bottle clunked as it fell to the floor but, valiantly, it did not smash.

Benedict frantically jangled the keys in his fingertips as the sound of the engine reverberated through the vehicle. He tore through the car park, leaving a trail of smoke, finally declaring himself to the broad daylight of the city streets and busy traffic.

He raced through the streets, without any care for the vehicles that swerved and snaked and spun out of his way. He ran through red lights with complete disregard for those who obeyed the street signs and traffic lights.

The Secret Service had converged upon their target and a flurry of black-suited men surrounded the house in strategic fashion. The front door was shoved open by a broad-shouldered agent. Elisha screamed. Her voice was muted by an agent who smothered her lips with his gloved hand. A second agent tackled her, causing her to drop to her knees, winded by the attack. She wrestled with the men but was easily overpowered. The gloved hand slipped to her chin in all the chaos and she seized the opportunity to scream again. Paul heard her from upstairs.

He charged down the stairs and found his sister beneath three sets of hands that indecently gripped her body, shoulders and head. He landed his feet at the centre of six identical black shoes as the cluster indiscriminately dragged her through the front door. Paul violently ripped at one of the men who hung over his sister, but he was quickly set upon by the alliance. Outnumbered and outgunned, he was swiftly tangled up like knotted yarn.

Paul was resolute. Fuelled by his love. An athletic agent pulled a pistol from his covert harness in a fluid movement, recognising the power beneath him. He crashed the butt of the pistol into the side of Paul's head with a single, damning blow. It landed heavily, silencing the animal.

Paul's vision was blurred as he wandered back into a semi-conscious state. His body was drained of energy. Numbed by the cranium blow. He squinted, studying the melee of men carrying his sister away from him. Elisha wriggled desperately, like a jackal. The exertion left her breathless and she drifted into unconsciousness. Her limp body was callously thrown into the back of a black vehicle as Paul still battled his blurred vision.

The Secret Service vehicle travelled at rip-roaring speed, eventually turning right into a disused expanse. Grass was erupting through the grey, cracking and crumbling concrete, eroding slowly and painfully to greenery. Biscuit-brown trees stood tall at the edges of the wasteland and monitored the grass that was growing through it. The area was surrounded by a rusted metal fence that the trees leant upon.

The car stopped suddenly. Elisha's wakening body was dragged out of the vehicle and she was propped up between two suited men. They carried her to the rear of the vehicle.

Benedict slammed on the brakes as he arced his car through the last corner of its journey. The brakes jammed the tyres, causing the vehicle to skid to a stop. He swung himself out of the sports car and sprinted through the undergrowth that surrounded his vehicle. The foliage around him was thick and thatched together. Benedict jumped over fallen trees and ran towards the car park.

Elisha had sunk to her knees. Her legs were weary and she was overcome with fear. One of the agents had a firm grasp on her upper arm, preventing her from slumping to the ground. Elisha was aware of her predicament and searched the horizon frantically.

Benedict ran, oblivious to the scratching and biting branches of the trees. His outstretched hands crashed abruptly onto the rusted metal fence and his eyes widened. Elisha was surrounded by her abductors. She saw him looking intently and despairingly at her.

'Benedict!' she attempted to shout, gasping.

An agent pulled a handgun from his holster and revelled in the moment. His right hand rose steadily from his waist. The motion jolted as his forefinger squeezed the trigger. The bullet collided with Elisha's head, causing it to snap backwards violently. Her body fell sideways. Benedict's outstretched hands slid down the metal fence as he fell to his knees on the grass-covered concrete. The agent who had been holding Elisha upright had sidestepped quickly upon seeing the other agent's gun rise. Her blood smudged his white shirt. He saw Benedict's descent and pulled a gun from his waistline. He shot in the direction of the grief-stricken onlooker. The agents rattled shots at the metal fence. Gunfire scarred the trees.

Benedict clambered to his feet and began to backtrack. He vomited as a hail of bullets whistled through the air. He arched his body and took short steps through difficult terrain. Benedict was overwhelmed with grief and his coordination eluded him. The agents ran and shot in sequence. The fleeing man studied the obstacles before him, conscious that he was struggling to land his rushed footsteps. His frailty caused him to collide with a branch from a tree yet to fall.

Benedict bolted from his chair in a haze of perspiration. His feet sent the Macallan bottle spinning across the room, smashing against the wall. The noise jolted his senses. He thought of Elisha. His heart pounded. The presentiment channelled his thoughts.

Chapter Forty-Two

WISDOM

I've been told that you must wear something red

On the second day of surveillance, Bravo Golf One and Bravo Golf Two arrived early to relieve the night watch, who were slumped in their vehicle, lost between wakefulness and sleep. The night workers were relieved to see the day shift, whose punctuality that morning was fuelled by the previous evening's scolding by their superior, Major Ed.

On the first day, Golf One and Golf Two had parked up outside Elisha's address and enjoyed a mid-morning coffee courtesy of the elegant lady. Both had marvelled at her beauty and flirted more than married men should. The coffee was an arabica blend. Bold and intense. Ellis had spoiled its darkened flavour with the request and delivery of a single sugar.

An undercover officer dressed in an oversized hoody had jogged past the coffee chatter. Their interaction with the subject filtered back to base. Back to Ed.

The man with a lapel full of medals had summoned them to his office at the end of the shift. It was a small office for such a large character—perfect for amplifying an already powerful voice. He began to chastise them both at a fiercely close distance, so much so that Logan and Ellis could feel the words on their skin. Both had been required to stand for their dressing down. Being the closest, Logan bore the brunt of the major's wrath; his ears were ringing like a tambourine by the time they left the room. A large part of what Ed had shouted at them was inaudible in its raging delivery. But what they both now knew was that:

1. They were not to fraternise with the subject of their surveillance.

2. They were not to accept coffee and exchange pleasantries with the aforementioned subject of their surveillance, and

3. Surveillance was, as defined, a practice best carried out from afar.

They whimpered away from Major Ed's office without discussing the day's misdemeanours. The young men were from Burlington, Vermont—it wasn't a job requirement and did not benefit their role or nurture their irresponsibility; it only served to fill the time on their shifts with conversations of hometown stories. Hometown glories. It was days like this that made them long for home.

On the second day, both arrived early. Eager to please. Ready to serve. They parked a healthy distance from the slender subject of their surveillance. The night watch reminded the rookies of their previous day's lack of professionalism with a parting gesture representing the sipping of coffee and exaggerated, protruding pinkie fingers. They drove away from their post, snorting with laughter.

The second day for the Burlington boys was far more frigid than the first; they spent less time talking and more time watching. Their objective resonated in their subconscious. *'It is your sole purpose to observe and not to protect, you are to report any hint of contact with Benedict Maven and await back-up.'*

The fire alarm was piercing. It caused the entire news team on floor eleven to cover their ears and shuffle like netted salmon through the open-plan office. The adjoining corridor provided momentary order, streamlining the transition through the exit to the concrete stairwell. It was no coincidence that those who appeared on camera were decidedly lighter on their feet.

Benedict had entered the Black Rock offices nearly fifteen minutes earlier and was standing, poised, beside the industrial staircase of the fire escape that would soon harbour several hundred people. He struck a solitary match and reached up to the smoke detector. The flame danced merrily, proud of the chaos it was about to cause. The fire alarm began to sound.

Benedict raced down the stairs two at a time and took a seat below ground level at the base of the building. He gently blew out the flame that travelled towards his fingers and listened for the stampede. He sat patiently as the sound of descent echoed through the space above him, amplified by the whirling concrete vacuum.

The mass exodus was complete and the day outside was comfortably cold. The crowd were toasty, warmed by the excitable chitter chatter that such a fracas brings. A young mother of one was at the centre of it. She was the chief gossiper, empowered by the promise of rumours and the drama of drama. The scrum of workers listened to the high flyer. There was little else for them to do. They were gathered in the designated assembly area and their offices were in full view. Far enough to avoid any fire but close enough to see that there wasn't one. The New York day continued around them. It seldom stopped, even for flash crowds.

Benedict allowed seven minutes to pass and then began his ascent. He leaned into the fire exit door on the eleventh floor and entered the studio. It had been left ajar by its last user, a loud-mouthed director and mother of one, Alexa Carey. The room was still buzzing with activity despite its emptiness.

The brash colours of daytime television were enough to confuse the elderly and cradle the young. The solitary occupant ignored the flickering and walked across the wide room. He was holding a small envelope, addressed to no-one but destined for everyone. Within its sealed confines lay a single compact audio cassette, a narrative of Elisha's letter, read aloud by its creator.

Alexa's desk held a framed picture of her spritely blonde-haired boy. Benedict acknowledged the photo before placing the envelope into her cluttered desk drawer, it would be discovered the following day.

He continued his journey to the far corner of the studio. It was minimal, its bland backdrop was preceded by a semi-circle of laminate flooring and spotlights. He ignored the sheen of the screen and nudged camera four into a more formal position. He pressed the record button. The red light at its brow flashed and he addressed the unmanned lens.

'New York City is under imminent attack. There are fifty-four bombs hidden in the boroughs and bridges of Brooklyn and Manhattan. Immediate evacuation is required. Please do not panic. The Patriot Act will assist those closest to the Manhattan coast. Those in Brooklyn should head east beyond Hempstead. Those in Upper Manhattan should head north beyond New Rochelle.'

Elisha's afternoon nap was heavy and she woke up with weighty eyes and lackadaisical senses. She sighed at the sight of her cup with its edges stained by the stagnant skin of her now undrinkable drink. The sound of the front door opening and closing stirred her senses and a voice jolted her body as the words travelled up to her.

'Hello, Lish—you here?' Paul wasn't expecting an answer but got one nevertheless.

'Yes, I'm up here, I must have dozed off.'

Paul's face was as rosy as an apple and glistening with perspiration. Between breaths he untied his running shoes and set them against the bottom step of the stairs.

Elisha's voice bounded down the stairs ahead of her. 'You had better not leave those sweaty sneakers there, mister!' Their eyes met.

'I'd worry less about where I leave my runners and more about your laziness, missy.' It was playful sibling banter that threatened to spiral out of control, and so Paul offered a pardon, remembering that it was her house he was living in. 'I'm only joking, sis. It's damn cold out there. Do you want a brew?'

'Oh, that would be lovely, I wasted mine.' She showed Paul the cold cappuccino she was carrying.

He threw a sweaty arm onto her sleepy shoulders as she drew level with him. 'Come on, sleepyhead,' he said, and they wandered into the kitchen.

The night was drawing in; Elisha adjusted the window blinds and flicked the switch of the living room lamp. Paul was busy beneath the shower, singing erroneous lyrics to timeless melodies. She giggled at her brother's monotone made-up chorus and rested her slender frame into her chair.

She turned on the television; her first thought was to turn the volume up and drown out Paul's 'singing'. Her finger was firmly pressed upon the volume-up button; it was Benedict's voice that blared out from behind the black screen.

The picture settled a second after she heard his dulcet tones. It showed Benedict and a series of scrolling bulletins all set in bold letters and primary colours. She watched it loop twice before she truly absorbed its content.

The shower stopped. Paul hummed the tune to the song he had just stopped singing, conscious that the sound of spraying water would no longer mask his voice. The acoustic clammy shower room breathed in relief as Paul opened the door. He stood on the landing and shouted to his sister, 'Have you seen the boys in blue today? Or, should I say, the boys in black?'

There was no reply. Elisha was transfixed by the screen before her. Paul heard Benedict's voice blasting from the living room and he shouted again. 'Lish!'

Paul scurried down the stairs wearing only a towel. He saw his sister perched forward on her chair, gawping at the screen. 'What's up? Have they found Benedict?'

She corrected him abruptly. 'No, it's New York, it's another terrorist attack.'

Before Paul could swallow any detail of the sensational story, the front door crashed open. It startled the siblings, despite them recognising the intruder's face and uniform.

Ellis was overcome with an excited delirium, fuelled by his fear and willingness. He bounded into the hallway wildly, like a character from a Roald Dahl story.

He drew his breath and spoke abruptly. 'You need to come with me.'

'Where?' Paul demanded.

'The docks—Pier Eleven—transport has been arranged for you.' He took another breath and looked Paul up and down. 'Please put some clothes on, we have to go now.' Even in his panic he was polite.

Paul pulled his sister up from the edge of her chair and dragged her to the stairs. 'Come on, Lish, we need to go.'

The fidgety agent at the bottom of the staircase allowed them to reach the penultimate step before he threw more words skywards. 'Put something red on.'

Paul and Elisha turned back and looked quizzingly at the random demand. The agent spoke again in an urgent clarity. 'I've been told that you must wear something red—just put something red on...quickly, we need to go.'

The agent was at the bottom of a cascade of orders. A Chinese whisper. Major Ed had in fact ordered the imminent collection of Benedict's allies the moment the transmission had echoed through the CC1s, specifying that they were to be placed aboard the red tanker. The disseminated order had been jumbled, courtesy of muffled radio transmissions, and by the time the message had reached Ellis, he had concluded that the subjects were to wear red. It was an insignificant error.

The Burlington boy watched brother and sister scale the final step before darting in opposite directions like repelling atoms. Major Ed's instruction resounded in his head. '*She is our only chance of finding him, do not lose her.*'

Paul began to rifle through his drawers and threw neatly piled clothes onto his bed. He pulled a red cable-knit sweater over his head and loose stonewashed jeans over his waist.

Elisha was staring into her wardrobe. Unlike Paul, she was defying the man downstairs and was not frantically looking for something to wear. Each end of the clothes rail held a cluster of hanging garments, as if they had been separated like curtains. But in the middle of the rail, between the two clusters of clothes, a single garment dangled— a red shift dress. Her shoe collection, which was usually neatly lined up beneath her clothes, had been shoved to one side. In their place, and directly below the red dress, lay the Rubik's cube. The dress hung directly above the cube like a giant exclamation mark.

The Burlington boy shouted impatiently from downstairs. 'Come on—we have to go!' He was growing queasy, feeling the pressure of his task, and had shuffled up onto the third stair.

Elisha didn't question her rearranged wardrobe. She pulled the dress from the rail and onto her body. Atop the pile of shoes was a pair of black ankle boots, her favourite Isabel Marants. She slid her feet into them and closed the wardrobe doors. The mirror beside the closet reflected her bohemian beauty.

Paul saw that the agent had climbed to the seventh step and barged into his sister's room. 'Lish, we need to go.'

He saw the red dress; his baffled expression caused her to answer an unasked question. 'It's the only red thing I have.'

'You can't just wear that, sis, it's freezing out there. I'll grab you a coat.' He chivalrously ran back into his bedroom.

The agent was on the eleventh step. Elisha and Paul both exited their respective bedrooms and met at the top of the stairs. She mouthed concise words to her brother, conscious that the agent was almost upon them.

'He's here.' Paul nodded once. He knew who is sister was referring to.

The agent cut through their silent conversation without questioning it. He was out of his depth. Nervous. 'Please—we have to leave NOW.'

Paul placed a thick, padded black coat around his sister's shoulders and quickly pulled her left arm through its sleeve. The agent ushered them both towards the stairs. Elisha steadied herself by pushing her right hand through the coat sleeve and landing it firmly onto the stair rail.

The trio descended at a demented pace, driven by its tunnel-visioned tail. The anxious agent slammed the front door behind them, and Elisha and Paul were bundled into the rear of the waiting vehicle like smugglers' treasure—the first part of his mission was complete.

All four corners of the Black Rock news studio were deserted. Bewilderment had replaced business-as-usual and the studio doors were still recovering from the onrush of a fleeing crew. No one had taken responsibility for turning the lights off before they left, and a silent floor was complemented by a steady hum of overhead lights. The multitude of television screens played Benedict's transmission on repeat; a bold message rolled beneath the beautiful and eloquent man.

'IMMINENT TERRORIST ATTACK ON NEW YORK CITY—IT IS OF PARAMOUNT IMPORTANCE THAT ALL

PERSONS IN BROOKLYN AND MANHATTAN EVACUATE IMMEDIATELY.'

The repeated sequence of colours, patterns and words was somewhat hypnotic. The floor cameras dotted around the expansive room drooped their heads like dying tulips.

Maggie watched as the last of her fleeing customers scrambled out through the diner's door. It was only then that the constant jangling of the bell above the door frustrated her. The radio gave life to the TV graphic, narrated slowly and calmly by an unknown man. Maggie turned off the television and radio; by now, the words had begun to overlap each other through their respective channels. It was as annoying as it was alarming. Maggie had watched and heard it all countless times in the last fifteen minutes.

Natasha had been the only one who had said goodbye to her; she had been assured that Maggie her employer, Maggie her friend would follow her after closing the shop—convincing words that Maggie never intended to act upon. Maggie collected the plates that decorated unoccupied tables and wiped down the still-warm seats. She pinched a French fry from a plate and savoured its taste; she smiled and spoke aloud to an empty space. 'Compliments to the chef.'

The bell jangled again, and a draught caused by crowds of people running past wafted into the diner. Maggie peered out from the kitchen; the soap suds clung to her fingers as she held up her hand to the intruder, shouting in a polite voice, 'We're closed!'

A man closed the door softly behind himself and took the hat from his head like a cowboy; he put it to his chest and then threw a raised voice back to Maggie. 'Sorry, ma'am, can I get a black coffee?'

Maggie walked to the hatless man and the splendid voice she knew, rubbing her soapy hands into an apron that held a thousand stains. Mr Hatten lent a familiar smile as Maggie's eyes lit up in recognition; he spoke again. 'You'd better make that a coffee to go.'

They both laughed marvellously as madness surrounded them. Mr Hatten tipped his head as Maggie took his hat from his gifted hands. 'Margaret.'

She responded to the seductive sounding of her name with a satirical question. 'So, why isn't a strapping young man like yourself running frantically for the Staten Island ferry?'

He watched her place his trilby onto the counter and then allowed her to turn before answering between chuckles. 'I am far too old, ma'am. New York is my home, if I'm going to bow out then I'll go to the sound of rapture in my best attire.' He tugged at the lapels of his navy-blue suit and fixed his cherry-red tie.

'You look very handsome, Mr Hatten. This one is on me—'

'Please call me John, we can escape the formalities on such a special occasion.'

The coffee was served, and Maggie took a seat opposite him. Mr Hatten hadn't spoken openly to anyone in his entire life, but the unmarried man began to speak without being prompted. Maggie sensed the importance of the moment and settled her hands around her coffee cup.

'I was the middle child of three. All boys. Times were tough. Money was tight. It was the quintessential middle-of-the-century childhood. My dad was a carpenter who cared for a drop of whiskey. He was a brilliant man who never had time for words or devotion. He always had his head in a book and a cup of bourbon at his side. He had encyclopaedic knowledge and I would often marvel at him from afar—you know, he was the type of man who could spoil crosswords.'

Mr Hatten fell into another sentence before even taking a breath. 'My mother was a hard woman; I think having three boys had taken its toll on her, compounded by my father's undiagnosed depression. It wasn't so common back then, you know, but it existed. They were just children with children. The youngest of us all was my beautiful brother Peter. His nutmeg hair curled uncontrollably. He was three when he died. Polio. The epidemic of fifty-two. And to think that three years later one needle could have prevented it. Salk's vaccine.

'My father didn't say a single word during the journey back to our house. I remember hearing the front door open and close in the middle of the night and never thought to question it. They found him four days later in the icy cold waters of the shipyard. He never really spoke, you know—I can't even remember the sound of his voice. I was seven.

'My mother's hair turned white overnight, and she slowly wandered out of this world and into her own. She was sectioned about a month or so later and us boys were placed into care. I never saw my brother again. You know, the last time we were together was at Peter and my father's funeral. They held them on the same day. The whole town turned out. I remember reading a chapter in front of the congregation and seeing my mother smile from within her chasm of grief. I learnt then how powerful words can be.

'I ended up graduating out of Northeastern University in journalism, and before writing words for a living I worked in a place not too dissimilar to this fine establishment you have here, young lady. That's what I love about this place—the smell of it, it reminds me of being young, it reminds me of Peter.' John felt the last few words wobble in between his breaths; he felt his eyes moistening and settled his quiver with a quote from his favourite painter, Edvard Munch, that encapsulated his life in a sentence.

'Sickness, insanity and death were the angels that surrounded my cradle and they have followed me throughout my life.'

John hadn't spoken like this before and, following this surge of honesty, he felt a weight lift from his shoulders that had unknowingly buckled him for years. Maggie recognised his moment of disclosure and the state of freedom he was now wallowing in; she allowed him to talk uninterrupted, freely, avoiding all opportunity to question. She wanted to know why he hadn't seen his brother again, but she refrained from asking.

John's brother had in fact followed a path littered with drugs and crime, soon falling to a lonely death in the Chicago projects in a murder unsolved. It was the glaring omission of his family anecdote.

Maggie owed him her story in return and cleared her throat in preparation. She was humbled that the man across from her had allowed her a snapshot of his life. He had refrained from offering her the atrocities of a Vietnamese battlefield and became increasingly conscious that she had observed for far too long. 'Anyway, enough about me.'

John relinquished his command of the conversation and offered Maggie an open question. 'So, why aren't you travelling across the Brooklyn Bridge to a safer shore?'

Maggie took a breath. 'This is my home, I built this diner from nothing into a retreat where all types of folk share stories. I am thankful that you've shared yours. My husband passed away nearly twenty years ago. Cancer. It was a long and ungraceful death. In the end, I couldn't bear to look at him—sounds awful, I know, but he was ghostly, as if he had wandered into the afterlife long before he left us.'

Mr Hatten rested his gifted hands upon hers. 'Us?'

'My daughter and me. She was eight. She grew up to be a delightful person and I know that her father would be extremely proud of her.'

John was beginning to enjoy the sound of his voice. 'Shouldn't you be with her?'

'I've called, but the networks are jammed, and anyway she's on the other side of the world—Australia, she emigrated a few years ago, she's married and has two stepchildren. But the beach life isn't for me, it's been a long time since I wore a bikini. I've visited a few times but this is where I belong. After her father died, I threw myself into this place and encouraged her to travel. Her father would often read her stories of Captain James Cook and Christopher Columbus. History and travel, they were his things—he was a stupidly intelligent man, I wish you could have met him—you know, the type of man who could spoil any quiz show.'

John and Margaret shared a smile. 'How did you meet?' asked John.

'We met like people meet, exchanged smiles, and we were entwined from that day on. Marie was eight when her dad passed away. This place was my sanctuary. Marie grew into quite the darling—oh, you should see her, John—so stylish, a fashion designer, pattern-maker, and all that falls in between. That's her there.' She pointed to a vintage-style black-and-white photograph on the wall beside the front door; it was protected by a heavy bold frame. It showed a girl of nineteen standing on an empty city street. Striking enough to rival a Norma Jean image.

'That's her? Well, well, I've been coming here for years and you've never mentioned it.'

'You never asked, you were too busy scribbling in between sips.'

'Too true, I guess the spoken word was never my forte.'

'Then you should have written it down.'

Mr Hatten stood up, laughed, and walked towards the photograph he had overlooked for years; he shook his head at the girl's beauty and his ignorance. Maggie went to follow him but was ordered to remain seated by a simple flick of John's writing hand. She obliged and tentatively settled down into her seat. The chaos of a hysterical city outside was muffled by double-glazed windows, and what sound remained was drowned out by this man talking to a woman.

John walked to the kitchen for more filtered coffee. Maggie was as content as she ever had been. She looked to the photograph and felt a warmth blanket her. She shouted to the wandering man, 'Can you remember it?'

'Remember what?'

'The reading for your brother.'

'Charles Dickens—I can recall each of his words as if they were my last.'

Mr Hatten emerged from the kitchen and spoke eloquently. 'When death strikes down the innocent and young, for every fragile form from which he lets the panting spirit free, a hundred virtues rise, in shapes of mercy, charity, and love, to walk the world and bless it. Of every tear that sorrowing mortals shed on such green graves, some good is born, some gentler nature comes.'

The Patriot Act had been passed in the absence of Benedict, during October 2001. Its main purpose was to allow the government to identify, monitor and survey those who threatened their great country. Under the provisions of this act, an evacuation procedure had been devised in the unlikely event of an attack on American borders. It was the brainchild of a naval commander, Walter G Edmunds, who had provided evacuation procedures based on trade routes along the coastlines of America. The East Coast operation had been enacted as soon as his secretary had saluted him, served him a coffee and informed him of Benedict's latest transmission. The piers along the Hudson River and East River were chosen as evacuation points. Upper Bay and Lower Bay were the designated corridors of escape to the coastal path beyond the Jersey Bight.

It was a simple plan. For any coastal city threatened and requiring urgent evacuation, three ports would provide instant sanctuary for occupants of the city in plight, supported by the stockpiling of cargo ships at designated rigs set across the North Atlantic Ocean. The three chosen ports would be allocated a colour—either red, white or blue, according to distance from the threatened city. The respective ports would illuminate all other tankers, liners and trading ships with their assigned colour and flock to the aide of fellow Americans. Each port had designated areas for docking off the coast, marked clearly and precisely in the red, the white or the blue of America. Three areas were clearly illuminated by bright halogen lights.

RED—Charleston, South Carolina, beyond Sullivan's Island.

BLUE—Saint Simons Island in Brunswick, Georgia.

WHITE—Galveston, Texas, beyond the tip of Bolivar Peninsular.

It was organised chaos, but it was chaos nonetheless. There was an amplified murmur that overawed everyone there. It caused each and every person to stoop lower and turn their best ear to commands being thrown at them from loudspeakers. Families jostled for position and tried desperately to remain united amongst an avalanche of people.

The car carrying Paul and Elisha arrived at the last checkpoint. The area was supposed to be sterile, allowing the privileged to board harmoniously and methodically. But best plans had been laid to rest and, now, clusters of people swept like spilled oil across the final checkpoint of the docks. The piers were overflowing with colour—red, white and blue, like an Independence Day parade, but it was more of a parody; here, people were colliding like drunken fools. The night sky had thickened.

The car stopped amidst the pandemonium. A stocky agent forcefully opened the passenger door with his heavy right hand and used his left to protect Elisha as he commanded her to step out of the car. Paul could see that there were far too many people pressed against his door for it to be opened. He slid across the back seat of the government car and followed his sister into the cauldron of noise and colour. Elisha's body stiffened upon hearing the noise, the screaming. The sound of panic. Paul huddled beside her and both were ushered towards the furthest end of the dock, which was ever so slightly less chaotic.

The harbour was being flooded by people continually seeping in like wayward waterfalls. The situation overwhelmed Elisha enough that she could not feel her footsteps. Paul put his arm under hers, sensing that her feet were flailing. She could see Paul's mouth moving and his eyes fixed wildly on hers.

'Are you OK?' he mouthed.

Elisha's ears had been blocked by the burbling of this place, a rushing, raking sound had filled her head. Paul shouted at her and shook her by the shoulders. 'Elisha!'

She came to life, as if she had woken after an anaesthetic; she replied loudly and drowsily, 'What?'

'Are you OK?' he threw back.

She zeroed in on her brother and composed herself. 'Yes, yes, I'm OK.'

She pushed her way past a wave of New Yorkers that threatened to separate the siblings. The stocky agent had forged through the crowd and was loitering a few steps ahead. He kept glancing back to Elisha, who was now gripping her brother's hand tightly and shouting into his ear. 'I have to see him, Paul—I need to see him.'

He could see the determination in her eyes and was resigned to the seriousness of her words; he shouted back, 'Lish, you don't even know where he is!'

'But he knows where I'll be, he will keep me safe, I know it.' She squeezed at his hand to settle his fluster.

Agents at the checkpoints were struggling to maintain order and by now were just trying to manage the herd of evacuees drowning the dockyard. The colossal tankers and ships were lined in filtered formation like race cars. Inflatable coloured tunnels had been attached to the dock and thrown to the choppy sea. People were scurrying like mice in a maze to them and through them.

The agent accompanying the siblings had now been divided from them by the mass of crazed people who craved the tunnels to the tankers. The slow shuffle had edged him away from Elisha and Paul like tectonic plates. He watched intently, hoping that they would fuse back together. He shouted for them.

Paul pulled Elisha across a path of people in order to get closer to the man whose name he still did not know. He caught his sister's eye and nodded to a nearby alley opening that filtered away from the harbour and towards the evacuated city. The alley was empty of people but clogged with old fishermen's boxes. Elisha saw her brother's gesture and warmed at their sibling intuition.

Paul swung his sister away and then tumbled theatrically into the agent and tackled him to the ground. The people immediately behind the agent fell forward. Amongst all the commotion, Elisha shot towards the darkened alley. It smelt awful. The girl in the red dress smelt freedom.

Agent Earl battled for composure beneath the trampling of people. Paul tugged at the agent's jacket in an attempt to regain his own balance but, more importantly, to upset the agent's. They jostled like alley cats—selfishly, and yet kicked out selflessly, realising the stampede threatened them both in their precarious predicament.

The alley was horrific but there was a distant light at its end. A heavenly light. Elisha began to move towards it without hesitation, without breathing. She was especially thankful that Paul had insisted she wear the oversized coat. It protected her petite body. It snagged on every sharp edge and slimed horribly as she ran the gauntlet of a dumping ground of old lines, nets and decaying fish. She leapt fittingly like a salmon over the last set of boxes that had a ghastly eggy liquid solidifying upon them. She threw the coat to the ground in disgust and in celebration, and she took a gulp of fresh air as her reward.

Agent Earl's radio had fallen from its holster, unclipped by the clash with Paul. It crunched like brittle toffee as a heavy Harlem man named Deontay landed his basketball sneaker upon it. It was only as

Paul found his feet that he truly appreciated the spectacle of it all. The docks were overwhelmed by evacuees, infantry and mass confusion. Helicopters were hovering above the sea, causing it to ripple like warm chocolate. There were supersize tankers, spiralling tunnels and floodlights, all set in different colours under the blackened night sky. The colours of the American flag.

Elisha approached Catherine Street. The street had been stripped of its usual hustle and bustle. She looked ahead to the diner where she had first shared pancakes with the man who had emptied New York City with mere words. She faintly heard the door's bell.

Local law enforcement officers were leading an older couple away from the diner. The couple were holding hands. The gentleman wore a trilby. The officers displayed no such solicitude to their elders; they were piqued at having to leave their original post in order to pull the protesting pair into the back of their patrol car. The rear door was emphatically slammed shut.

Elisha ducked behind the pillar of a high-rise building until the car had raced out of view towards the docks. The sound of its engine echoed throughout the vacant street. Elisha's shoulder was stung by the cold surface of the concrete pillar. She pulled away from it and walked towards the unoccupied, unguarded diner.

The storm rapidly drew its strength from the Atlantic Ocean. The mammoth force hurled itself at the dainty island set idyllically in the Caribbean Sea. The cloud circled at phenomenal speed above the American isle, swirling like the shell of a giant garden snail.

Mr and Mrs Carter were awake, courtesy of the broken rum glass. A ghostly howl surrounded their detached room at the Dechambeau Hotel. Mrs Carter clung to her husband as the ceiling above them began clunking beneath the hurricane they were perilously oblivious to. 'Bill…what's happening?'

The couple scrambled to the oak door directly opposite the glass doors that displayed the evilness of mother nature outside. The beach was a battlefield of spinning sand; violent tornado-like vortices sprung up like booby traps. The hurricane raged, whistling and whirling as if it were enjoying its temper. Mr Carter landed his left hand on the brass door handle, but the door had been sucked shut by a force they could not yet feel.

The ceiling of their detached abode was torn from the walls. The glass-door wall was the only foundation that resisted the power, causing the ceiling to peel back, like the lid from a tin of sardines. A colossal airstream barrelled into the room and yanked the married couple off the floor. Mr Carter's right arm squeezed around his wife's neck as he tried desperately to hold them together.

He screamed in blind panic, 'CAD—HOLD ON!'

The force within the room had confused itself and was bouncing back and forth trying to return to its creator overhead. Its energy caused the contents of the room to collide cataclysmically. Mr Carter was fading; his left hand was slipping from the door handle. His white knuckles finally released their grip, causing the anniversary couple to be thrown the length of the room. They slammed horribly into what remained of the ceiling. Mrs Carter took the brunt of the force and was smashed repeatedly against a nook that had been created by the damaged roof. Her arms and legs flailed helplessly as if she were possessed by the Devil himself.

The couple's collision had caused Mr Carter to become jammed beneath the ceiling that was killing his wife with repeated blows. Mr Carter looked up, and the last image he saw was that of his wife being sucked upwards through a gap created by her own body. He saw the contorted, lifeless body of his sweetheart disappear into a black sky before he was wrenched against the crumbling ceiling like a child's doll thrown in a tantrum. The power of the whirlwind instantly stole the breath from his lungs and the life from his heart.

A day later, a search and rescue helicopter hovered high and alone above Mount Eagle Point. The devastation below was astronomical. An island levelled. The pilot scanned the horizon. Out at sea were the landmarks of his homeland. Floating, sinking or sunken. The ocean was as calm as he had ever seen it, exhausted by the previous day's exertion. The pilot zoomed his attention to two cadavers bobbing beside each other on the water's surface. William and Cadence. Two visitors to the island, celebrating twenty-five years of marriage, who had involuntarily adhered to their Catholic vows.

Chapter Forty-Three

RECKONING

Defying the ache of his heart that pulled at his entire body like an anchor

A defining click resulted in New York's oxygen being gulped in an instant. The explosions cut through Central Park like Armageddon. The tremor ripped through the city streets—gobbling, chewing up and spitting out everything in its path. A raging ball of fire followed, incinerating the destruction left behind by the phantom. The series of blasts compounded into one enormous flash that illuminated the park and the city.

The explosion caused Elisha to run to the nearest structure; her red dress flurried behind her as she dashed to the doorway of Maggie's Diner.

Benedict threw a detonator to the puddled ground and watched smoke and flames rise into the sky. He was in plain view of the city's cameras. Unhidden. Alarms echoed from vehicles and buildings, filling the side streets with a cacophony of sirens and whistles and bells. Ash and dust feathered to the ground, falling like gothic snow. A swinging electrical cable provided a violent firework display as it arced relentlessly. Runaway flames were busy peeling cars of their colour, as the soot-covered buildings cast a heavy darkness over the deserted streets. Isolated fires simmered and hissed in the rain, no longer powered by the explosion that had created them. There was chaos, but no one screamed.

Benedict looked up at the raindrops as they fell onto his skin and savoured the peacefulness of freedom. His hair fell like a gloopy mess to his forehead, causing each and every droplet to run an identical course down his nose and onto his lips. He tasted the rain.

Central Park was engulfed by all the mesmeric colours between yellow and red. The beautiful green and New York grey had been marvelled and mused at for nearly one hundred and fifty years by tourists and locals alike. Now the rectangle of fire overwhelmed the empty city; a wall of flames stretched from 59th Street to 110th Street and was the width of three avenues on either side of the park. It was a moving entity, bubbling and swaying like an apocalyptic war dance.

The pond, the lake and the reservoir reflected the night fire that was both magical and deadly. It crippled the foliage that sat on the banks of the still waters. The cloud of smoke was fanned as the rain fell to quell the sting of the fire. The raindrops fizzed as they landed on the flames, evaporating almost instantly, but there was a storm brewing on the night skyline. Benedict walked with purpose away from the frenzy. The drizzle had drifted into a resilient downpour, battling the flames. Fire and Water. Benedict continued to walk away from the duel. He walked with a precognitive disposition. New York City was deserted, dying.

Elisha waited as a maze of flames scoffed the scattering rain. From beyond the heat's haziness, a solitary figure walked towards her. It was him. She took a deep breath and felt her body sigh. The fire was a backdrop to his staggered movement. Elisha stepped from the confines of Maggie's doorway and wandered towards him. The rain began to fall more heavily. It caused her to squint and cower slightly under the sting of heaven's water.

The wind had grown stronger and caused her red dress to flutter wildly. She quivered in the cold and in the eyes of the dashing man before her. The water had sucked the red dress to her skin, causing it to perfectly caress her waistline and ripple slightly at the hem like a mermaid's tail. The storm gathered momentum in the sky above.

Benedict's wet hair hung over his face. His eyes widened as he walked to meet the lady in red. He flicked back his hair and looked at her intently, fiercely. Elisha steadied herself and plotted a path along Catherine Street through the deepening puddles. The rain tried desperately to intervene, casting a slight mist between them. It was enough to mask Benedict's movement. He edged onto Cherry Street, further away from Elisha and closer to the arched pillar of Manhattan Bridge. She shouted desperately, 'BENEDICT!'

He shouted back, knowing her thoughts, 'I CAN'T PROTECT YOU.'

Elisha took small steps towards him, but he mirrored her movement, shuffling backwards, stopping only when she did. Elisha understood that this was as far as she could go. The rain concealed her tears, but they fell anyway. She was exhausted by the pull of love on her body and shouted hopelessly, 'I LOVE YOU!'

Benedict was weakened by a feeling he could not explain. 'ELISHA—' He composed himself and sucked up the strength to call out again. 'THIS WORLD WILL SPIN WITHOUT YOU— WITHOUT ME.'

He began to shuffle again, defying the ache of his heart that pulled at his entire body like an anchor. Elisha was frozen by the moment and watched Benedict stumbling away from her. She had forgotten the cold. The pair pierced the camouflage of weather and looked deep into each other's eyes. They were disturbed by a sickening chant that echoed from behind Elisha. She spun, searching for the sound, and looked back at Benedict, the target of their frenzy. He too was drawn to the deathly chorus and flicked his attention between the girl and an advancing mob.

A wave of vigilantes swept towards her, armed with weapons of choice. An eerie lull preceded a chorus of chanting. The only words discernible were 'MURDERER', 'DEVIL', 'KILLER'.

The pack of people hunted Benedict and dismissed the woman in their peripheral line of sight. They were focused. Insatiable. She turned away from the crazy crowd and looked to the man she loved. 'BENEDICT!'

Benedict theatrically bowed to Elisha, turned slightly and ran. Two helicopters marked B1 and B2 appeared from the grey clouds above. Their blades spoiled the symmetry of the rain. Water sprayed into the air as Benedict's feet gained traction in the puddles. Elisha's hair and red garment rippled in the vacuum of the helicopter's draught. They swept over her to begin their pursuit of America's most wanted man. Her true love.

The mob followed the storm-riding helicopters. Elisha fell to her knees as the crazed group ran beyond her, pursuing Benedict with purpose. A strike of lightning illuminated Benedict and the frenzied mob that chased him. The helicopters whipped themselves away from the bridge and the scolding phenomenon. The resultant thunder soothed them. It reminded them that the lightning had passed. The deadly mission continued.

The crowd that was closing in on Benedict was a disturbing demographic. It housed the good, the bad and the ugly. They were united in their purpose. They sought Benedict's blood. They had crashed around the city streets like a tsunami. A large section had clustered at the front of the group, leaving a small trail and another large group behind, like honey dripping from a spoon. Benedict knew those who chased him. Each had their own motive for his murder.

Harold found himself at the front of the second group. He was a forty-seven-year-old businessman and family man. People naturally warmed to him. He had watched his only son, Dylan, plummet from the North Tower on September 11. Harold cursed the news reporters and journalists who referred to Dylan as a 'jumper', and always believed that it was Benedict's hands that had 'pushed' his son from that burning building. Rage burned within him.

The group in front of Harold was led by a boy of nineteen, dressed top to toe in black. He wore a balaclava that only revealed his piercing hazel-brown eyes. His name was Joaquin. He had watched his uncle hanged publicly over a year ago and swore to avenge him. Joaquin was part of a syndicate of men who trafficked southern European women and girls from their shanty homes to dingy American hostels and brothels.

Joaquin was an impressionable boy, young and naive. His uncle had been his only remaining relative. He was his father, his hero and his friend. Of the hundreds of women Joaquin had tricked, trapped and deceived into believing the American dream, three had fallen into the eternal sleep. They had been raped, savaged and murdered by the rugged hands of his uncle, the ex-fisherman, the alcoholic. Joaquin refused to believe it. He had shouted Spanish words when his uncle was fatally punished for his crimes. Joaquin carried a knife. It hindered his running.

The mob was stretching further apart. A solitary black vehicle swerved between the two main clusters, forcing those who were sprinkled between them to join one or the other. The black vehicle that had dissected the groups had opened a path for fourteen identical black vehicles to follow. The crowds watched the vehicles zoom between them and cursed their advantage. The black formation had Benedict in their sights. Nonetheless, those on foot regrouped and began to march as one, like Nazis. They began to chant like Nazis.

Benedict reached the eighty-foot arched structure. He clambered up the wet temporary scaffolding that decorated the stone pillar. His grip was strong and resolute.

The black swarm screeched to a stop beneath his vantage point and marvelled at his athleticism. They watched as their prey scaled the wall of stone and metal, beyond firing point. The leader of the black pack interrupted the occasion, realising that Benedict had lured them to a dead end. 'Circle back to the foot of the bridge—flush subject to Dumbo!'

Benedict skipped over the safety fencing and landed himself onto the empty Manhattan Bridge. It was eerily silent. The vehicles below him spun in sequence and rushed to its north end. Benedict took a moment to gather his thoughts and looked over Cherry Street to the girl in the red dress. He paused, swallowed a breath and turned away. He ran southwards and looked back over his shoulder to the open road.

The silence was soon undone as a black snake of vehicles broke through an unnecessary road block and slithered onto the bridge. They had converged at the northern entrance. Benedict watched the string of vehicles fall into formation, aligning like a series of arrowheads. His trickery had afforded him the promise of escape.

Benedict thought of Harold's son and Elisha but there was no time for such sentiment. All lanes of the bridge were occupied by the purring black panthers, glistening beneath the street lights and the dark storm. Their headlights shone nakedly onto the empty rising road as Benedict disappeared over the subtle brow.

The columns of the bridge were heavy and weathered. They stretched high up into thick clouds. Moisseiff's design cantilevered perfectly between the city suburbs, perched over the glossy black water, which had been turned into a pattern of polka dots by the falling rain.

Benedict had the second half of the bridge to himself. He ran freely along the bridge's softly sloping edge. Liberated. Hunted. He tried to swallow the panorama that surrounded him but his mind was blocked by a single image of the girl in the red dress.

The wind accelerated the roar of fifteen vehicles and two helicopters over the bow of the bridge to Benedict's ears. The helicopters hovered like birds of prey and the cars announced themselves onto the highest point of the bridge like a pack of wolves.

Each one growled and relished the pack formation. The lead arrow-point drivers drew their weapons and swept downhill.

The helicopters threw their searchlights onto Benedict's scrambling figure. The lead vehicles began to fire. The ripple of rapid gunfire ripped through the stretched circles of light and towards their target. Benedict zigzagged like a pinball beyond their deadliness.

The volley of gunfire had hypnotised the driver of the most advanced vehicle, which veered under his gusto into the adjacent lane and nudged the shoulder of the second. The glance at top speed stiffened the wheels of the lead vehicle, which burnt as the tread jammed against the grain of the road. The wheels pointed to the horizon beyond the bridge; the car followed, swerving fatally at top speed. The driver frantically tried to correct the steering wheel and stamped on the brakes. The wheel locked. The car crashed, leapt over the concrete ledge and off the side of the bridge into an apparently weightless flight. But gravity soon found the soaring black object and tugged it towards the earth's core. Oxygen ripped into each orifice of the falling vehicle. It sparked into ignition, combusting the fuel that had once given the car life. The explosion was spellbinding.

Fourteen other drivers looked back over their shoulders to the rising fizz of white smoke. The helicopters' blades sucked up the cloud and sliced it into a thousand pieces. The lead helicopter pilot castigated the pack, distorted by grief, commanding them to obey his orders. 'HOLD YOUR FIRE! We have an uninterrupted view of the subject in a continued sterile area, maintain a visual and await command.'

Benedict looked beyond the blades of Bravo One and Bravo Two. They blocked the moon for split seconds at a time, causing a slow-motion strobe sequence. He didn't marvel at it for more than a second or two; instead he drew his gaze to a postmodern high-rise, whose symmetry of windows reflected headlights, search lights and the night sky.

Benedict neared the end of the bridge and skipped an adjoining barricade, announcing himself into Dumbo, in the borough of Brooklyn. His reflection decorated the entrance to the building. He ran towards the rusty-bricked structure, divided into three by a central spine of gunmetal grey. The centre block rose from the base of Sands Street to the tip of the roof. The searchlights temporarily blinded him as they reflected heavily off the clear pane before him. He shielded his eyes but the sound of black cars screeching around the corner focused his wits.

The rain fell monotonously onto the windows of the building. The lashing caused Benedict to fumble with the chain around his neck. He pulled it from beneath his soaked top. It held a silver cross that sparkled in the light. He grasped the cross and yanked it sharply away from his chest. The chain snapped and slithered from his shoulders, falling into a puddle below.

Benedict rolled the cross in his hand and used the bottom stepped edge to place it into a lock that inconspicuously decorated the doorway. He turned the adapter key in an anticlockwise direction, which in turn revealed a digital keypad. Water dripped onto the lime-green digits upon the raised squares. Benedict tapped the keypad five times, shielding the numbers selected from Bravo Two's on-board cameras. *8–1–0–1–8*. The doors opened automatically. Benedict stepped through and accepted the invitation out of the rain. The doors closed and deadlocked behind him.

His shoes squelched through an abandoned reception area. It was largely made of marble; bright lights illuminated the coving of the ceilings; leather Barcelona chairs lined the entrance. Benedict made his way through the swanky area to the elevator, which was set on the outer edge of the building, a short distance from the entrance.

The metal doors of the elevator were cumbersome but closed softly and securely. Opposite the entrance was a floor-to-ceiling mirror, with a chrome rail across it. To the left stood a polished grey wall. The outer edge was made of thick glass, shaded in a soft black. The translucent tone allowed its rider to enjoy the vista of the New York bridges and the Manhattan skyline. It was often the business deal clincher for property tycoons and their investors.

Benedict selected the top floor and then landed his tired hands onto the chrome rail. His body welcomed the rest and the oversized mirror welcomed his image. The elevator rose swiftly, silently. The reflection of night shielded Benedict's rise. The helicopters threw their lights onto the building, searching for their target. The toned glass caused the light to rebound down onto the street. Benedict arched backwards, still holding the rail, and saw himself in the mirror. He took a despondent deep breath and looked beyond the glass to the craziness that followed him.

The Secret Service agents converged on the entrance; the helicopters watched from above. Two agents frantically tried and failed to open the door that Benedict's cross had unlocked. One of the two shot at the lock with his handgun in a flamboyant rage. The bullet scarred the glass before deflecting and disappearing into the darkness of the street.

The rain continued to fall as Benedict rose. The helicopters looked down upon this rising man and the mob, and the agents looked up. Benedict allowed them to blur into the forefront of his view as he gathered the colour of the city in the background. The storm loitered; swirling above the sea. The rain fell diagonally, directed by the storm's tailwinds. The moonlight shimmered through the puzzle of clouds. The view was sensational.

Chapter Forty-Four

MALEVOLENCE

Suckle on wisdom without provocation. Allow temporary empowerment and bask in the silence of contentment.

'Is Billy bullying you?' asked the principal.

Benedict replied unequivocally, 'Yes, Mr Hart. He takes my money every morning.'

Mr Hart's response to Benedict's admission was no knee-jerk reaction. He was a wholesome man with frugal ways and unrivalled patience who spent weekends traipsing through dew-soaked fields in a khaki wax jacket. He had marvelled at birds in flight and forage ever since his father had put a pair of vintage binoculars around his neck. It was a quality the principal had acquired—to observe without being observed.

The black marks beside Billy's name had blotted to a severe smudge, threatening to blacken the pristine pages of Mr Hart's register. Billy was burdened with social and economic failings, courtesy of his wayward parents, but Mr Hart had given him too many chances, watched him resist too many subtle interventions and wasted too many words on the boy and his father. In his head and in his heart, the decision was final.

Mr Hart had only met the widowed man once but had shared a plethora of phone conversations with him. Granted, Mr Benter seldom answered the phone, but when he did, he preferred only to listen to his own words and skirted prying questions like a seasoned politician. He was a loud, highly functioning drunk fuelled by grief and guilt.

The home-time bell rang, and Mr Hart observed the flock of fleeing children soaring through the gates. He scythed between them like a wolf amongst bison and ushered Billy to one side. He pressed a sealed envelope into Billy's hands and then spoke clearly to avoid confusion.

'That's the end of the road for you, son. Give this to your dad and tell him that you are no longer a student at this school.'

He offered no explanation to the subject of the letter, who already knew its content. Within the letter was a request for its reader to attend its writer's office, but the principal knew there would be no protest knock at his door. It was not a decision landed upon by any judgement of social and economic deprivation, but some apples are just rotten, and given the freedom of a healthy cart, they will willingly infect it. The educational system was by no means tailored to the survival of the fittest but driven to eradicate those who cared least for its values. It was simple science. The evolution of education.

Billy snatched the letter from the birdwatcher, unaware of the opportunity he had wasted. Yes, his hardships had shaped his soul, but the blame for his failings fell solely upon his own shrugged shoulders. The school had done everything to nurture him but his objection to authority was purposeful. It was merely a footnote to his story that his makers cared more for red wine than their bloodline.

Mr Hart placed his hand upon the boy's shoulder and watched him dismiss it in an instant. Billy walked nonchalantly to the gates. The principal was crestfallen but felt certain that he had not failed the boy as he watched him disappear from his view.

The man walked with a despondent slump, weighed down by his mood and heavy black trench coat. The coat swamped his slim, wiry frame and reached just below his knees. He was dressed entirely in black. His pupils were devoid of emotion—empty whirlpools of black. His skin was pale.

The clock struck ten. He walked with purpose towards the school entrance. He walked briskly—in spite of his heavy coat and hefty black leather boots—fuelled by his adrenaline. A St Christopher pendant bounced against his chest, momentarily blessed by the morning sun. Billy's index finger and thumb caressed the ridges on its surface before tucking it back into the confines of darkness beneath his jacket.

He reached out and allowed his right hand to slide up the handrail at the school's entrance. It was refreshingly cold and steadied his nerve. The school motto decorated the glass doors. It was colourful; Billy was captivated by its shimmer and whispered the motto to himself. 'To dare is to dream.'

He pushed at the door with his ice-cold hand and it creaked open. His boots squeaked on the polished vinyl hallways. He looked at a glass cabinet in the hallway; it was crammed full of medals, shields and cups, achievements of students past and present. He marvelled at his reflection, riveted by his own darkness. He reached into the left breast of his coat and took hold of a sawn-off, twelve-gauge Remington shotgun. Billy revelled in its power and held it proudly by his side. He walked towards the nearest classroom.

The room was modest in size—desks were arranged neatly and there was a hum of nonsensical chatter. Billy slowly turned the brass doorknob with his left hand and held the shotgun firmly in his right, white-knuckled. The classroom was full. Instantly the chatter hushed and each child zoomed their attention to the intruder. The teacher took one look at the figure in black and instantly recognised his dark desire. She rushed at him with her hands in a wild frenzy but the entrant raised his weapon quickly, as if practised. He steadied it effortlessly with his left hand and squeezed at the resistance of the trigger. The barrel kicked into the air. The shotgun's blast was too loud for the room and rang in the children's ears. The power of the gun reverberated through Billy's body, causing him to stagger backwards from the recoil. He collided with the door and then tamed the flailing gun within his hands.

He looked at his victim, a prim and proper young woman ripped apart by his cartridge. She had fallen into a distorted heap on the floor. Dead. Her warm blood had sprung unorthodox patterns of red across her front-row students.

Billy spun round. He allowed a moment to pass and soaked up the hysteria of screaming children. He settled his shotgun and lowered its pitch.

Ellie Perivale was as whimsical as the rhyme in her name. A blonde bundle of joy, eight years old. The impact of sound had spun the feather-light girl from her third-row chair and she collided with an adjacent desk. She stumbled to her feet and saw a man in black poised before her. Her classmates were already fighting for position, calling upon an unlearned, inbuilt human instinct to survive. Ellie could see that her friends were screaming by their widened mouths, but she could not hear them. Instead, a piercing buzz was busy confusing her wits. It unbalanced her. She instinctively stretched her jaw and then raised her hands to cradle the pain of perforation. A young boy crashed into her slender shoulder, spinning her sideward; she tumbled again and was trampled by a flurry of friends. The children from the front row were heading for the sanctuary of the furthest wall and cared little for the placement of their feet. The knotted collision of arms and legs had unwittingly caused Ellie to face the front of the room and she watched the man casually move the gun's barrel side to side like a huntsman. Her teacher lay lifeless beside his black boots.

Billy shot again and again at no one in particular, revelling in the madness like a demented Nazi. He watched the children collide horribly in panic and pain until the sound of chaos simmered down. A series of gunpowder flashes lit up the room. Dead weights landed upon Ellie's timid body, sucking away her energy and breath. She shuffled desperately with her small hands to pull herself out from the crush but her panicked movement was easily detected. The gunman shot again.

The first time he took aim was when the children were all piled on top of each other and truly defenceless. He reloaded and shot another six times until he was convinced that the classroom was entirely still. Soon enough he could only hear his own heavy breathing and racing heart. He was exhausted by his efforts and sucked several times at the air of death before him; twenty-five small bodies and that of their teacher carelessly torn apart. He raised the weapon to his chin and looked madly at the far wall. It was covered with paintings of the brightest and most innocent of colours. He accepted that he was at the end of his life and pulled the trigger.

The bold letters above the collection of paintings were stained with blood. *Lincoln Elementary. Classroom Two. To Dare is to Dream.*

Chapter Forty-Five

SACRIFICE

Nurture an unadorned faithfulness and be an adherent of a utilitarian nature. Eternal light can illuminate the darkest of dominions.

The anticipation and excitement at the Tropicana Field stadium was palpable. The Tampa Bay Devil Rays were five home runs clear of their rivals the New York Yankees. Both teams occupied the dizzy heights at the top of the Major League Baseball Championship. The Rays were on the cusp of glory and history.

The blue and red crowd jostled for position. The Tampa Bay pitcher, Declan Jarr, caressed a baseball between his taped fingers and a solitary tanned leather glove. Odejio 'OD' Roho envisaged the crispness of a home run and focused on the man who teased the stitched ball. Remnants of orange dirt drifted through the air, a reminder of the previous play.

Jarr drew his knee to his chest and concealed the ball momentarily within the secrecy of his delivery. His elastic arm hurled backwards and summoned the torque that was needed to toss the ball at over one hundred miles per hour. His fingertips were the last thing to feel the smooth leather before the ball hurled towards the athletic OD. It corkscrewed through the open air.

OD was the Yankees' star man; his eyes were as white as the ball that rocketed towards him. He focused on it and slowed his mind, condemning the delivery to a manageable hitting speed. OD swung his bat in anticipation of connection but was stunned mid-swing by a shuddering whoosh beyond the stadium. It caused the bat to slip from his grasp and soar towards the pitcher.

The thunderous noise unbalanced Jarr, who sank to his knees. The crowd ignored his stumble and instead looked high up to a celestial blue sky and saw a jumbo jet careering towards them at the speed of sound. The startling image was so inconceivable it failed to form in their cognisance. They gawped at the fuselage and the four enormous engines that hung from the wings. It rocketed towards them. People cowered and spun but moved little.

The aircraft containing tonnes of fuel crashed into the stadium, cockpit first. The foundations of the stadium shuddered to the core; the spectators were bathed in a moment of silence before the aircraft summoned the strength to decimate everything and everyone. It did not discriminate, scooping up the stadium and field effortlessly. The shockwave rippled like an earthquake before an unstoppable undercurrent of heat incinerated each and every person in its path.

A satellite image looked down towards earth; an uninterrupted view of explosions spoiled the planet's majesty. An unknown voice narrated a sombre truth as explosions erupted like popping candy across America—St Petersburg, Minnesota, Texas, San Francisco, Miami and Colorado.

'Today we mourn the deaths of over two hundred thousand friends, family and loved ones. No words can explain the horror that was unleashed by so few but had such a profound effect on so many. We have been led to believe that the foiled terrorist attack of September 11 has triggered this catastrophic and barbaric event. This coordinated terrorist attack on Major League Baseball stadiums across America is the largest attack on democracy since April 19, 1995, when, in Oklahoma City, a car bomb exploded outside a federal office building, killing one hundred and sixty-eight people.'

Chapter Forty-Six

SAVIOUR

Embrace those around you and be an unfaltering shield against the vile, the ungodly and the immoral.

Benedict floored the accelerator pedal of the stolen Porsche. The car caterwauled as its engine leapt into another dimension of speed and whooshed past pedestrians and street artists, who all spun like tops in the chaos of sound. His peripheral vision was a horizontal blur of colour. Benedict was at the mercy of the vehicle's raw power, and yet he tamed its frenzy with an occasional flick of its steering wheel like a rodeo cowboy.

A pursuing black spot tried desperately to veer into a defined view, hanging onto the coat tails of the vanishing vehicle's vapour. Agent Six barked over his headset, 'Eastbound, Thirty-Third—he's getting away.'

The adrenaline-crazed Agent Four joined the chase, screeching from a side street, and arced in front of Agent Six, taking the lead. Agent Six was annoyed but slightly relieved. He fell back into the formation of identical SUVs.

Agent Four was now the lead vehicle and announced it via his headset. He was just three car lengths away from Benedict. Four shifted his vehicle sharply to the left, in a wild attempt to close the gap on Benedict. His eyes widened to the colour of impending doom—a dull red.

A family car innocently ambled along the street before him. Agent Four was the embodiment of horror. He slammed his foot on the brake pedal. His gloved hands pushed against the steering wheel as he willed every ounce of his strength to stamp on the brakes and avoid the five-door station wagon. The four wheels locked unforgivingly.

His vehicle tore through the family car and its occupants. The force of the impact pulled and pushed them, cruelly catapulting and crushing them amongst the mangled wreckage.

Agent Four's airbag had deployed causing his head to plunge into a pillow of air. The SUV gasped and settled but was barely damaged. Its driver staggered onto the street and walked wearily to the family car. A randomness of boiled sweets was strewn amongst the bodies and the blood.

Chapter Forty-Seven

FOUNDATION

Purge yourself when troublesome thoughts threaten your spirit, raze all to the ground and begin again more purely.

Benedict declared the forthcoming state of emergency at a meeting with the Mayor of New York City and various fat cats—representatives of large corporations, lawyers and real-estate holders, who all had supreme influence over the city. The hundred-year warning was a difficult notion to sell and was met with a trickling of murmurs and unrest, as Benedict had known it would be. At a later meeting they all claimed to have delved wholeheartedly into various alternatives to protect New York from collapse in a hundred years, but the Manhattan skyline was maintained by the pockets of people blinded by lavish lifestyles and net gain and, ultimately, people are people—fuelled by human instinct and tainted by the lust of acquisition.

Benedict allowed the pantomime to play out in his mind but, ultimately, he knew it would be a fruitless gabfest that need not be entertained. He knew that those who calculated profit margins annually would fall long before the city towers tumbled to salt water in the twenty-second century and that, contrary to a president's words, you could in fact escape the responsibility of tomorrow by evading it today and for the rest of your life.

The attacks of September 11 had crippled the city's spirit and structure. Beneath the settling and unsettling rubble lay the Hudson River, lurking, poised, ready to swell into new-found territory.

Many moons ago, the docks, wharfs and landfill had increased the tips of Lower Manhattan, causing the outer edge of the city to effectively balance on water. The World Trade complex had originally been steadied. A slurry wall had merged concrete, steel and clay to create a bathtub around the buildings, protecting them from the water, silt and soil of the Hudson. One hundred panels, each stretching twenty-two feet wide and seven storeys deep, were interlocked and set beyond the bedrock of the bay. Now, the remnants of the wall had long since disintegrated into the rising river, weakening the diagonal ties that held the city to the basin.

The tranquil ponds of the nineteenth-century Central Park were slowly and slyly fusing to the Hudson like a disease. The people of New York City were oblivious to the shifting and swelling of the sea beneath them. Conspiracy theorists had speculated for an eternity that the city would one day sink into its surrounding water. The ice-cap pages penned by weirdly wonderful men and women had been ignored due to a flurry of fantastical 'far-out' theories that the average citizen did not believe. It blurred the sincerity of the work at times, and made the part-time scientists seem less credible.

Lower Manhattan would collapse into the Hudson and the Atlantic Ocean in December 2104. Eight hundred thousand people would die on that fateful day. A further one million would die later as a result of injury or waterborne diseases.

Benedict's 'terrorist attack' of 2002 would enlighten city officials as to the crumbling footings of the park. A series of slurry walls would be fitted thereafter that would see the city out until earth's doomsday six millennia later. Fire crews and civilians would be spared the effort of extinguishing the flames that soared above the buildings. The impending *perfect storm* would overpower its fiery rival within three days of the explosion. The charred Central Park would be re-steadied, re-grow and re-flourish. It would one day hold a plaque dedicated to a man named Benedict Maven.

Chapter Forty-Eight

APOCALYPSE

Believe that there is purpose for pain. Natural selection cares little for creed, colour and compassion. Its fleeting depravity is necessary for the betterment of existence.

An incandescent reporter interrupted the shenanigans. 'Enough about Bobby, Lucy and his lucky stars—if you have this power, what will you do with it? Can you cure cancer?'

Benedict paused before speaking.

'Yes—I can cure cancer,' he proclaimed.

The room murmured in disbelief, drawn to his answer. The answer permeated throughout America. Throughout the world. Strangers shared the news.

The leaves of Massachusetts' Chester-Blandford Forest were late to change. The greenery had outlasted the season and the autumnal colour appeared much later than normal. Climate change had that effect—it could change colours and conquer cities.

The land had stodged to a muddy, gritty texture like warm porridge—the Netherlands' Delta Works project had fought valiantly in resistance to the slowly rising tides; the series of dams, levees and sluices had been converged upon by salty water—overpowered, chewed up and swallowed by the sea. Those who had remained watched agonisingly as their beloved country fell to an unabashed power. The Netherlands was stripped of its country status long before the last of the Dutch were forced to flee. Japan, Vietnam, Bangladesh, Myanmar, Thailand, Philippines, and Malaysia had no populations and no self-governing political entities, and after falling below sea level, they too, fell into history.

Continents had been crippled by the fattening ocean. Asia had lost entire countries and was now a retreating series of slim islands, like protruding blue veins. Britain had thinned and clogged unhealthily like smoker's lungs.

Entire forests had been felled by machines fit for purpose. Sent to destroy one of earth's greatest natural resources, the trees—the longest-living organisms on the planet. The wonders of the world had been torn down and shaped into timber-framed houses. Log fires burned long into the nights.

The world's zoos had conferred at length with the World Wildlife Organisation and governing bodies, but ultimately, they had been resigned to a final decision. They had decided with heavy hearts that all of the animals enclosed would be spared a long suffering. Their time in captivity had been claustrophobic, but those entertained by them had funded their food supply. Now the crowds had diminished, falling to a life of subsistence on a crumbling, overcrowded earth. Those who had volunteered and worked at the zoos had long since waved goodbye to the animals they cared for. The only solace was that the animals would not die slow lingering deaths of starvation or thirst. Those animals close enough to their natural habitat, or to a habitat where they might thrive, were afforded the chance of life. The release clause stipulated that these animals would be saved from a sleepy needle to fend for themselves in a pre-apocalyptic world.

Toronto Zoo was officially the last zoo to release polar bears. A total of nine were introduced to the icy regions of Churchill. Northern Canada was littered with sporadic icy plates, scattered like lilies in a Monet painting. Within a year, all nine polar bears had perished. Drowned. Exhausted. Extinct.

An image of an emaciated polar bear was no longer treated with any contempt or pity. Its image was worn, torn and tattered on a large billboard poster in Piccadilly Circus. The people of London didn't even acknowledge it anymore. It had caused an uproar during its first year and saw nearly a million people pledging money to the 'Save The Bear' fund. The charity, much like the polar bears, had dwindled away to nothing over time. Starved of fish. Starved of money.

The world's water levels had risen considerably. The ice caps had melted due to a severe unmanageable increase in carbon emissions and a world that had too many people upon it.

Officially, four fifths of the world had swelled with water. Towering buildings across the entire east coast of Australia protruded horribly from the ocean, like stalagmites. The sewer systems in the cities had failed, polluting the streets with sewerage and a godawful stench. Sydney's wharfs had released their grip upon the yachts and boats they harboured, causing them to roam like freed animals between buildings. A few of the higher beachfront properties protruded, stacked together in a line amidst a mass of water. They would eventually crumble. Empires built on sand.

The Opera House sails peeked out of the sea like toes in a bathtub; the iconic building would also fall prey to the ocean's acidification that crippled the foundations of all that it encountered, making holes in concrete, like Japanese knotweed. The city was being squeezed into submission—drowning from the recurrence of vicious waves and smothered by a thick fog from the sky down. Eventually the ocean would swallow everything the city had.

It had been deemed financially unviable by the senate to try to save the national landmarks and the nation's most illustrious federal agencies. NASA was in the final stages of closure. Too many of its launch pads and research centres had been eaten up by the world's seas. The last official NASA mission belonged to Bart Sykes, who was subsequently stranded in space. The astronaut had uploaded a hundred images prior to opening the escape hatch of Idaho Two and taking his own life. It was the first and last suicide in space. The last thing he felt before unconscious suffocation was a bubbling sensation on his tongue caused by the absence of pressure in the vacuum of space. It caused the saliva on his tongue to boil at body temperature. It was unpleasant, those last fourteen seconds exposed to space without any protective clothing and without oxygen. His brain had wilted into submission before his circulatory system was blocked entirely by the thickening of his blood.

A rocket scientist named Christian Kayman was the first on earth to view the pictures he had sent, and for once he didn't need to rely on his qualifications to interpret them. It showed a three-dimensional image of earth spinning slowly like a bowling ball on its axis. With each rotation a new, almost identical image of the earth replaced the last. There were ninety-nine other images in total, each subtly different to the last. The final image saw the first and last of the sequence placed side by side. Both spun slowly. One hundred years of subtle differences revealed a profound truth.

The blue marble had been truly spoiled and split. The continents had broken into smaller chunks and resembled an unfinished puzzle. Antarctica had almost entirely disappeared, melted under the supreme power of the sun's ultraviolet, ultra-violent radiation. The patchwork of decaying, greying land had been joined by huge welts of hickory-brown hypoxia sediment—dead zones of water sucked clean of its oxygen. Jaundiced garbage islands had grown to the size of small countries and were a breeding ground of disease and bacteria. The blue marble was no longer a shiny, pretty, spherical organism; it was dying, scarred and discoloured like a petrified ball of wood.

The astronaut's final gesture was as easy to understand as ABC; it was entitled the Apocalypse Breme Chart and made for gloriously sad viewing—far sadder than that of an emaciated polar bear.

Chapter Forty-Nine

PURITY

Marvel at this beautiful life and surrender to the premise of unrequited love.

It was a Thursday evening. Elisha had prepared dinner—Brunswick stew, with her not-so-secret ingredients, English peas and black pepper, for added zest and zip. Andy's favourite.

Andy was severely withdrawn and had been wilting drastically for nearly a month. He had reluctantly attended the local doctor's office, but despite the partial breakthrough with the man who held a pad, a pen and a pocket watch, Andrew was unhealed and in a constant daze of depression.

The doctor, a young fellow with sincere diction, had prescribed amitriptyline to help his patient sleep, but it wasn't the sleeplessness that troubled Andy. It was the constant drone of life and the subconscious bubble that he bounded around in that was his undoing. Andy would often spend his afternoons engrossed in slumber, lost in life.

The void that had entered him since his father's death had swelled. It had eaten away at his gregarious defences and he was now riddled with nihilism. Nothing fulfilled him. He had drifted so far from the beauty of the world that he could no longer see it or feel its occasional warmth. Elisha too, was lost in her partner's wallow. The broken man barely spoke to her and when he did it was out of courtesy to avoid further prying. Andy was dismissive, distant and disillusioned.

Elisha prepared the table and called to Andy who was staring blankly at evening television, unaware of what he was watching, placated only by its background noise. 'Food's ready, honey,' she shouted, with a genuine attempt to deter Andy's hidden oppressor.

He mustered what was left of his afternoon energy and bumbled into the kitchen like a brainwashed soldier adhering to instruction. He was devoid of emotion. Drained.

Elisha saw the apparition before her and tried again. 'Alright, darling?'

Andy did not reply and abruptly took his seat at the table. He looked beyond the condiments to the brisket-juiced board atop the counter.

Elisha was optimistic and leaned over her lost soul, laying a dishful of stew before him and then placing her hand in the centre of his back. She kissed the top of his head and began unintentionally to prod the sleeping volcano. 'How are you feeling?' she said enthusiastically.

Andy shrugged and mumbled, 'OK, I guess.'

Elisha was unconvinced but undeterred; she settled into her own chair directly opposite him. She tried again, cosseting him as if he was a child. 'Come on, darling, tuck in while it's still warm—it's your favourite…chicken and brisket.' She was trying. She was failing.

She took a spoonful from the bowl before her and ate it, hoping that the burly man would mirror her movement. He did not indulge her—instead he dipped his spoon and twisted it back and forth like a petulant teen. Elisha had been stepping upon eggshells for far too long and felt a sudden surge of annoyance boil within her. She cracked. 'Andy, don't play with it, eat it.'

Still there was nothing in return, not even a glance. The shell of a man before her was captivated by his spoon, dancing to the tune of his hand within the brisket broth. 'Andy, snap out of it, we can't go on like this!'

He looked up, disgusted at her outburst and, with an impulse to destroy, he calmly pronounced, 'I'm not hungry,' and slid the bowl insolently to one side. The volcano began to grumble within him.

Elisha was dumbfounded by his contempt but tried to remain patient. She stood up and coolly collected the dish that Andy had abandoned. She took two steps towards the kitchen sink but succumbed to her rage, softly declaring the final blow. 'You are going the same way as your father.'

Andy erupted from his chair. The drastic motion caused his chair to fall backwards and crash to the floor; the sound further compelled his rage. 'WHAT DID YOU FUCKING SAY?'

Elisha clunked the bowl into the sink and spun with venom. 'You—you are heading for an early grave just like your dad.'

Andy threw his arm out towards his antagonist and gripped her by her clothing at the centre of her back. Elisha had never seen such a violent outburst in all the years she had known Andy, but now he was beyond reason. He held her tightly at the cusp of her neck, restricting her movement, and then growled at her through clenched teeth, 'Don't you fucking dare—who the fuck do you think you are?'

'I'm your fucking fiancée, remember? Now get the hell off me.' Elisha tried to pull away from him, but his grip was strong. 'Andrew, let me go,' she ordered.

The builder's eyes were glazed. There was no release.

Elisha shouted again as if she was trying to wake a sleepwalker. 'Let me go!'

He shoved her to the kitchen wall and pinned her against it by pushing his right hand solidly around her throat. Elisha kicked her legs in resistance, but he squeezed his hand and callously shook his head before lifting her off the ground. He held her momentarily at his eye level and snarled, 'Don't you ever talk about my dad.'

It was the catalyst for his madness. He dropped his fiancée and watched her slump to the floor in a heap of breathlessness. He laughed cruelly at her wheezing and coughing. Elisha was yet to cry; the fear and shock had not yet allowed her to register her sadness. She curled her body, hoping that Andy would leave the kitchen.

He paced back and forth, compelled by his demons.

Elisha's sadness finally overwhelmed her and she began to sob in between breaths. She started to crawl towards the living room.

Andy felt no remorse and was indulging in a moment of lucidity in which he decided that nothing he did mattered to him. The sound of shuffling and blubbering distracted and annoyed him. His eyes began to bulge as they filled with evil.

Elisha saw him looking at her with the wildest of stares as he moved towards her. 'Andrew…'

He grabbed the uppermost part of her left arm and pulled her to her feet with ease, fuelled by an impulsive rage. Elisha was exhausted.

Andy had repressed his hurt for too many years. He was an outgoing character with innermost demons. The last three months had seen him disappear within himself. He seldom spoke, instead choosing to hum through any form of human contact. It appeared joyous at first, and to those on the fringes of his life, but it disturbed Elisha.

It was the drone that had persuaded her to make an appointment with the doctor's office. The doctor had been polite and professional, but for all of Andy's most recent faults, he, ironically, had a gift for self-preservation—easily convincing the graduate from the school of medicine at Stony Brook that he had been saved by a ten-minute conversation and a packet of tablets.

Andy was now in the grip of his psychosis. He held Elisha effortlessly with his weakest arm and reached for her bowl of food upon the table. 'You think this fucking food is gonna make me better, do you?' he snarled in a disturbingly soft voice before launching the bowl beyond her. It smashed into twenty pieces, causing the contents to decorate the wall like abstract art. He rolled his left hand into his fiancée's hair, gripping it and thrusting her into an arc position. The slop of stew dripped down the wall; Andy pushed her face towards it, goading her. 'You fucking eat it!'

Elisha summoned the strength to straighten her body and grabbed the hand that was controlling her. Andy shrugged her flailing arms away from his own and landed a solid clenched fist to the side of her head. It dazed her enough that he now held her entire weight by her hair; he reached out to the kitchen counter and grabbed the granite mortar dish. He swung it wildly with a complete twist of his body, bludgeoning the woman he loved over the head. There was a disturbing crack like the sound of warming ice.

He released his grip and watched her sag to the kitchen floor. He dropped the inanimate object beside her. Blood began to dribble from her left ear. Her breathing was sporadic and short. Her head was still. Shut down by trauma, only her bottom lip moved subtly, sucking at the air in anguish for a few moments, then it was still too. She was dead.

Andy didn't dwell on the swelling of blood. He walked towards the front door with an inner tranquillity. He felt no sadness but was aware of the consequences of such acts. He opened the door and stepped out in his black socks into the coldness of the impending night. The temperature sucked at his lungs, reminding him that he was alive. The chill seeped into the house that Elisha Carter and Andrew Birchill had called home and began to thicken her seeping blood.

The subway station was sparsely populated with New Yorkers oblivious to the shoeless man that had joined them. He was ice cold to touch, but no one touched him as he walked beyond them all, unchallenged and unhindered, to the far end of the platform.

The street above harboured a last quarter moon. The Brooklyn Bridge was a sight to behold on this crisp night. Those beneath the city streets were oblivious to the splendour of the evening and concentrated the entirety of their attention upon a dark tunnel. The train rattled towards its destination and the city dwellers squeezed together, ready to board. Andy looked to the shuffling movement but did not engage in it. Instead he perched at the end of the platform in a place where the train's doors would not land.

The bitter cold had completely taken over his body and, even before he became the unknown man in tomorrow's papers, he no longer knew who he was himself. He leapt out into the train's path as it rattled into the station.

Chapter Fifty

CHARITY

Deny vulgar indulgence. Be defined by the people around you and the magnanimous deeds you do.

Elisha sat on the sofa she had become acutely accustomed to. Her upset state was palpable; her little nip of brandy had done nothing to help. She shuffled in her seat. Benedict's letter shook in her hands. She tried to steady it, desperately willing her hands not to shake. She momentarily held the letter in one hand and roughly wiped away tears with her other.

Benedict stood beside a casino table. His posture kindled power. He wore a black suit that fitted him perfectly. Tailored and tight. He toyed with a cocktail stick that he held between his teeth. A gathering crowd stood behind him; each person jostled for a position closer to the table, closer to him. Stacks of casino chips towered high above the green felt. They were branded with the stamp of the casino—a flouncy coat of arms. The towers had been stacked in a compulsive manner by their owner's delicate hands. Benedict looked intently towards the impressive casino ceiling and pondered his winnings.

Benedict held a briefcase loosely in his left hand; it tapped occasionally against his left knee. His brogues clicked on the ground as he walked towards a church.

An old nun sat stoically on a rickety chair behind a small wooden desk. The grandeur of the church eclipsed her. She was frail and withered but she was blessed with unrelenting faith. It was one of her many virtues.

Benedict approached the desk and nodded in the nun's direction. Her eyes were sunken beneath her soft and slackened skin. She offered him a warm and friendly smile. Benedict lifted the briefcase and carefully placed it on the desk.

The nun looked down to her feet and pushed backwards on her chair in an attempt to stand and properly greet Benedict. Her curved body had difficulty in straightening. By the time she had stood upright, Benedict's brogues had clicked and echoed out of the nun's degenerating sight. She squinted into the distance, but the apparition had completely disappeared. The nun was too weak to shout and instead turned her attention to the briefcase.

She fumbled at the clips and slowly opened the lid. She rested her hand upon the cross that dangled from her neck. An expression of utter amazement appeared on her face, causing her skin to tighten. Her surprise seemed to invigorate her, fuelling her to shout to her sisters who were at the top of the church steps. The briefcase was full of United States dollars, neatly piled and bound. She offered a silent prayer to her saviour and then to the stranger.

Chapter Fifty-One

NOBILITY

Savour the pursuit of divinity and the occasional brilliance of people. They will be the preservation of peace and the salvation of life.

The hall was the nucleus of the ceremony and people had gathered like clusters of atoms within it. Those who had jostled politely for seats wore retro waistcoats and dicky bows. There was more than one person wearing a monocle.

The chairperson walked onto the stage under the gleam of the lights. He was greeted by the eccentric audience who tapped a quiet applause. He leaned forward slightly and grasped the chrome microphone stand, quickly positioning it for his comfort. With a sharp clearing of his throat he began. 'Einstein's theory of relativity has long been a physicist's idolisation, but now, ladies and gentlemen, this is no more. This year's worthy recipient of the Nobel Prize has successfully fused quantum mechanics with relativity. Ladies and gentlemen, put your hands together for the founder of quantum gravity—Gregory James.'

Dr James stood to rapturous applause. He had been walked through the presentation earlier that day. Mrs James stood up beside her husband and embraced him intently. Dr James kissed her on the cheek before he walked timidly onto the stage. The audience stood in acknowledgement of his achievement. Only his fellow scientists appreciated the dramatic and world-changing effects that such a discovery would hold in its power. The rest of the would depend upon it but, ultimately, take it for granted.

Dr James was immersed in the warm glow of the stage lights. He walked tentatively to the chairperson, who presented him with a golden medal. Dr James turned and scanned the standing crowd for Mrs James. He found her. Her pride was evident. Dr James stepped up to the microphone. He was a humble man but confident in his ability. He sipped at the glass of water from the table beside the microphone and spoke delicately. 'Thank you,' he began, raising his hand to quieten the applause. 'Thank you...thank you.'

Dr James was fluent in the language of science; he continued with confidence. 'The Theory of Everything is a term for the ultimate theory of the universe—a set of equations capable of describing all phenomena that have been observed, or that will ever be observed. A beautiful example of it is the equation of conventional non-relativistic quantum mechanics, which describes the everyday world of human beings—air, water, rocks, fire and so on. Such a theory gives us the ability to read and understand the mind of God.' He paused before his last few words and delivered a gesture of inverted commas with his brilliant hands. He was outwardly atheist; scientists were expected to be, but inwardly he truly did believe in some sort of higher power.

With another gesture he invited the audience to observe the projected video behind him. 'As you can see, a substance called wurtzite boron nitride is suspended by opposing wires. You would be fooled into thinking this is a diamond—it is much more robust. It is also far more stable in oxygen when extreme temperatures are placed upon it. Paradoxically, its strength comes from its atom flexibility.'

He turned to the screen and spoke again. 'Just coming into shot is a laser—but, again, don't be fooled into thinking this is just any laser—the laser in question provides ten petawatts of power. To put that into perspective, ladies and gentlemen, it's five billion times more powerful than a lighthouse; it can produce all of the sun's solar energy that falls on earth in one picosecond—or a trillionth of a second—and if fired at ordinary matter, the matter would be vaporised instantly, leading to an extremely hot and dense ionised gas commonly known as plasma.'

The audience listened attentively. Dr James continued. 'To find plasma on earth, ladies and gentlemen, would be like finding a needle in a quattuordecillion bales of hay—that's forty-five zeros, by the way.' He smirked and revelled in the collective laughter. He waited for the laughter to cease before speaking again. 'It provides us with a glimpse into the conditions of the early universe—the Big Bang. In essence, we can travel back in time.'

Dr James turned to the screen once again and continued his lecture. 'As you can see from the image, the laser has been fired upon the substance suspended. Within a fraction of a second, a small explosion has fragmented the nitrate into invisible plasma.'

The audience was spellbound.

'The ionised gas expands exponentially from the aforementioned explosion and settles dome-like around its creator—just like that of the ozone layer. The laser is fired once again and, under careful examination, notice how it fragments on impact with the invisible shield and dissipates thereafter. Even a laser of this magnitude cannot pierce the invisible barrier.'

Dr James allowed the audience to absorb his words, and then allowed the subsequent applause to die down somewhat before he delivered his finale. 'Ladies and gentlemen, we are now in the process of fixing the ozone layer that protects our existence, and we can now predict natural disasters, tectonic shifts, wind change, rainfall and ocean moonlight movement—this will allow us to pre-empt or mitigate destructive acts of nature and preserve humanity as we know it—and did I mention we can prevent some forms of cancer?'

The audience shuffled in their seats, questioning the Nobel man's purposeful afterthought. Dr James answered their disbelief. 'Yes, you heard me correctly. The photoluminescence—otherwise known as ultraviolet light can be significantly reduced; in turn, forms of skin cancer, such as nonmelanoma and cell carcinoma can be averted.'

Before the last word left his lips, the hall was sparkling with euphoria. All eyes looked towards him, illuminated by the spotlight. Dr James felt like God.

Chapter Fifty-Two

RETRIBUTION

Quell the evilness of men or suffer the malevolence of children. Absolute sin will be punished evermore, final breaths immortalised by the weakness of the soul.

Frank's heavy frame was intimidating. His shoulders were firm and, due to the size of his back muscles, his upper arms protruded instead of hanging straight down by his sides. He was colossal.

The sound of falling water echoed from an upstairs bathroom. Frank kicked off his surfer sandals and slithered like a python towards the stairs. The predator crept to the top of the stairs; each step groaned as it felt the burden of the heavy man.

Katie lived alone, distanced from her parents, whose munificence had fuelled her independence. She would often turn heads and had a beauty desired by most—a slender frame and a softness that drew even the heaviest of hearts to her. It was Frank she had desired. A butch man who was vehemently disapproved of by her estranged parents. That was her intention.

Frank shuddered as his feet touched the cold bathroom tiles; his fingers tightened as they clenched unwittingly and uncontrollably to a fist. Frank was all too familiar with his hands; they were the tools of his labour.

The bathroom was humid; the steamy haze clung to every surface and concealed Frank's presence. Katie continued to lather herself under the shower's spray. Foam bubbles fell from her silky-smooth skin, swirling around her painted toenails. She closed her eyes as the water drenched her face.

Frank grasped the chrome handle on the shower door and pulled it sharply—it startled Katie, exposing her beauty and displeasure.

'Frank? Get out!' She reached for the towel that hung next to the shower.

Frank placed his right hand upon the towel, preventing her from obtaining it. She threw a punch at his face, but he laughed it away. Her naked skin aroused his appetite. 'Don't spoil the view, I just wanted to see you,' he said calmly.

Katie was terrified and vulnerable but addressed her ex-boyfriend with forced confidence. 'Frank—I told you—it's over!' Frank looked at her blankly as if her words had evaporated into thin air. It unnerved her, and her tone of voice changed instantly. 'Frank, please leave, it's over.'

'It ain't over till I say it's over.' He grabbed a handful of Katie's wet hair and yanked her downwards, causing her to arch into submission; droplets of water showered Frank's gigantic arm. His enormous hand shifted slightly and took a bigger chunk of his ex-girlfriend's hair; she stooped further, like a scolded dog submitting to its owner's command. He pulled her violently out of the shower, causing her feet to slip on the wet, soapy porcelain. Her arms flailed in an attempt to steady herself, reaching first for the sink and then the large hand that was controlling her.

She gripped Frank's wrist and tried to pull it towards the crown of her head to avoid further pain as she screamed, 'LET ME GO!'

Frank dragged her across the bathroom. Her balance eluded her. She had to relent her grip on her captor's hand as Frank edged out of the bathroom. She flung her hands out and caught hold of the door frame, but still Frank pulled her towards him. He was enjoying her struggle, prolonging it. She clung hopelessly by her fingernails to the door's edge but the odds were stacked against her. Frank was immensely strong and the door was wet with condensation. Katie was exhausted; the fear and pain had drowned her will. She knew Frank's power. She tried to scream but could only manage a whimper. Frank placed his free hand over her mouth and then hauled her defenceless frame from the room.

He leered at her exposed body for a moment as her heels dragged across the floor. He wrapped his arms around her. She kicked out with a sudden burst of cornered energy, but it was useless. Frank tightened his grip, contorting her—sucking away the last of her spirit.

Katie was flung onto her bed like laundry. She struggled to regain her breath from Frank's death grip and crumpled into a cocoon to protect her dignity and prevent further punishment. Her clammy skin sank into the cotton duvet. She was cold. Katie turned to face Frank but was unable to speak; instead her eyes pleaded with his malice. She didn't struggle; the adrenaline that had coursed through her body had totally diminished. She was too exhausted and too petite to fight back. She accepted what was about to happen. She thought of her mother and focused on the shower's hum in the background—she longed for her parents.

Katie's parents had lost their little girl during her teenage rebellion. They had questioned their parenting. They hadn't seen their princess for over a year. They had spoken briefly at Christmas on the phone but parted with an argument. Katie took pleasure in telling them she was living with Frank in New York. They were unaware of the recent split.

Frank flipped her body like a playing card. She didn't resist the motion as she spun smoothly onto her front, her face smothered in the pillow's softness.

The bed buckled under his weight. He unbuttoned his camouflage surfer shorts and they fell to the floor beside the bed; he kicked them away from his feet. Katie's fingers clenched and corkscrewed the bed linen. The weight of Frank smothered her; his huge torso pinned her to the bed. Overpowering. Suffocating. Katie thought of her parents' voices and took solace in their comforting tone. She focused on them intently.

Katie barely moved until Frank's hand pushed at the back of her head, drowning her in the comfort of her pillow. She gasped for air as she felt his weight relent. Frank had decided he had finished. He yanked horribly at her head, twisting her towards him. He squashed her rosy cheeks together with his right hand's thumb and index finger. His palm masked her lips. She was silent; she stared sharply at the animal that knelt over her. His hand slid from her cheeks to her slender neckline. He drew at his cheeks and sucked at his gums; he spat onto her face—his gummy saliva stained the beautiful girl's face and ran slowly over her cheek. It repulsed her. She felt the warm stickiness as it trickled to the pillow.

Frank rose from the bed and it creaked with relief. He reached for his discarded shorts, pulled them on, and buttoned them slowly like a satisfied punter. Katie lay naked and molested upon contorted bed sheets. Her mind was as blank as the ceiling.

Frank announced his departure by repeating his words, 'It ain't over till I say it's over.'

The stair treads creaked individually as he walked down the stairs to the front door. Katie heard the snap of the front door latch as it closed. Frank was gone—she longed for her parents. The shower still hummed cheerfully.

Faint sirens echoed through a typical affluent suburban street. Everything about this street oozed class. The lampposts were vintage and released a compassionate glow onto a wide walkway. The gardens were striped in two shades of green, edged with flowers and bespoke garden ornaments. The houses were detached, flat bricked, each window and doorway crested with ornate nineteenth-century craftsmanship.

Dwayne Trigg stood tall in front of a navy-blue door. He was out of place. His face didn't fit the neighbourhood. He wore black fingerless leather gloves that were ridged with chrome beads. He raised his right hand and knocked the door three times. He looked to his left and the glowing street corner. His simplistic black tattoo mingled with his African-American skin. The tattoo was unassuming—a circle and a triangle.

Dwayne was gratified to hear the sound of a latch loosening at the front door. He quickly looked forward, eyes fixed on the door as it swung open. He was greeted politely by the occupant.

'Hello, sir,' said David.

Without any warning, Dwayne pushed David forcefully to his chest. David stumbled backwards, his arms flailing; his elbow slammed against the door as he tried desperately to regain his balance. His left hand reached unconsciously to the floor to soften his fall. It was inevitable; Dwayne was too big, too powerful.

Dwayne entered the fallen man's home. His motorcycle boots scraped the hallway's parquet and squeaked as he stepped forward to the fallen host. David scrambled to the living room in fear, his hands and feet scurrying like a toddler. Dwayne's footsteps followed him, further squeaking on the freshly polished floor that smelt of fresh lemon.

David scrambled to a seated position against the oak coffee table that sat pleasantly upon a shaggy cream rug. He looked up at the uninvited guest. Dwayne was dressed entirely in black, his leather jacket revealing his burly frame.

Photo frames adorned every wall, and every available cabinet space was full of achievements, accolades and holiday memories. A simple family home.

'Where's your fucking money and car keys, you white fool?'

'I'll give you anything, please—just don't hurt me.' David had never experienced violence. He cared little for confrontation.

Dwayne was enraged at David's failure to answer the question succinctly and commanded, 'I said give me your fucking car keys and your money!'

David panicked. His heart pounded wildly, so much so that he could feel his blood pumping at the side of his temple. His delay incensed Dwayne who was already numb, courtesy of cocaine. Dwayne reacted and kicked cruelly at David's face. David's head crashed like a wrecking ball into the edge of the oak table, fracturing his skull. The whites of his forgiving eyes began to turn blood-red. Dwayne knelt over David who began to convulse uncontrollably.

Dwayne didn't seem to acknowledge the family man's distress and instead he crashed his elbow onto the man's face, enraged at his insolence. Each blow lacked remorse. Dwayne pummelled David's head repeatedly with callous elbows until his blood coloured the rug.

Dwayne stopped suddenly and began frantically to search David's home, ridding the blood from his face and elbows with a neatly folded tea towel from the kitchen. He returned to the living room moments later. He flicked at a wad of notes in his right hand and grinned. His teeth glistened a dull shade of gold in the subdued living room lighting. He jangled a set of keys between his fingers and glanced at the groaning man surrounded by family photographs.

Dwayne was fidgety; the drugs had befriended his bloodstream and he staggered erratically into the hallway. He reached for the door and edged beyond it. The lemony smell drifted into the street for a mere moment before the blue door closed behind him.

Chapter Fifty-Three

FORGIVENESS

Relinquish the burdens of rage and seek out those who are worthy of forgiveness

The old man seemed to be a regular, cloddishly stooped over on his stool. Michael watched him fumble with a newspaper and awkwardly sip his coffee. Michael studied the old man's hands; they were wrinkly but supple. He held the newspaper and coffee cup gingerly.

Michael turned his attention to the waitress. She had painted nails and blonde hair, an impassive but impressive-looking girl, jaded by part-time work. Michael focused on her blonde locks, which had absorbed some of the grease that hung in the air. The kitchen beyond her was a muddle of chaos. Michael watched the plump chef flipping prime pounds of beef and drowning fries in bubbling oil. The smell was inviting but the messy clutter unnerved him.

Michael's personal despair and inner anguish was lessened by his analysis of others—those who are most judgemental are often battling inner imperfections. Michael slouched further into his stool, weighed down by the censorious chip on his shoulder. He was out of work and had fallen into a murky depression. His mood was often the catalyst for wild marital arguments and scathing verbal attacks upon his children. Those closest to him often bore the brunt of his sadness.

The bell above the door jangled loudly. Michael was poised, ready to critique the strangers that entered. He watched the two beautiful people who walked in. They were obviously happy. Their happiness exhausted him. He couldn't bear to look at them. He thought of his own wife and his kitchen drawer full of unpaid bills. He tried to suppress his melancholy, but the black dog on his shoulders grew stronger.

The old man's stool scraped across the chequered floor causing Michael to turn sharply. He watched the pensioner walk towards him and felt his gentle hand upon his shoulder for a moment. Michael drew breath but did not speak. Nor did the old man; instead he tipped his head towards the owner, Maggie, who was standing in the kitchen. 'Ma'am.'

Maggie waved and said goodbye from the confines of the kitchen. Michael was stalled momentarily by the stranger's gesture of kindness but was drawn back to his people watching. He looked to the attractive couple, who caught his movement. Both looked back at him, causing Michael to turn away quickly. He decided not to snoop any further and instead occupied his mind with his newspaper, embarrassed at his prying. He delved into the newspaper's vacancy section and sighed despondently.

Michael's misophonia threatened to overwhelm him. Natasha's picking and Maggie's scraping was becoming too much. He tried to steady himself and took a solitary breath, but the sound of laughter stole him away from a practised moment of clarity. He looked towards the giggling pair and watched the elegant lady roll a pink flower between her fingertips. He was maddened by her happiness and only saw the sadness in flowers. He yanked his stool across the tiled floor and marched to the restroom.

He splashed cold water over his reddened eyes and stared at himself in the mirror. He was ashamed at what he had become; suffocated by his own guilt. He contemplated suicide.

Elisha wriggled from her seat; Benedict was ready with her coat and held it for her while she slid her arms into the sleeves. She headed for the door as Benedict ambled to the counter. He stood beside an unoccupied stool and turned the pages of the tatty newspaper. Its owner had yet to return. Benedict removed the lid of a red felt-tip pen that he had retrieved from his pocket. Natasha ogled the beautiful man. Benedict tipped his head towards her but looked instead towards Maggie. 'Thank you, Margaret.'

Maggie's heart fluttered as the handsome man penned something discreetly onto the newspaper. She hadn't been addressed that way since her husband's passing. Her voice crackled with emotion. 'Have a lovely day, sir.'

Michael returned from the restroom. He looked to the door of the diner as it slammed shut. He was happy that the perfect couple had left; it spared him any further evaluation. He sat on his padded stool and rubbed his brow. He looked dumbfounded at the newspaper before him—a thick red circle had caught his attention. The circled advert introduced a social enterprise vacancy. Beneath the circle were three boldly scribbled words—*I forgive you.*

Michael rushed to the door and fumbled with it in his haste; his anguish was manifested by the furious jangling of the bell before he skidded onto the street outside. He circled frantically, scanning his surroundings, but the striking man had disappeared.

Michael stood confidently in his black three-piece suit, looking out over New York's skyline. The modern office was vast. Family pictures dressed his desk. He heard a sharp tapping on the large glass double doors. His view of the panorama was interrupted but he acknowledged the sound with a mere flick of his fingers, gesturing for the tapper to enter.

Jim Thatcher pushed open the door and entered the room. Michael was still captivated by his view of the skyline and didn't turn towards his guest. He knew it was Jim—he had been expecting his associate. Jim quickly looked at a reflection of himself in a wall-mounted gilded mirror. He was happy with his tailored suit and puffed out his chest to admire his jacket's fit. He flicked at his fringe with his fingertips. His buoyant quiff revealed a slight blemish on his hairline. A small scar on the top of his forehead lent itself perfectly to the sweep of his brown hair. It was a reminder of his squandered youth and how a single schoolyard blow had redirected his rebellious path.

Michael turned and greeted his associate. Their business relationship was beyond formality and they addressed each other with a solitary nod.

'Jim, today is a very important day—our Red Circle brand has acquired its first million in corporate fundraising, I had the report earlier.' Jim revelled in the man's words but didn't interrupt.

'Yep, one million from absolutely nothing—to say I'm proud of you is an understatement.'

Jim jumped in, 'Proud of *us*. I couldn't have done it without you, Michael.'

Michael stood up and began to saunter around the office. He continued to speak candidly. 'Most of our competitors are still more concerned with their own subsistence and shareholders—some seem to focus solely on the "I" in charity. I know it's been a struggle, but you did a great job convincing our investors and trustees. And I do believe that a man's true wealth is the good he does in this world.'

Michael was seldom so expressive. Jim widened his eyes before speaking. 'I agree. That's very poetical.'

Michael chuckled and spoke with humility. 'Not my words—an Arab prophet came up with them a few thousand years ago.'

He looked to a large emblem upon the wall—a red glassy disc perched delightfully—the focal point of the monochrome office. Michael threw his voice up towards it, causing Jim to look up at it too. 'It doesn't represent the sun, you know.'

'Does it not?' Jim questioned.

'No—and I never once said it did. Some freelance free-living journalist once suggested that it represented the sun and I just allowed her to believe it…and, henceforth, everyone thought it was that and I never had the heart to correct them.'

Jim was baffled. Michael sensed this and addressed it. 'But its perception is quite insignificant.'

Jim chipped in but recognised the man's philosophical state so spoke quietly, not to disturb his rhythm. 'I always thought it represented the sun—you know, the circle of life.'

Michael barely noticed Jim's remark and continued to speak profoundly. 'It represents forgiveness.'

Jim sensed his fragility and offered soft words. 'Forgiveness for what?'

'I killed a baby's parents.' Michael paused and took a shallow breath. 'March 2, 1976—I remember it like it was yesterday. I've wanted to tell you about this for the longest time.'

Michael refrained from any further wandering and returned to his desk. Jim watched him settle into his seat.

Michael rummaged in his desk drawer and pulled out a framed newspaper print—a job advert circled in thick red ink with three words written beneath it: *I forgive you.*

He held it for a moment before placing it precisely upon his desk. He looked up to Jim and said, 'Take a seat, my friend.'

Chapter Fifty-Four

MAVEN

Perfectly absorbed within a posture of penitence

The rooftop welcomed the solitary man. The shady skyline was majestically backlit by the moon's glow, which coloured the puddles around him with a deep, blackened sheen. Rain was hurled by the wind against Benedict's face and body. He was captivated by a brilliance that caused his features to shimmer. It was a defining moment. It was a divine moment.

Benedict savoured the tranquillity and looked out over the city that had betrayed him. The storm continued to whisper and silently summoned its power. Bravo One and Bravo Two descended, spoiling his fleeting moment of clarity. Their searchlights beamed down, and their tail lights flashed intermittently, in time and sequence like Morse code. The helicopters approached quickly, violently arching backwards to a standing hover above Benedict. He was in their sights.

Benedict darted from his position beneath them. His movement caused the pilots to softly engage the rudder pedal and adjust their vantage to accommodate his strides. The tails circled in opposite directions like synchronised swimmers. Benedict was captured by their light. There was no negotiation. The crew doors violently crashed open and shuddered against the runners. In a sweeping motion, the helicopters' armaments swung into view. The M134

Miniguns spewed fire that lit up the rooftop. Benedict dived to his right and scrambled behind the enormous air conditioning units, his back pressed against the stainless-steel surface.

The initial burst of incendiary rounds cascaded out of control. It took a mere two seconds to steady and then centred on the man that stooped behind the wall of metal. Shards of molten bullets ricocheted overhead, puncturing the rooftop, tearing through the wet air with trails of diffused vapour. It was as marvellous as it was merciless. Benedict was calm, in spite of the raging tempest around him. Trapped by crossfire, he thought of his parents and contemplated the New York skyline which burned like the apocalypse.

Elisha looked on from the sanctuary of Manhattan. Her eyes unbelieving of the stormy Brooklyn sky. She had forgotten the rain. Blinded by her love.

The constant whip of gunfire was unrelenting, cutting through the altitude and the pinnacle of night. The searchlights struggled to focus on their prey, occasionally peeking into the openness of airspace, spinning and stretching wildly into nothingness as the pilots rode the storm.

The sight caused Elisha's heart to ache in helplessness and she damned the helicopters that were intent on killing the man she loved. The rain began to lash down, its thickening caused her to shield her eyes. Lightning flashed above the rooftop, momentarily blessing the sky with light. The shockwave widened her eyes and spun the devils that spat fire.

Bravo One and Bravo Two plummeted from the roaring sky, scorned by the wrath of nature. Elisha watched the helicopters spin like lighthouse beacons before they disappeared from her view. She looked to the heavens and pondered the reality of divine intervention.

Benedict watched the dramatic descent of his illuminators. He revelled in his solitude and looked intently at the bridge set against the fiery city. A trickle of reddened light peered through the shadow of night like alpenglow. He relished its beauty. In that moment, he was a child. A boy. A man.

He walked towards the building's edge. He stepped onto a raised concrete lip and balanced upon its outermost edge. He stretched his arms out wide and raised his chest, welcoming the cold night to the entirety of his body. He tilted his head back slightly and drew breath. The rain lashed down upon him. He was at one with the elements, perfectly absorbed within a posture of penitence.

Benedict recalled the words of his letter. His mind was filled with an image of Elisha. He shouted to the sky, to his creator, but the storm sucked the sound from his voice. It began to bleed the spirit from his soul.

'I forbid you to repent my sins, I tread forth within sacred communion.'

Printed in Great Britain
by Amazon